THE ESSENTIAL HEMINGWAY

Ernest Hemingway

arrow books

Published by Arrow Books in 2004

13 15 17 19 20 18 16 14

First published in the United Kingdom in 1947 by Jonathan Cape Ltd

Fiesta first published 1927
A Farewell to Arms first published 1929
To Have and Have Not first published 1937
For Whom the Bell Tolls first published 1941
In Our Time first published 1926
Men Without Women first published 1928
Winner Take Nothing first published 1934
The First Forty-Nine first published 1939
Death in the Afternoon first published 1932

Arrow Books
The Random House Group Limited
20 Vauxhall Bridge Road, London, SW1V 2SA

Random House Australia (Pty) Limited
20 Alfred Street, Milsons Point, Sydney, New South Wales 2061, Australia

Random House New Zealand Limited
18 Poland Road, Glenfield, Auckland 10, New Zealand

Random House (Pty) Limited
Endulini, 5a Jubilee Road, Parktown 2193, South Africa

The Random House Group Limited Reg. No. 954009

www.randomhouse.co.uk

A CIP catalogue record for this book is available from the British Library

Papers used by Random House are natural, recyclable products made from
wood grown in sustainable forests. The manufacturing processes conform
to the environmental regulations of the country of origin

ISBN 0 09 933931 5

Typeset by SX Composing DTP, Rayleigh, Essex
Printed and bound by Cox & Wyman Ltd, Reading, Berkshire

Contents

THE NOVELS

THE STORIES

The Novels

'FIESTA'
(THE SUN ALSO RISES)
BOOK ONE

Chapter 1

Robert Cohn was once middleweight boxing champion of
Princeton. Do not think that I am very much impressed by that
as a boxing title, but it meant a lot to Cohn. He cared nothing
for boxing, in fact he disliked it, but he learned it painfully and
thoroughly to counteract the feeling of inferiority and shyness
he had felt on being treated as a Jew at Princeton. There was a
certain inner comfort in knowing he could knock down
anybody who was snooty to him, although, being very shy and
a thoroughly nice boy, he never fought except in the gym. He
was Spider Kelly's star pupil. Spider Kelly taught all his young
gentlemen to box like featherweights, no matter whether they
weighed one hundred and five or two hundred and five
pounds. But it seemed to fit Cohn. He was really very fast. He
was so good that Spider promptly overmatched him and got
his nose permanently flattened. This increased Cohn's distaste
for boxing, but it gave him a certain satisfaction of some
strange sort, and it certainly improved his nose. In his last year
at Princeton he read too much and took to wearing spectacles.
I never met anyone of his class who remembered him. They did
not even remember that he was middleweight boxing
champion.

I mistrust all frank and simple people, especially when their
stories hold together, and I always had a suspicion that perhaps
Robert Cohn had never been middleweight boxing champion,
and that perhaps a horse had stepped on his face, or that maybe

his mother had been frightened or seen something, or that he had, maybe, bumped into something as a young child, but I finally had somebody verify the story from Spider Kelly. Spider Kelly not only remembered Cohn. He had often wondered what had become of him.

Robert Cohn was a member, through his father, of one of the richest Jewish families in New York, and through his mother of one of the oldest. At the military school where he prepped for Princeton, and played a very good end on the football team, no one had made him race-conscious. No one had ever made him feel he was a Jew, and hence any different from anybody else, until he went to Princeton. He was a nice boy, a friendly boy, and very shy, and it made him bitter. He took it out in boxing, and he came out of Princeton with painful self-consciousness and the flattened nose, and was married by the first girl who was nice to him. He was married five years, had three children, lost most of the fifty thousand dollars his father left him, the balance of the estate having gone to his mother, hardened into a rather unattractive mould under domestic unhappiness with a rich wife; and just when he had made up his mind to leave his wife she left him and went off with a miniature-painter. As he had been thinking for months about leaving his wife and had not done it because it would be too cruel to deprive her of himself, her departure was a very healthful shock.

The divorce was arranged and Robert Cohn went out to the Coast. In California he fell among literary people and, as he still had a little of the fifty thousand left, in a short time he was backing a review of the Arts. The review commenced publication in Carmel, California, and finished in Province-town, Massachusetts. By that time Cohn, who had been regarded purely as an angel, and whose name had appeared on the editorial page merely as a member of the advisory board, had become the sole editor. It was his money and he discovered he liked the authority of editing. He was sorry when the magazine became too expensive and he had to give it up.

By that time, though, he had other things to worry about. He had been taken in hand by a lady who hoped to rise with the magazine. She was very forceful, and Cohn never had a

4

chance of not being taken in hand. Also he was sure that he loved her. When this lady saw that the magazine was not going to rise, she became a little disgusted with Cohn and decided that she might as well get what there was to get while there was still something available, so she urged that they go to Europe, where Cohn could write. They came to Europe, where the lady had been educated, and stayed three years. During these three years, the first spent in travel, the last two in Paris, Robert Cohn had two friends, Braddocks and myself. Braddocks was his literary friend. I was his tennis friend.

The lady who had him, her name was Frances, found toward the end of the second year that her looks were going, and her attitude toward Robert changed from one of careless possession and exploitation to the absolute determination that he should marry her. During this time Robert's mother had settled an allowance on him, about three hundred dollars a month. During two years and a half I do not believe that Robert Cohn looked at another woman. He was fairly happy, except that, like many people living in Europe, he would rather have been in America, and he had discovered writing. He wrote a novel, and it was not really such a bad novel as the critics later called it, although it was a very poor novel. He read many books, played bridge, played tennis, and boxed at a local gymnasium.

I first became aware of his lady's attitude toward him one night after the three of us had dined together. We had dined at l'Avenue's and afterward went to the Café de Versailles for coffee. We had several *fines* after the coffee, and I said I must be going. Cohn had been talking about the two of us going off somewhere on a weekend trip. He wanted to get out of town and get in a good walk. I suggested we fly to Strasbourg and walk up to Saint Odile, or somewhere or other in Alsace. 'I know a girl in Strasbourg who can show us the town,' I said.

Somebody kicked me under the table. I thought it was accidental and went on: 'She's been there two years and knows everything there is to know about the town. She's a swell girl.'

I was kicked again under the table and, looking, saw Frances, Robert's lady, her chin lifting and her face hardening.

'Hell,' I said, 'why go to Strasbourg? We could go up to Bruges, or to the Ardennes.'

Cohn looked relieved. I was not kicked again. I said good-night and went out. Cohn said he wanted to buy a paper and would walk to the corner with me. 'For God's sake,' he said, 'what did you say that about the girl in Strasbourg for? Didn't you see Frances?'

'No, why should I? If I know an American girl that lives in Strasbourg what the hell is it to Frances?'

'It doesn't make any difference. Any girl. I couldn't go, that would be all.'

'Don't be silly.'

'You don't know Frances. Any girl at all. Didn't you see the way she looked?'

'Oh, well,' I said, 'let's go to Senlis.'

'Don't get sore.'

'I'm not sore. Senlis is a good place and we can stay at the Grand Cerf and take a hike in the woods and come home.'

'Good, that will be fine.'

'Well, I'll see you to-morrow at the courts,' I said.

'Good-night, Jake,' he said, and started back to the café.

'You forgot to get your paper,' I said.

'That's so.' He walked with me up to the kiosk at the corner. 'You are not sore, are you, Jake?' He turned with the paper in his hand.

'No, why should I be?'

'See you at tennis,' he said. I watched him walk back to the café holding his paper. I rather liked him and evidently she led him quite a life.

Chapter 2

That winter Robert Cohn went over to America with his novel, and it was accepted by a fairly good publisher. His going made an awful row I heard, and I think that was where Frances lost him, because several women were nice to him in New York, and when he came back he was quite changed. He was more enthusiastic about America than ever, and he was not so simple, and he was not so nice. The publishers had praised his novel pretty highly and it rather went to his head. Then several women had put themselves out to be nice to him, and his horizons had all shifted. For four years his horizon had been absolutely limited to his wife. For three years, or almost three years, he had never seen beyond Frances. I am sure he had never been in love in his life.

He had married on the rebound from the rotten time he had in college, and Frances took him on the rebound from his discovery that he had not been everything to his first wife. He was not in love yet but he realized that he was an attractive quantity to women, and that the fact of a woman caring for him and wanting to live with him was not simply a divine miracle. This changed him so that he was not so pleasant to have around. Also, playing for higher stakes than he could afford in some rather steep bridge games with his New York connections, he had held cards and won several hundred dollars. It made him rather vain of his bridge game, and he talked several times of how a man could always make a living at bridge if he were ever forced to.

Then there was another thing. He had been reading W. H. Hudson. That sounds like an innocent occupation, but Cohn had read and reread *The Purple Land*. *The Purple Land* is a very sinister book if read too late in life. It recounts splendid imaginary amorous adventures of a perfect English gentleman in an intensely romantic land, the scenery of which is very well described. For a man to take it at thirty-four as a guidebook to what life holds is about as safe as it would be for a man of the same age to enter Wall Street direct from a French convent, equipped with a complete set of the more practical Alger books. Cohn, I believe, took every word of *The Purple Land* as literally as though it had been an R. G. Dun report. You understand me, he made some reservations, but on the whole the book to him was sound. It was all that was needed to set him off. I did not realize the extent to which it had set him off until one day he came into my office.

'Hello, Robert,' I said. 'Did you come in to cheer me up?'

'Would you like to go to South America, Jake?' he asked.

'No.'

'Why not?'

'I don't know. I never wanted to go. Too expensive. You can see all the South Americans you want in Paris anyway.'

'They're not the real South Americans.'

'They look awfully real to me.'

I had a boat train to catch with a week's mail stories, and only half of them written.

'Do you know any dirt?' I asked.

'No.'

'None of your exalted connections getting divorces?'

'No; listen, Jake. If I handled both our expenses, would you go to South America with me?'

'Why me?'

'You can talk Spanish. And it would be more fun with two of us.'

'No,' I said, 'I like this town and I go to Spain in the summertime.'

'All my life I've wanted to go on a trip like that,' Cohn said. He sat down. 'I'll be too old before I can ever do it.'

'Don't be a fool,' I said. 'You can go anywhere you want. You've got plenty of money.'

'I know. But I can't get started.'

'Cheer up,' I said. 'All countries look just like the moving pictures.'

But I felt sorry for him. He had it badly.

'I can't stand it to think my life is going so fast and I'm not really living it.'

'Nobody ever lives their life all the way up except bull-fighters.'

'I'm not interested in bull-fighters. That's an abnormal life. I want to go back in the country in South America. We could have a great trip.'

'Did you ever think about going to British East Africa to shoot?'

'No, I wouldn't like that.'

'I'd go there with you.'

'No; that doesn't interest me.'

'That's because you never read a book about it. Go on and

8

read a book all full of love affairs with the beautiful shiny black princesses.'

'I want to go to South America.'

He had a hard, Jewish, stubborn, streak.

'Come on downstairs and have a drink.'

'Aren't you working?'

'No,' I said. We went down the stairs to the café on the ground floor. I had discovered that was the best way to get rid of friends. Once you had a drink all you had to say was: 'Well, I've got to get back and get off some cables,' and it was done. It is very important to discover graceful exits like that in the newspaper business, where it is such an important part of the ethics that you should never seem to be working. Anyway, we went downstairs to the bar and had a whisky and soda. Cohn looked at the bottles in bins around the walls. 'This is a good place,' he said.

'There's a lot of liquor,' I agreed.

'Listen, Jake,' he leaned forward on the bar. 'Don't you ever get the feeling that all your life is going by and you're not taking advantage of it? Do you realize you've lived nearly half the time you have to live already?'

'Yes, every once in a while.'

'Do you know that in about thirty-five years more we'll be dead?'

'What the hell, Robert,' I said. 'What the hell.'

'I'm serious.'

'It's one thing I don't worry about,' I said.

'You ought to.'

'I've had plenty to worry about one time or other. I'm through worrying.'

'Well, I want to go to South America.'

'Listen, Robert, going to another country doesn't make any difference. I've tried all that. You can't get away from yourself by moving from one place to another. There's nothing to that.'

'But you've never been to South America.'

'South America hell! If you went there the way you feel now it would be exactly the same. This is a good town. Why don't you start living your life in Paris?'

9

'I'm sick of Paris, and I'm sick of the Quarter.'

'Stay away from the Quarter. Cruise around by yourself and see what happens to you.'

'Nothing happens to me. I walked alone all one night and nothing happened except a bicycle cop stopped me and asked to see my papers.'

'Wasn't the town nice at night?'

'I don't care for Paris.'

So there you were. I was sorry for him, but it was not a thing you could do anything about, because right away you ran up against the two stubbornnesses: South America could fix it and he did not like Paris. He got the first idea out of a book, and I suppose the second came out of a book too.

'Well,' I said, 'I've got to go upstairs and get off some cables.'

'Do you really have to go?'

'Yes, I've got to get these cables off.'

'Do you mind if I come up and sit around the office?'

'No, come on up.'

He sat in the outer room and read the papers, and the editor and publisher and I worked hard for two hours. Then I sorted out the carbons, stamped on a by-line, put the stuff in a couple of big manila envelopes and rang for a boy to take them to the Gare St Lazare. I went out into the other room and there was Robert Cohn asleep in the big chair. He was asleep with his head on his arms. I did not like to wake him up, but I wanted to lock the office and shove off. I put my hand on his shoulder. He shook his head. 'I can't do it,' he said, and put his head deeper into his arms. 'I can't do it. Nothing will make me do it.'

'Robert,' I said, and shook him by the shoulder. He looked up. He smiled and blinked.

'Did I talk out loud just then?'

'Something. But it wasn't clear.'

'God, what a rotten dream!'

'Did the typewriter put you to sleep?'

'Guess so. I didn't sleep all last night.'

'What was the matter?'

'Talking,' he said.

I could picture it. I have a rotten habit of picturing the

10

bedroom scenes of my friends. We went out to the Café Napolitain to have an *apéritif* and watch the evening crowd on the Boulevard.

Chapter 3

It was a warm spring night and I sat at a table on the terrace of the Napolitain after Robert had gone, watching it get dark and the electric signs come on, and the red and green stop-and-go traffic-signal, and the crowd going by, and the horse-cabs clippety-clopping along at the edge of the solid taxi traffic, and the *poules* going by, singly and in pairs, looking for the evening meal. I watched a good-looking girl walk past the table and watched her go up the street and lost sight of her, and watched another, and then saw the first one coming back again. She went by once more and I caught her eye, and she came over and sat down at the table. The waiter came up.

'Well, what will you drink?' I asked.

'Pernod.'

'That's not good for little girls.'

'Little girl yourself. Dites garçon, un pernod.'

'A pernod for me, too.'

'What's the matter?' she asked. 'Going on a party?'

'Sure. Aren't you?'

'I don't know. You never know in this town.'

'Don't you like Paris?'

'No.'

'Why don't you go somewhere else?'

'Isn't anywhere else.'

'You're happy, all right.'

'Happy, hell!'

Pernod is greenish imitation absinthe. When you add water it turns milky. It tastes like liquorice and it has a good uplift, but it drops you just as far. We sat and drank it, and the girl looked sullen.

'Well,' I said, 'are you going to buy me a dinner?'

She grinned and I saw why she made a point of not laughing. With her mouth closed she was a rather pretty girl. I paid for the saucers and we walked out to the street. I hailed a horse-cab and the driver pulled up at the curb. Settled back in the slow, smoothly rolling *fiacre* we moved up the Avenue de l'Opéra, passed the locked doors of the shops, their windows lighted, the Avenue broad and shiny and almost deserted. The cab passed the New York *Herald* bureau with the window full of clocks.

'What are all the clocks for?' she asked.

'They show the hour all over America.'

'Don't kid me.'

We turned off the Avenue up the Rue des Pyramides, through the traffic of the Rue de Rivoli, and through a dark gate into the Tuileries. She cuddled against me and I put my arm around her. She looked up to be kissed. She touched me with one hand and I put her hand away.

'Never mind.'

'What's the matter? You sick?'

'Yes.'

'Everybody's sick. I'm sick, too.'

We came out of the Tuileries into the light and crossed the Seine and then turned up the Rue des Saints Pères.

'You oughtn't to drink pernod if you're sick.'

'You neither.'

'It doesn't make any difference with me. It doesn't make any difference with a woman.'

'What are you called?'

'Georgette. How are you called?'

'Jacob.'

'That's a Flemish name.'

'American too.'

'You're not Flamand?'

'No, American.'

'Good, I detest Flamands.'

By this time we were at the restaurant. I called to the *cocher* to stop. We got out and Georgette did not like the looks of the place. 'This is no great thing of a restaurant.'

12

'No,' I said. 'Maybe you would rather go to Foyot's. Why don't you keep the cab and go on?'

I had picked her up because of a vague sentimental idea that it would be nice to eat with someone. It was a long time since I had dined with a *poule,* and I had forgotten how dull it could be. We went into the restaurant, passed Madame Lavigne at the desk and into a little room. Georgette cheered up a little under the food.

'It isn't bad here,' she said. 'It isn't chic, but the food is all right.'

'Better than you eat in Liège.'

'Brussels, you mean.'

We had another bottle of wine and Georgette made a joke. She smiled and showed all her bad teeth, and we touched glasses. 'You're not a bad type,' she said. 'It's a shame you're sick. We get on well. What's the matter with you, anyway?'

'I got hurt in the war,' I said.

'Oh, that dirty war.'

We would probably have gone on and discussed the war and agreed that it was in reality a calamity for civilization, and perhaps would have been better avoided. I was bored enough. Just then from the other room some one called: 'Barnes! I say, Barnes! Jacob Barnes!'

'It's a friend calling me,' I explained, and went out.

There was Braddocks at a big table with a party: Cohn, Frances Clyne, Mrs Braddocks, several people I did not know.

'You're coming to the dance, aren't you?' Braddocks asked.

'What dance?'

'Why, the dancings. Don't you know we've revived them?' Mrs Braddocks put in.

'You must come, Jake. We're all going,' Frances said from the end of the table. She was tall and had a smile.

'Of course, he's coming,' Braddocks said. 'Come in and have coffee with us, Barnes.'

'Right.'

'And bring your friend,' said Mrs Braddocks laughing. She was a Canadian and had all their easy social graces.

'Thanks, we'll be in,' I said. I went back to the small room.

'Who are your friends?' Georgette asked.

13

'Writers and artists.'

'There are lots of those on this side of the river.'

'Too many.'

'I think so. Still, some of them make money.'

'Oh, yes.'

We finished the meal and the wine. 'Come on,' I said. 'We're going to have coffee with the others.'

Georgette opened her bag, made a few passes at her face as she looked in the little mirror, re-defined her lips with the lipstick, and straightened her hat.

'Good,' she said.

We went into the room full of people and Braddocks and the men at his table stood up.

'I wish to present my fiancée, Mademoiselle Georgette Leblanc,' I said. Georgette smiled that wonderful smile, and we shook hands all round.

'Are you related to Georgette Leblanc, the singer?' Mrs Braddocks asked.

'Connais pas,' Georgette answered.

'But you have the same name,' Mrs Braddocks insisted cordially.

'No,' said Georgette. 'Not at all. My name is Hobin.'

'But Mr Barnes introduced you as Mademoiselle Georgette Leblanc. Surely he did,' insisted Mrs Braddocks, who in the excitement of talking French was liable to have no idea what she was saying.

'He's a fool,' Georgette said.

'Oh, it was a joke, then,' Mrs Braddocks said.

'Yes,' said Georgette. 'To laugh at.'

'Did you hear that, Henry?' Mrs Braddocks called down the table to Braddocks. 'Mr Barnes introduced his fiancée as Mademoiselle Leblanc, and her name is actually Hobin.'

'Of course, darling. Mademoiselle Hobin, I've known her for a very long time.'

'Oh, Mademoiselle Hobin,' Frances Clyne called, speaking French very rapidly and not seeming so proud and astonished as Mrs Braddocks at its coming out really French. 'Have you been in Paris long? Do you like it here? You love Paris, do you not?'

14

'Who's she?' Georgette turned to me. 'Do I have to talk to her?'

She turned to Frances, sitting smiling, her hands folded, her head poised on her long neck, her lips pursed ready to start talking again.

'No, I don't like Paris. It's expensive and dirty.'

'Really? I find it so extraordinarily clean. One of the cleanest cities in all Europe.'

'I find it dirty.'

'How strange! But perhaps you have not been here very long.'

'I've been here long enough.'

'But it does have nice people in it. One must grant that.'

Georgette turned to me. 'You have nice friends.'

Frances was a little drunk and would have liked to have kept it up but the coffee came, and Lavigne with the liqueurs, and after that we all went out and started for Braddocks's dancing-club.

The dancing-club was a *bal musette* in the Rue de la Montagne Sainte Geneviève. Five nights a week the working people of the Panthéon quarter danced there. One night a week it was the dancing-club. On Monday nights it was closed. When we arrived it was quite empty, except for a policeman sitting near the door, the wife of the proprietor back of the zinc bar, and the proprietor himself. The daughter of the house came downstairs as we went in. There were long benches, and tables ran across the room, and at the far end a dancing-floor.

'I wish people would come earlier,' Braddocks said. The daughter came up and wanted to know what we would drink. The proprietor got up on a high stool beside the dancing-floor and began to play the accordion. He had a string of bells around one of his ankles and beat time with his foot as he played. Everyone danced. It was hot and we came off the floor perspiring.

'My God,' Georgette said. 'What a box to sweat in!'

'It's hot.'

'Hot, my God!'

'Take off your hat.'

'That's a good idea.'

15

Someone asked Georgette to dance, and I went over to the bar. It was really very hot and the accordion music was pleasant in the hot night. I drank a beer, standing in the doorway and getting the cool breath of wind from the street. Two taxis were coming down the steep street. They both stopped in front of the Bal. A crowd of young men, some in jerseys and some in their shirt-sleeves, got out. I could see their hands and newly washed, wavy hair in the light from the door. The policeman standing by the door looked at me and smiled. They came in. As they went in, under the light I saw hands, wavy hair, white faces, grimacing, gesturing, talking. With them was Brett. She looked very lovely, and she was very much with them.

One of them saw Georgette and said: 'I do declare. There is an actual harlot. I'm going to dance with her, Lett. You watch me.'

The tall, dark one, called Lett, said: 'Don't you be rash.'

The wavy blond one answered: 'Don't you worry, dear.' And with them was Brett.

I was very angry. Somehow they always made me angry. I know they are supposed to be amusing, and you should be tolerant, but I wanted to swing on one, anyone, anything to shatter that superior, simpering composure. Instead, I walked down the street and had a beer at the bar at the next Bal. The beer was not good and I had a worse cognac to take the taste out of my mouth. When I came back to the Bal there was a crowd on the floor and Georgette was dancing with the tall blond youth, who danced big-hippily, carrying his head on one side, his eyes lifted as he danced. As soon as the music stopped another one of them asked her to dance. She had been taken up by them. I knew then that they would all dance with her. They are like that.

I sat down at a table. Cohn was sitting there. Frances was dancing. Mrs Braddocks brought up somebody and introduced him as Robert Prentiss. He was from New York by way of Chicago, and was a rising new novelist. He had some sort of an English accent. I asked him to have a drink.

'Thanks so much,' he said, 'I've just had one.'

'Have another.'

'Thanks, I will then.'

16

We got the daughter of the house over and each had a *fine à l'eau*.

'You're from Kansas City, they tell me,' he said.

'Yes.'

'Do you find Paris amusing?'

'Yes.'

'Really?'

I was a little drunk. Not drunk in any positive sense but just enough to be careless.

'For God's sake,' I said, 'yes. Don't you?'

'Oh, how charmingly you get angry,' he said. 'I wish I had that faculty.'

I got up and walked over toward the dancing-floor. Mrs Braddocks followed me. 'Don't be cross with Robert,' she said. 'He's still only a child, you know.'

'I wasn't cross,' I said. 'I just thought perhaps I was going to throw up.'

'Your fiancée is having a great success,' Mrs Braddocks looked out on the floor where Georgette was dancing in the arms of the tall, dark one, called Lett.

'Isn't she?' I said.

'Rather,' said Mrs Braddocks.

Cohn came up. 'Come on, Jake,' he said, 'have a drink.' We walked over to the bar. 'What's the matter with you? You seem all worked up over something?'

'Nothing. This whole show makes me sick is all.'

Brett came up to the bar.

'Hello, you chaps.'

'Hello, Brett,' I said. 'Why aren't you tight?'

'Never going to get tight any more. I say, give a chap a brandy and soda.'

She stood holding the glass and I saw Robert Cohn looking at her. He looked a great deal as his compatriot must have looked when he saw the promised land. Cohn, of course, was much younger. But he had that look of eager, deserving expectation.

Brett was damned good-looking. She wore a slipover jersey sweater and a tweed skirt, and her hair was brushed back like a boy's. She started all that. She was built with curves like the hull of a racing yacht, and you missed none of it with that wool jersey.

'It's a fine crowd you're with, Brett,' I said.

'Aren't they lovely? And you, my dear. Where did you get it?'

'At the Napolitain.'

'And have you had a lovely evening?'

'Oh, priceless,' I said.

Brett laughed. 'It's wrong of you, Jake. It's an insult to all of us. Look at Frances there, and Jo.'

This for Cohn's benefit.

'It's in restraint of trade,' Brett said. She laughed again.

'You're wonderfully sober,' I said.

'Yes. Aren't I? And when one's with the crowd I'm with, one can drink in such safety, too.'

The music started and Robert Cohn said: 'Will you dance this with me, Lady Brett?'

Brett smiled at him. 'I've promised to dance this with Jacob,' she laughed. 'You've a hell of a biblical name, Jake.'

'How about the next?' asked Cohn.

'We're going,' Brett said. 'We've a date up at Montmartre.'

Dancing, I looked over Brett's shoulder and saw Cohn, standing at the bar, still watching her.

'You've made a new one there,' I said to her.

'Don't talk about it. Poor chap. I never knew it till just now.'

'Oh, well,' I said. 'I suppose you like to add them up.'

'Don't talk like a fool.'

'You do.'

'Oh, well. What if I do?'

'Nothing,' I said. We were dancing to the accordion and someone was playing the banjo. It was hot and I felt happy. We passed close to Georgette dancing with another one of them.

'What possessed you to bring her?'

'I don't know, I just brought her.'

'You're getting damned romantic.'

'No, bored.'

'Now?'

'No, not now.'

'Let's get out of here. She's well taken care of.'

'Do you want to?'

'Would I ask you if I didn't want to?'

We left the floor and I took my coat off a hanger on the wall and put it on. Brett stood by the bar. Cohn was talking to her. I stopped at the bar and asked them for an envelope. The patronne found one. I took a fifty-franc note from my pocket, put it in the envelope, sealed it, and handed it to the patronne.

'If the girl I came with asks for me, will you give her this?' I said. 'If she goes out with one of those gentlemen, will you save this for me?'

'C'est entendu, Monsieur,' the patronne said. 'You go now? So early?'

'Yes,' I said.

We started out the door. Cohn was still talking to Brett. She said good night and took my arm. 'Good night, Cohn,' I said. Outside in the street we looked for a taxi.

'You're going to lose your fifty francs,' Brett said.

'Oh, yes.'

'No taxis.'

'We could walk up to the Panthéon and get one.'

'Come on and we'll get a drink in the pub next door and send for one.'

'You wouldn't walk across the street.'

'Not if I could help it.'

We went into the next bar and I sent a waiter for a taxi.

'Well,' I said, 'we're out away from them.'

We stood against the tall zinc bar and did not talk and looked at each other. The waiter came and said the taxi was outside. Brett pressed my hand hard. I gave the waiter a franc and we went out. 'Where should I tell him?' I asked.

'Oh, tell him to drive around.'

I told the driver to go to the Parc Montsouris, and got in, and slammed the door. Brett was leaning back in the corner, her eyes closed. I got in and sat beside her. The cab started with a jerk.

'Oh, darling, I've been so miserable,' Brett said.

19

Chapter 4

The taxi went up the hill, passed the lighted square, then on into the dark, still climbing, and levelled out onto a dark street behind St Etienne du Mont, went smoothly down the asphalt, passed the trees and the standing bus at the Place de la Contrescarpe, then turned on to the cobbles of the Rue Mouffetard. There were lighted bars and late open shops on each side of the street. We were sitting apart and we jolted close together going down the old street. Brett's hat was off. Her head was back. I saw her face in the lights from the open shops, then it was dark, then I saw her face clearly as we came out on the Avenue des Gobelins. The street was torn up and men were working on the car-tracks by the light of acetylene flares. Brett's face was white and the long line of her neck showed in the bright light of the flares. The street was dark again and I kissed her. Our lips were tight together and then she turned away and pressed against the corner of the seat, as far away as she could get. Her head was down.

'Don't touch me,' she said. 'Please don't touch me.'

'What's the matter?'

'I can't stand it.'

'Oh, Brett.'

'You mustn't. You must know. I can't stand it, that's all. Oh, darling, please understand!'

'Don't you love me?'

'Love you? I simply turn all to jelly when you touch me.'

'Isn't there anything we can do about it?'

She was sitting up now. My arm was around her and she was leaning back against me, and we were quite calm. She was looking into my eyes with that way she had of looking that made you wonder whether she really saw out of her own eyes. They would look on and on after every one else's eyes in the world would have stopped looking. She looked as though there were nothing on earth she would not look at like that, and really she was afraid of so many things.

'And there's not a damn thing we could do,' I said.

'I don't know,' she said. 'I don't want to go through that hell again.'

'We'd better keep away from each other.'

'But, darling, I have to see you. It isn't all that you know.'

'No, but it always gets to be.'

'That's my fault. Don't we pay for all the things we do, though?'

She had been looking into my eyes all the time. Her eyes had different depths, sometimes they seemed perfectly flat. Now you could see all the way into them.

'When I think of the hell I've put chaps through. I'm paying for it all now.'

'Don't talk like a fool,' I said. 'Besides, what happened to me is supposed to be funny. I never think about it.'

'Oh, no. I'll lay you don't.'

'Well, let's shut up about it.'

'I laughed about it too, myself, once.' She wasn't looking at me. 'A friend of my brother's came home that way from Mons. It seemed like a hell of a joke. Chaps never know anything, do they?'

'No,' I said. 'Nobody ever knows anything.'

I was pretty well through with the subject. At one time or another I had probably considered it from most of its various angles, including the one that certain injuries or imperfections are a subject of merriment while remaining quite serious for the person possessing them.

'It's funny,' I said. 'It's very funny. And it's a lot of fun, too, to be in love.'

'Do you think so?' Her eyes looked flat again.

'I don't mean fun that way. In a way it's an enjoyable feeling.'

'No,' she said. 'I think it's hell on earth.'

'It's good to see each other.'

'No. I don't think it is.'

'Don't you want to?'

'I have to.'

21

We were sitting now like two strangers. On the right was the Parc Montsouris. The restaurant where they have the pool of live trout and where you can sit and look out over the park was closed and dark. The driver leaned his head around.

'Where do you want to go?' I asked. Brett turned her head away.

'Oh, go to the Select.'

'Café Select,' I told the driver. 'Boulevard Montparnasse.' We drove straight down, turning around the Lion de Belfort that guards the passing Montrouge trams. Brett looked straight ahead. On the Boulevard Raspail, with the lights of Montparnasse in sight, Brett said: 'Would you mind very much if I asked you to do something?'

'Don't be silly.'

'Kiss me just once more before we get there.'

When the taxi stopped I got out and paid. Brett came out putting on her hat. She gave me her hand as she stepped down. Her hand was shaky. 'I say, do I look too much of a mess?' She pulled her man's felt hat down and started in for the bar. Inside, against the bar and at tables, were most of the crowd who had been at the dance.

'Hello, you chaps,' Brett said. 'I'm going to have a drink.'

'Oh, Brett! Brett!' the little Greek portrait-painter, who called himself a duke, and whom everybody called Zizi, pushed up to her. 'I got something fine to tell you.'

'Hello, Zizi,' Brett said.

'I want you to meet a friend,' Zizi said. A fat man came up. 'Count Mippipopolous, meet my friend Lady Ashley.'

'How do you do?' said Brett.

'Well, does your ladyship have a good time here in Paris?' asked Count Mippipopolous, who wore an elk's tooth on his watch-chain.

'Rather,' said Brett.

'Paris is a fine town all right,' said the count. 'But I guess you have pretty big doings yourself over in London.'

'Oh, yes,' said Brett. 'Enormous.'

Braddocks called to me from a table. 'Barnes,' he said, 'have a drink. That girl of yours got in a frightful row.'

'What about?'

'Something the patronne's daughter said. A corking row. She was rather splendid, you know. Showed her yellow card and demanded the patronne's daughter's too. I say it was a row.'

'What finally happened?

'Oh, some one took her home. Not a bad-looking girl. Wonderful command of the idiom. Do stay and have a drink.'

'No,' I said. 'I must shove off. Seen Cohn?'

'He went home with Frances,' Mrs Braddocks put in.

'Poor chap, he looks awfully down,' Braddocks said.

'I dare say he is,' said Mrs Braddocks.

'I have to shove off,' I said. 'Good night.'

I said good night to Brett at the bar. The count was buying champagne. 'Will you take a glass of wine with us, sir?' he asked.

'No. Thanks awfully. I have to go.'

'Really going?' Brett asked.

'Yes,' I said. 'I've got a rotten headache.'

'I'll see you to-morrow?'

'Come in at the office.'

'Hardly.'

'Well, where will I see you?'

'Anywhere around five clock.'

'Make it the other side of town then.'

'Good. I'll be at the Crillon at five.'

'Try and be there,' I said.

'Don't worry,' Brett said. 'I've never let you down, have I?'

'Heard from Mike?'

'Letter to-day.'

'Good night, sir,' said the count.

I went out on to the sidewalk and walked down toward the Boulevard St Michel, passed the tables of the Rotonde, still crowded, looked across the street at the Dôme, its tables running out to the edge of the pavement. Someone waved at me from a table, I did not see who it was, and went on. I wanted to get home. The Boulevard Montparnasse was deserted. Lavigne's was closed tight, and they were stacking the tables outside the Closerie des Lilas. I passed Ney's statue standing among the new-leaved chestnut-trees in the arc-light.

23

There was a faded purple wreath leaning against the base. I stopped and read the inscription: from the Bonapartist Groups, some date; I forget. He looked very fine, Marshal Ney in his top-boots, gesturing with his sword among the green new horse-chestnut leaves. My flat was just across the street, a little way down the Boulevard St Michel.

There was a light in the concierge's room and I knocked on the door and she gave me my mail. I wished her good night and went upstairs. There were two letters and some papers. I looked at them under the gaslight in the dining-room. The letters were from the States. One was a bank statement. It showed a balance of $2,432.60. I got out my cheque-book and deducted four cheques drawn since the first of the month, and discovered I had a balance of $1,832.60. I wrote this on the back of the statement. The other letter was a wedding announcement. Mr and Mrs Aloysius Kirby announce the marriage of their daughter Katherine – I knew neither the girl nor the man she was marrying. They must be circularizing the town. It was a funny name. I felt sure I could remember anybody with a name like Aloysius. It was a good Catholic name. There was a crest on the announcement. Like Zizi the Greek duke. And that count. The count was funny. Brett had a title, too. Lady Ashley. To hell with Brett. To hell with you, Lady Ashley.

I lit the lamp beside the bed, turned off the gas, and opened the wide windows. The bed was far back from the windows, and I sat with the windows open and undressed by the bed. Outside a night train, running on the street-car tracks, went by carrying vegetables to the markets. They were noisy at night when you could not sleep. Undressing, I looked at myself in the mirror of the big armoire beside the bed. That was a typically French way to furnish a room. Practical, too, I suppose. Of all the ways to be wounded. I suppose it was funny. I put on my pyjamas and got into bed. I had the two bull-fight papers, and I took their wrappers off. One was orange. The other yellow. They would both have the same news, so whichever I read first would spoil the other. *Le Toril* was the better paper, so I started to read it. I read it all the way through, including the Petite Correspondance and the

Cornigrams. I blew out the lamp. Perhaps I would be able to sleep.

My head started to work. The old grievance. Well, it was a rotten way to be wounded and flying on a joke front like the Italian. In the Italian hospital we were going to form a society. It had a funny name in Italian. I wonder what became of the others, the Italians. That was in the Ospedale Maggiore in Milano, Padiglione Ponte. The next building was the Padiglione Zonda. There was a statue of Ponte, or maybe it was Zonda. That was where the liaison colonel came to visit me. That was funny. That was about the first funny thing. I was all bandaged up. But they had told him about it. Then he made that wonderful speech: 'You, a foreigner, an Englishman (any foreigner was an Englishman), have given more than your life.' What a speech! I would like to have it illuminated to hang in the office. He never laughed. He was putting himself in my place, I guess. 'Che mala fortuna! Che mala fortuna!'

I never used to realize it, I guess. I try and play it along and just not make trouble for people. Probably I never would have had any trouble if I hadn't run into Brett when they shipped me to England. I suppose she only wanted what she couldn't have. Well, people were that way. To hell with people. The Catholic Church had an awfully good way of handling all that. Good advice, anyway. Not to think about it. Oh, it was swell advice. Try and take it sometime. Try and take it.

I lay awake thinking and my mind jumping around. Then I couldn't keep away from it, and I started to think about Brett and all the rest of it went away. I was thinking about Brett and my mind stopped jumping around and started to go in sort of smooth waves. Then all of a sudden I started to cry. Then after a while it was better and I lay in bed and listened to the heavy trams go by and way down the street, and then I went to sleep.

I woke up. There was a row going on outside. I listened and I thought I recognized a voice. I put on a dressing-gown and went to the door. The concierge was talking down-stairs. She was very angry. I heard my name and called down the stairs.

'Is that you, Monsieur Barnes?' the concierge called.

'Yes. It's me.'

'There's a species of woman here who's waked the whole

street up. What kind of dirty business at this time of night! She says she must see you. I've told her you're asleep.'

Then I heard Brett's voice. Half asleep I had been sure it was Georgette. I don't know why. She could not have known my address.

'Will you send her up, please?'

Brett came up the stairs. I saw she was quite drunk. 'Silly thing to do,' she said. 'Make an awful row. I say, you weren't asleep, were you?'

'What did you think I was doing?'

'Don't know. What time is it?'

I looked at the clock. It was half-past four. 'Had no idea what hour it was,' Brett said. 'I say, can a chap sit down? Don't be cross, darling. Just left the count. He brought me here.'

'What's he like?' I was getting brandy and soda and glasses.

'Just a little,' said Brett. 'Don't try and make me drunk. The count? Oh, rather. He's quite one of us.'

'Is he a count?'

'Here's how. I rather think so, you know. Deserves to be, anyhow. Knows hell's own amount about people. Don't know where he got it all. Owns a chain of sweetshops in the States.'

She sipped at her glass.

'Think he called it a chain. Something like that. Linked them all up. Told me a little about it. Damned interesting. He's one of us, though. Oh, quite. No doubt. One can always tell.'

She took another drink.

'How do I buck on about all this? You don't mind, do you? He's putting up for Zizi, you know.'

'Is Zizi really a duke, too?'

'I shouldn't wonder. Greek, you know. Rotten painter. I rather liked the count.'

'Where did you go with him?'

'Oh, everywhere. He just brought me here now. Offered me ten thousand dollars to go to Biarritz with him. How much is that in pounds?'

'Around two thousand.'

'Lot of money. I told him I couldn't do it. He was awfully nice about it. Told him I knew too many people in Biarritz.'

Brett laughed.

'I say, you are slow on the up-take,' she said. I had only sipped my brandy and soda. I took a long drink.

'That's better. Very funny,' Brett said. 'Then he wanted me to go to Cannes with him. Told him I knew too many people in Cannes. Monte Carlo. Told him I knew too many people in Monte Carlo. Told him I knew too many people everywhere. Quite true, too. So I asked him to bring me here.'

She looked at me, her hand on the table, her glass raised. 'Don't look like that,' she said. 'Told him I was in love with you. True, too. Don't look like that. He was damn nice about it. Wants to drive us out to dinner to-morrow night. Like to go?'

'Why not?'

'I'd better go now.'

'Why?'

'Just wanted to see you. Damned silly idea. Want to get dressed and come down? He's got the car just up the street.'

'The count?'

'Himself. And a chauffeur in livery. Going to drive me around and have breakfast in the Bois. Hampers. Got it all at Zelli's. Dozen bottles of Mumms. Tempt you?'

'I have to work in the morning,' I said. 'I'm too far behind you now to catch up and be any fun.'

'Don't be an ass.'

'Can't do it.'

'Right. Send him a tender message?'

'Anything. Absolutely.'

'Good night, darling.'

'Don't be sentimental.'

'You make me ill.'

We kissed good night and Brett shivered. 'I'd better go,' she said. 'Good night, darling.'

'You don't have to go.'

'Yes.'

We kissed again on the stairs and as I called for the cordon the concierge muttered something behind her door. I went back upstairs and from the open window watched Brett walking up the street to the big limousine drawn up to the kerb under the arc-light. She got in and it started off. I turned around. On the table was an empty glass and a glass half-full of brandy and soda. I took them both out to the kitchen and poured the half-full glass down the sink. I turned off the gas in the dining-room, kicked off my slippers sitting on the bed, and got into bed. This was Brett, that I had felt like crying about. Then I thought of her walking up the street and stepping into the car, as I had last seen her, and of course in a little while I felt like hell again. It is awfully easy to be hard-boiled about everything in the daytime, but at night it is another thing.

Chapter 5

In the morning I walked down the Boulevard to the Rue Soufflot for coffee and brioche. It was a fine morning. The horse-chestnut trees in the Luxembourg gardens were in bloom. There was the pleasant early-morning feeling of a hot day. I read the papers with the coffee and then smoked a cigarette. The flower-women were coming up from the market and arranging their daily stock. Students went by going up to the law school, or down to the Sorbonne. The Boulevard was busy with trams and people going to work. I got on an S bus and rode down to the Madeleine, standing on the black platform. From the Madeleine I walked along the Boulevard des Capucines to the Opéra, and up to my office. I passed the man with the jumping frogs and the man with the boxer toys. I stepped aside to avoid walking into the thread with which his girl assistant manipulated the boxers. She was standing looking away, the thread in her folded hands. The man was urging two tourists to buy. Three more tourists had stopped and were watching. I walked on behind a man who was pushing a roller that printed the name CINZANO on the sidewalk in damp letters. All along people were going to work. It felt pleasant to be going to work. I walked across the avenue and turned in to my office.

Up-stairs in the office I read the French morning papers,

smoked, and then sat at the typewriter and got off a good morning's work. At eleven o'clock I went over to the Quai d'Orsay in a taxi and went in and sat with about a dozen correspondents, while the foreign-office mouthpiece, a young *Nouvelle-Revue-Française* diplomat in horn-rimmed spectacles, talked and answered questions for half an hour. The President of the Council was in Lyons making a speech, or, rather he was on his way back. Several people asked questions to hear themselves talk and there were a couple of questions asked by news service men who wanted to know the answers. There was no news. I shared a taxi back from the Quai d'Orsay with Woolsey and Krum.

'What do you do nights, Jake?' asked Krum. 'I never see you around.'

'Oh, I'm over in the Quarter.'

'I'm coming over some night. The Dingo. That's the great place, isn't it?'

'Yes. That, or this new dive, the Select.'

'I've meant to get over,' said Krum. 'You know how it is, though, with a wife and kids.'

'Playing any tennis?' Woolsey asked.

'Well, no,' said Krum. 'I can't say I've played any this year. I've tried to get away, but Sunday's it's always rained, and the courts are so damned crowded.'

'The Englishmen all have Saturday off,' Woolsey said.

'Lucky beggars,' said Krum. 'Well, I'll tell you. Some day I'm not going to be working for an agency. Then I'll have plenty of time to get out in the country.'

'That's the thing to do. Live out in the country and have a little car.'

'I've been thinking some about getting a car next year.'

I banged on the glass. The chauffeur stopped. 'Here's my street,' I said. 'Come in and have a drink.'

'Thanks, old man,' Krum said. Woolsey shook his head. 'I've got to file that line he got off this morning.'

I put a two-franc piece in Krum's hand.

'You're crazy, Jake,' he said. 'This is on me.'

'It's all on the office, anyway.'

'Nope. I want to get it.'

I waved good-bye. Krum put his head out. 'See you at the lunch on Wednesday.'

'You bet.'

I went to the office in the elevator. Robert Cohn was waiting for me. 'Hello, Jake,' he said. 'Going out to lunch?'

'Yes. Let me see if there is anything new.'

'Where will we eat?'

'Anywhere.'

I was looking over my desk. 'Where do you want to eat?'

'How about Wetzel's? They've got good hors d'œuvres.'

In the restaurant we ordered hors d'œuvres and beer. The sommelier brought the beer, tall, beaded on the outside of the steins, and cold. There were a dozen different dishes of hors d'œuvres.

'Have any fun last night?' I asked.

'No. I don't think so.'

'How's the writing going?'

'Rotten. I can't get this second book going.'

'That happens to everybody.'

'Oh, I'm sure of that. It gets me worried, though.'

'Thought any more about going to South America?'

'I mean that.'

'Well, why don't you start off?'

'Frances.'

'Well,' I said, 'take her with you.'

'She wouldn't like it. That isn't the sort of thing she likes. She likes a lot of people around.'

'Tell her to go to hell.'

'I can't. I've got certain obligations to her.'

He shoved the sliced cucumbers away and took a pickled herring.

'What do you know about Lady Brett Ashley, Jake?'

'Her name's Lady Ashley. Brett's her own name. She's a nice girl,' I said. 'She's getting a divorce and she's going to marry Mike Campbell. He's over in Scotland now. Why?'

'She's a remarkably attractive woman.'

'Isn't she?'

'There's a certain quality about her, a certain fineness. She seems to be absolutely fine and straight.'

30

'She's very nice.'

'I don't know how to describe the quality,' Cohn said. 'I suppose it's breeding.'

'You sound as though you liked her pretty well.'

'I do. I shouldn't wonder if I were in love with her.'

'She's a drunk,' I said. 'She's in love with Mike Campbell, and she's going to marry him. He's going to be rich as hell some day.'

'I don't believe she'll ever marry him.'

'Why not?'

'I don't know. I just don't believe it. Have you known her a long time?'

'Yes,' I said. 'She was a V. A. D. in a hospital I was in during the war.'

'She must have been just a kid then.'

'She's thirty-four now.'

'When did she marry Ashley?'

'During the war. Her own true love had just kicked off with the dysentery.'

'You talk sort of bitter.'

'Sorry. I didn't mean to. I was just trying to give you the facts.'

'I don't believe she would marry anybody she didn't love.'

'Well,' I said. 'She's done it twice.'

'I don't believe it.'

'Well,' I said, 'don't ask me a lot of fool questions if you don't like the answers.'

'I didn't ask you that.'

'You asked me what I knew about Brett Ashley.'

'I didn't ask you to insult her.'

'Oh, go to hell.'

He stood up from the table his face white, and stood there white and angry behind the little plates of hors d'œuvres.

'Sit down,' I said. 'Don't be a fool.'

'You've got to take that back.'

'Oh, cut out the prep-school stuff.'

'Take it back.'

'Sure. Anything. I never heard of Brett Ashley. How's that?'

'No. Not that. About me going to hell.'

31

'Oh, don't go to hell,' I said. 'Stick around. We're just starting lunch.'

Cohn smiled again and sat down. He seemed glad to sit down. What the hell would he have done if he hadn't sat down? 'You say such damned insulting things, Jake.'

'I'm sorry. I've got a nasty tongue. I never mean it when I say nasty things.'

'I know it,' Cohn said. 'You're really about the best friend I have, Jake.'

God help you, I thought. 'Forget what I said,' I said out loud. 'I'm sorry.'

'It's all right. It's fine. I was just sore for a minute.'

'Good. Let's get something else to eat.'

After we finished the lunch we walked up to the Café de la Paix and had coffee. I could feel Cohn wanted to bring up Brett again, but I held him off it. We talked about one thing and another, and I left him to come to the office.

Chapter 6

At five o'clock I was in the Hotel Crillon waiting for Brett. She was not there, so I sat down and wrote some letters. They were not very good letters but I hoped their being on Crillon stationery would help them. Brett did not turn up, so about quarter to six I went down to the bar and had a Jack Rose with George the barman. Brett had not been in the bar either, and so I looked for her upstairs on my way out, and took a taxi to the Café Select. Crossing the Seine I saw a string of barges being towed empty down the current, riding high, the bargemen at the sweeps as they came toward the bridge. The river looked nice. It was always pleasant crossing bridges in Paris.

The taxi rounded the statue of the inventor of the semaphore engaged in doing same, and turned up the Boulevard Raspail, and I sat back to let that part of the ride pass. The

Boulevard Raspail always made dull riding. It was like a certain stretch on the P.L.M. between Fontainebleau and Montereau that always made me feel bored and dead and dull until it was over. I suppose it is some association of ideas that makes those dead places in a journey. There are other streets in Paris as ugly as the Boulevard Raspail. It is a street I do not mind walking down at all. But I cannot stand to ride along it. Perhaps I had read something about it once. That was the way Robert Cohn was about all of Paris. I wondered where Cohn got that incapacity to enjoy Paris. Possibly from Mencken. Mencken hates Paris, I believe. So many young men get their likes and dislikes from Mencken.

The taxi stopped in front of the Rotonde. No matter what café in Montparnasse you ask a taxi-driver to bring you to from the right bank of the river, they always take you to the Rotonde. Ten years from now it will probably be the Dôme. It was near enough, anyway. I walked past the sad tables of the Rotonde to the Select. There were a few people inside at the bar, and outside, alone, sat Harvey Stone. He had a pile of saucers in front of him, and he needed a shave.

'Sit down,' said Harvey, 'I've been looking for you.'

'What's the matter?'

'Nothing. Just looking for you.'

'Been out to the races?'

'No. Not since Sunday.'

'What do you hear from the States?'

'Nothing. Absolutely nothing.'

'What's the matter?'

'I don't know. I'm through with them. I'm absolutely through with them.'

He leaned forward and looked me in the eye.

'Do you want to know something, Jake?'

'Yes.'

'I haven't had anything to eat for five days.'

I figured rapidly back in my mind. It was three days ago that Harvey had won two hundred francs from me shaking poker dice in the New York Bar.

'What's the matter?'

'No money. Money hasn't come,' he paused. 'I tell you it's

strange, Jake. When I'm like this I just want to be alone. I want to stay in my own room. I'm like a cat.'

I felt in my pocket.

'Would a hundred help you any, Harvey?'

'Yes.'

'Come on. Let's go and eat.'

'There's no hurry. Have a drink.'

'Better eat.'

'No. When I get like this I don't care whether I eat or not.'

We had a drink. Harvey added my saucer to his own pile.

'Do you know Mencken, Harvey?'

'Yes. Why?'

'What's he like?'

'He's all right. He says some pretty funny things. Last time I had dinner with him we talked about Hoffenheimer. "The trouble is," he said, "he's a garter snapper." That's not bad.'

'That's not bad.'

'He's through now,' Harvey went on. 'He's written about all the things he knows, and now he's on all the things he doesn't know.'

'I guess he's all right,' I said. 'I just can't read him.'

'Oh, nobody reads him now,' Harvey said, 'except the people that used to read the Alexander Hamilton Institute.'

'Well,' I said. 'That was a good thing, too.'

'Sure,' said Harvey. So we sat and thought deeply for a while.

'Have another port?'

'All right,' said Harvey.

'There comes Cohn,' I said. Robert Cohn was crossing the street.

'That moron,' said Harvey. Cohn came up to our table.

'Hello, you bums,' he said.

'Hello, Robert,' Harvey said. 'I was just telling Jake here that you're a moron.'

'What do you mean?'

'Tell us right off. Don't think. What would you rather do if you could do anything you wanted?'

Cohn started to consider.

'Don't think. Bring it right out.'

34

'I don't know,' Cohn said. 'What's it all about, anyway?'

'I mean what would you rather do. What comes into your head first. No matter how silly it is.'

'I don't know,' Cohn said. 'I think I'd rather play football again with what I know about handling myself, now.'

'I misjudged you,' Harvey said. 'You're not a moron. You're only a case of arrested development.'

'You're awfully funny, Harvey,' Cohn said. 'Some day somebody will push your face in.'

Harvey Stone laughed. 'You think so. They won't, though. Because it wouldn't make any difference to me. I'm not a fighter.'

'It would make a difference to you if anybody did it.'

'No, it wouldn't. That's where you make your big mistake. Because you're not intelligent.'

'Cut it out about me.'

'Sure,' said Harvey. 'It doesn't make any difference to me. You don't mean anything to me.'

'Come on, Harvey,' I said. 'Have another porto.'

'No,' he said. 'I'm going up the street and eat. See you later, Jake.'

He walked out and up the street. I watched him crossing the street through the taxis, small, heavy, slowly sure of himself in the traffic.

'He always gets me sore,' Cohn said. 'I can't stand him.'

'I like him,' I said. 'I'm fond of him. You don't want to get sore at him.'

'I know it,' Cohn said. 'He just gets on my nerves.'

'Write this afternoon?'

'No. I couldn't get it going. It's harder to do than my first book. I'm having a hard time handling it.'

The sort of healthy conceit that he had when he returned from America early in the spring was gone. Then he had been sure of his work, only with these personal longings for adventure. Now the sureness was gone. Somehow I feel I have not shown Robert Cohn clearly. The reason is that until he fell in love with Brett, I never heard him make one remark that would, in any way, detach him from other people. He was nice to watch on the tennis-court, he had a good body, and he kept it in shape; he handled his cards well at bridge, and he had a funny sort of undergraduate quality about him. If he were in a crowd nothing he said stood out. He wore what used to be called polo shirts at school, and may be called that still, but he was not professionally youthful. I do not believe he thought about his clothes much. Externally he had been formed at Princeton. Internally he had been moulded by the two women who had trained him. He had a nice, boyish sort of cheerfulness that had never been trained out of him, and I probably have not brought it out. He loved to win at tennis. He probably loved to win as much as Lenglen, for instance. On the other hand, he was not angry at being beaten. When he fell in love with Brett his tennis game went all to pieces. People beat him who had never had a chance with him. He was very nice about it.

Anyhow, we were sitting on the terrace of the Café Select, and Harvey Stone had just crossed the street.

'Come on up to the Lilas,' I said.

'I have a date.'

'What time?'

'Frances is coming here at seven-fifteen.'

'There she is.'

Frances Clyne was coming toward us from across the street. She was a very tall girl who walked with a great deal of movement. She waved and smiled. We watched her cross the street.

'Hello,' she said, 'I'm so glad you're here, Jake. I've been wanting to talk to you.'

'Hello, Frances,' said Cohn. He smiled.

'Why, hello, Robert. Are you here?' She went on, talking rapidly. 'I've had the darndest time. This one' – shaking her head at Cohn – 'didn't come home for lunch.'

'I wasn't supposed to.'

'Oh, I know. But you didn't say anything about it to the cook. Then I had a date myself, and Paula wasn't at her office. I went to the Ritz and waited for her, and she never came, and of course I didn't have enough money to lunch at the Ritz –'

'What did you do?'

'Oh, went out, of course.' She spoke in a sort of imitation

joyful manner. 'I always keep my appointments. No one keeps theirs, nowadays. I ought to know better. How are you, Jake, anyway?'

'Fine.'

'That was a fine girl you had at the dance, and then went off with that Brett one.'

'Don't you like her?' Cohn asked.

'I think she's perfectly charming. Don't you?'

Cohn said nothing.

'Look, Jake. I want to talk with you. Would you come over with me to the Dôme? You'll stay here, won't you, Robert? Come on, Jake.'

We crossed the Boulevard Montparnasse and sat down at a table. A boy came up with the *Paris Times*, and I bought one and opened it.

'What's the matter, Frances?'

'Oh, nothing,' she said, 'except that he wants to leave me.'

'How do you mean?'

'Oh, he told every one that we were going to be married, and I told my mother and everyone, and now he doesn't want to do it.'

'What's the matter?'

'He's decided he hasn't lived enough. I knew it would happen when he went to New York.'

She looked up, very bright-eyed and trying to talk inconsequentially.

'I wouldn't marry him if he doesn't want to. Of course I wouldn't. I wouldn't marry him now for anything. But it does seem to me to be a little late now, after we've waited three years, and I've just gotten my divorce.'

I said nothing.

'We were going to celebrate so, and instead we've just had scenes. It's so childish. We have dreadful scenes, and he cries and begs me to be reasonable, but he says he just can't do it.'

'It's rotten luck.'

'I should say it is rotten luck. I've wasted two years and a half on him now. And I don't know now if any man will ever want to marry me. Two years ago I could have married anybody I wanted, down at Cannes. All the old ones that wanted to marry somebody chic and settle down were crazy about me. Now I don't think I could get anybody.'

'Sure, you could marry anybody.'

'No, I don't believe it. And I'm fond of him, too. And I'd like to have children. I always thought we'd have children.'

She looked at me very brightly. 'I never liked children much, but I don't want to think I'll never have them. I always thought I'd have them and then like them.'

'He's got children.'

'Oh, yes. He's got children, and he's got money, and he's got a rich mother, and he's written a book, and nobody will publish my stuff, nobody at all. It isn't bad, either. And I haven't got any money at all. I could have had alimony, but I got the divorce the quickest way.'

She looked at me again very brightly.

'It isn't right. It's my own fault and it's not, too. I ought to have known better. And when I tell him he just cries and says he can't marry. Why can't he marry? I'd be a good wife. I'm easy to get along with. I leave him alone. It doesn't do any good.'

'It's a rotten shame.'

'Yes, it is a rotten shame. But there's no use talking about it, is there? Come on, let's go back to the café.'

'And of course there isn't anything I can do.'

'No. Just don't let him know I talked to you. I know what he wants.' Now for the first time she dropped her bright, terribly cheerful manner. 'He wants to go back to New York alone, and be there when his book comes out so when a lot of little chickens like it. That's what he wants.'

'Maybe they won't like it. I don't think he's that way. Really.'

'You don't know him like I do, Jake. That's what he wants to do. I know it. I know it. That's why he doesn't want to marry. He wants to have a big triumph this fall all by himself.'

'Want to go back to the café?'

'Yes. Come on.'

We got up from the table – they had never brought us a drink – and started across the street toward the Select, where Cohn sat smiling at us from behind the marble-topped table.

38

'Well, what are you smiling at?' Frances asked him. 'Feel pretty happy?'

'I was smiling at you and Jake with your secrets.'

'Oh, what I've told Jake isn't any secret. Everybody will know it soon enough. I only wanted to give Jake a decent version.'

'What was it? About your going to England?'

'Yes, about my going to England. Oh, Jake! I forgot to tell you. I'm going to England.'

'Isn't that fine!'

'Yes, that's the way it's done in the very best families. Robert's sending me. He's going to give me two hundred pounds and then I'm going to visit friends. Won't it be lovely? The friends don't know about it, yet.'

She turned to Cohn and smiled at him. He was not smiling now.

'You were only going to give me a hundred pounds, weren't you, Robert? But I made him give me two hundred. He's really very generous. Aren't you, Robert?'

I do not know how people could say such terrible things to Robert Cohn. There are people to whom you could not say insulting things. They give you a feeling that the world would be destroyed, would actually be destroyed before your eyes, if you said certain things. But here was Cohn taking it all. Here it was, all going on right before me, and I did not even feel an impulse to try and stop it. And this was friendly joking to what went on later.

'How can you say such things, Frances?' Cohn interrupted.

'Listen to him. I'm going to England. I'm going to visit friends. Ever visit friends that didn't want you? Oh, they'll have to take me, all right. "How do you do, my dear? Such a long time since we've seen you. And how is your dear mother?" Yes, how is my dear mother? She put all her money into French war bonds. Yes, she did. Probably the only person in the world that did. "And what about Robert?" or else very careful talking around Robert. "You must be most careful not to mention him, my dear. Poor Frances has had a most unfortunate experience." Won't it be fun, Robert? Don't you think it will be fun, Jake?'

She turned to me with that terribly bright smile. It was very satisfactory to her to have an audience for this.

'And where are you going to be, Robert? It's my own fault, all right. Perfectly my own fault. When I made you get rid of your little secretary on the magazine I ought to have known you'd get rid of me the same way. Jake doesn't know about that. Should I tell him?'

'Shut up, Frances, for God's sake.'

'Yes, I'll tell him. Robert had a little secretary on the magazine. Just the sweetest little thing in the world, and he thought she was wonderful, and then I came along and he thought I was pretty wonderful, too. So I made him get rid of her, and he had brought her to Provincetown from Carmel when he moved the magazine, and he didn't even pay her fare back to the coast. All to please me. He thought I was pretty fine, then. Didn't you, Robert?

'You mustn't misunderstand, Jake, it was absolutely platonic with the secretary. Not even platonic. Nothing at all, really. It was just that she was so nice. And he did that just to please me. Well, I suppose that we that live by the sword shall perish by the sword. Isn't that literary, though? You want to remember that for your next book, Robert.

'You know Robert is going to get material for a new book. Aren't you, Robert? That's why he's leaving me. He's decided I don't film well. You see, he was so busy all the time that we were living together, writing on this book, that he doesn't remember anything about us. So now he's going out and get some new material. Well, I hope he gets something frightfully interesting.

'Listen, Robert, dear. Let me tell you something. You won't mind, will you? Don't have scenes with your young ladies. Try not to. Because you can't have scenes without crying, and then you pity yourself so much you can't remember what the other person's said. You'll never be able to remember any conversations that way. Just try and be calm. I know it's awfully hard. But remember, it's for literature. We all ought to make sacrifices for literature. Look at me. I'm going to England without a protest. All for literature. We must all help young writers. Don't you think

40

so, Jake? But you're not a young writer. Are you, Robert? You're thirty-four. Still, I suppose that is young for a great writer. Look at Hardy. Look at Anatole France. He just died a little while ago. Robert doesn't think he's any good, though. Some of his French friends told him. He doesn't read French very well himself. He wasn't a good writer like you are, was he, Robert? Do you think he ever had to go and look for material? What do you suppose he said to his mistresses when he wouldn't marry them? I wonder if he cried, too? Oh, I've just thought of something.' She put her gloved hand up to her lips. 'I know the real reason why Robert won't marry me, Jake. It's just come to me. They've sent it to me in a vision in the Café Select. Isn't it mystic? Some day they'll put a tablet up. Like at Lourdes. Do you want to hear, Robert? I'll tell you. It's so simple. I wonder why I never thought about it. Why, you see, Robert's always wanted to have a mistress, and if he doesn't marry me, why, then he's had one. She was his mistress for over two years. See how it is? And if he marries me, like he's always promised he would, that would be the end of all the romance. Don't you think that's bright of me to figure that out? It's true, too. Look at him and see if it's not. Where are you going, Jake?'

'I've got to go in and see Harvey Stone a minute.'

Cohn looked up as I went in. His face was white. Why did he sit there? Why did he keep on taking it like that?

As I stood against the bar looking out I could see them through the window. Frances was talking on to him, smiling brightly, looking into his face each time she asked: 'Isn't it so, Robert?' Or maybe she did not ask that now. Perhaps she said something else. I told the barman I did not want anything to drink and went out through the side door. As I went out the door I looked back through the two thicknesses of glass and saw them sitting there. She was still talking to him. I went down a side street to the Boulevard Raspail. A taxi came along and I got in and gave the driver the address of my flat.

41

Chapter 7

As I started up the stairs the concierge knocked on the glass of the door of her lodge, and as I stopped she came out. She had some letters and a telegram.

'Here is the post. And there was a lady here to see you.'

'Did she leave a card?'

'No. She was with a gentleman. It was the one who was here last night. In the end I find she is very nice.'

'Was she with a friend of mine?'

'I don't know. He was never here before. He was very large. Very, very large. She was very nice. Very, very nice. Last night she was, perhaps, a little –' She put her head on one hand and rocked it up and down. 'I'll speak perfectly frankly, Monsieur Barnes. Last night I found her not so gentille. Last night I formed another idea of her. But listen to what I tell you. She is très, très gentille. She is of very good family. It is a thing you can see.'

'They did not leave any word?'

'Yes. They said they would be back in an hour.'

'Send them up when they come.'

'Yes, Monsieur Barnes. And that lady, that lady there is someone. An eccentric, perhaps, but quelqu'une, quelqu'une!'

The concierge, before she became a concierge, had owned a drink-selling concession at the Paris racecourses. Her life-work lay in the pelouse, but she kept an eye on the people of the pesage, and she took great pride in telling me which of my guests were well brought up, which were of good family, who were sportsmen, a French word pronounced with the accent on the men. The only trouble was that people who did not fall into any of those three categories were very liable to be told there was no one home, chez Barnes. One of my friends, an extremely underfed-looking painter, who was obviously to Madame Duzinell neither well brought up, of good family, nor a sportsman, wrote me a letter asking if I could get him a pass to get by the concierge so he could come up and see me occasionally in the evenings.

I went up to the flat wondering what Brett had done to the concierge. The wire was a cable from Bill Gorton, saying he was arriving on the *France*. I put the mail on the table, went back to the bedroom, undressed and had a shower. I was rubbing down when I heard the door-bell pull. I put on a bathrobe and slippers and went to the door. It was Brett. Back of her was the count. He was holding a great bunch of roses.

'Hello, darling,' said Brett. 'Aren't you going to let us in?'

'Come on. I was just bathing.'

'Aren't you the fortunate man? Bathing.'

'Only a shower. Sit down, Count Mippipopolous. What will you drink?'

'I don't know whether you like flowers, sir,' the count said, 'but I took the liberty of just bringing these roses.'

'Here, give them to me.' Brett took them. 'Get me some water in this, Jake.' I filled the big earthenware jug with water in the kitchen, and Brett put the roses in it, and placed them in the centre of the dining-room table.

'I say. We have had a day.'

'You don't remember anything about a date with me at the Crillon?'

'No. Did we have one? I must have been blind.'

'You were quite drunk, my dear,' said the count.

'Wasn't I, though? And the count's been a brick, absolutely.'

'You've got hell's own drag with the concierge now.'

'I ought to have. Gave her two hundred francs.'

'Don't be a damned fool.'

'His,' she said, and nodded at the count.

'I thought we ought to give her a little something for last night. It was very late.'

'He's wonderful,' Brett said. 'He remembers everything that's happened.'

'So do you, my dear.'

'Fancy,' said Brett. 'Who'd want to? I say, Jake, *do* we get a drink?'

'You get it while I go in and dress. You know where it is.'

'Rather.'

While I dressed I heard Brett put down glasses and then a siphon, and then heard them talking. I dressed slowly, sitting on the bed. I felt tired and pretty rotten. Brett came in the room, a glass in her hand, and sat on the bed.

'What's the matter, darling? Do you feel rocky?'

She kissed me coolly on the forehead.

'Oh, Brett, I love you so much.'

'Darling,' she said. Then: 'Do you want me to send him away?'

'No. He's nice.'

'I'll send him away.'

'No, don't.'

'Yes, I'll send him away.'

'You can't just like that.'

'Can't I, though? You stay here. He's mad about me, I tell you.'

She was gone out of the room. I lay face down on the bed. I was having a bad time. I heard them talking but I did not listen. Brett came in and sat on the bed.

'Poor old darling.' She stroked my head.

'What did you say to him?' I was lying with my face away from her. I did not want to see her.

'Sent him for champagne. He loves to go for champagne.'

Then later: 'Do you feel better, darling? Is the head any better?'

'It's better.'

'Lie quiet. He's gone to the other side of town.'

'Couldn't we live together, Brett? Couldn't we just live together?'

'I don't think so. I'd just *tromper* you with everybody. You couldn't stand it.'

'I stand it now.'

'That would be different. It's my fault, Jake. It's the way I'm made.'

'Couldn't we go off in the country for a while?'

'It wouldn't be any good. I'll go if you like. But I couldn't live quietly in the country. Not with my own true love.'

'I know.'

'Isn't it rotten? There isn't any use my telling you I love you.'

'You know I love you.'

'Let's not talk. Talking's all bilge. I'm going away from you, and then Michael's coming back.'

'Why are you going away?'

'Better for you. Better for me.'

'When are you going?'

'Soon as I can.'

'Where?'

'San Sebastian.'

'Can't we go together?'

'No. That would be a hell of an idea after we'd just talked it out.'

'We never agreed.'

'Oh, you know as well as I do. Don't be obstinate, darling.'

'Oh, sure,' I said. 'I know you're right. I'm just low, and when I'm low I talk like a fool.'

I sat up, leaned over, found my shoes beside the bed and put them on. I stood up.

'Don't look like that, darling.'

'How do you want me to look?'

'Oh, don't be a fool. I'm going away tomorrow.'

'Tomorrow?'

'Yes. Didn't I say so? I am.'

'Let's have a drink, then. The count will be back.'

'Yes. He should be back. You know he's extraordinary about buying champagne. It means any amount to him.'

We went into the dining-room. I took up the brandy bottle and poured Brett a drink and one for myself. There was a ring at the bell-pull. I went to the door and there was the count. Behind him was the chauffeur carrying a basket of champagne.

'Where should I have him put it, sir?' asked the count.

'In the kitchen,' Brett said.

'Put it in there, Henry,' the count motioned. 'Now go down and get the ice.' He stood looking after the basket inside the kitchen door. 'I think you'll find that's very good wine,' he said. 'I know we don't get much of a chance to judge good

45

wine in the States now, but I got this from a friend of mine that's in the business.'

'Oh, you always have someone in the trade,' Brett said.

'This fellow raises the grapes. He's got thousands of acres of them.'

'What's his name?' asked Brett. 'Veuve Cliquot?'

'No,' said the count. 'Mumms. He's a baron.'

'Isn't it wonderful,' said Brett. 'We all have titles. Why haven't you a title, Jake?'

'I assure you, sir,' the count put his hand on my arm. 'It never does a man any good. Most of the time it costs you money.'

'Oh, I don't know. It's damned useful sometimes,' Brett said.

'I've never known it to do me any good.'

'You haven't used it properly. I've had hell's own amount of credit on mine.'

'Do sit down, count,' I said. 'Let me take that stick.'

The count was looking at Brett across the table under the gaslight. She was smoking a cigarette and flicking the ashes on the rug. She saw me notice it. 'I say, Jake, I don't want to ruin your rugs. Can't you give a chap an ash-tray?'

I found some ash-trays and spread them around. The chauffeur came up with a bucket full of salted ice. 'Put two bottles in it, Henry,' the count called.

'Anything else, sir?'

'No. Wait down in the car.' He turned to Brett and to me. 'We'll want to ride out to the Bois for dinner?'

'If you like,' Brett said. 'I couldn't eat a thing.'

'I always like a good meal,' said the count.

'Should I bring the wine in, sir?' asked the chauffeur.

'Yes. Bring it in, Henry,' said the count. He took out a heavy pigskin cigar-case and offered it to me. 'Like to try a real American cigar?'

'Thanks,' I said. 'I'll finish the cigarette.'

He cut off the end of his cigar with a gold cutter he wore on one end of his watch-chain.

'I like a cigar to really draw,' said the count. 'Half the cigars you smoke don't draw.'

He lit the cigar, puffed at it, looking across the table at Brett. 'And when you're divorced, Lady Ashley, then you won't have a title.'

'No. What a pity.'

'No,' said the count. 'You don't need a title. You got class all over you.'

'Thanks. Awfully decent of you.'

'I'm not joking you,' the count blew a cloud of smoke. 'You got the most class of anybody I ever seen. You got it. That's all.'

'Nice of you,' said Brett. 'Mummy would be pleased. Couldn't you write it out, and I'll send it in a letter to her.'

'I'd tell her, too,' said the count. 'I'm not joking you. I never joke people. Joke people and you make enemies. That's what I always say.'

'You're right,' Brett said. 'You're terribly right. I always joke people and I haven't a friend in the world. Except Jake here.'

'You don't joke him.'

'That's it.'

'Do you, now?' asked the count. 'Do you joke him?'

Brett looked at me and wrinkled up the corners of her eyes.

'No,' she said. 'I wouldn't joke him.'

'See,' said the count. 'You don't joke him.'

'This is a hell of a dull talk,' Brett said. 'How about some of that champagne?'

The count reached down and twirled the bottles in the shiny bucket. 'It isn't cold, yet. You're always drinking, my dear. Why don't you just talk?'

'I've talked too ruddy much. I've talked myself all out to Jake.'

'I should like to hear you really talk, my dear. When you talk to me you never finish your sentence at all.'

'Leave 'em for you to finish. Let anyone finish them as they like.'

'It is a very interesting system,' the count reached down and gave the bottles a twirl. 'Still I would like to hear you talk some time.'

'Isn't he a fool?' Brett asked.

'Now,' the count brought up a bottle. 'I think this is cool.'

I brought a towel and he wiped the bottle dry and held it up. 'I like to drink champagne from magnums. The wine is better but it would have been too hard to cool.' He held the bottle, looking at it. I put out the glasses.

'I say. You might open it,' Brett suggested.

'Yes, my dear. Now I'll open it.'

It was amazing champagne.

'I say that is wine,' Brett held up her glass. 'We ought to toast something. "Here's to royalty".'

'This wine is too good for toast-drinking, my dear. You don't want to mix emotions up with a wine like that. You lose the taste.'

Brett's glass was empty.

'You ought to write a book on wines, count,' I said.

'Mr Barnes,' answered the count, 'all I want out of wines is to enjoy them.'

'Let's enjoy a little more of this,' Brett pushed her glass forward. The count poured very carefully. 'There, my dear. Now you enjoy that slowly, and then you can get drunk.'

'Drunk? Drunk?'

'My dear, you are charming when you are drunk.'

'Listen to the man.'

'Mr Barnes,' the count poured my glass full. 'She is the only lady I have ever known who was as charming when she was drunk as when she was sober.'

'You haven't been around much, have you?'

'Yes, my dear. I have been around very much. I have been around a very great deal.'

'Drink your wine,' said Brett. 'We've all been around. I dare say Jake here has seen as much as you have.'

'My dear, I am sure Mr Barnes has seen a lot. Don't think I don't think so, sir. I have seen a lot, too.'

'Of course you have, my dear,' Brett said. 'I was only ragging.'

'I have been in seven wars and four revolutions,' the count said.

'Soldiering?' Brett asked.

'Sometimes, my dear. And I have got arrow wounds. Have you ever seen arrow wounds?'

'Let's have a look at them.'

The count stood up, unbuttoned his vest, and opened his shirt. He pulled up the undershirt onto his chest and stood, his chest black, and big stomach muscles bulging under the light.

'You see them?'

Below the line where his ribs stopped were two raised white welts. 'See on the back where they come out.' Above the small of the back were the same two scars, raised as thick as a finger.

'I say. Those are something.'

'Clean through.'

The count was tucking in his shirt.

'Where did you get those?' I asked.

'In Abyssinia. When I was twenty-one years old.'

'What were you doing?' asked Brett. 'Were you in the army?'

'I was on a business trip, my dear.'

'I told you he was one of us. Didn't I?' Brett turned to me. 'I love you, count. You're a darling.'

'You make me very happy, my dear. But it isn't true.'

'Don't be an ass.'

'You see, Mr Barnes, it is because I have lived very much that now I can enjoy everything so well. Don't you find it like that?'

'Yes. Absolutely.'

'I know,' said the count. 'That is the secret. You must get to know the values.'

'Doesn't anything ever happen to your values?' Brett asked.

'No. Not any more.'

'Never fall in love?'

'Always,' said the count. 'I am always in love.'

'What does that do to your values?'

'That, too, has got a place in my values.'

'You haven't any values. You're dead, that's all.'

'No, my dear. You're not right. I'm not dead at all.'

We drank three bottles of the champagne and the count left the basket in my kitchen. We dined at a restaurant in the Bois. It was a good dinner. Food had an excellent place in the count's values. So did wine. The count was in fine form during the meal. So was Brett. It was a good party.

'Where would you like to go?' asked the count after dinner. We were the only people left in the restaurant. The two waiters were standing over against the door. They wanted to go home.

'We might go up on the hill,' Brett said. 'Haven't we had a splendid party?'

The count was beaming. He was very happy.

'You are very nice people,' he said. He was smoking a cigar again. 'Why don't you get married, you two?'

'We want to lead our own lives,' I said.

'We have our careers,' Brett said. 'Come on. Let's get out of this.'

'Have another brandy,' the count said.

'Get it on the hill.'

'No. Have it here where it is quiet.'

'You and your quiet,' said Brett. 'What is it men feel about quiet?'

'We like it,' said the count. 'Like you like noise, my dear.'

'All right,' said Brett. 'Let's have one.'

'Sommelier!' the count called.

'Yes, sir.'

'What is the oldest brandy you have?'

'Eighteen eleven, sir.'

'Bring us a bottle.'

'I say. Don't be ostentatious. Call him off, Jake.'

'Listen, my dear. I get more value for my money in old brandy than in any other antiquities.'

'Got many antiquities?'

'I got a houseful.'

Finally we went up to Montmartre. Inside Zelli's it was crowded, smoky, and noisy. The music hit you as you went in. Brett and I danced. It was so crowded we could barely move. The nigger drummer waved at Brett. We were caught in the jam, dancing in one place in front of him.

'Hahre you?'

'Great.'

'Thaats good.'

He was all teeth and lips.

'He's a great friend of mine,' Brett said. 'Damn good drummer.'

The music stopped and we started toward the table where

50

the count sat. Then the music started again and we danced. I looked at the count. He was sitting at the table smoking a cigar. The music stopped again.

'Let's go over.'

Brett started toward the table. The music started and again we danced, tight in the crowd.

'You are a rotten dancer, Jake. Michael's the best dancer I know.'

'He's splendid.'

'He's got his points.'

'I like him,' I said. 'I'm damned fond of him.'

'I'm going to marry him,' Brett said. 'Funny. I haven't thought about him for a week.'

'Don't you write him?'

'Not I. Never write letters.'

'I'll bet he writes to you.'

'Rather. Damned good letters, too.'

'When are you going to get married?'

'How do I know? As soon as we can get the divorce. Michael's trying to get his mother to put up for it.'

'Could I help you?'

'Don't be an ass. Michael's people have loads of money.'

The music stopped. We walked over to the table. The count stood up.

'Very nice,' he said. 'You looked very, very nice.'

'Don't you dance, count?' I asked.

'No. I'm too old.'

'Oh, come off it,' Brett said.

'My dear, I would do it if I would enjoy it. I enjoy to watch you dance.'

'Splendid,' Brett said. 'I'll dance again for you some time. I say. What about your little friend, Zizi?'

'Let me tell you. I support that boy, but I don't want to have him around.'

'He is rather hard.'

'You know I think that boy's got a future. But personally I don't want him around.'

'Jake's rather the same way.'

'He gives me the willies.'

51

'Well,' the count shrugged his shoulders. 'About his future, you can't ever tell. Anyhow, his father was a great friend of my father.'

'Come on. Let's dance.' Brett said.

We danced. It was crowded and close.

'Oh, darling,' Brett said, 'I'm so miserable.'

I had that feeling of going through something that has all happened before. 'You were happy a minute ago.'

The drummer shouted: 'You can't two time –'

'It's all gone.'

'What's the matter?'

'I don't know. I just feel terrible.'

'. . . . . .' the drummer chanted. Then turned to his sticks.

'Want to go?'

I had the feeling as in a nightmare of it all being something repeated, something I had been through and that now I must go through again.

'. . . . . .' the drummer sang softly.

'Let's go,' said Brett. 'You don't mind?'

'. . . . . .' the drummer shouted and grinned at Brett.

'All right,' I said. We got out from the crowd. Brett went to the dressing-room.

'Brett wants to go,' I said to the count. He nodded. 'Does she? That's fine. You take the car. I'm going to stay here for a while, Mr Barnes.'

We shook hands.

'It was a wonderful time,' I said. 'I wish you would let me get this.' I took a note out of my pocket.

'Mr Barnes, don't be ridiculous,' the count said.

Brett came over with her wrap on. She kissed the count and put her hand on his shoulder to keep him from standing up. As we went out the door I looked back and there were three girls at his table. We got into the big car. Brett gave the chauffeur the address of her hotel.

'No, don't come up,' she said at the hotel. She had rung and the door was unlatched.

'Really?'

'No. Please.'

'Good night, Brett,' I said. 'I'm sorry you feel rotten.'

'Good night, Jake. Good night, darling. I won't see you again.' We kissed standing at the door. She pushed me away. We kissed again. 'Oh, don't!' Brett said.

She turned quickly and went into the hotel. The chauffeur drove me around to my flat. I gave him twenty francs and he touched his cap and said: 'Good night, sir,' and drove off. I rang the bell. The door opened and I went upstairs and went to bed.

BOOK TWO

Chapter 8

I did not see Brett again until she came back from San Sebastian. One card came from her from there. It had a picture of the Concha, and said: 'Darling. Very quiet and healthy. Love to all the chaps. BRETT.'

Nor did I see Robert Cohn again. I heard Frances had left for England and I had a note from Cohn saying he was going out in the country for a couple of weeks, he did not know where, but that he wanted to hold me to the fishing-trip in Spain we had talked about last winter. I could reach him always, he wrote, through his bankers.

Brett was gone. I was not bothered by Cohn's troubles, I rather enjoyed not having to play tennis, there was plenty of work to do, I went often to the races, dined with friends, and put in some extra time at the office getting things ahead so I could leave it in charge of my secretary when Bill Gorton and I should shove off to Spain the end of June. Bill Gorton arrived, put up a couple of days at the flat and went off to Vienna. He was very cheerful and said the States were wonderful. New York was wonderful. There had been a grand theatrical season and a whole crop of great young light heavyweights. Any one of them was a good prospect to grow up, put on weight and trim Dempsey. Bill was very happy. He had made a lot of money on his last book, and was going to make a lot more. We had a good time while he was in Paris, and then he went off to Vienna. He was coming back in three weeks and we would leave for Spain to get in some fishing and go to the fiesta at Pamplona. He wrote that Vienna was wonderful. Then a card from Budapest: 'Jake, Budapest is wonderful.' Then I got a wire: 'Back on Monday.'

Monday evening he turned up at the flat. I heard his taxi stop and went to the window and called to him; he waved and started upstairs carrying his bags. I met him on the stairs, and took one of the bags.

'Well,' I said, 'I hear you had a wonderful trip.'

'Wonderful,' he said. 'Budapest is absolutely wonderful.'

'How about Vienna?'

'Not so good, Jake. Not so good. It seemed better than it was.'

'How do you mean?' I was getting glasses and a siphon.

'Tight, Jake. I was tight.'

'That's strange. Better have a drink.'

Bill rubbed his forehead. 'Remarkable thing,' he said. 'Don't know how it happened. Suddenly it happened.'

'Last long?'

'Four days, Jake. Lasted just four days.'

'Where did you go?'

'Don't remember. Wrote you a post-card. Remember that perfectly.'

'Do anything else?'

'Not so sure. Possible.'

'Go on. Tell me about it.'

'Can't remember. Tell you anything I could remember.'

'Go on. Take that drink and remember.'

'Might remember a little,' Bill said. 'Remember something about a prize-fight. Enormous Vienna prize-fight. Had a nigger in it. Remember the nigger perfectly.'

'Go on.'

'Wonderful nigger. Looked like Tiger Flowers, only four times as big. All of a sudden everybody started to throw things. Not me. Nigger'd just knocked local boy down. Nigger put up his glove. Wanted to make a speech. Then local white boy hit him. Then he knocked white boy cold. Then everybody commenced to throw chairs. Nigger went home with us in our car. Couldn't get his clothes. Wore my coat. Remember the whole thing now. Big sporting evening.'

'What happened?'

'Loaned the nigger some clothes and went around with him to try and get his money. Claimed nigger owed them money on account of wrecking hall. Wonder who translated? Was it me?'

'Probably it wasn't you.'

'You're all right. Wasn't me at all. Was another fellow. Think we called him the local Harvard man. Remember him now. Studying music.'

'How'd you come out?'

'Not so good, Jake. Injustice everywhere. Promoter claimed nigger promised let local boy stay. Claimed nigger violated contract. Can't knock out Vienna boy in Vienna. "My God, Mister Gorton," said nigger, "I didn't do nothing in there for forty minutes but try and let him stay. That white boy musta ruptured himself swinging at me. I never did hit him".'

'Did you get any money?'

'No money, Jake. All we could get was nigger's clothes. Somebody took his watch, too. Splendid nigger. Big mistake to have come to Vienna. Not so good, Jake. Not so good.'

'What became of the nigger?'

'Went back to Cologne. Lives there. Married. Got a family. Going to write me a letter and send me the money I loaned him. Wonderful nigger. Hope I gave him the right address.'

'You probably did.'

'Well, anyway, let's eat,' said Bill. 'Unless you want me to tell you some more travel stories.'

'Go on.'

'Let's eat.'

We went downstairs and out onto the Boulevard St Michel in the warm June evening.

'Where will we go?'

'Want to eat on the island?'

'Sure.'

We walked down the Boulevard. At the juncture of the Rue Denfert-Rochereau with the Boulevard is a statue of two men in flowing robes.

'I know who they are.' Bill eyed the monument. 'Gentlemen who invented pharmacy. Don't try and fool me on Paris.'

We went on.

'Here's a taxidermist's,' Bill said. 'Want to buy anything? Nice stuffed dog?'

'Come on,' I said. 'You're pie-eyed.'

'Pretty nice stuffed dogs,' Bill said. 'Certainly brighten up your flat.'

'Come on.'

'Just one stuffed dog. I can take 'em or leave 'em alone. But listen, Jake. Just one stuffed dog.'

'Come on.'

'Mean everything in the world to you after you bought it. Simple exchange of values. You give them money. They give you a stuffed dog.'

'We'll get one on the way back.'

'All right. Have it your own way. Road to hell paved with unbought stuffed dogs. Not my fault.'

We went on.

'How'd you feel that way about dogs so sudden?'

'Always felt that way about dogs. Always been a great lover of stuffed animals.'

We stopped and had a drink.

'Certainly like to drink,' Bill said. 'You ought to try it some-times, Jake.'

'You're about a hundred and forty-four ahead of me.'

'Ought not to daunt you. Never be daunted. Secret of my success. Never been daunted. Never been daunted in public.'

'Where were you drinking?'

'Stopped at the Crillon. George made me a couple of Jack Roses. George's a great man. Know the secret of his success? Never been daunted.'

'You'll be daunted after about three more pernods.'

'Not in public. If I begin to feel daunted I'll go off by myself. I'm like a cat that way.'

'When did you see Harvey Stone?'

'At the Crillon. Harvey was just a little daunted. Hadn't eaten for three days. Doesn't eat any more. Just goes off like a cat. Pretty sad.'

'He's all right.'

'Splendid. Wish he wouldn't keep going off like a cat, though. Makes me nervous.'

58

'What'll we do tonight?'

'Doesn't make any difference. Only let's not get daunted. Suppose they got any hard-boiled eggs here? If they had hard-boiled eggs here we wouldn't have to go all the way down to the island to eat.'

'Nix,' I said. 'We're going to have a regular meal.'

'Just a suggestion,' said Bill. 'Want to start now?'

'Come on.'

We started on again down the Boulevard. A horse-cab passed us. Bill looked at it.

'See that horse-cab? Going to have that horse-cab stuffed for you for Christmas. Going to give all my friends stuffed animals. I'm a nature-writer.'

A taxi passed, someone in it waved, then banged for the driver to stop. The taxi backed up to the kerb. In it was Brett.

'Beautiful lady,' said Bill. 'Going to kidnap us.'

'Hullo!' Brett said. 'Hullo!'

'This is Bill Gorton. Lady Ashley.'

Brett smiled at Bill. 'I say I'm just back. Haven't bathed even. Michael comes in tonight.'

'Good. Come on and eat with us, and we'll all go to meet him.'

'Must clean myself.'

'Oh, rot! Come on.'

'Must bathe. He doesn't get in till nine.'

'Come and have a drink, then, before you bathe.'

'Might do that. Now you're not talking rot.'

We got in the taxi. The driver looked around.

'Stop at the nearest bistro,' I said.

'We might as well go to the Closerie,' Brett said. 'I can't drink these rotten brandies.'

'Closerie des Lilas.'

Brett turned to Bill.

'Have you been in this pestilential city long?'

'Just got in today from Budapest.'

'How was Budapest?'

'Wonderful. Budapest was wonderful.'

'Ask him about Vienna.'

'Vienna,' said Bill, 'is a strange city.'

'Very much like Paris,' Brett smiled at him, wrinkling the corners of her eyes.

'Exactly,' Bill said. 'Very much like Paris at this moment.'

'You *have* a good start.'

Sitting out on the terraces of the Lilas Brett ordered a whisky and soda, I took one, too, and Bill took another pernod.

'How are you, Jake?'

'Great,' I said. 'I've had a good time.'

Brett looked at me. 'I was a fool to go away,' she said. 'One's an ass to leave Paris.'

'Did you have a good time?'

'Oh, all right. Interesting. Not frightfully amusing.'

'See anybody?'

'No, hardly anybody. I never went out.'

'Didn't you swim?'

'No. Didn't do a thing.'

'Sounds like Vienna,' Bill said.

Brett wrinkled up the corners of her eyes at him.

'So that's the way it was in Vienna.'

'It was like everything in Vienna.'

Brett smiled at him again.

'You've a nice friend, Jake.'

'He's all right,' I said. 'He's a taxidermist.'

'That was in another country,' Bill said. 'And besides all the animals were dead.'

'One more,' Brett said, 'and I must run. Do send the waiter for a taxi.'

'There's a line of them. Right out in front.'

'Good.'

We had the drink and put Brett into her taxi.

'Mind you're at the Select around ten. Make him come. Michael will be there.'

'We'll be there,' Bill said. The taxi started and Brett waved.

'Quite a girl,' Bill said. 'She's damned nice. Who's Michael?'

'The man she's going to marry.'

'Well, well,' Bill said. 'That's always just the stage I meet anybody. What'll I send them? Think they'd like a couple of stuffed race-horses?'

'We better eat.'

'Is she really Lady something or other?' Bill asked in the taxi on our way down to the Ile Saint Louis.

'Oh, yes. In the stud-book and everything.'

'Well, well.'

We ate dinner at Madame Lecomte's restaurant on the far side of the island. It was crowded with Americans and we had to stand up and wait for a place. Someone had put it in the American Women's Club list as a quaint restaurant on the Paris quais as yet untouched by Americans, so we had to wait forty-five minutes for a table. Bill had eaten at the restaurant in 1918, and right after the armistice, and Madame Lecomte made a great fuss over seeing him.

'Doesn't get us a table, though,' Bill said. 'Grand woman, though.'

We had a good meal, a roast chicken, new green beans, mashed potatoes, a salad, and some apple-pie and cheese.

'You've got the world here all right,' Bill said to Madame Lecomte. She raised her hand. 'Oh, my God!'

'You'll be rich.'

'I hope so.'

After the coffee and a *fine* we got the bill, chalked up the same as ever on a slate, that was doubtless one of the 'quaint' features, paid it, shook hands, and went out.

'You never come here any more, Monsieur Barnes,' Madame Lecomte said.

'Too many compatriots.'

'Come at lunch-time. It's not crowded then.'

'Good. I'll be down soon.'

We walked along under the trees that grew out over the river on the Quai d'Orléans side of the island. Across the river were the broken walls of old houses that were being torn down.

'They're going to cut a street through.'

'They would,' Bill said.

We walked on and circled the island. The river was dark and a bateau mouche went by, all bright with lights, going fast and quiet up and out of sight under the bridge. Down the river was Notre Dame squatting against the night sky. We crossed to the left bank of the Seine by the wooden footbridge from the Quai de Béthune, and stopped on the bridge and looked down the

61

river at Notre Dame. Standing on the bridge the island looked dark, the houses were high against the sky, and the trees were shadows.

'It's pretty grand,' Bill said. 'God, I love to get back.'

We leaned on the wooden rail of the bridge and looked up the river to the lights of the big bridges. Below the water was smooth and black. It made no sound against the piles of the bridge. A man and a girl passed us. They were walking with their arms around each other.

We crossed the bridge and walked up the Rue du Cardinal Lemoine. It was steep walking, and we went all the way up to the Place Contrescarpe. The arc-lights shone through the leaves of the trees in the square, and underneath the trees was an S bus ready to start. Music came out of the door of the Nègre Joyeux. Through the window of the Café Aux Amateurs I saw the long zinc bar. Outside on the terrace working people were drinking. In the open kitchen of the Amateurs a girl was cooking potato-chips in oil. There was an iron pot of stew. The girl ladled some onto a plate for an old man who stood holding a bottle of red wine in one hand.

'Want to have a drink?'

'No,' said Bill. 'I don't need it.'

We turned to the right off the Place Contrescarpe, walking along smooth narrow streets with high old houses on both sides. Some of the houses jutted out toward the street. Others were cut back. We came onto the Rue du Pot de Fer and followed it along until it brought us to the rigid north and south of the Rue Saint Jacques and then walked south, past Val de Grâce, set back behind the courtyard and the iron fence, to the Boulevard du Port Royal.

'What do you want to do?' I asked. 'Go up to the café and see Brett and Mike?'

'Why not?'

We walked along Port Royal until it became Montparnasse, and then on past the Lilas, Lavigne's, and all the little cafés, Damoy's, crossed the street to the Rotonde, past its lights and tables to the Select.

Michael came toward us from the tables. He was tanned and healthy-looking.

'Hel-lo, Jake,' he said. 'Hel-lo! Hel-lo! How are you, old lad?'

'You look very fit, Mike.'

'Oh, I am. I'm frightfully fit. I've done nothing but walk. Walk all day long. One drink a day with my mother at tea.'

Bill had gone into the bar. He was standing talking with Brett, who was sitting on a high stool, her legs crossed. She had no stockings on.

'It's good to see you, Jake,' Michael said. 'I'm a little tight, you know. Amazing, isn't it? Did you see my nose?'

There was a patch of dried blood on the bridge of his nose.

'An old lady's bags did that,' Mike said. 'I reached up to help her with them and they fell on me.'

Brett gestured at him from the bar with her cigarette-holder and wrinkled the corners of her eyes.

'An old lady,' said Mike. 'Her bags *fell* on me.'

'Let's go in and see Brett. I say, she is a piece. You *are* a lovely lady, Brett. Where did you get that hat?'

'Chap bought it for me. Don't you like it?'

'It's a dreadful hat. Do get a good hat.'

'Oh, we've so much money now,' Brett said. 'I say, haven't you met Bill yet? You *are* a lovely host, Jake.'

She turned to Mike. 'This is Bill Gorton. This drunkard is Mike Campbell. Mr. Campbell is an undischarged bankrupt.'

'Aren't I, though? You know I met my ex-partner yesterday in London. Chap who did me in.'

'What did he say?'

'Bought me a drink. I thought I might as well take it. I say, Brett, you *are* a lovely piece. Don't you think she's beautiful?'

'Beautiful. With this nose?'

'It's a lovely nose. Go on, point it at me. Isn't she a lovely piece?'

'Couldn't we have kept the man in Scotland?'

'I say, Brett, let's turn in early.'

'Don't be indecent, Michael. Remember there are ladies at this bar.'

'Isn't she a lovely piece? Don't you think so, Jake?'

'There's a fight tonight,' Bill said. 'Like to go?'

'Fight,' said Mike. 'Who's fighting?'

'Ledoux and somebody.'

'He's very good, Ledoux,' Mike said. 'I'd like to see it, rather' – he was making an effort to pull himself together – 'but I can't go. I had a date with this thing here. I say, Brett, do get a new hat.'

Brett pulled the felt hat down far over one eye and smiled out from under it. 'You two run along to the fight. I'll have to be taking Mr. Campbell home directly.'

'I'm not tight,' Mike said. 'Perhaps just a little. I say, Brett, you are a lovely piece.'

'Go on to the fight,' Brett said. 'Mr. Campbell's getting difficult. What are these outbursts of affection, Michael?'

'I say, you are a lovely piece.'

We said good night. 'I'm sorry I can't go,' Mike said. Brett laughed. I looked back from the door. Mike had one hand on the bar and was leaning toward Brett, talking. Brett was looking at him quite coolly, but the corners of her eyes were smiling.

Outside on the pavement I said: 'Do you want to go to the fight?'

'Sure,' said Bill. 'If we don't have to walk.'

'Mike was pretty excited about his girl friend,' I said in the taxi.

'Well,' said Bill. 'You can't blame him such a hell of a lot.'

Chapter 9

The Ledoux–Kid Francis fight was the night of June 20th. It was a good fight. The morning after the fight I had a letter from Robert Cohn, written from Hendaye. He was having a very quiet time, he said, bathing, playing some golf and much bridge. Hendaye had a splendid beach, but he was anxious to start on the fishing-trip. When would I be down? If I would buy him a double-tapered line he would pay me when I came down.

That same morning I wrote Cohn from the office that Bill and I would leave Paris on the 25th unless I wired him otherwise, and would meet him at Bayonne, where we could get a bus over the mountains to Pamplona. The same evening about seven o'clock I stopped in at the Select to see Michael and Brett. They were not there, and I went over to the Dingo. They were inside sitting at the bar.

'Hello, darling.' Brett put out her hand.

'Hello, Jake,' Mike said. 'I understand I was tight last night.'

'Weren't you, though,' Brett said. 'Disgraceful business.'

'Look,' said Mike, 'when do you go down to Spain? Would you mind if we came down with you?'

'It would be grand.'

'You wouldn't mind, really? I've been at Pamplona, you know. Brett's mad to go. You're sure we wouldn't just be a bloody nuisance?'

'Don't talk like a fool.'

'I'm a little tight, you know. I wouldn't ask you like this if I weren't. You're sure you don't mind?'

'Oh, shut up, Michael,' Brett said. 'How can the man say he'd mind now? I'll ask him later.'

'But you don't mind, do you?'

'Don't ask that again unless you want to make me sore. Bill and I go down on the morning of the 25th.'

'By the way, where is Bill?' Brett asked.

'He's out at Chantilly dining with some people.'

'He's a good chap.'

'Splendid chap,' said Mike. 'He is, you know.'

'You don't remember him,' Brett said.

'I do. Remember him perfectly. Look, Jake, we'll come down, the night of the 24th. Brett can't get up in the morning.'

'Indeed not!'

'If our money comes and you're sure you don't mind.'

'It will come, all right. I'll see to that.'

'Tell me what tackle to send for.'

'Get two or three rods with reels, and lines, and some flies.'

'I won't fish,' Brett put in.

'Get two rods, then, and Bill won't have to buy one.'

65

'Right,' said Mike. 'I'll send a wire to the keeper.'

'Won't it be splendid,' Brett said. 'Spain! We *will* have fun.'

'The 25th. When is that?'

'Saturday.'

'We *will* have to get ready.'

'I say,' said Mike, 'I'm going to the barber's.'

'I must bathe,' said Brett. 'Walk up to the hotel with me, Jake. Be a good chap.'

'We *have* got the loveliest hotel,' Mike said. 'I think it's a brothel!'

'We left our bags here at the Dingo when we got in, and they asked us at this hotel if we wanted a room for the afternoon only. Seemed frightfully pleased we were going to stay all night.'

'I believe it's a brothel,' Mike said. 'And *I* should know.'

'Oh, shut it and go and get your hair cut.'

Mike went out. Brett and I sat at the bar.

'Have another?'

'Might.'

'I needed that,' Brett said.

We walked up the Rue Delambre.

'I haven't seen you since I've been back,' Brett said.

'No.'

'How *are* you, Jake?'

'Fine.'

Brett looked at me. 'I say,' she said, 'is Robert Cohn going on this trip?'

'Yes. Why?'

'Don't you think it will be a bit rough on him?'

'Why should it?'

'Who did you think I went down to San Sebastian with?'

'Congratulations,' I said.

We walked along.

'What did you say that for?'

'I don't know. What would you like me to say?'

We walked along and turned a corner.

'He behaved rather well, too. He gets a little dull.'

'Does he?'

'I rather thought it would be good for him.'

'You might take up social service.'

'Don't be nasty.'

'I won't.'

'Didn't you really know?'

'No,' I said. 'I guess I didn't think about it.'

'Do you think it will be too rough on him?'

'That's up to him,' I said. 'Tell him you're coming. He can always not come.'

'I'll write him and give him a chance to pull out of it.'

I did not see Brett again until the night of June 24th.

'Did you hear from Cohn?'

'Rather. He's keen about it.'

'My God!'

'I thought it was rather odd myself.'

'Says he can't wait to see me.'

'Does he think you're coming alone?'

'No. I told him we were all coming down together. Michael and all.'

'He's wonderful.'

'Isn't he?'

They expected their money the next day. We arranged to meet at Pamplona. They would go directly to San Sebastian and take the train from there. We would all meet at the Montoya in Pamplona. If they did not turn up on Monday at the latest we would go on ahead up to Burguete in the mountains, to start fishing. There was a bus to Burguete. I wrote out an itinerary so they could follow us.

Bill and I took the morning train from the Gare d'Orsay. It was a lovely day, not too hot, and the country was beautiful from the start. We went back into the diner and had breakfast. Leaving the dining-car I asked the conductor for tickets for the first service.

'Nothing until the fifth.'

'What's this?'

There were never more than two servings of lunch on that train, and always plenty of places for both of them.

'They're all reserved,' the dining-car conductor said. 'There will be a fifth service at three-thirty.'

'This is serious,' I said to Bill.

'Give him ten francs.'

'Here,' I said. 'We want to eat in the first service.'

The conductor put the ten francs in his pocket.

'Thank you,' he said. 'I would advise you gentlemen to get some sandwiches. All the places for the first four services were reserved at the office of the company.'

'You'll go a long way, brother,' Bill said to him in English. 'I suppose if I'd given you five francs you would have advised us to jump off the train.'

'Comment?'

'Go to hell!' said Bill. 'Get the sandwiches made and a bottle of wine. You tell him, Jake.'

'And send it up to the next car.' I described where we were.

In our compartment were a man and his wife and their young son.

'I suppose you're Americans, aren't you?' the man asked. 'Having a good trip?'

'Wonderful,' said Bill.

'That's what you want to do. Travel while you're young. Mother and I always wanted to get over, but we had to wait a while.'

'You could have come over ten years ago, if you'd wanted to,' the wife said. 'What you always said was: "See America first!" I will say we've seen a good deal, take it one way and another.'

'Say, there's plenty of Americans on this train,' the husband said. 'They've got seven cars of them from Dayton, Ohio. They've been on a pilgrimage to Rome, and now they're going down to Biarritz and Lourdes.'

'So, that's what they are. Pilgrims. Goddam Puritans,' Bill said.

'What part of the States you boys from?'

'Kansas City,' I said. 'He's from Chicago.'

'You both going to Biarritz?'

'No. We're going fishing in Spain.'

'Well, I never cared for it, myself. There's plenty that do out where I come from, though. We got some of the best fishing in the State of Montana. I've been out with the boys, but I never cared for it any.'

'Mighty little fishing you did on them trips,' his wife said.

He winked at us.

'You know how the ladies are. If there's a jug goes along, or a case of beer, they think it's hell and damnation.'

'That's the way men are,' his wife said to us. She smoothed her comfortable lap. 'I voted against prohibition to please him, and because I like a little beer in the house, and then he talks that way. It's a wonder they ever find anyone to marry them.'

'Say,' said Bill, 'do you know that gang of Pilgrim Fathers have cornered the dining-car until half past three this afternoon?'

'How do you mean? They can't do a thing like that.'

'You try and get seats.'

'Well, Mother, it looks as though we better go back and get another breakfast.'

She stood up and straightened her dress.

'Will you boys keep an eye on our things? Come on, Hubert.'

They all three went up to the wagon restaurant. A little while after they were gone a steward went through announcing the first service, and pilgrims, with their priests, commenced filing down the corridor. Our friend and his family did not come back. A waiter passed in the corridor with our sandwiches and the bottle of Chablis, and we called him in.

'You're going to work to-day,' I said.

He nodded his head. 'They start now, at ten-thirty.'

'When do we eat?'

'Huh! When do I eat?'

He left two glasses for the bottle, and we paid him for the sandwiches and tipped him.

'I'll get the plates,' he said, 'or bring them with you.'

We ate the sandwiches and drank the Chablis and watched the country out of the window. The grain was just beginning to ripen and the fields were full of poppies. The pastureland was green, and there were fine trees, and sometimes big rivers and chateaux off in the trees.

At Tours we got off and bought another bottle of wine, and when we got back in the compartment the gentleman from Montana and his wife and his son, Hubert, were sitting comfortably.

'Is there good swimming in Biarritz?' asked Hubert.

'That boy's just crazy till he can get in the water,' his mother said. 'It's pretty hard on youngsters travelling.'

'There's good swimming,' I said. 'But it's dangerous when it's rough.'

'Did you get a meal?' Bill asked.

'We sure did. We set right there when they started to come in, and they must have just thought we were in the party. One of the waiters said something to us in French, and then they just sent three of them back.'

'They thought we were snappers, all right,' the man said. 'It certainly shows you the power of the Catholic Church. It's a pity you boys ain't Catholics. You could get a meal, then, all right.'

'I am,' I said. 'That's what makes me so sore.'

Finally at a quarter past four we had lunch. Bill had been rather difficult at the last. He buttonholed a priest who was coming back with one of the returning streams of pilgrims.

'When do us Protestants get a chance to eat, Father?'

'I don't know anything about it. Haven't you got tickets?'

'It's enough to make a man join the Klan,' Bill said. The priest looked back at him.

Inside the dining-car the waiters served the fifth successive table d'hôte meal. The waiter who served us was soaked through. His white jacket was purple under the arms.

'He must drink a lot of wine.'

'Or wear purple undershirts.'

'Let's ask him.'

'No. He's too tired.'

The train stopped for half an hour at Bordeaux and we went out through the station for a little walk. There was not time to get in to the town. Afterward we passed through the Landes and watched the sun set. There were wide fire-gaps cut through the pines, and you could look up them like avenues and see wooded hills way off. About seven-thirty we had dinner and watched the country through the open window in the diner. It was all sandy pine country full of heather. There were little clearings with houses in them, and once in a while we passed a sawmill. It got dark and we could feel the country hot and sandy and dark outside of the window, and about nine

70

o'clock we got into Bayonne. The man and his wife and Hubert all shook hands with us. They were going on to La Négresse to change to Biarritz.

'Well, I hope you have lots of luck,' he said.

'Be careful about those bull-fights.'

'Maybe we'll see you at Biarritz,' Hubert said.

We got off with our bags and rod-cases and passed through the dark station and out to the lights and the line of cabs and hotel buses. There, standing with the hotel runners, was Robert Cohn. He did not see us at first. Then he started forward.

'Hello, Jake. Have a good trip?'

'Fine,' I said. 'This is Bill Gorton.'

'How are you?'

'Come on,' said Robert. 'I've got a cab.' He was a little near-sighted. I had never noticed it before. He was looking at Bill, trying to make him out. He was shy, too.

'We'll go up to my hotel. It's all right. It's quite nice.'

We got into the cab, and the cabman put the bags up on the seat beside him and climbed up and cracked his whip, and we drove over the dark bridge and into the town.

'I'm awfully glad to meet you,' Robert said to Bill. 'I've heard so much about you from Jake and I've read your books. Did you get my line, Jake?'

The cab stopped in front of the hotel and we all got out and went in. It was a nice hotel, and the people at the desk were very cheerful, and we each had a good small room.

Chapter 10

In the morning it was bright, and they were sprinkling the streets of the town, and we all had breakfast in a café. Bayonne is a nice town. It is like a very clean Spanish town and it is on a big river. Already, so early in the morning, it was very hot on the bridge across the river. We walked out on the bridge and then took a walk through the town.

I was not at all sure Mike's rods would come from Scotland in time, so we hunted a tackle store and finally bought a rod for Bill upstairs over a drygoods store. The man who sold the tackle was out, and we had to wait for him to come back. Finally he came in, and we bought a pretty good rod cheap, and two landing-nets.

We went out into the street again and took a look at the cathedral. Cohn made some remark about it being a very good example of something or other I forget what. It seemed like a nice cathedral, nice and dim, like Spanish churches. Then we went up past the old fort and out to the local Syndicat d'Initiative office, where the bus was supposed to start from. There they told us the bus service did not start until July 1st. We found out at the tourist office what we ought to pay for a motor-car to Pamplona and hired one at a big garage just around the corner from the Municipal Theatre for four hundred francs. The car was to pick us up at the hotel in forty minutes, and we stopped at the café on the square where we had eaten breakfast, and had a beer. It was hot, but the town had a cool, fresh, early-morning smell and it was pleasant sitting in the café. A breeze started to blow, and you could feel that the air came from the sea. There were pigeons out in the square, and the houses were a yellow, sun-baked colour, and I did not want to leave the café. But we had to go to the hotel to get our bags packed and pay the bill. We paid for the beers, we matched and I think Cohn paid, and went up to the hotel. It was only sixteen francs apiece for Bill and me, with ten per cent added for the service, and we had the bags sent down and waited for Robert Cohn. While we were waiting I saw a cockroach on the parquet floor that must have been at least three inches long. I pointed him out to Bill and then put my shoe on him. We agreed he must have just come in from the garden. It was really an awfully clean hotel.

Cohn came down, finally, and we all went out to the car. It was a big, closed car, with a driver in a white duster with blue collar and cuffs, and we had him put the back of the car down. He piled in the bags and we started off up the street and out of the town. We passed some lovely gardens and had a good look back at the town, and then we were out in the country, green and rolling, and the road climbing all the time. We passed lots of Basques with oxen, or cattle, hauling carts along the road, and nice farmhouses, low roofs, and all white-plastered. In the Basque country the land all looks very rich and green and the houses and villages look well-off and clean. Every village had a pelota court and on some of them kids were playing in the hot sun. There were signs on the walls of the churches saying it was forbidden to play pelota against them, and the houses in the villages had red-tiled roofs, and then the road turned off and commenced to climb and we were going way up close along a hillside, with a valley below and hills stretched off back toward the sea. You couldn't see the sea. It was too far away. You could see only hills and more hills, and you knew where the sea was.

We crossed the Spanish frontier. There was a little stream and a bridge, and Spanish carabineers, with patent-leather Bonaparte hats, and short guns on their backs, on one side, and on the other fat Frenchmen in képis and moustaches. They only opened one bag and took the passports in and looked at them. There was a general store and inn on each side of the line. The chauffeur had to go in and fill out some papers about the car and we got out and went over to the stream to see if there were any trout. Bill tried to talk some Spanish to one of the carabineers, but it did not go very well. Robert Cohn asked, pointing with his finger, if there were any trout in the stream, and the carabineer said yes, but not many.

I asked him if he ever fished, and he said no, that he didn't care for it.

Just then an old man with long, sunburned hair and beard, and clothes that looked as though they were made of gunny-sacking, came striding up to the bridge. He was carrying a long staff, and he had a kid slung on his back, tied by the four legs, the head hanging down.

The carabineer waved him back with his sword. The man turned without saying anything, and started back up the white road into Spain.

'What's the matter with the old one?' I asked.

'He hasn't got any passport.'

I offered the guard a cigarette. He took it and thanked me.

'What will he do?' I asked.

The guard spat in the dust.

'Oh, he'll just wade across the stream.'

'Do you have much smuggling?'

'Oh,' he said, 'they go through.'

The chauffeur came out, folding up the papers and putting them in the inside pocket of his coat. We all got in the car and it started up the white dusty road into Spain. For a while the country was much as it had been; then, climbing all the time, we crossed the top of a col, the road winding back and forth on itself, and then it was really Spain. There were long brown mountains and a few pines and far-off forests of beech-trees on some of the mountainsides. The road went along the summit of the col and then dropped down, and the driver had to honk, and slow up, and turn out to avoid running into two donkeys that were sleeping in the road. We came down out of the mountains and through an oak forest, and there were white cattle grazing in the forest. Down below there were grassy plains and clear streams, and then we crossed a stream and went through a gloomy little village, and started to climb again. We climbed up and up and crossed another high col and turned along it, and the road ran down to the right, and we saw a whole new range of mountains off to the south, all brown and baked-looking and furrowed in strange shapes.

After a while we came out of the mountains, and there were trees along both sides of the road, and a stream and ripe fields of grain, and the road went on, very white and straight ahead, and then lifted to a little rise, and off on the left was a hill with an old castle, with buildings close around it and a field of grain going right up to the walls and shifting in the wind. I was up in front with the driver and I turned around. Robert Cohn was asleep, but Bill looked and nodded his head. Then we crossed a wide plain, and there was a big river off on the right shining in the sun from between the line of trees, and away off you could see the plateau of Pamplona rising out of the plain, and the walls of the city, and the great brown cathedral, and the broken skyline of the other churches. In back of the plateau were the mountains, and every way you looked there were other mountains, and ahead the road stretched out white across the plain going toward Pamplona.

We came into the town on the other side of the plateau, the road slanting up steeply and dustily with shade-trees on both sides, and then levelling out through the new part of town they are building up outside the old walls. We passed the bull-ring, high and white and concrete-looking in the sun, and then came into the big square by a side street and stopped in front of the Hotel Montoya.

The driver helped us down with the bags. There was a crowd of kids watching the car, and the square was hot, and the trees were green, and the flags hung on their staffs, and it was good to get out of the sun and under the shade of the arcade that runs all the way around the square. Montoya was glad to see us, and shook hands and gave us good rooms looking out on the square, and then we washed and cleaned up and went downstairs in the dining-room for lunch. The driver stayed for lunch, too, and afterward we paid him and he started back to Bayonne.

There are two dining-rooms in the Montoya. One is upstairs on the second floor and looks out on the square. The other is down one floor below the level of the square and has a door that opens on the back street that the bulls pass along when they run through the streets early in the morning on their way to the ring. It is always cool in the downstairs dining-room and we had a very good lunch. The first meal in Spain was always a shock with the hors d'œuvres, an egg course, two meat courses, vegetables, salad, and dessert and fruit. You have to drink plenty of wine to get it all down. Robert Cohn tried to say he did not want any of the second meat course, but we would not interpret for him, and so the waitress brought him something else as a replacement, a plate of cold meats, I think. Cohn had been rather nervous ever since we had met at Bayonne. He did not know whether we knew Brett had been with him at San Sebastian, and it made him rather awkward.

'Well,' I said, 'Brett and Mike ought to get in tonight.'

'I'm not sure they'll come,' Cohn said.

'Why not?' Bill said. 'Of course they'll come.'

'They're always late,' I said.

'I rather think they're not coming,' Robert Cohn said.

He said it with an air of superior knowledge that irritated both of us.

'I'll bet you fifty pesetas they're here tonight,' Bill said. He always bets when he is angered, and so he usually bets foolishly.

'I'll take it,' Cohn said. 'Good. You remember it, Jake. Fifty pesetas.'

'I'll remember it myself,' Bill said. I saw he was angry and wanted to smooth him down.

'It's a sure thing they'll come,' I said. 'But maybe not tonight.'

'Want to call it off?' Cohn asked.

'No. Why should I? Make it a hundred if you like.'

'All right. I'll take that.'

'That's enough,' I said. 'Or you'll have to make a book and give me some of it.'

'I'm satisfied.' Cohn said. He smiled. 'You'll probably win it back at bridge, anyway.'

'You haven't got it yet,' Bill said.

We went out to walk around under the arcade to the Café Iruña for coffee. Cohn said he was going over and get a shave.

'Say,' Bill said to me, 'have I got any chance on that bet?'

'You've got a rotten chance. They've never been on time anywhere. If their money doesn't come it's a cinch they won't get in tonight.'

'I was sorry as soon as I opened my mouth. But I had to call him. He's all right, I guess, but where does he get this inside stuff? Mike and Brett fixed it up with us about coming down here.'

I saw Cohn coming over across the square.

'Here he comes.'

'Well, let him not get superior and Jewish.'

'The barber-shop's closed,' Cohn said. 'It's not open till four.'

We had coffee at the Iruña, sitting in comfortable wicker chairs looking out from the cool of the arcade at the big square. After a while Bill went to write some letters and Cohn went over to the barber-shop. It was still closed, so he decided to go up to the hotel and get a bath, and I sat out in front of the café and then went for a walk in the town. It was very hot, but I kept on the shady side of the streets and went through the market and had a good time seeing the town again. I went to the Ayuntamiento and found the old gentleman who subscribes for the bull-fight tickets for me every year, and he had gotten the money I sent him from Paris and renewed my subscriptions, so that was all set. He was the archivist, and all the archives of the town were in his office. That has nothing to do with the story. Anyway, his office had a green baize door and a big wooden door, and when I went out I left him sitting among the archives that covered all the walls, and I shut both the doors, and as I went out of the building into the street the porter stopped me to brush off my coat.

'You must have been in a motor-car,' he said.

The back of the collar and the upper part of the shoulders were grey with dust.

'From Bayonne.'

'Well, well,' he said. 'I knew you were in a motor-car from the way the dust was.' So I gave him two copper coins.

At the end of the street I saw the cathedral and walked up toward it. The first time I ever saw it I thought the façade was ugly but I liked it now. I went inside. It was dim and dark and the pillars went high up, and there were people praying, and it smelt of incense, and there were some wonderful big windows. I knelt and started to pray and prayed for everybody I thought of, Brett and Mike and Bill and Robert Cohn and myself, and all the bull-fighters, separately for the ones I liked, and lumping all the rest, then I prayed for myself again, and while I was praying for myself I found I was getting sleepy, so I prayed that the bull-fights would be good, and that it would be a fine fiesta, and that we would get some fishing. I wondered if there was anything else I might pray for, and I thought I would like to have some money, so I prayed that I would make a lot of money, and then I started to think how I would make it, and thinking of making money reminded me of the count, and I started wondering about where he was, and regretting I hadn't seen him since that night in Montmartre, and about something funny Brett told me about him, and as all the time I was kneeling with my forehead on the wood in front of me, and was thinking of myself as praying, I was a little ashamed, and regretted that I was such a rotten Catholic, but realized there was nothing I could do about it, at least for a while, and maybe never, but that anyway it was a grand religion, and I only wished I felt religious and maybe I would the next time; and then I was out in the hot sun on the steps of the cathedral, and the forefinger and the thumb of my right hand were still damp, and I felt them dry in the sun. The sunlight was hot and hard, and I crossed over beside some buildings, and walked back along side-streets to the hotel.

At dinner that night we found that Robert Cohn had taken a bath, had had a shave and a haircut and a shampoo, and something put on his hair afterward to make it stay down. He was nervous, and I did not try to help him any. The train was due in at nine o'clock from San Sebastian, and, if Brett and Mike were coming, they would be on it. At twenty minutes to nine we were not half through dinner. Robert Cohn got up from the table and said he would go to the station. I said I would go with him, just to devil him. Bill said he would be damned if he would leave his dinner. I said we would be right back.

We walked to the station. I was enjoying Cohn's nervousness. I hoped Brett would be on the train. At the station the train was late, and we sat on a baggage-truck and waited outside in the dark. I have never seen a man in civil life as nervous as Robert Cohn – nor as eager. I was enjoying it. It was lousy to enjoy it, but I felt lousy. Cohn had a wonderful quality of bringing out the worst in anybody.

After a while we heard the train-whistle way off below on the other side of the plateau, and then we saw the headlight coming up the hill. We went inside the station and stood with a crowd of people just back of the gates, and the train came in and stopped, and everybody started coming out through the gates.

They were not in the crowd. We waited till everybody had gone through and out of the station and gotten into buses, or taken cabs, or were walking with their friends or relatives through the dark into the town.

'I knew they wouldn't come,' Robert said. We were going back to the hotel.

'I thought they might,' I said.

Bill was eating fruit when we came in and finishing a bottle of wine.

'Didn't come, eh?'

'No.'

'Do you mind if I give you that hundred pesetas in the morning, Cohn?' Bill asked. 'I haven't changed any money here yet.'

'Oh, forget about it,' Robert Cohn said. 'Let's bet on something else. Can you bet on bull-fights?'

'You could,' Bill said, 'but you don't need to.'

'It would be like betting on the war,' I said. 'You don't need any economic interest.'

'I'm very curious to see them,' Robert said.

Montoya came up to our table. He had a telegram in his hand. 'It's for you.' He handed it to me.

It read: 'Stopped night San Sebastian.'

'It's from them,' I said. I put it in my pocket. Ordinarily I should have handed it over.

'They've stopped over in San Sebastian,' I said. 'Send their regards to you.'

Why I felt that impulse to devil him I do not know. Of course I do know. I was blind, unforgivingly jealous of what had happened to him. The fact that I took it as a matter of course did not alter that any. I certainly did hate him. I do not think I ever really hated him until he had that little spell of superiority at lunch – that and when he went through all that barbering. So I put the telegram in my pocket. The telegram came to me, anyway.

'Well,' I said. 'We ought to pull out on the noon bus for Burguete. They can follow us if they get in tomorrow night.'

There were only two trains up from San Sebastian, an early-morning train and the one we had just met.

'That sounds like a good idea,' Cohn said.

'The sooner we get on the stream the better.'

'It's all one to me when we start,' Bill said. 'The sooner the better.'

We sat in the Iruña for a while and had coffee and then took a little walk out to the bull-ring and across the field and under the trees at the edge of the cliff and looked down at the river in the dark, and I turned in early. Bill and Cohn stayed out in the café quite late, I believe, because I was asleep when they came in.

In the morning I bought three tickets for the bus to Burguete. It was scheduled to leave at two o'clock. There was nothing earlier. I was sitting over at the Iruña reading the papers when I saw Robert Cohn coming across the square. He came up to the table and sat down in one of the wicker chairs.

'This is a comfortable café,' he said. 'Did you have a good night, Jake?'

'I slept like a log.'

'I didn't sleep very well. Bill and I were out late, too.'

'Where were you?'

'Here. And after it shut we went over to that other café. The old man there speaks German and English.'

'The Café Suizo.'

'That's it. He seems like a nice old fellow. I think it's a better café than this one.'

'It's not so good in the daytime,' I said. 'Too hot. By the way, I got the bus tickets.'

'I'm not going up today. You and Bill go on ahead.'

'I've got your ticket.'

'Give it to me. I'll get the money back.'

'It's five pesetas.'

Robert Cohn took out a silver five-peseta piece and gave it to me.

'I ought to stay,' he said. 'You see I'm afraid there's some sort of misunderstanding.'

'Why?' I said. 'They may not come here for three or four days now if they start on parties at San Sebastian.'

'That's just it,' said Robert. 'I'm afraid they expected to meet me at San Sebastian, and that's why they stopped over.'

'What makes you think that?'

'Well, I wrote suggesting it to Brett.'

'Why in hell didn't you stay there and meet them, then?' I started to say, but I stopped. I thought that idea would come to him by itself, but I do not believe it ever did.

He was being confidential now and it was giving him

pleasure to be able to talk with the understanding that I knew there was something between him and Brett.

'Well, Bill and I will go up right after lunch,' I said.

'I wish I could go. We've been looking forward to this fishing all winter.' He was being sentimental about it. 'But I ought to stay. I really ought. As soon as they come I'll bring them right up.'

'Let's find Bill.'

'I want to go over to the barber-shop.'

'See you at lunch.'

I found Bill up in his room. He was shaving.

'Oh, yes, he told me all about it last night,' Bill said. 'He's a great little confider. He said he had a date with Brett at San Sebastian.'

'The lying bastard!'

'Oh, no,' said Bill. 'Don't get sore. Don't get sore at this stage of the trip. How did you ever happen to know this fellow, anyway?'

'Don't rub it in.'

Bill looked around, half-shaved, and then went on talking into the mirror while he lathered his face.

'Didn't you send him with a letter to me in New York last winter? Thank God, I'm a travelling man. Haven't you got some more Jewish friends you could bring along?' He rubbed his chin with his thumb, looked at it, and then started scraping again.

'You've got some fine ones yourself.'

'Oh, yes. I've got some darbs. But not alongside of this Robert Cohn. The funny thing is he's nice, too. I like him. But he's just so awful.'

'He can be damn nice.'

'I know it. That's the terrible part.'

I laughed.

'Yes. Go on and laugh,' said Bill. 'You weren't out with him last night until two o'clock.'

'Was he very bad?'

'Awful. What's all this about him and Brett, anyway? Did she ever have anything to do with him?'

He raised his chin up and pulled it from side to side.

'Sure. She went down to San Sebastian with him.'

'What a damn-fool thing to do. Why did she do that?'

'She wanted to get out of town and she can't go anywhere alone. She said she thought it would be good for him.'

'What bloody-fool things people do. Why didn't she go off with some of her own people? Or you?' – he slurred that over – 'or me? Why not me?' He looked at his face carefully in the glass, put a big dab of lather on each cheek-bone. 'It's an honest face. It's a face any woman would be safe with.'

'She'd never seen it.'

'She should have. All women should see it. It's a face that ought to be thrown on every screen in the country. Every woman ought to be given a copy of this face as she leaves the altar. Mothers should tell their daughters about this face. My son' – he pointed the razor at me – 'go west with this face and grow up with the country.'

He ducked down to the bowl, rinsed his face with cold water, put on some alcohol and then looked at himself carefully in the glass, pulling down his long upper lip.

'My God!' he said, 'isn't it an awful face?'

He looked in the glass.

'And as for this Robert Cohn,' Bill said, 'he makes me sick, and he can go to hell, and I'm damn glad he's staying here so we won't have him fishing with us.'

'You're damn right.'

'We're going trout-fishing. We're going trout-fishing in the Irati River, and we're going to get tight now at lunch on the wine of the country, and then take a swell bus ride.'

'Come on. Let's go over to the Iruña and start,' I said.

Chapter 11

It was baking hot in the square when we came out after lunch with our bags and the rod-case to go to Burguete. People were on top of the bus, and others were climbing up a ladder. Bill went up and Robert sat beside Bill to save a place for me, and I went back in the hotel to get a couple of bottles of wine to take with us. When I came out the bus was crowded. Men and women were sitting on all the baggage and boxes on top, and the women all had their fans going in the sun. It certainly was hot. Robert climbed down and I fitted into the place he had saved on the one wooden seat that ran across the top.

Robert Cohn stood in the shade of the arcade waiting for us to start. A Basque with a big leather wine-bag in his lap lay across the top of the bus in front of our seat, leaning back against our legs. He offered the wine-skin to Bill and to me, and when I tipped it up to drink he imitated the sound of a klaxon motor-horn so well and so suddenly that I spilled some of the wine, and everybody laughed. He apologized and made me take another drink. He made the klaxon again a little later, and it fooled me the second time. He was very good at it. The Basques liked it. The man next to Bill was talking to him in Spanish and Bill was not getting it, so he offered the man one of the bottles of wine. The man waved it away. He said it was too hot and he had drunk too much at lunch. When Bill offered the bottle the second time he took a long drink, and then the bottle went all over that part of the bus. Every one took a drink very politely, and then they made us cork it up and put it away. They all wanted us to drink from their leather wine-bottles. They were peasants going up into the hills.

Finally, after a couple more false klaxons, the bus started, and Robert Cohn waved good-bye to us, and all the Basques waved good-bye to him. As soon as we started out on the road outside of town it was cool. It felt nice riding high up and close under the trees. The bus went quite fast and made a good breeze, and as we went out along the road with the dust powdering the trees and down the hill, we had a fine view, back through the trees, of the town rising up from the bluff above the river. The Basque lying against my knees pointed out the view with the neck of the wine-bottle, and winked at us. He nodded his head.

'Pretty nice, eh?'

'These Basques are swell people,' Bill said.

The Basque lying against my legs was tanned the colour of

saddle-leather. He wore a black smock like all the rest. There were wrinkles in his tanned neck. He turned around and offered his wine-bag to Bill. Bill handed him one of our bottles. The Basque wagged a forefinger at him and handed the bottle back, slapping in the cork with the palm of his hand. He shoved the wine-bag up.

'Arriba! Arriba!' he said. 'Lift it up.'

Bill raised the wine-skin and let the stream of wine spurt out and into his mouth, his head tipped back. When he stopped drinking and tipped the leather bottle down a few drops ran down his chin.

'No! No!' several Basques said. 'Not like that.' One snatched the bottle away from the owner, who was himself about to give a demonstration. He was a young fellow and he held the wine-bottle at full arms' length and raised it high up, squeezing the leather bag with his hand so the stream of wine hissed into his mouth. He held the bag out there, the wine making a flat, hard trajectory into his mouth, and he kept on swallowing smoothly and regularly.

'Hey!' the owner of the bottle shouted. 'Whose wine is that?'

The drinker waggled his little finger at him and smiled at us with his eyes. Then he bit the stream off sharp, made a quick lift with the wine-bag and lowered it down to the owner. He winked at us. The owner shook the wine-skin sadly.

We passed through a town and stopped in front of the posada, and the driver took on several packages. Then we started on again, and outside the town the road commenced to mount. We were going through farming country with rocky hills that sloped down into the fields. The grain-fields went up the hillsides. Now as we went higher there was a wind blowing the grain. The road was white and dusty, and the dust rose under the wheels and hung in the air behind us. The road climbed up into the hills and left the rich grain-fields below. Now there were only patches of grain on the bare hillsides and on each side of the water-courses. We turned sharply out to the side of the road to give room to pass to a long string of six mules, following one after the other, hauling a high-hooded wagon loaded with freight. The wagon and the mules were covered with dust. Close behind was another string of mules and another wagon. This was loaded with lumber, and the arriero driving the mules leaned back and put on the thick wooden brakes as we passed. Up here the country was quite barren and the hills were rocky and hard-baked clay furrowed by the rain.

We came around a curve into a town, and on both sides opened out a sudden green valley. A stream went through the centre of the town and fields of grapes touched the houses.

The bus stopped in front of a posada and many of the passengers got down, and a lot of the baggage was unstrapped from the roof from under the big tarpaulins and lifted down. Bill and I got down and went into the posada. There was a low, dark room with saddles and harness, and hayforks made of white wood, and clusters of canvas rope-soled shoes and hams and slabs of bacon and white garlics and long sausages hanging from the roof. It was cool and dusky, and we stood in front of a long wooden counter with two women behind it serving drinks. Behind them were shelves stacked with supplies and goods.

We each had an aguardiente and paid forty centimes for the two drinks. I gave the woman fifty centimes to make a tip, and she gave me back the copper piece, thinking I had misunderstood the price.

Two of our Basques came in and insisted on buying a drink. So they bought a drink and then we bought a drink, and then they slapped us on the back and bought another drink. Then we bought, and then we all went out into the sunlight and the heat, and climbed back on top of the bus. There was plenty of room now for everyone to sit on the seat, and the Basque who had been lying on the tin roof now sat between us. The woman who had been serving drinks came out wiping her hands on her apron and talked to somebody inside the bus. Then the driver came out swinging two flat leather mail-pouches and climbed up, and everybody waving we started off.

The road left the green valley at once, and we were up in the hills again. Bill and the wine-bottle Basque were having a conversation. A man leaned over from the other side of the seat and asked in English: 'You're Americans?'

'Sure.'

'I been there,' he said. 'Forty years ago.'

He was an old man, as brown as the others, with the stubble of a white beard.

'How was it?'

'What you say?'

'How was America?'

'Oh, I was in California. It was fine.'

'Why did you leave?'

'What you say?'

'Why did you come back here?'

'Oh! I come back to get married. I was going to go back but my wife she don't like to travel. Where you from?'

'Kansas City.'

'I been there,' he said. 'I been in Chicago, St. Louis, Kansas City, Denver, Los Angeles, Salt Lake City.'

He named them carefully.

'How long were you over?'

'Fifteen years. Then I come back and got married.'

'Have a drink?'

'All right,' he said. 'You can't get this in America, eh?'

'There's plenty if you can pay for it.'

'What you come over here for?'

'We're going to the fiesta at Pamplona.'

'You like the bull-fights?'

'Sure. Don't you?'

'Yes,' he said. 'I guess I like them.'

Then after a little:

'Where you go now?'

'Up to Burguete to fish.'

'Well,' he said, 'I hope you catch something.'

He shook hands and turned around to the back seat again. The other Basques had been impressed. He sat back comfortably and smiled at me when I turned around to look at the country. But the effort of talking American seemed to have tired him. He did not say anything after that.

The bus climbed steadily up the road. The country was barren and rocks stuck up through the clay. There was no grass beside the road. Looking back we could see the country spread out below. Far back the fields were squares of green and brown on the hillsides. Making the horizon were the brown mountains. They were strangely shaped. As we climbed higher the horizon kept changing. As the bus ground slowly up the road we could see other mountains coming up in the south. Then the road came over the crest, flattened out, and went into a forest. It was a forest of cork oaks, and the sun came through the trees in patches, and there were cattle grazing back in the trees. We went through the forest and the road came out and turned along a rise of land, and out ahead of us was a rolling green plain, with dark mountains beyond it. These were not like the brown, heat-baked mountains we had left behind. These were wooded and there were clouds coming down from them. The green plain stretched off. It was cut by fences and the white of the road showed through the trunks of a double line of trees that crossed the plain toward the north. As we came to the edge of the rise we saw the red roofs and white houses of Burguete ahead strung out on the plain, and away off on the shoulder of the first dark mountain was the gray metal-sheathed roof of the monastery of Roncevalles.

'There's Roncevaux,' I said.

'Where?'

'Way off there where the mountains start.'

'It's cold up here,' Bill said.

'It's high,' I said. 'It must be twelve hundred metres.'

'It's awful cold,' Bill said.

The bus levelled down onto the straight line of road that ran to Burguete. We passed a crossroads and crossed a bridge over a stream. The houses of Burguete were along both sides of the road. There were no side-streets. We passed the church and the school-yard, and the bus stopped. We got down and the driver handed down our bags and the rod-case. A carabineer in his cocked hat and yellow leather cross-straps came in.

'What's in there?' he pointed to the rod-case.

I opened it and showed him. He asked to see our fishing permits and I got them out. He looked at the date and then waved us on.

'Is that all right?' I asked.

'Yes. Of course.'

We went up the street, past the whitewashed stone houses, families sitting in their doorways watching us, to the inn.

The fat woman who ran the inn came out from the kitchen and shook hands with us. She took off her spectacles, wiped them, and put them on again. It was cold in the inn and the wind was starting to blow outside. The woman sent a girl upstairs with us to show the room. There were two beds, a washstand, a clothes-chest, and a big, framed steel-engraving of Nuestra Señora de Roncevalles. The wind was blowing against the shutters. The room was on the north side of the inn. We washed, put on sweaters, and came downstairs into the dining-room. It had a stone floor, low ceiling, and was oak-panelled. The shutters were all up and it was so cold you could see your breath.

'My God!' said Bill. 'It can't be this cold tomorrow. I'm not going to wade a stream in this weather.'

There was an upright piano in the far corner of the room beyond the wooden tables and Bill went over and started to play.

'I got to keep warm,' he said.

I went out to find the woman and ask her how much the room and board was. She put her hands under her apron and looked away from me.

'Twelve pesetas.'

'Why, we only paid that in Pamplona.'

She did not say anything, just took off her glasses and wiped them on her apron.

'That's too much,' I said. 'We didn't pay more than that at a big hotel.'

'We've put in a bathroom.'

'Haven't you got anything cheaper?'

'Not in the summer. Now is the big season.'

We were the only people in the inn. Well, I thought, it's only a few days.

'Is the wine included?'

'Oh, yes.'

'Well,' I said. 'It's all right.'

I went back to Bill. He blew his breath at me to show how cold it was, and went on playing. I sat at one of the tables and looked at the pictures on the wall. There was one panel of rabbits, dead, one of pheasants, also dead, and one panel of dead ducks. The panels were all dark and smoky-looking. There was a cupboard full of liqueur bottles. I looked at them all. Bill was still playing. 'How about a hot rum punch?' he said. 'This isn't going to keep me warm permanently.'

I went out and told the woman what a rum punch was and how to make it. In a few minutes a girl brought a stone pitcher, steaming, into the room. Bill came over from the piano and we drank the hot punch and listened to the wind.

'There isn't too much rum in that.'

I went over to the cupboard and brought the rum bottle and poured a half-tumblerful into the pitcher.

'Direct action,' said Bill. 'It beats legislation.'

The girl came in and laid the table for supper.

'It blows like hell up here,' Bill said.

The girl brought in a big bowl of hot vegetable soup and the wine. We had fried trout afterward and some sort of a stew and a big bowl full of wild strawberries. We did not lose money on the wine, and the girl was shy but nice about bringing it. The old woman looked in once and counted the empty bottles.

After supper we went upstairs and smoked and read in bed to keep warm. Once in the night I woke and heard the wind blowing. It felt good to be warm and in bed.

Chapter 12

When I woke in the morning I went to the window and looked out. It had cleared and there were no clouds on the mountains. Outside under the window were some carts and an old diligence, the wood of the roof cracked and split by the weather. It must have been left from the days before the motor-buses. A goat hopped up on one of the carts and then to the roof of the diligence. He jerked his head at the other goats below and when I waved at him he bounded down.

Bill was still sleeping, so I dressed, put on my shoes outside in the hall, and went downstairs. No one was stirring downstairs, so I unbolted the door and went out. It was cool outside in the early morning and the sun had not yet dried the dew that had come when the wind died down. I hunted around in the shed behind the inn and found a sort of mattock, and went down toward the stream to try and dig some worms for bait. The stream was clear and shallow but it did not look trouty. On the grassy bank where it was damp I drove the mattock into the earth and loosened a chunk of sod. There were worms underneath. They slid out of sight as I lifted the sod and I dug carefully and got a good many. Digging at the edge of the damp ground I filled two empty tobacco-tins with worms and sifted dirt onto them. The goats watched me dig.

When I went back into the inn the woman was down in the kitchen, and I asked her to get coffee for us, and that we wanted a lunch. Bill was awake and sitting on the edge of the bed.

'I saw you out of the window,' he said. 'Didn't want to interrupt you. What were you doing? Burying your money?'

'You lazy bum!'

'Been working for the common good? Splendid. I want you to do that every morning.'

'Come on,' I said. 'Get up.'

'What? Get up? I never get up.'

He climbed into bed and pulled the sheet up to his chin.

'Try and argue me into getting up.'

I went on looking for the tackle and putting it all together in the tackle-bag.

'Aren't you interested?' Bill asked.

'I'm going down and eat.'

'Eat? Why didn't you say eat? I thought you just wanted me to get up for fun. Eat? Fine. Now you're reasonable. You go out and dig some more worms and I'll be right down.'

'Oh, go to hell!'

'Work for the good of all.' Bill stepped into his under-clothes. 'Show irony and pity.'

I started out of the room with the tackle-bag, the nets, and the rod-case.

'Hey! come back!'

90

I put my head in the door.

'Aren't you going to show a little irony and pity?'

I thumbed my nose.

'That's not irony.'

As I went down-stairs I heard Bill singing, 'Irony and Pity. When you're feeling . . . Oh, give them Irony and Give them Pity. Oh, give them Irony. When they're feeling . . . Just a little irony. Just a little pity . . .' He kept on singing until he came downstairs. The tune was: 'The Bells are Ringing for Me and my Gal.' I was reading a week-old Spanish paper.

'What's all this irony and pity?'

'What? Don't you know about Irony and Pity?'

'No. Who got it up?'

'Everybody. They're mad about it in New York. It's just like the Fratellinis used to be.'

The girl came in with the coffee and buttered toast. Or, rather, it was bread toasted and buttered.

'Ask her if she's got any jam,' Bill said. 'Be ironical with her.'

'Have you got any jam?'

'That's not ironical. I wish I could talk Spanish.'

The coffee was good and we drank it out of big bowls. The girl brought in a glass dish of raspberry jam.

'Thank you.'

'Hey! that's not the way,' Bill said. 'Say something ironical. Make some crack about Primo de Rivera.'

'I could ask her what kind of a jam they think they've gotten into in the Riff.'

'Poor,' said Bill. 'Very poor. You can't do it. That's all. You don't understand irony. You have no pity. Say something pitiful.'

'Robert Cohn.'

'Not so bad. That's better. Now why is Cohn pitiful? Be ironic.'

He took a big gulp of coffee.

'Aw, hell!' I said. 'It's too early in the morning.'

'There you go. And you claim you want to be a writer, too. You're only a newspaper man. An expatriated newspaper man. You ought to be ironical the minute you get out of bed. You ought to wake up with your mouth full of pity.'

'Go on,' I said. 'Who did you get this stuff from?'

'Everybody. Don't you read? Don't you ever see anybody? You know what you are? You're an expatriate. Why don't you live in New York? Then you'd know these things. What do you want me to do? Come over here and tell you every year?'

'Take some more coffee,' I said.

'Good. Coffee is good for you. It's the caffeine in it. Caffeine, we are here. Caffeine puts a man on her horse and a woman in his grave. You know what's the trouble with you? You're an expatriate. One of the worst type. Haven't you heard that? Nobody that ever left their own country ever wrote anything worth printing. Not even in the newspapers.'

He drank the coffee.

'You're an expatriate. You've lost touch with the soil. You get precious. Fake European standards have ruined you. You drink yourself to death. You become obsessed by sex. You spend all your time talking, not working. You are an expatriate, see? You hang around cafés.'

'It sounds like a swell life,' I said. 'When do I work?'

'You don't work. One group claims women support you. Another group claims you're impotent.'

'No,' I said. 'I just had an accident.'

'Never mention that,' Bill said. 'That's the sort of thing that can't be spoken of. That's what you ought to work up into a mystery. Like Henry's bicycle.'

He had been going splendidly, but he stopped. I was afraid he thought he had hurt me with that crack about being impotent. I wanted to start him again.

'It wasn't a bicycle,' I said. 'He was riding horseback.'

'I heard it was a tricycle.'

'Well,' I said. 'A plane is sort of like a tricycle. The joystick works the same way.'

'But you don't pedal it.'

'No,' I said, 'I guess you don't pedal it.'

'Let's lay off that,' Bill said.

'All right. I was just standing up for the tricycle.'

'I think he's a good writer, too,' Bill said. 'And you're a hell of a good guy. Anybody ever tell you you were a good guy?'

'I'm not a good guy.'

'Listen. You're a hell of a good guy, and I'm fonder of you than anybody on earth. I couldn't tell you that in New York. It'd mean I was a faggot. That was what the Civil War was about. Abraham Lincoln was a faggot. He was in love with General Grant. So was Jefferson Davis. Lincoln just freed the slaves on a bet. The Dred Scott case was framed by the Anti-Saloon League. Sex explains it all. The Colonel's Lady and Judy O'Grady are Lesbians under their skin.'

He stopped.

'Wanted to hear some more?'

'Shoot,' I said.

'I don't know any more. Tell you some more at lunch.'

'Old Bill,' I said.

'You bum.'

We packed the lunch and two bottles of wine in the rucksack, and Bill put it on. I carried the rod-case and the landing-nets slung over my back. We started up the road and then went across a meadow and found a path that crossed the fields and went toward the woods on the slope of the first hill. We walked across the fields on the sandy path. The fields were rolling and grassy and the grass was short from the sheep grazing. The cattle were up in the hills. We heard their bells in the woods.

The path crossed a stream on a foot-log. The log was surfaced off, and there was a sapling bent across for a rail. In the flat pool beside the stream tadpoles spotted the sand. We went up a steep bank and across the rolling fields. Looking back we saw Burguete, white houses and red roofs, and the white road with a truck going along it and the dust rising.

Beyond the fields we crossed another faster-flowing stream. A sandy road led down to the ford and beyond into the woods. The path crossed the stream on another foot-log below the ford, and joined the road, and we went into the woods.

It was a beech wood and the trees were very old. Their roots bulked above the ground and the branches were twisted. We walked on the road between the thick trunks of the old beeches and the sunlight came through the leaves in light patches on the grass. The trees were big, and the foliage was thick but it was not gloomy. There was no undergrowth, only the smooth grass, very green and fresh, and the big grey trees well spaced as though it were a park.

'This is country,' Bill said.

The road went up a hill and we got into thick woods, and the road kept on climbing. Sometimes it dipped down but rose again steeply. All the time we heard the cattle in the woods. Finally, the road came out on the top of the hills. We were on the top of the height of land that was the highest part of the range of wooded hills we had seen from Burguete. There were wild strawberries growing on the sunny side of the ridge in a little clearing in the trees.

Ahead the road came out of the forest and went along the shoulder of the ridge of hills. The hills ahead were not wooded, and there were great fields of yellow gorse. Way off we saw the steep bluffs, dark with trees and jutting with grey stone, that marked the course of the Irati River.

'We have to follow this road along the ridge, cross these hills, go through the woods on the far hills, and come down to the Irati valley,' I pointed out to Bill.

'That's a hell of a hike.'

'It's too far to go and fish and come back the same day, comfortably.'

'Comfortably. That's a nice word. We'll have to go like hell to get there and back and have any fishing at all.'

It was a long walk and the country was very fine, but we were tired when we came down the steep road that led out of the wooded hills into the valley of the Rio de la Fabrica.

The road came out from the shadow of the woods into the hot sun. Ahead was a river-valley. Beyond the river was a steep hill. There was a field of buckwheat on the hill. We saw a white house under some trees on the hillside. It was very hot and we stopped under some trees beside a dam that crossed the river.

Bill put the pack against one of the trees and we jointed up the rods, put on the reels, tied on leaders, and got ready to fish.

'You're sure this thing has trout in it?' Bill asked.

'It's full of them.'

'I'm going to fish a fly. You got any McGintys?'

'There some in there.'

'You going to fish bait?'

94

'Yeah. I'm going to fish the dam here.'

'Well, I'll take the fly-book, then.' He tied on a fly. 'Where'd I better go? Up or down?'

'Down is the best. They're plenty up above, too.'

Bill went down the bank.

'Take a worm can.'

'No, I don't want one. If they won't take a fly I'll just flick it around.'

Bill was down below watching the stream.

'Say,' he called up against the noise of the dam. 'How about putting the wine in that spring up the road?'

'All right,' I shouted. Bill waved his hand and started down the stream. I found the two wine-bottles in the pack, and carried them up the road to where the water of a spring flowed out of an iron pipe. There was a board over the spring and I lifted it and, knocking the corks firmly into the bottles, lowered them down into the water. It was so cold my hand and wrist felt numbed. I put back the slab of wood, and hoped nobody would find the wine.

I got my rod that was leaning against the tree, took the bait-can and landing-net, and walked out onto the dam. It was built to provide a head of water for driving logs. The gate was up, and I sat on one of the squared timbers and watched the smooth apron of water before the river tumbled into the falls. In the white water at the foot of the dam it was deep. As I baited up, a trout shot up out of the white water into the falls and was carried down. Before I could finish baiting, another trout jumped at the falls, making the same lovely arc and disappearing into the water that was thundering down. I put on a good-sized sinker and dropped into the white water close to the edge of the timbers of the dam.

I did not feel the first trout strike. When I started to pull up I felt that I had one and brought him, fighting and bending the rod almost double, out of the boiling water at the foot of the falls, and swung him up and onto the dam. He was a good trout, and I banged his head against the timber so that he quivered out straight, and then slipped him into my bag.

While I had him on, several trout had jumped at the falls. As

95

soon as I baited up and dropped in again I hooked another and brought him in the same way. In a little while I had six. They were all about the same size. I laid them out, side by side, all their heads pointing the same way, and looked at them. They were beautifully coloured and firm and hard from the cold water. It was a hot day, so I slit them all and shucked out the insides, gills and all, and tossed them over across the river. I took the trout ashore, washed them in the cold, smoothly heavy water above the dam, and then picked some ferns and packed them all in the bag, three trout on a layer of ferns, then another layer of ferns, then three more trout, and then covered them with ferns. They looked nice in the ferns, and now the bag was bulky, and I put it in the shade of the tree.

It was very hot on the dam, so I put my worm-can in the shade with the bag, and got a book out of the pack and settled down under the tree to read until Bill should come up for lunch.

It was a little past noon and there was not much shade, but I sat against the trunk of two of the trees that grew together, and read. The book was something by A. E. W. Mason, and I was reading a wonderful story about a man who had been frozen in the Alps and then fallen into a glacier and disappeared, and his bride was going to wait twenty-four years exactly for his body to come out on the moraine, while her true love waited too, and they were still waiting when Bill came up.

'Get any?' he asked. He had his rod and his bag and his net all in one hand, and he was sweating. I hadn't heard him come up, because of the noise from the dam.

'Six. What did you get?'

Bill sat down, opened up his bag, laid a big trout on the grass. He took out three more, each one a little bigger than the last, and laid them side by side in the shade from the tree. His face was sweaty and happy.

'How are yours?'

'Smaller.'

'Let's see them.'

'They're packed.'

'How big are they really?'

96

'They're all about the size of your smallest.'

'You're not holding out on me?'

'I wish I were.'

'Get them all on worms?'

'Yes.'

'You lazy bum!'

Bill put the trout in the bag and started for the river, swinging the open bag. He was wet from the waist down and I knew he must have been wading the stream.

I walked up the road and got out the two bottles of wine. They were cold. Moisture beaded on the bottles as I walked back to the trees. I spread the lunch on a newspaper, and uncorked one of the bottles and leaned the other against a tree. Bill came up drying his hands, his bag plump with ferns.

'Let's see that bottle,' he said. He pulled the cork, and tipped up the bottle and drank. 'Whew! That makes my eyes ache.'

'Let's try it.'

The wine was icy cold and tasted faintly rusty.

'That's not such filthy wine,' Bill said.

'The cold helps it,' I said.

We unwrapped the little parcels of lunch.

'Chicken.'

'There's hard-boiled eggs.'

'Find any salt?'

'First the egg,' said Bill. 'Then the chicken. Even Bryan could see that.'

'He's dead. I read it in the paper yesterday.'

'No. Not really?'

'Yes. Bryan's dead.'

Bill laid down the egg he was peeling.

'Gentlemen,' he said, and unwrapped a drumstick from a piece of newspaper. 'I reverse the order. For Bryan's sake. As a tribute to the Great Commoner. First the chicken; then the egg.'

'Wonder what day God created the chicken?'

'Oh,' said Bill, sucking the drumstick, 'how should we know? We should not question. Our stay on earth is not for long. Let us rejoice and believe and give thanks.'

'Eat an egg.'

Bill gestured with the drumstick in one hand and the bottle of wine in the other.

'Let us rejoice in our blessings. Let us utilize the fowls of the air. Let us utilize the produce of the vine. Will you utilize a little, brother?'

'After you, brother.'

Bill took a long drink.

'Utilize a little, brother,' he handed me the bottle. 'Let us not doubt, brother. Let us not pry into the holy mysteries of the hen-coop with simian fingers. Let us accept on faith and simply say – I want you to join with me in saying – What shall we say, brother?' He pointed the drumstick at me and went on. 'Let me tell you. We will say, and I for one am proud to say – and I want you to say with me, on your knees, brother. Let no man be ashamed to kneel here in the great out-of-doors. Remember the woods were God's first temples. Let us kneel and say: "Don't eat that, Lady – that's Mencken".'

'Here,' I said. 'Utilize a little of this.'

We uncorked the other bottle.

'What's the matter?' I said. 'Didn't you like Bryan?'

'I loved Bryan,' said Bill. 'We were like brothers.'

'Where did you know him?'

'He and Mencken and I all went to Holy Cross together.'

'And Frankie Frisch.'

'It's a lie. Frankie Frisch went to Fordham.'

'Well,' I said, 'I went to Loyola with Bishop Manning.'

'It's a lie,' Bill said. 'I went to Loyola with Bishop Manning myself.'

'You're cock-eyed,' I said.

'On wine?'

'Why not?'

'It's the humidity,' Bill said. 'They ought to take this damn humidity away.'

'Have another shot.'

'Is this all we've got?'

'Only the two bottles.'

'Do you know what you are?' Bill looked at the bottle affectionately.

'No,' I said.

'You're in the pay of the Anti-Saloon League.'

'I went to Notre Dame with Wayne B. Wheeler.'

'It's a lie,' said Bill. 'I went to Austin Business College with Wayne B. Wheeler. He was class president.'

'Well,' I said, 'the saloon must go.'

'You're right there, old classmate,' Bill said. 'The saloon must go, and I will take it with me.'

'You're cock-eyed.'

'On wine?'

'On wine.'

'Well, maybe I am.'

'Want to take a nap?'

'All right.'

We lay with our heads in the shade and looked up into the trees.

'You asleep?'

'No,' Bill said. 'I was thinking.'

I shut my eyes. It felt good lying on the ground.

'Say,' Bill said, 'what about this Brett business?'

'What about it?'

'Were you ever in love with her?'

'Sure.'

'For how long?'

'Off and on for a hell of a long time.'

'Oh, hell!' Bill said. 'I'm sorry, fella.'

'It's all right,' I said. 'I don't give a damn any more.'

'Really?'

'Really. Only I'd a hell of a lot rather not talk about it.'

'You aren't sore I asked you?'

'Why the hell should I be?'

'I'm going to sleep,' Bill said. He put a newspaper over his face.

'Listen, Jake,' he said, 'are you really a Catholic?'

'Technically.'

'What does that mean?'

'I don't know.'

'All right, I'll go to sleep now,' he said. 'Don't keep me awake by talking so much.'

I went to sleep, too. When I woke up Bill was packing the

rucksack. It was late in the afternoon and the shadow from the trees was long and went out over the dam. I was stiff from sleeping on the ground.

'What did you do? Wake up?' Bill asked. 'Why didn't you spend the night?' I stretched and rubbed my eyes.

'I had a lovely dream,' Bill said. 'I don't remember what it was about, but it was a lovely dream.'

'I don't think I dreamt.'

'You ought to dream,' Bill said. 'All our biggest business men have been dreamers. Look at Ford. Look at President Coolidge. Look at Rockefeller. Look at Jo Davidson.'

I disjointed my rod and Bill's and packed them in the rod-case. I put the reels in the tackle-bag. Bill had packed the rucksack and we put one of the trout-bags in. I carried the other.

'Well,' said Bill, 'have you got everything?'

'The worms.'

'Your worms. Put them in there.'

He had the pack on his back and I put the worm-cans in one of the outside flap pockets.

'You got everything now?'

I looked around on the grass at the foot of the elm-trees.

'Yes.'

We started up the road into the woods. It was a long walk home to Burguete, and it was dark when we came down across the fields to the road, and along the road between the houses of the town, their windows lighted, to the inn.

We stayed five days at Burguete and had good fishing. The nights were cold and the days were hot, and there was always a breeze even in the heat of the day. It was hot enough so that it felt good to wade in a cold stream, and the sun dried you when you came out and sat on the bank. We found a stream with a pool deep enough to swim in. In the evenings we played three-handed bridge with an Englishman named Harris, who had walked over from Saint Jean Pied de Port and was stopped at the inn for the fishing. He was very pleasant and went with us twice to the Irati River. There was no word from Robert Cohn nor from Brett and Mike.

Chapter 13

One morning I went down to breakfast and the Englishman, Harris, was already at the table. He was reading the paper through spectacles. He looked up and smiled.

'Good morning,' he said. 'Letter for you. I stopped at the post and they gave it me with mine.'

The letter was at my place at the table, leaning against a coffee-cup. Harris was reading the paper again. I opened the letter. It had been forwarded from Pamplona. It was dated San Sebastian, Sunday:

DEAR JAKE,

We got here Friday, Brett passed out on the train, so brought her here for 3 days' rest with old friends of ours. We go to Montoya Hotel Pamplona Tuesday, arriving at I don't know what hour. Will you send a note by the bus to tell us what to do to rejoin you all on Wednesday. All our love and sorry to be late, but Brett was really done in and will be quite all right by Tues. and is practically so now. I know her so well and try to look after her but it's not so easy. Love to all the chaps.

MICHAEL.

'What day of the week is it?' I asked Harris.

'Wednesday, I think. Yes, quite. Wednesday. Wonderful how one loses track of the days up here in the mountains.'

'Yes. We've been here nearly a week.'

'I hope you're not thinking of leaving?'

'Yes. We'll go in on the afternoon bus, I'm afraid.'

'What a rotten business. I had hoped we'd all have another go at the Irati together.'

'We have to go into Pamplona. We're meeting people there.'

'What rotten luck for me. We've had a jolly time here at Burguete.'

'Come on in to Pamplona. We can play some bridge there, and there's going to be a damned fine fiesta.'

'I'd like to. Awfully nice of you to ask me. I'd best stop on here, though. I've not much more time to fish.'

'You want those big ones in the Irati.'

'I say, I do, you know. They're enormous trout there.'

'I'd like to try them once more.'

'Do. Stop over another day. Be a good chap.'

'We really have to get into town,' I said.

'What a pity.'

After breakfast Bill and I were sitting warming in the sun on a bench out in front of the inn and talking it over. I saw a girl coming up the road from the centre of the town. She stopped in front of us and took a telegram out of the leather wallet that hung against her skirt.

'Por ustedes?'

I looked at it. The address was: 'Barnes, Burguete.'

'Yes. It's for us.'

She brought out a book for me to sign, and I gave her a couple of coppers. The telegram was in Spanish: 'Vengo Jueves Cohn.'

I handed it to Bill.

'What does the word Cohn mean?' he asked.

'What a lousy telegram!' I said. 'He could send ten words for the same price. "I come Thursday." That gives you a lot of dope, doesn't it?'

'It gives you all the dope that's of interest to Cohn.'

'We're going in, anyway,' I said. 'There's no use trying to move Brett and Mike out here and back before the fiesta. Should we answer it?'

'We might as well,' said Bill. 'There's no need for us to be snooty.'

We walked up to the post-office and asked for a telegraph blank.

'What will we say?' Bill asked.

' "Arriving to-night." That's enough.'

We paid for the message and walked back to the inn. Harris

was there and the three of us walked up to Roncevalles. We went through the monastery .

'It's a remarkable place,' Harris said, when we came out. 'But you know I'm not much on those sort of places.'

'Me either,' Bill said.

'It's a remarkable place, though,' Harris said. 'I wouldn't not have seen it. I'd been intending coming up each day.'

'It isn't the same as fishing, though, is it?' Bill asked. He liked Harris.

'I say not.'

We were standing in front of the old chapel of the monastery.

'Isn't that a pub across the way?' Harris asked. 'Or do my eyes deceive me?'

'It has the look of a pub,' Bill said.

'It looks to me like a pub,' I said.

'I say,' said Harris, 'let's utilize it.' He had taken up utilizing from Bill.

We had a bottle of wine apiece. Harris would not let us pay. He talked Spanish quite well, and the innkeeper would not take our money.

'I say. You don't know what it's meant to me to have you chaps up here.'

'We've had a grand time, Harris.'

Harris was a little tight.

'I say. Really you don't know how much it means. I've not had much fun since the war.'

'We'll fish together again, some time. Don't you forget it, Harris.'

'We must. We *have* had such a jolly good time.'

'How about another bottle around?'

'Jolly good idea,' said Harris.

'This is mine,' said Bill. 'Or we don't drink it.'

'I wish you'd let me pay for it. It *does* give me pleasure, you know.'

'This is going to give me pleasure,' Bill said.

The innkeeper brought in the fourth bottle. We had kept the same glasses. Harris lifted his glass.

'I say. You know this does utilize well.'

Bill slapped him on the back.

'Good old Harris.'

'I say. You know my name isn't really Harris. It's Wilson-Harris. All one name. With a hyphen, you know.'

'Good old Wilson-Harris,' Bill said. 'We call you Harris because we're so fond of you.'

'I say, Barnes. You don't know what this all means to me.'

'Come on and utilize another glass,' I said.

'Barnes. Really, Barnes, you can't know. That's all.'

'Drink up, Harris.'

We walked back down the road from Roncevalles with Harris between us. We had lunch at the inn and Harris went with us to the bus. He gave us his card, with his address in London and his club and his business address, and as we got on the bus he handed us each an envelope. I opened mine and there were a dozen flies in it. Harris had tied them himself. He tied all his own flies.

'I say, Harris –' I began.

'No, no!' he said. He was climbing down from the bus. 'They're not first-rate flies at all. I only thought if you fished them some time it might remind you of what a good time we had.'

The bus started. Harris stood in front of the post-office. He waved. As we started along the road he turned and walked back toward the inn.

'Say, wasn't that Harris nice?' Bill said.

'I think he really did have a good time.'

'Harris? You bet he did.'

'I wish he'd come into Pamplona.'

'He wanted to fish.'

'Yes. You couldn't tell how English would mix with each other, anyway.'

'I suppose not.'

We got into Pamplona late in the afternoon and the bus stopped in front of the Hotel Montoya. Out in the plaza they were stringing electric-light wires to light the plaza for the fiesta. A few kids came up when the bus stopped, and a custom officer for the town made all the people getting down from the bus open their bundles on the sidewalk. We went into the hotel and on the stairs I met Montoya. He shook hands with us, smiling in his embarrassed way.

'Your friends are here,' he said.

'Mr Campbell?'

'Yes. Mr Cohn and Mr Campbell and Lady Ashley.'

He smiled as though there were something I would hear about.

'When did they get in?'

'Yesterday. I've saved you the rooms you had.'

'That's fine. Did you give Mr Campbell the room on the plaza?'

'Yes. All the rooms we looked at.'

'Where are our friends now?'

'I think they went to the pelota.'

'And how about the bulls?'

Montoya smiled. 'Tonight,' he said. 'Tonight at seven o'clock they bring in the Villar bulls, and to-morrow come the Miuras. Do you all go down?'

'Oh, yes. They've never seen a desencajonada.'

Montoya put his hand on my shoulder.

'I'll see you there.'

He smiled again. He always smiled as though bull-fighting were a very special secret between the two of us; a rather shocking but really very deep secret that we knew about. He always smiled as though there were something lewd about the secret to outsiders, but that it was something that we understood. It would not do to expose it to people who would not understand.

'You're friend, is he aficionado, too?' Montoya smiled at Bill.

'Yes. He came all the way from New York to see the San Fermines.'

'Yes?' Montoya politely disbelieved. 'But he's not aficionado like you.'

He put his hand on my shoulder again embarrassedly.

'Yes,' I said. 'He's a real aficionado.'

'But he's not aficionado like you are.'

Aficion means passion. An aficionado is one who is passionate about the bull-fights. All the good bull-fighters stayed at Montoya's hotel; that is, those with aficion stayed there. The commercial bull-fighters stayed once, perhaps, and then did not come back. The good ones came each year. In Montoya's room were their photographs. The photographs were dedicated to Juanito Montoya or to his sister. The photographs of bull-fighters Montoya had really believed in were framed. Photographs of bull-fighters who had been without aficion Montoya kept in a drawer of his desk. They often had the most flattering inscriptions. But they did not mean anything. One day Montoya took them all out and dropped them in the waste-basket. He did not want them around.

We often talked about bulls and bull-fighters. I had stopped at the Montoya for several years. We never talked for very long at a time. It was simply the pleasure of discovering what we each felt. Men would come in from distant towns and before they left Pamplona stop and talk for a few minutes with Montoya about bulls. These men were aficionados. Those who were aficionados could always get rooms even when the hotel was full. Montoya introduced me to some of them. They were always very polite at first, and it amused them very much that I should be an American. Somehow it was taken for granted that an American could not have aficion. He might simulate it or confuse it with excitement, but he could not really have it. When they saw that I had aficion, and there was no password, no set questions that could bring it out, rather it was a sort of oral spiritual examination with the questions always a little on the defensive and never apparent, there was this same embarrassed putting the hand on the shoulder, or a 'Buen hombre.' But nearly always there was the actual touching. It seemed as though they wanted to touch you to make it certain.

Montoya could forgive anything of a bull-fighter who had aficion. He could forgive attacks of nerves, panic, bad unexplainable actions, all sorts of lapses. For one who had aficion he could forgive anything. At once he forgave me all my friends. Without his ever saying anything they were simply a little something shameful between us, like the spilling open of the horses in bull-fighting.

Bill had gone upstairs as we came in, and I found him washing and changing in his room.

'Well,' he said, 'talk a lot of Spanish?'

'He was telling me about the bulls coming in tonight.'

'Let's find the gang and go down.'

'All right. They'll probably be at the café.'

'Have you got tickets?'

'Yes. I got them for all the unloadings.'

'What's it like?' He was pulling his cheek before the glass, looking to see if there were unshaved patches under the line of the jaw.

'It's pretty good,' I said. 'They let the bulls out of the cages one at a time, and they have steers in the corral to receive them and keep them from fighting, and the bulls tear in at the steers and the steers run around like old maids trying to quiet them down.'

'Do they ever gore the steers?'

'Sure. Sometimes they go right after them and kill them.'

'Can't the steers do anything?'

'No. They're trying to make friends.'

'What do they have them in for?'

'To quiet down the bulls and keep them from breaking their horns against the stone walls, or goring each other.'

'Must be swell being a steer.'

We went down the stairs and out of the door and walked across the square toward the café Iruña. There were two lonely looking ticket-houses standing in the square. Their windows, marked, SOL, SOL Y SOMBRA, and SOMBRA, were shut. They would not open until the day before the fiesta.

Across the square the white wicker tables and chairs of the Iruña extended out beyond the arcade to the edge of the street. I looked for Brett and Mike at the tables. There they were. Brett and Mike and Robert Cohn. Brett was wearing a Basque beret. So was Mike. Robert Cohn was bare-headed and wearing his spectacles. Brett saw us coming and waved. Her eyes crinkled up as we came up to the table.

'Hello, you chaps!' she called.

Brett was happy. Mike had a way of getting an intensity of feeling into shaking hands. Robert Cohn shook hands because we were back.

'Where the hell have you been?' I asked.

'I brought them up here,' Cohn said.

'What rot,' Brett said. 'We'd have gotten here earlier if you hadn't come.'

'You'd never have gotten here.'

'What rot! You chaps are brown. Look at Bill.'

'Did you get good fishing?' Mike asked. 'We wanted to join you.'

'It wasn't bad. We missed you.'

'I wanted to come,' Cohn said, 'but I thought I ought to bring them.'

'You bring us. What rot.'

'Was it really good?' Mike asked. 'Did you take many?'

'Some days we took a dozen apiece. There was an Englishman up there.'

'Named Harris,' Bill said. 'Ever know him, Mike? He was in the war, too.'

'Fortunate fellow,' Mike said. 'What times we had. How I wish those dear days were back.'

'Don't be an ass.'

'Were you in the war, Mike?' Cohn asked.

'Was I not.'

'He was a very distinguished soldier,' Brett said. 'Tell them about the time your horse bolted down Piccadilly.'

'I'll not. I've told that four times.'

'You never told me,' Robert Cohn said.

'I'll not tell that story. It reflects discredit on me.'

'Tell them about your medals.'

'I'll not. That story reflects great discredit on me.'

'What story's that?'

'Brett will tell you. She tells all the stories that reflect discredit on me.'

'Go on. Tell it, Brett.'

'Should I?'

'I'll tell it myself.'

'What medals have you got, Mike?'

'I haven't got any medals.'

'You must have some.'

'I suppose I've the usual medals. But I never sent in for

them. One time there was this wopping big dinner and the Prince of Wales was to be there, and the cards said medals will be worn. So naturally I had no medals, and I stopped at my tailor's and he was impressed by the invitation, and I thought that's a good piece of business, and I said to him: "You've got to fix me up with some medals." He said: "What medals, sir?" And I said: "Oh, any medals. Just give me a few medals." So he said: "What medals *have* you, sir?" And I said: "How should I know?" Did he think I spent all my time reading the bloody gazette? "Just give me a good lot. Pick them out yourself." So he got some medals, you know, miniature medals, and handed me the box, and I put it in my pocket and forgot it. Well, I went to the dinner, and it was the night they'd shot Henry Wilson, so the Prince didn't come and the King didn't come, and no one wore any medals, and all these coves were busy taking off their medals, and I had mine in my pocket.'

He stopped for us to laugh.

'Is that all?'

'That's all. Perhaps I didn't tell it right.'

'You didn't,' said Brett. 'But no matter.'

We were all laughing.

'Ah, yes,' said Mike. 'I know now. It was a damn dull dinner, and I couldn't stick it, so I left. Later on in the evening I found the box in my pocket. What's this? I said. Medals? Bloody military medals? So I cut them all off their backing – you know, they put them on a strip – and gave them all around. Gave one to each girl. Form of souvenir. They thought I was hell's own shakes of a soldier. Give away medals in a night club. Dashing fellow.'

'Tell the rest,' Brett said.

'Don't you think that was funny?' Mike asked. We were all laughing. 'It was. I swear it was. Any rate, my tailor wrote me and wanted the medals back. Sent a man around. Kept on writing for months. Seems some chap had left them to be cleaned. Frightfully military cove. Set hell's own store by them.' Mike paused. 'Rotten luck for the tailor,' he said.

'You don't mean it,' Bill said. 'I should think it would have been grand for the tailor.'

'Frightfully good tailor. Never believe it to see me now,'

Mike said. 'I used to pay him a hundred pounds a year just to keep him quiet. So he wouldn't send me any bills. Frightful blow to him when I went bankrupt. It was right after the medals. Gave his letters rather a bitter tone.'

'How did you go bankrupt?' Bill asked.

'Two ways,' Mike said. 'Gradually and then suddenly.'

'What brought it on?'

'Friends,' said Mike. 'I had a lot of friends. False friends. Then I had creditors, too. Probably had more creditors than anybody in England.'

'Tell them about in the court,' Brett said.

'I don't remember,' Mike said. 'I was just a little tight.'

'Tight!' Brett exclaimed. 'You were blind!'

'Extraordinary thing,' Mike said. 'Met my former partner the other day. Offered to buy me a drink.'

'Tell them about your learned counsel,' Brett said.

'I will not,' Mike said. 'My learned counsel was blind, too. I say this is a gloomy subject. Are we going down and see these bulls unloaded or not?'

'Let's go down.'

We called the waiter, paid, and started to walk through the town. I started off walking with Brett, but Robert Cohn came up and joined her on the other side. The three of us walked along, past the Ayuntamiento with the banners hung from the balcony, down past the market and down past the steep street that led to the bridge across the Arga. There were many people walking to go and see the bulls, and carriages drove down the hill and across the bridge, the drivers, the horses, and the whips rising above the walking people in the street. Across the bridge we turned up a road to the corrals. We passed a wine-shop with a sign in the window: Good Wine 30 Centimes A Litre.

'That's where we'll go when funds get low,' Brett said.

The woman standing in the door of the wine-shop looked at us as we passed. She called to someone in the house and three girls came to the window and stared. They were staring at Brett.

At the gate of the corrals two men took tickets from the people that went in. We went in through the gate. There were trees inside and a low, stone house. At the far end was the stone wall of the corrals, with apertures in the stone that were like loopholes running all along the face of each corral. A ladder led up to the top of the wall, and people were climbing up the ladder and spreading down to stand on the walls that separated the two corrals. As we came up the ladder, walking across the grass under the trees, we passed the big, grey painted cages with the bulls in them. There was one bull in each travelling-box. They had come by train from a bull-breeding ranch in Castile, and had been unloaded off flat-cars at the station and brought up here to be let out of their cages into the corrals. Each cage was stencilled with the name and the brand of the bull-breeder.

We climbed up and found a place on the wall looking down into the corral. The stone walls were whitewashed, and there was straw on the ground and wooden feed-boxes and water-troughs set against the wall.

'Look up there,' I said.

Beyond the river rose the plateau of the town. All along the old walls and ramparts people were standing. The three lines of fortifications made three black lines of people. Above the walls there were heads in the windows of the houses. At the far end of the plateau boys had climbed into the trees.

'They must think something is going to happen,' Brett said.

'They want to see the bulls.'

Mike and Bill were on the other wall across the pit of the corral. They waved to us. People who had come late were standing behind us, pressing against us when other people crowded them.

'Why don't they start?' Robert Cohn asked.

A single mule was hitched to one of the cages and dragged it up against the gate in the corral wall. The men shoved and lifted it with crowbars into position against the gate. Men were standing on the wall ready to pull up the gate of the corral and then the gate of the cage. At the other end of the corral a gate opened and two steers came in, swaying their heads and trotting, their lean flanks swinging. They stood together at the far end, their heads toward the gate where the bull would enter.

111

'They don't look happy,' Brett said.

The men on top of the wall leaned back and pulled up the door of the corral. Then they pulled up the door of the cage.

I leaned way over the wall and tried to see into the cage. It was dark. Someone rapped on the cage with an iron bar. Inside something seemed to explode. The bull, striking into the wood from side to side with his horns, made a great noise. Then I saw a dark muzzle and the shadow of horns, and then, with a clattering on the wood in the hollow box, the bull charged and came out into the corral, skidding with his forefeet in the straw as he stopped, his head up, the great hump of muscle on his neck swollen tight, his body muscles quivering as he looked up at the crowd on the stone walls. The two steers backed away against the wall, their heads sunken, their eyes watching the bull.

The bull saw them and charged. A man shouted from behind one of the boxes and slapped his hat against the planks, and the bull before he reached the steer, turned, gathered himself and charged where the man had been, trying to reach him behind the planks with a half-dozen quick, searching drives with the right horn.

'My God, isn't he beautiful?' Brett said. We were looking right down on him.

'Look how he knows how to use his horns,' I said. 'He's got a left and a right just like a boxer.'

'Not really?'

'You watch.'

'It goes too fast.'

'Wait. There'll be another one in a minute.'

They had backed up another cage into the entrance. In the far corner a man, from behind one of the plank shelters, attracted the bull, and while the bull was facing away the gate was pulled up and a second bull came out into the corral.

He charged straight for the steers and two men ran out from behind the planks and shouted, to turn him. He did not change his direction and the men shouted: 'Hah! Hah! Toro!' and waved their arms; the two steers turned sideways to take the shock, and the bull drove into one of the steers.

'Don't look,' I said to Brett. She was watching, fascinated.

'Fine,' I said. 'If it doesn't buck you.'

'I saw it,' she said. 'I saw him shift from his left to his right horn.'

'Damn good!'

The steer was down now, his neck stretched out, his head twisted, he lay the way he had fallen. Suddenly the bull left off and made for the other steer which had been standing at the far end, his head swinging, watching it all. The steer ran awkwardly and the bull caught him, hooked him lightly in the flank, and then turned away and looked up at the crowd on the walls, his crest of muscle rising. The steer came up to him and made as though to nose at him and the bull hooked perfunctorily. The next time he nosed at the steer and then the two of them trotted over to the other bull.

When the next bull came out, all three, the two bulls and the steer, stood together, their heads side by side, their horns against the newcomer. In a few minutes the steer picked the new bull up, quieted him down, and made him one of the herd. When the last two bulls had been unloaded the herd were all together.

The steer who had been gored had gotten to his feet and stood against the stone wall. None of the bulls came near him, and he did not attempt to join the herd.

We climbed down from the wall with the crowd, and had a last look at the bulls through the loopholes in the wall of the corral. They were all quiet now, their heads down. We got a carriage outside and rode up to the café. Mike and Bill came in half an hour later. They had stopped on the way for several drinks.

We were sitting in the café.

'That's an extraordinary business,' Brett said.

'Will those last ones fight as well as the first?' Robert Cohn asked. 'They seemed to quiet down awfully fast.'

'They all know each other,' I said. 'They're only dangerous when they're alone, or only two or three of them together.'

'What do you mean, dangerous?' Bill said. 'They all looked dangerous to me.'

'They only want to kill when they're alone. Of course, if you went in there you'd probably detach one of them from the herd, and he'd be dangerous.'

113

'That's too complicated,' Bill said. 'Don't you ever detach me from the herd, Mike.'

'I say,' Mike said, 'they *were* fine bulls, weren't they? Did you see their horns?'

'Did I not,' said Brett. 'I had no idea what they were like.'

'Did you see the one hit that steer?' Mike asked. 'That was extraordinary.'

'It's no life being a steer,' Robert Cohn said.

'Don't you think so?' Mike said. 'I would have thought you'd loved being a steer, Robert.'

'What do you mean, Mike?'

'They lead such a quiet life. They never say anything and they're always hanging about so.'

We were embarrassed. Bill laughed. Robert Cohn was angry. Mike went on talking.

'I should think you'd love it. You'd never have to say a word. Come on, Robert. Do say something. Don't just sit there.'

'I said something, Mike. Don't you remember? About the steers.'

'Oh, say something more. Say something funny. Can't you see we're all having a good time here?'

'Come off it, Michael. You're drunk,' Brett said.

'I'm not drunk. I'm quite serious. *Is* Robert Cohn going to follow Brett around like a steer all the time?'

'Shut up, Michael. Try and show a little breeding.'

'Breeding be damned. Who has any breeding, anyway, except the bulls? Aren't the bulls lovely? Don't you like them, Bill? Why don't you say something, Robert? Don't sit there looking like a bloody funeral. What if Brett did sleep with you? She's slept with lots of better people than you.'

'Shut up,' Cohn said. He stood up. 'Shut up, Mike.'

'Oh, don't stand up and act as though you were going to hit me. That won't make any difference to me. Tell me, Robert. Why do you follow Brett around like a poor bloody steer? Don't you know you're not wanted? I know when I'm not wanted. Why don't you know when you're not wanted? You came down to San Sebastian where you weren't wanted, and followed Brett around like a bloody steer. Do you think that's right?'

114

'Shut up. You're drunk.'

'Perhaps I am drunk. Why aren't you drunk? Why don't you ever get drunk, Robert? You know you didn't have a good time at San Sebastian because none of our friends would invite you on any of the parties. You can't blame them hardly. Can you? I asked them to. They wouldn't do it. You can't blame them, now. Can you? Now, answer me. Can you blame them?'

'Go to hell, Mike.'

'I can't blame them. Can you blame them? Why do you follow Brett around? Haven't you any manners? How do you think it makes *me* feel?'

'You're a splendid one to talk about manners,' Brett said. 'You've such lovely manners.'

'Come on, Robert,' Bill said.

'What do you follow her around for?'

Bill stood up and took hold of Cohn.

'Don't go,' Mike said. 'Robert Cohn's going to buy a drink.'

Bill went off with Cohn. Cohn's face was sallow. Mike went on talking. I sat and listened for a while. Brett looked disgusted.

'I say, Michael, you might not be such a bloody ass,' she interrupted. 'I'm not saying he's not right, you know.' She turned to me.

The emotion left Mike's voice. We were all friends together.

'I'm not so damn drunk as I sounded,' he said.

'I know you're not,' Brett said.

'We're none of us sober,' I said.

'I didn't say anything I didn't mean.'

'But you put it so badly,' Brett laughed.

'He was an ass, though. He came down to San Sebastian where he damn well wasn't wanted. He hung around Brett and just *looked* at her. It made me damned well sick.'

'He did behave very badly,' Brett said.

'Mark you. Brett's had affairs with men before. She tells me all about everything. She gave me this chap Cohn's letters to read. I wouldn't read them.'

'Damned noble of you.'

'No, listen, Jake. Brett's gone off with men. But they

weren't ever Jews, and they didn't come and hang about afterward.'

'Damned good chaps,' Brett said. 'It's all rot to talk about it. Michael and I understand each other.'

'She gave me Robert Cohn's letters. I wouldn't read them.'

'You wouldn't read any letters, darling. You wouldn't read mine.'

'I can't read letters,' Mike said. 'Funny, isn't it?'

'You can't read anything.'

'No. You're wrong there. I read quite a bit. I read when I'm at home.'

'You'll be writing next,' Brett said. 'Come on, Michael. Do buck up. You've got to go through with this thing now. He's here. Don't spoil the fiesta.'

'Well, let him behave, then.'

'He'll behave. I'll tell him.'

'You'll tell him, Jake. Tell him either he must behave or get out.'

'Yes,' I said, 'it would be nice for me to tell him.'

'Look, Brett. Tell Jake what Robert calls you. That *is* perfect, you know.'

'Oh, no. I can't.'

'Go on. We're all friends. Aren't we all friends, Jake?'

'I can't tell him. It's too ridiculous.'

'I'll tell him.'

'You won't, Michael. Don't be an ass.'

'He calls her Circe,' Mike said. 'He claims she turns men into swine. Damn good. I wish I were one of these literary chaps.'

'He'd be good, you know,' Brett said. 'He writes a good letter.'

'I know,' I said. 'He wrote me from San Sebastian.'

'That was nothing,' Brett said. 'He can write a damned amusing letter.'

'She made me write that. She was supposed to be ill.'

'I damned well was, too.'

'Come on,' I said, 'we must go in and eat.'

'How should I meet Cohn?' Mike said.

'Just act as though nothing had happened.'

116

shut my eyes because the room would go round and round. If I kept on reading that feeling would pass.

I heard Brett and Robert Cohn come up the stairs. Cohn said good night outside the door and went on up to his room. I heard Brett go into the room next door. Mike was already in bed. He had come in with me an hour before. He woke as she came in, and they talked together. I heard them laugh. I turned off the light and tried to go to sleep. It was not necessary to read any more. I could shut my eyes without getting the wheeling sensation. But I could not sleep. There is no reason why because it is dark you should look at things differently from when it is light. The hell there isn't!

I figured that all out once, and for six months I never slept with the electric light off. That was another bright idea. To hell with women, anyway. To hell with you, Brett Ashley.

Women made such swell friends. Awfully swell. In the first place, you had to be in love with a woman to have a basis of friendship. I had been having Brett for a friend. I had not been thinking about her side of it. I had been getting something for nothing. That only delayed the presentation of the bill. The bill always came. That was one of the swell things you could count on.

I thought I had paid for everything. Not like the woman pays and pays and pays. No idea of retribution or punishment. Just exchange of values. You gave up something and got something else. Or you worked for something. You paid some way for everything that was any good. I paid my way into enough things that I liked, so that I had a good time. Either you paid by learning about them, or by experience, or by taking chances, or by money. Enjoying living was learning to get your money's worth and knowing when you had it. You could get your money's worth. The world was a good place to buy in. It seemed like a fine philosophy. In five years, I thought, it will seem just as silly as all the other fine philosophies I've had.

Perhaps that wasn't true, though. Perhaps as you went along you did learn something. I did not care what it was all about. All I wanted to know was how to live in it. Maybe if you found out how to live in it you learned from that what it was all about.

I wished Mike would not behave so terribly to Cohn, though. Mike was a bad drunk. Brett was a good drunk. Bill was a good drunk. Cohn was never drunk. Mike was unpleasant after he passed a certain point. I liked to see him hurt Cohn. I wished he would not do it, though, because afterward it made me disgusted at myself. That was morality; things that made you disgusted afterward. No, that must be immorality. That was a large statement. What a lot of bilge I could think up at night. What rot, I could hear Brett say it. What rot! When you were with English you got into the habit of using English expressions in your thinking. The English spoken language – the upper classes, anyway – must have fewer words than the Eskimo. Of course I didn't know anything about the Eskimo. Maybe the Eskimo was a fine language. Say the Cherokee. I didn't know anything about the Cherokee, either. The English talked with inflected phrases. One phrase to mean everything. I like them, though. I liked the way they talked. Take Harris. Still Harris was not the upper classes.

I turned on the light again and read. I read the Turgenieff. I knew that now, reading it in the oversensitized state of my mind after much too much brandy, I would remember it somewhere, and afterwards it would seem as though it had really happened to me. I would always have it. That was another good thing you paid for and then had. Some time along toward daylight I went to sleep.

The next two days in Pamplona were quiet, and there were no more rows. The town was getting ready for the fiesta. Workmen put up the gate-posts that were to shut off the side streets when the bulls were released from the corrals and came running through the streets in the morning on their way to the ring. The workmen dug holes and fitted in the timbers, each timber numbered for its regular place. Out on the plateau beyond the town employees of the bull-ring exercised picador horses, galloping them stiff-legged on the hard, sun-baked fields behind the bull-ring. The big gate of the bull-ring was open, and inside the amphitheatre was being swept. The ring was rolled and sprinkled, and carpenters replaced weakened or cracked planks in the barrera. Standing at the edge of the smooth rolled sand you could look up in the empty stands and see old women sweeping out the boxes.

Outside, the fence that led from the last street of the town to the entrance of the bull-ring was already in place and made a long pen; the crowd would come running down with the bulls behind them on the morning of the day of the first bull-fight. Out across the plain, where the horse and cattle fair would be, some gipsies had camped under the trees. The wine and aguardiente sellers were putting up their booths. One booth advertised ANIS DEL TORO. The cloth sign hung against the planks in the hot sun. In the big square that was the centre of the town there was no change yet. We sat in the white wicker chairs on the terrasse of the café and watched the motor-buses come in and unload peasants from the country coming in to the market, and we watched the buses fill up and start out with peasants sitting with their saddle-bags full of the things they had bought in the town. The tall gray motor-buses were the only life of the square except for the pigeons and the man with a hose who sprinkled the gravelled square and watered the streets.

In the evening was the paseo. For an hour after dinner everyone, all the good-looking girls, the officers from the garrison, all the fashionable people of the town, walked in the street on one side of the square while the café tables filled with the regular after-dinner crowd.

During the morning I usually sat in the café and read the Madrid papers and then walked in the town or out into the country. Sometimes Bill went along. Sometimes he wrote in his room. Robert Cohn spent the mornings studying Spanish or trying to get a shave at the barber-shop. Brett and Mike never got up until noon. We all had a vermouth at the café. It was a quiet life and no one was drunk. I went to church a couple of times, once with Brett. She said she wanted to hear me go to confession, but I told her that not only was it impossible but it was not as interesting as it sounded, and, besides, it would be in a language she did not know. We met Cohn as we came out of church, and although it was obvious he had followed us, yet he was very pleasant and nice, and we all three went for a walk out to the gipsy camp, and Brett had her fortune told.

It was a good morning, there were high white clouds above the mountains. It had rained a little in the night and it was fresh and cool on the plateau, and there was a wonderful view. We all felt good and we felt healthy, and I felt quite friendly to Cohn. You could not be upset about anything on a day like that.

That was the last day before the fiesta.

Chapter 15

At noon of Sunday, July 6th, the fiesta exploded. There is no other way to describe it. People had been coming in all day from the country, but they were assimilated in the town and you did not notice them. The square was as quiet in the hot sun as on any other day. The peasants were in the outlying wine-shops. There they were drinking, getting ready for the fiesta. They had come in so recently from the plains and the hills that it was necessary that they make their shifting in values gradually. They could not start in paying café prices. They got their money's worth in the wine-shops. Money still had a definite value in hours worked and bushels of grain sold. Late in the fiesta it would not matter what they paid, nor where they bought.

Now on the day of the starting of the fiesta of San Fermin they had been in the wine-shops of the narrow streets of the town since early morning. Going down the streets in the morning on the way to mass in the cathedral, I heard them singing through the open doors of the shops. They were warming up. There were many people at the eleven o'clock Mass. San Fermin is also a religious festival.

I walked down the hill from the cathedral and up the street to the café on the square. It was a little before noon. Robert Cohn and Bill were sitting at one of the tables. The marble-topped tables and the white wicker chairs were gone. They were replaced by cast-iron tables and severe folding chairs. The café was like a battleship stripped for action. Today the waiters did not leave you alone all morning to read without asking if you wanted to order something. A waiter came up as soon as I sat down.

'What are you drinking?' I asked Bill and Robert.

'Sherry,' Cohn said.

'Jerez,' I said to the waiter.

Before the waiter brought the sherry the rocket that announced the fiesta went up in the square. It burst and there was a grey ball of smoke high up above the Theatre Gayarre, across on the other side of the plaza. The ball of smoke hung in the sky like a shrapnel burst, and as I watched, another rocket came up to it, trickling smoke in the bright sunlight. I saw the bright flash as it burst and another little cloud of smoke appeared. By the time the second rocket had burst there were so many people in the arcade, that had been empty a minute before, that the waiter, holding the bottle high up over his head, could hardly get through the crowd to our table. People were coming into the square from all sides, and down the street we heard the pipes and the fifes and the drums coming. They were playing the *riau-riau* music, the pipes shrill and the drums pounding, and behind them came the men and boys dancing. When the fifers stopped they all crouched down in the street, and when the reed-pipes and the fifes shrilled, and the flat, dry hollow drums tapped it out again, they all went up in the air dancing. In the crowd you saw only the heads and shoulders of the dancers going up and down.

In the square a man, bent over, was playing on a reed-pipe, and a crowd of children were following him shouting, and pulling at his clothes. He came out of the square, the children following him, and piped them past the café and down a side street. We saw his blank pockmarked face as he went by, piping, the children close behind him shouting and pulling at him.

'He must be the village idiot,' Bill said. 'My God! look at that!'

Down the street came dancers. The street was solid with dancers, all men. They were all dancing in time behind their own fifers and drummers. They were a club of some sort, and all wore workmen's blue smocks, and red handkerchiefs around their necks, and carried a great banner on two poles. The banner danced up and down with them as they came down surrounded by the crowd.

'Hurray for Wine! Hurray for the Foreigners!' was painted on the banner.

'Where are the foreigners?' Robert Cohn asked.

'We're the foreigners,' Bill said.

All the time rockets were going up. The café tables were all full now. The square was emptying of people and the crowd was filling the cafés.

'Where's Brett and Mike?' Bill asked.

'I'll go and get them,' Cohn said.

'Bring them here.'

The fiesta was really started. It kept up day and night for seven days. The dancing kept up, the drinking kept up, the noise went on. The things that happened could only have happened during a fiesta. Everything became quite unreal finally and it seemed as though nothing could have any consequences. It seemed out of place to think of consequences during the fiesta. All during the fiesta you had the feeling, even when it was quiet, that you had to shout any remark to make it heard. It was the same feeling about any action. It was a fiesta and it went on for seven days.

That afternoon was the big religious procession. San Fermin was translated from one church to another. In the procession were all the dignitaries, civil and religious. We could not see them because the crowd was too great. Ahead of the formal procession and behind it danced the *riau-riau* dancers. There was one mass of yellow shirts dancing up and down in the crowd. All we could see of the procession through the closely pressed people that crowded all the side streets and kerbs were the great giants, cigar-store Indians, thirty feet high, Moors, a King and Queen, whirling and waltzing solemnly to the *riau-riau*.

They were all standing outside the chapel where San Fermin and the dignitaries had passed in leaving a guard of soldiers, the giants, with the men who danced in them standing beside their resting frames, and the dwarfs moving with their whacking

124

bladders through the crowd. We started inside and there was a smell of incense and people filing back into the church, but Brett was stopped just inside the door because she had no hat, so we went out again and along the street that ran back from the chapel into town. The street was lined on both sides with people keeping their place at the kerb for the return of the procession. Some dancers formed a circle around Brett and started to dance. They wore big wreaths of white garlics around their necks. They took Bill and me by the arms and put us in the circle. Bill started to dance, too. They were all chanting. Brett wanted to dance but they did not want her to. They wanted her as an image to dance around. When the song ended with the sharp *riau-riau!* they rushed us into a wine-shop.

We stood at the counter. They had Brett seated on a wine-cask. It was dark in the wine-shop and full of men singing, hard-voiced singing. Back of the counter they drew the wine from casks. I put down money for the wine, but one of the men picked it up and put it back in my pocket.

'I want a leather wine-bottle,' Bill said.

'There's a place down the street,' I said. 'I'll go get a couple.'

The dancers did not want me to go out. Three of them were sitting on the high wine-cask beside Brett, teaching her to drink out of the wine-skins. They had hung a wreath of garlics around her neck. Some one insisted on giving her a glass. Somebody was teaching Bill a song. Singing it into his ear. Beating time on Bill's back.

I explained to them that I would be back. Outside in the street I went down the street looking for the shop that made leather wine-bottles. The crowd was packed on the sidewalks and many of the shops were shuttered, and I could not find it. I walked as far as the church, looking on both sides of the street. Then I asked a man and he took me by the arm and led me to it. The shutters were up but the door was open.

Inside it smelled of fresh tanned leather and hot tar. A man was stencilling completed wine-skins. They hung from the roof in bunches. He took one down, blew it up, screwed the nozzle tight, and then jumped on it.

'See! It doesn't leak.'

'I want another one, too. A big one.'

He took down a big one that would hold a gallon or more, from the roof. He blew it up, his cheeks puffing ahead of the wine-skin, and stood on the bota holding on to a chair.

'What are you going to do? Sell them in Bayonne?'

'No. Drink out of them.'

He slapped me on the back.

'Good man. Eight pesetas for the two. The lowest price.'

The man who was stencilling the new ones and tossing them into a pile stopped.

'It's true,' he said. 'Eight pesetas is cheap.'

I paid and went out and along the street to the wine-shop. It was darker than ever inside and very crowded. I did not see Brett and Bill, and someone said they were in the back room. At the counter the girl filled the two wine-skins for me. One held two litres. The other held five litres. Filling them both cost three pesetas sixty céntimos. Someone at the counter, that I had never seen before, tried to pay for the wine, but I finally paid for it myself. The man who had wanted to pay then bought me a drink. He would not let me buy one in return, but said he would take a rinse of the mouth from the new wine-bag. He tipped the big five-litre bag up and squeezed it so the wine hissed against the back of his throat.

'All right,' he said, and handed back the bag.

In the back room Brett and Bill were sitting on barrels surrounded by the dancers. Everybody had his arms on everybody else's shoulders, and they were all singing. Mike was sitting at a table with several men in their shirt-sleeves, eating from a bowl of tuna fish, chopped onions and vinegar. They were all drinking wine and mopping up the oil and vinegar with pieces of bread.

'Hello, Jake. Hello!' Mike called. 'Come here. I want you to meet my friends. We're all having an hors-d'œuvre.'

I was introduced to the people at the table. They supplied their names to Mike and sent for a fork for me.

'Stop eating their dinner, Michael,' Brett shouted from the wine-barrels.

'I don't want to eat up your meal,' I said when someone handed me a fork.

'Eat,' he said. 'What do you think it's here for?'

I unscrewed the nozzle of the big wine-bottle and handed it around. Everyone took a drink, tipping the wine-skin at arm's length.

Outside, above the singing, we could hear the music of the procession going by.

'Isn't that the procession?' Mike asked.

'Nada,' some one said. 'It's nothing. Drink up. Lift the bottle.'

'Where did they find you?' I asked Mike.

'Someone brought me here,' Mike said. 'They said you were here.'

'Where's Cohn?'

'He's passed out,' Brett called. 'They've put him away somewhere.'

'Where is he?'

'I don't know.'

'How should we know,' Bill said. 'I think he's dead.'

'He's not dead,' Mike said. 'I know he's not dead. He's just passed out on Anis del Mono.'

As he said Anis del Mono one of the men at the table looked up, brought out a bottle from inside his smock, and handed it to me.

'No,' I said. 'No, thanks!'

'Yes. Yes. Arriba! Up with the bottle!'

I took a drink. It tasted of liquorice and warmed all the way. I could feel it warming in my stomach.

'Where the hell is Cohn?'

'I don't know,' Mike said. 'I'll ask. Where is the drunken comrade?' he asked in Spanish.

'You want to see him?'

'Yes,' I said.

'Not me,' said Mike. 'This gent.'

The Anis del Mono man wiped his mouth and stood up.

'Come on.'

In a back room Robert Cohn was sleeping quietly on some wine-casks. It was almost too dark to see his face. They had covered him with a coat and another coat was folded under his head. Around his neck and on his chest was a big wreath of twisted garlics.

'Let him sleep,' the man whispered. 'He's all right.'

Two hours later Cohn appeared. He came into the front room still with the wreath of garlics around his neck. The Spaniards shouted when he came in. Cohn wiped his eyes and grinned.

'I must have been sleeping,' he said.

'Oh, not at all,' Brett said.

'You were only dead,' Bill said.

'Aren't we going to go and have some supper?' Cohn asked.

'Do you want to eat?'

'Yes. Why not? I'm hungry.'

'Eat those garlics, Robert,' Mike said. 'I say. Do eat those garlics.'

Cohn stood there. His sleep had made him quite all right.

'Do let's go and eat,' Brett said. 'I must get a bath.'

'Come on,' Bill said. 'Let's translate Brett to the hotel.'

We said good-bye to many people and shook hands with many people and went out. Outside it was dark.

'What time is it do you suppose?' Cohn asked.

'It's tomorrow,' Mike said. 'You've been asleep two days.'

'No,' said Cohn, 'what time is it?'

'It's ten o'clock.'

'What a lot we've drunk.'

'You mean what a lot *we've* drunk. You went to sleep.'

Going down the dark streets to the hotel we saw the sky-rockets going up in the square. Down the side streets that led to the square we saw the square solid with people, those in the centre all dancing.

It was a big meal at the hotel. It was the first meal of the prices being doubled for the fiesta, and there were several new courses. After the dinner we were out in the town. I remember resolving that I would stay up all night to watch the bulls go through the streets at six o'clock in the morning, and being so sleepy that I went to bed around four o'clock. The others stayed up.

My own room was locked and I could not find the key, so I

128

went upstairs and slept on one of the beds in Cohn's room. The fiesta was going on outside in the night, but I was too sleepy for it to keep me awake. When I woke it was the sound of the rocket exploding that announced the release of the bulls from the corrals at the edge of town. They would race through the streets and out to the bull-ring. I had been sleeping heavily and I woke feeling I was too late. I put on a coat of Cohn's and went out on the balcony. Down below the narrow street was empty. All the balconies were crowded with people. Suddenly a crowd came down the street. They were all running, packed close together. They passed along and up the street toward the bull-ring and behind them came more men running faster, and then some stragglers who were really running. Behind them was a little bare space, and then the bulls, galloping, tossing their heads up and down. It all went out of sight around the corner. One man fell, rolled to the gutter, and lay quiet. But the bulls went right on and did not notice him. They were all running together.

After they went out of sight a great roar came from the bull-ring. It kept on. Then finally the pop of the rocket that meant the bulls had gotten through the people in the ring and into the corrals. I went back in the room and got into bed. I had been standing on the stone balcony in bare feet. I knew our crowd must have all been out at the bull-ring. Back in bed, I went to sleep.

Cohn woke me when he came in. He started to undress and went over and closed the window because the people on the balcony of the house just across the street were looking in.

'Did you see the show?' I asked.

'Yes. We were all there.'

'Anybody get hurt?'

'One of the bulls got into the crowd in the ring and tossed six or eight people.'

'How did Brett like it?'

'It was all so sudden there wasn't any time for it to bother anybody.'

'I wish I'd been up.'

'We didn't know where you were. We went to your room but it was locked.'

129

'Where did you stay up?'

'We danced at some club.'

'I got sleepy,' I said.

'My gosh! I'm sleepy now,' Cohn said. 'Doesn't this thing ever stop?'

'Not for a week.'

Bill opened the door and put his head in.

'Where were you, Jake?'

'I saw them go through from the balcony. How was it?'

'Grand.'

'Where you going?'

'To sleep.'

No one was up before noon. We ate at tables set out under the arcade. The town was full of people. We had to wait for a table. After lunch we went over to the Iruña. It had filled up, and as the time for the bull-fight came it got fuller, and the tables were crowded closer. There was a close, crowded hum that came every day before the bull-fight. The café did not make this same noise at any other time, no matter how crowded it was. This hum went on, and we were in it and a part of it.

I had taken six seats for all the fights. Three of them were barreras, the first row at the ring-side, and three were sobrepuertos, seats with wooden backs, half-way up the amphitheatre. Mike thought Brett had best sit high up for her first time, and Cohn wanted to sit with them. Bill and I were going to sit in the barreras, and I gave the extra ticket to a waiter to sell. Bill said something to Cohn about what to do and how to look so he would not mind the horses. Bill had seen one season of bull-fights.

'I'm not worried about how I'll stand it. I'm only afraid I may be bored,' Cohn said.

'You think so?'

'Don't look at the horses, after the bull hits them,' I said to Brett. 'Watch the charge and see the picador try and keep the bull off, but then don't look again until the horse is dead if it's been hit.'

'I'm a little nervy about it,' Brett said. 'I'm worried whether I'll be able to go through with it all right.'

130

'You'll be all right. There's nothing but that horse part that will bother you, and they're only in for a few minutes with each bull. Just don't watch when it's bad.'

'She'll be all right,' Mike said. 'I'll look after her.'

'I don't think you'll be bored,' Bill said.

'I'm going over to the hotel to get the glasses and the wine-skin,' I said. 'See you back here. Don't get cock-eyed.'

'I'll come along,' Bill said. Brett smiled at us.

We walked around through the arcade to avoid the heat of the square.

'That Cohn gets me,' Bill said. 'He's got this Jewish superiority so strong that he thinks the only emotion he'll get out of the fight will be being bored.'

'We'll watch him with the glasses,' I said.

'Oh, to hell with him!'

'He spends a lot of time there.'

'I want him to stay there.'

In the hotel on the stairs we met Montoya.

'Come on,' said Montoya. 'Do you want to meet Pedro Romero?'

'Fine,' said Bill. 'Let's go see him.'

We followed Montoya up a flight and down the corridor.

'He's in room number eight,' Montoya explained. 'He's getting dressed for the bull-fight.'

Montoya knocked on the door and opened it. It was a gloomy room with a little light coming in from the window on the narrow street. There were two beds separated by a monastic partition. The electric light was on. The boy stood very straight and unsmiling in his bull-fighting clothes. His jacket hung over the back of a chair. They were just finishing winding his sash. His black hair shone under the electric light. He wore a white linen shirt and the sword-handler finished his sash and stood up and stepped back. Pedro Romero nodded, seeming very far away and dignified when we shook hands. Montoya said something about what great aficionados we were, and that we wanted to wish him luck. Romero listened very seriously. Then he turned to me. He was the best-looking boy I have ever seen.

'You go to the bull-fight,' he said in English.

'You know English,' I said, feeling like an idiot.

'No,' he answered, and smiled.

One of three men who had been sitting on the beds came up and asked us if we spoke French. 'Would you like me to interpret for you? Is there anything you would like to ask Pedro Romero?'

We thanked him. What was there that you would like to ask? The boy was nineteen years old, alone except for his sword-handler, and the three hangers-on, and the bull-fight was to commence in twenty minutes. We wished him 'Mucha suerte,' shook hands, and went out. He was standing, straight and handsome and altogether by himself, alone in the room with the hangers-on as we shut the door.

'He's a fine boy, don't you think so?' Montoya asked.

'He's a good-looking kid,' I said.

'He looks like a torero,' Montoya said. 'He has the type.'

'He's a fine boy.'

'We'll see how he is in the ring,' Montoya said.

We found the big leather wine-bottle leaning against the wall in my room, took it and the field-glasses, locked the door, and went downstairs.

It was a good bull-fight. Bill and I were very excited about Pedro Romero. Montoya was sitting about ten places away. After Romero had killed his first bull Montoya caught my eye and nodded his head. This was a real one. There had not been a real one for a long time. Of the other two matadors, one was very fair and the other was passable. But there was no comparison with Romero, although neither of his bulls was much.

Several times during the bull-fight I looked up at Mike and Brett and Cohn, with the glasses. They seemed to be all right. Brett did not look upset. All three were leaning forward on the concrete railing in front of them.

'Let me take the glasses,' Bill said.

'Does Cohn look bored?' I asked.

'That kike!'

Outside the ring, after the bull-fight was over, you could not move in the crowd. We could not make our way through but had to be moved with the whole thing, slowly, as a glacier, back to town. We had that disturbed emotional feeling that always comes after a bull-fight, and the feeling of elation that comes after a good bull-fight. The fiesta was going on. The drums pounded and the pipe music was shrill, and everywhere the flow of the crowd was broken by patches of dancers. The dancers were in a crowd, so you did not see the intricate play of the feet. All you saw was the heads and shoulders going up and down, up and down. Finally, we got out of the crowd and made for the café. The waiter saved chairs for the others, and we each ordered an absinthe and watched the crowd in the square and the dancers.

'What do you suppose that dance is?' Bill asked.

'It's a sort of jota.'

'They're not all the same,' Bill said. 'They dance differently to all the different tunes.'

'It's swell dancing.'

In front of us on a clear part of the street a company of boys were dancing The steps were very intricate and their faces were intent and concentrated. They all looked down while they danced. Their rope-soled shoes tapped and spatted on the pavement. The toes touched. The heels touched. The balls of the feet touched. Then the music broke wildly and the step was finished and they were all dancing on up the street.

'Here come the gentry,' Bill said.

They were crossing the street.

'Hello, men,' I said.

'Hello, gents!' said Brett. 'You saved us seats? How nice.'

'I say,' Mike said, 'that Romero what'shisname is some-body. Am I wrong?'

'Oh, isn't he lovely,' Brett said. 'And those green trousers.'

'Brett never took her eyes off them.'

'I say, I must borrow your glasses tomorrow.'

'How did it go?'

'Wonderfully! Simply perfect. I say, it is a spectacle!'

'How about the horses?'

'I couldn't help looking at them.'

'She couldn't take her eyes off them,' Mike said. 'She's an extraordinary wench.'

'They do have some rather awful things happen to them,' Brett said. 'I couldn't look away, though.'

'Did you feel all right?'

'I didn't feel badly at all.'

'Robert Cohn did,' Mike put in. 'You were quite green, Robert.'

'The first horse did bother me,' Cohn said.

'You weren't bored, were you?' asked Bill.

Cohn laughed.

'No. I wasn't bored. I wished you'd forgive me that.'

'It's all right,' Bill said, 'so long as you weren't bored.'

'He didn't look bored,' Mike said. 'I thought he was going to be sick.'

'I never felt that bad. It was just for a minute.'

'*I* thought he was going to be sick. You weren't bored, were you, Robert?'

'Let up on that, Mike. I said I was sorry I said it.'

'He was, you know. He was positively green.'

'Oh, shove it along, Michael.'

'You mustn't ever get bored at your first bull-fight, Robert,' Mike said. 'It might make such a mess.'

'Oh, shove it along, Michael,' Brett said.

'He said Brett was a sadist,' Mike said. 'Brett's not a sadist. She's just a lovely, healthy wench.'

'Are you a sadist, Brett?' I asked.

'Hope not.'

'He said Brett was a sadist just because she has a good, healthy stomach.'

'Won't be healthy long.'

Bill got Mike started on something else than Cohn. The waiter brought the absinthe glasses.

'Did you really like it?' Bill asked Cohn.

'No, I can't say I liked it. I think it's a wonderful show.'

'Gad, yes! What a spectacle!' Brett said.

'I wish they didn't have the horse part,' Cohn said.

'They're not important,' Bill said. 'After a while you never notice anything disgusting.'

'It is a bit strong just at the start,' Brett said. 'There's a dreadful moment for me just when the bull starts for the horse.'

'The bulls were fine,' Cohn said.

'They were very good,' Mike said.

'I want to sit down below, next time.' Brett drank from her glass of absinthe.

'She wants to see the bull-fighters close by,' Mike said.

'They are something,' Brett said. 'That Romero lad is just a child.'

'He's a damned good-looking boy,' I said. 'When we were up in his room I never saw a better-looking kid.'

'How old do you suppose he is?'

'Nineteen or twenty.'

'Just imagine it.'

The bull-fight on the second day was much better than on the first. Brett sat between Mike and me at the barrera, and Bill and Cohn went up above. Romero was the whole show. I do not think Brett saw any other bull-fighter. No one else did either, except the hard-shelled technicians. It was all Romero. There were two other matadors, but they did not count. I sat beside Brett and explained to Brett what it was all about. I told her about watching the bull, not the horse, when the bulls charged the picadors, and got her to watching the picador place the point of his pic so that she saw what it was all about, so that it became more something that was going on with a definite end, and less of a spectacle with unexplained horrors. I had her watch how Romero took the bull away from a fallen horse with his cape, and how he held him with the cape and turned him, smoothly and suavely, never wasting the bull. She saw how Romero avoided every brusque movement and saved his bulls for the last when he wanted them, not winded and discomposed but smoothly worn down. She saw how close Romero always worked to the bull, and I pointed out to her the tricks the other bull-fighters used to make it look as though they were working closely. She saw why she liked Romero's cape-work and why she did not like the others.

Romero never made any contortions, always it was straight and pure and natural in line. The others twisted themselves like cork-screws, their elbows raised, and leaned against the flanks of the bull after his horns had passed, to give a faked look of danger. Afterward, all that was faked turned bad and gave an unpleasant feeling. Romero's bull-fighting gave real emotion, because he kept the absolutely purity of line in his movements and always quietly and calmly let the horns pass him close each time. He did not have to emphasize their closeness. Brett saw how something that was beautiful done close to the bull was ridiculous if it were done a little way off. I told her how since the death of Joselito all the bull-fighters had been developing a technique that simulated this appearance of danger in order to give a fake emotional feeling, while the bull-fighter was really safe. Romero had the old thing, the holding of his purity of line through the maximum of exposure, while he dominated the bull by making him realize he was unattainable, while he prepared him for the killing.

'I've never seen him do an awkward thing,' Brett said.

'You won't until he gets frightened,' I said.

'He'll never be frightened,' Mike said. 'He knows too damned much.'

'He knew everything when he started. The others can't ever learn what he was born with.'

'And God, what looks,' Brett said.

'I believe, you know, that she's falling in love with this bull-fighter chap,' Mike said.

'I wouldn't be surprised.'

'Be a good chap, Jake. Don't tell her anything more about him. Tell her how they beat their old mothers.'

'Tell me what drunks they are.'

'Oh, frightful,' Mike said. 'Drunk all day and spend all their time beating their poor old mothers.'

'He looks that way,' Brett said.

'Doesn't he?' I said.

They had hitched the mules to the dead bull and then the whips cracked, the men ran, and the mules, straining forward, their legs pushing, broke into a gallop, and the bull, one horn up, his head on its side, swept a swath smoothly across the sand and out the red gate.

'This next is the last one.'

'Not really,' Brett said. She leaned forward on the barrera. Romero waved his picadors to their places, then stood, his cape against his chest, looking across the ring to where the bull would come out.

After it was over we went out and were pressed tight in the crowd.

'These bull-fights are hell on one,' Brett said. 'I'm limp as a rag.'

'Oh, you'll get a drink,' Mike said.

The next day Pedro Romero did not fight. It was Miura bulls, and a very bad bull-fight. The next day there was no bull-fight scheduled. But all day and all night the fiesta kept on.

Chapter 16

In the morning it was raining. A fog had come over the mountains from the sea. You could not see the tops of the mountains. The plateau was dull and gloomy, and the shapes of the trees and the houses were changed. I walked out beyond the town to look at the weather. The bad weather was coming over the mountains from the sea.

The flags in the square hung wet from the white poles and the banners were wet and hung damp against the front of the houses, and in between the steady drizzle the rain came down and drove everyone under the arcades and made pools of water in the square, and the streets wet and dark and deserted; yet the fiesta kept up without any pause. It was only driven under cover.

The covered seats of the bull-ring had been crowded with people sitting out of the rain watching the concourse of Basque and Navarrais dancers and singers, and afterward the Val Carlos dancers in their costumes danced down the street in the rain, the drums sounding hollow and damp, and the chiefs of the bands riding ahead on their big, heavy-footed horses, their costumes wet, the horses' coats wet in the rain. The crowd was in the cafés and the dancers came in, too, and sat, their tight-wound white legs under the tables, shaking the water from their belled caps, and spreading their red and purple jackets over the chairs to dry. It was raining hard outside.

I left the crowd in the café and went over to the hotel to get shaved for dinner. I was shaving in my room when there was a knock on the door.

'Come in,' I recalled.

Montoya walked in.

'How are you?' he said.

'Fine,' I said.

'No bulls today.'

'No,' I said, 'nothing but rain.'

'Where are your friends?'

'Over at the Iruña.'

Montoya smiled his embarrassed smile.

'Look,' he said. 'Do you know the American ambassador?'

'Yes,' I said. 'Everybody knows the American ambassador.'

'He's here in town, now.'

'Yes,' I said. 'Everybody's seen them.'

'I've seen them, too,' Montoya said. He didn't say anything. I went on shaving.

'Sit down,' I said. 'Let me send for a drink.'

'No, I have to go.'

I finished shaving and put my face down into the bowl and washed it with cold water. Montoya was standing there looking more embarrassed.

'Look,' he said. 'I've just had a message from them at the Grand Hotel that they want Pedro Romero and Marcial Lalanda to come over for coffee tonight after dinner.'

'Well,' I said, 'it can't hurt Marcial any.'

'Marcial has been in San Sebastian all day. He drove over in a car this morning with Marquez. I don't think they'll be back tonight.'

Montoya stood embarrassed. He wanted me to say something.

'Don't give Romero the message,' I said.

'You think so?'

'Absolutely.'

Montoya was very pleased.

'I wanted to ask you because you were an American,' he said.

'That's what I'd do.'

'Look,' said Montoya. 'People take a boy like that. They

138

don't know what he's worth. They don't know what he means. Any foreigner can flatter him. They start this Grand Hotel business, and in one year they're through.'

'Like Algabeno,' I said.

'Yes, like Algabeno.'

'They're a fine lot,' I said. 'There's one American woman down here now that collects bull-fighters.'

'I know. They only want the young ones.'

'Yes,' I said. 'The old ones get fat.'

'Or crazy like Gallo.'

'Well,' I said, 'it's easy. All you have to do is not give him the message.'

'He's such a fine boy,' said Montoya. 'He ought to stay with his own people. He shouldn't mix in that stuff.'

'Won't you have a drink?' I asked.

'No,' said Montoya, 'I have to go.' He went out.

I went downstairs and out the door and took a walk around through the arcades around the square. It was still raining. I looked in at the Iruña for the gang and they were not there, so I walked on around the square and back to the hotel. They were eating dinner in the downstairs dining-room.

They were well ahead of me and it was no use trying to catch them. Bill was buying shoe-shines for Mike. Bootblacks opened the street door and each one Bill called over and started to work on Mike.

'This is the eleventh time my boots have been polished,' Mike said. 'I say, Bill is an ass.'

The bootblacks had evidently spread the report. Another came in.

'Limpia botas?' he said to Bill.

'No,' said Bill. 'For this Señor.'

The bootblack knelt down beside the one at work and started on Mike's free shoe that shone already in the electric light.

'Bill's a yell of laughter,' Mike said.

I was drinking red wine, and so far behind them that I felt a little uncomfortable about all this shoe-shining. I looked around the room. At the next table was Pedro Romero. He stood up when I nodded, and asked me to come over and meet a friend. His table was beside ours, almost touching. I met the friend, a Madrid bull-fight critic, a little man with a drawn face. I told Romero how much I liked his work, and he was very pleased. We talked Spanish and the critic knew a little French. I reached to our table for my wine-bottle but the critic took my arm. Romero laughed.

'Drink here,' he said in English.

He was very bashful about his English, but he was really very pleased with it, and as we went on talking he brought out words he was not sure of, and asked me about them. He was anxious to know the English for *Corrida de toros*, the exact translation. Bull-fight he was suspicious of. I explained that bull-fight in Spanish was the *lidia* of a *toro*. The Spanish word *corrida* means in English the running of bulls – the French translation is *Course de taureaux*. The critic put that in. There is no Spanish word for bull-fight.

Pedro Romero said he had learned a little English in Gibraltar. He was born in Ronda. That is not far above Gibraltar. He started bull-fighting in Malaga in the bull-fighting school there. He had only been at it three years. The bull-fight critic joked him about the number of *Malagueño* expressions he used. He was nineteen years old, he said. His older brother was with him as a banderillero, but he did not live in this hotel. He lived in a smaller hotel with the other people who worked for Romero. He asked me how many times I had seen him in the ring. I told him only three. It was really only two, but I did not want to explain after I had made the mistake.

'Where did you see me the other time? In Madrid?'

'Yes,' I lied. I had read the accounts of his two appearances in Madrid in the bull-fight papers, so I was all right.

'The first or the second time?'

'The first.'

'I was very bad,' he said. 'The second time I was better. You remember?' He turned to the critic.

He was not at all embarrassed. He talked of his work as something altogether apart from himself. There was nothing conceited or braggartly about him.

'I like it very much that you like my work,' he said. 'But you haven't seen it yet. Tomorrow, if I get a good bull, I will try and show it to you.'

When he said this he smiled, anxious that neither the bull-fight critic nor I would think he was boasting.

'I am anxious to see it,' the critic said. 'I would like to be convinced.'

'He doesn't like my work much.' Romero turned to me. He was serious.

The critic explained that he liked it very much, but that so far it had been incomplete.

'Wait till tomorrow, if a good one comes out.'

'Have you seen the bulls for tomorrow?' the critic asked me.

'Yes. I saw them unloaded.'

Pedro Romero leaned forward.

'What did you think of them?'

'Very nice,' I said. 'About twenty-six arrobas. Very short horns. Haven't you seen them?'

'Oh, yes,' said Romero.

'They won't weigh twenty-six arrobas,' said the critic.

'No,' said Romero.

'They've got bananas for horns,' the critic said.

'You call them bananas?' asked Romero. He turned to me and smiled. '*You* wouldn't call them bananas?'

'No,' I said. 'They're horns all right.'

'They're very short,' said Pedro Romero. 'Very, very short. Still, they aren't bananas.'

'I say, Jake,' Brett called from the next table, 'you *have* deserted us.'

'Just temporarily,' I said. 'We're talking bulls.'

'You *are* superior.'

'Tell him that bulls have no balls,' Mike shouted. He was drunk.

Romero looked at me inquiringly.

'Drunk,' I said. 'Borracho! Muy borracho!'

'You might introduce your friends,' Brett said. She had not stopped looking at Pedro Romero. I asked them if they would like to have coffee with us. They both stood up. Romero's face was very brown. He had very nice manners.

I introduced them all around and they started to sit down,

but there was not enough room, so we all moved over to the big table by the wall to have coffee. Mike ordered a bottle of Fundador and glasses for everybody. There was a lot of drunken talking.

'Tell him I think writing is lousy,' Bill said. 'Go on, tell him. Tell him I'm ashamed of being a writer.'

Pedro Romero was sitting beside Brett and listening to her.

'Go on. Tell him!' Bill said.

Romero looked up smiling.

'This gentleman,' I said, 'is a writer.'

Romero was impressed. 'This other one, too,' I said, pointing at Cohn.

'He looks like Villalta,' Romero said, looking at Bill. 'Rafael, doesn't he look like Villalta?'

'I can't see it,' the critic said.

'Really,' Romero said in Spanish. 'He looks a lot like Villalta. What does the drunken one do?'

'Nothing.'

'Is that why he drinks?'

'No. He's waiting to marry this lady.'

'Tell him bulls have no balls!' Mike shouted, very drunk, from the other end of the table.

'What does he say?'

'He's drunk.'

'Jake,' Mike called. 'Tell him bulls have no balls!'

'You understand?' I said.

'Yes.'

I was sure he didn't, so it was all right.

'Tell him Brett wants to see him put on those green pants.'

'Pipe down, Mike.'

'Tell him Brett is dying to know how he can get into those pants.'

'Pipe down.'

During this Romero was fingering his glass and talking with Brett. Brett was talking French and he was talking Spanish and a little English, and laughing.

Bill was filling the glasses.

'Tell him Brett wants to come into –'

'Oh, pipe down, Mike, for Christ's sake!'

Romero looked up smiling. 'Pipe down! I know that,' he said.

Just then Montoya came into the room. He started to smile at me, then he saw Pedro Romero with a big glass of cognac in his hand, sitting laughing between me and a woman with bare shoulders, at a table full of drunks. He did not even nod.

Montoya went out of the room. Mike was on his feet proposing a toast. 'Let's all drink to –' he began. 'Pedro Romero,' I said. Everybody stood up. Romero took it very seriously, and we touched glasses and drank it down, I rushing it a little because Mike was trying to make it clear that that was not at all what he was going to drink to. But it went off all right, and Pedro Romero shook hands with everyone and he and the critic went out together.

'My God! he's a lovely boy,' Brett said. 'And how I would love to see him get into those clothes. He must use a shoe-horn.'

'I started to tell him,' Mike began. 'And Jake kept interrupting me. Why do you interrupt me? Do you think you talk Spanish better than I do?'

'Oh, shut up. Mike! Nobody interrupted you.'

'No, I'd like to get this settled.' He turned away from me. 'Do you think you amount to something, Cohn? Do you think you belong here among us? People who are out to have a good time? For God's sake don't be so noisy, Cohn!'

'Oh, cut it out, Mike,' Cohn said.

'Do you think Brett wants you here? Do you think you add to the party? Why don't you say something?'

'I said all I had to say the other night, Mike.'

'I'm not one of you literary chaps.' Mike stood shakily and leaned against the table. 'I'm not clever. But I do know when I'm not wanted. Why don't you see when you're not wanted, Cohn? Go away. Go away, for God's sake. Take that sad Jewish face away. Don't you think I'm right?'

He looked at us.

'Sure,' I said. 'Let's all go over to the Iruña.'

'No. Don't you think I'm right? I love that woman.'

'Oh, don't start that again. Do shove it along, Michael,' Brett said.

'Don't you think I'm right, Jake?'

Cohn still sat at the table. His face had the sallow, yellow look it got when he was insulted, but somehow he seemed to be enjoying it. The childish, drunken heroics of it. It was his affair with a lady of title.

'Jake,' Mike said. He was almost crying. 'You know I'm right. Listen, you!' He turned to Cohn: 'Go away! Go away now!'

'But I won't go, Mike,' said Cohn.

'Then I'll make you!' Mike started toward him around the table. Cohn stood up and took off his glasses. He stood waiting, his face sallow, his hands fairly low, proudly and firmly waiting for the assault, ready to do battle for his lady love.

I grabbed Mike. 'Come on to the café,' I said. 'You can't hit him here in the hotel.'

'Good!' said Mike. 'Good idea!'

We started off. I looked back as Mike stumbled up the stairs and saw Cohn putting his glasses on again. Bill was sitting at the table pouring another glass of Fundador. Brett was sitting looking straight ahead at nothing.

Outside on the square it had stopped raining and the moon was trying to get through the clouds. There was a wind blowing. The military band was playing and the crowd was massed on the far side of the square where the fireworks specialist and his son were trying to send up fire balloons. A balloon would start up jerkily, on a great bias, and be torn by the wind or blown against the houses of the square. Some fell into the crowd. The magnesium flared and the fireworks exploded and chased about in the crowd. There was no one dancing in the square. The gravel was too wet.

Brett came out with Bill and joined us. We stood in the crowd and watched Don Manuel Orquito, the fireworks king, standing on a little platform, carefully starting the balloons with sticks, standing above the heads of the crowd to launch the balloons off into the wind. The wind brought them all down, and Don Manuel Orquito's face was sweaty in the light of his complicated fireworks that fell into the crowd and charged and chased, sputtering and cracking, between the legs

of the people. The people shouted as each new luminous paper
bubble careened, caught fire, and fell.

'They're razzing Don Manuel,' Bill said.

'How do you know he's Don Manuel?' Brett said.

'His name's on the programme. Don Manuel Orquito, the
pirotecnico of esta ciudad.'

'Globos illuminados,' Mike said. 'A collection of globos
illuminados. That's what the paper said.'

The wind blew the band music away.

'I say, I wish one would go up,' Brett said. 'That Don
Manuel chap is furious.'

'He's probably worked for weeks fixing them to go off,
spelling out "Hail to San Fermin",' Bill said.

'Globos illuminados,' Mike said. 'A bunch of bloody globos
illuminados.'

'Come on,' said Brett. 'We can't stand here.'

'Her ladyship wants a drink,' Mike said.

'How you know things,' Brett said.

Inside, the café was crowded and very noisy. No one noticed
us come in. We could not find a table. There was a great noise
going on.

'Come on, let's get out of here,' Bill said.

Outside the paseo was going in under the arcade. There
were some English and Americans from Biarritz in sport
clothes scattered at the tables. Some of the women stared at the
people going by with lorgnettes. We had acquired, at some
time, a friend of Bill's from Biarritz. She was staying with
another girl at the Grand Hotel. The other girl had a headache
and had gone to bed.

'Here's the pub,' Mike said. It was the Bar Milano, a small,
tough bar where you could get food and where they danced in
the back room. We all sat down at a table and ordered a bottle
of Fundador. The bar was not full. There was nothing going on.

'This is a hell of a place,' Bill said.

'It's too early.'

'Let's take the bottle and come back later,' Bill said. 'I don't
want to sit here on a night like this.'

'Let's go and look at the English,' Mike said. 'I love to look
at the English.'

'They're awful,' Bill said. 'Where did they all come from?'

'They come from Biarritz,' Mike said. 'They come to see the last day of the quaint little Spanish festa.'

'I'll festa them,' Bill said.

'You're an extraordinarily beautiful girl.' Mike turned to Bill's friend. 'When did you come here?'

'Come off it, Michael.'

'I say, she *is* a lovely girl. Where have I been? Where have I been looking all this while? You're a lovely thing. *Have* we met? Come along with me and Bill. We're going to festa the English.'

'I'll festa them,' Bill said. 'What the hell are they doing at this fiesta?'

'Come on,' Mike said. 'Just us three. We're going to festa the bloody English. I hope you're not English? I'm Scotch. I hate the English. I'm going to festa them. Come on, Bill.'

Through the window we saw them, all three arm in arm going toward the café. Rockets were going up in the square.

'I'm going to sit here,' Brett said.

'I'll stay with you,' Cohn said.

'Oh, don't!' Brett said. 'For God's sake, go off somewhere. Can't you see Jake and I want to talk?'

'I didn't,' Cohn said. 'I thought I'd sit here because I felt a little tight.'

'What a hell of a reason for sitting with anyone. If you're tight, go to bed. Go on to bed.'

'Was I rude enough to him?' Brett asked. Cohn was gone. 'My God! I'm so sick of him!'

'He doesn't add much to the gaiety.'

'He depresses me so.'

'He's behaved very badly.'

'Damned badly. He had a chance to behave so well.'

'He's probably waiting just outside the door now.'

'Yes. He would. You know I do know how he feels. He can't believe it didn't mean anything.'

'I know.'

'Nobody else would behave as badly. Oh, I'm so sick of the whole thing. And Michael. Michael's been lovely, too.'

'It's been damned hard on Mike.'

'Yes. But he didn't need to be a swine.'

'Everybody behaves badly,' I said. 'Give them the proper chance.'

'You wouldn't behave badly.' Brett looked at me.

'I'd be as big an ass as Cohn,' I said.

'Darling, don't let's talk a lot of rot.'

'All right. Talk about anything you like.'

'Don't be difficult. You're the only person I've got, and I feel rather awful tonight.'

'You've got Mike.'

'Yes, Mike. Hasn't he been pretty?'

'Well,' I said, 'it's been damned hard on Mike, having Cohn around and seeing him with you.'

'Don't I know it, darling? Please don't make me feel any worse than I do.'

Brett was nervous as I had never seen her before. She kept looking away from me and looking ahead at the wall.

'Want to go for a walk?'

'Yes. Come on.'

I corked up the Fundador bottle and gave it to the bartender.

'Let's have one more drink of that,' Brett said. 'My nerves are rotten.'

We each drank a glass of the smooth amontillado brandy.

'Come on,' said Brett.

As we came out the door I saw Cohn walk out from under the arcade.

'He *was* there,' Brett said.

'He can't be away from you.'

'Poor devil!'

'I'm not sorry for him. I hate him, myself.'

'I hate him, too,' she shivered. 'I hate his damned suffering.'

We walked arm in arm down the side street away from the crowd and the lights of the square. The street was dark and wet, and we walked along it to the fortifications at the edge of town. We passed wine-shops with light coming out from their doors onto the black, wet street, and sudden bursts of music.

'Want to go in?'

'No.'

We walked out across the wet grass and on to the stone wall of the fortifications. I spread a newspaper on the stone and Brett sat down. Across the plain it was dark, and we could see the mountains. The wind was high up and took the clouds across the moon. Below us were the dark pits of the fortifications. Behind were the trees and the shadow of the cathedral, and the town silhouetted against the moon.

'Don't feel bad,' I said.

'I feel like hell,' Brett said. 'Don't let's talk.'

We looked out at the plain. The long lines of trees were dark in the moonlight. There were the lights of a car on the road climbing the mountain. Up on the top of the mountain we saw the lights of the fort. Below to the left was the river. It was high from the rain, and black and smooth. Trees were dark along the banks. We sat and looked out. Brett stared straight ahead. Suddenly she shivered.

'It's cold.'

'Want to walk back?'

'Through the park.'

We climbed down. It was clouding over again. In the park it was dark under the trees.

'Do you still love me, Jake?'

'Yes,' I said.

'Because I'm a goner,' Brett said.

'How?'

'I'm a goner. I'm mad about the Romero boy. I'm in love with him, I think.'

'I wouldn't be if I were you.'

'I can't help it. I'm a goner. It's tearing me all up inside.'

'Don't do it.'

'I can't help it. I've never been able to help anything.'

'You ought to stop it.'

'How can I stop it? I can't stop things. Feel that?'

Her hand was trembling.

'I'm like that all through.'

'You oughtn't to do it.'

'I can't help it. I'm a goner now, anyway. Don't you see the difference?'

'No.'

'I've got to do something. I've got to do something I really want to do. I've lost my self-respect.'

'You don't have to do that.'

'Oh, darling, don't be difficult. What do you think it's meant to have that damned Jew about, and Mike the way he's acted?'

'Sure.'

'I can't just stay tight all the time.'

'No.'

'Oh, darling, please stay by me. Please stay by me and see me through this.'

'Sure.'

'I don't say it's right. It is right though for me. God knows, I've never felt such a bitch.'

'What do you want me to do?'

'Come on,' Brett said. 'Let's go and find him.'

Together we walked down the gravel path in the park in the dark, under the trees and then out from under the trees and past the gate into the street that led into town.

Pedro Romero was in the café. He was at a table with other bull-fighters and bull-fight critics. They were smoking cigars. When we came in they looked up. Romero smiled and bowed. We sat down at a table half-way down the room.

'Ask him to come over and have a drink.'

'Not yet. He'll come over.'

'I can't look at him.'

'He's nice to look at,' I said.

'I've always done just what I wanted.'

'I know.'

'I do feel such a bitch.'

'Well,' I said.

'My God!' said Brett, 'the things a woman goes through.'

'Yes?'

'Oh, I do feel such a bitch.'

I looked across at the table. Pedro Romero smiled. He said something to the other people at his table, and stood up. He came over to our table. I stood up and we shook hands.

'Won't you have a drink?'

'You must have a drink with me,' he said. He seated himself, asking Brett's permission without saying anything. He had very nice manners. But he kept on smoking his cigar. It went well with his face.

'You like cigars?' I asked.

'Oh, yes. I always smoke cigars.'

It was part of his system of authority. It made him seem older. I noticed his skin. It was clear and smooth and very brown. There was a triangular scar on his cheek-bone. I saw he was watching Brett. He felt there was something between them. He must have felt it when Brett gave him her hand. He was being very careful. I think he was sure, but he did not want to make any mistake.

'You fight tomorrow?' I said.

'Yes,' he said. 'Algabeno was hurt today in Madrid. Did you hear?'

'No,' I said. 'Badly?'

He shook his head.

'Nothing. Here,' he showed his hand. Brett reached out and spread the fingers apart.

'Oh!' he said in English, 'you tell fortunes?'

'Sometimes. Do you mind?'

'No. I like it.' He spread his hand flat on the table. 'Tell me I live for always, and be a millionaire.'

He was still very polite, but he was surer of himself. 'Look,' he said, 'do you see any bulls in my hand?'

He laughed. His hand was very fine and the wrist was small.

'There are thousands of bulls,' Brett said. She was not at all nervous now. She looked lovely.

'Good,' Romero laughed. 'At a thousand duros apiece,' he said to me in Spanish. 'Tell me some more.'

'It's a good hand,' Brett said. 'I think he'll live a long time.'

'Say it to me. Not to your friend.'

'I said you'd live a long time.'

'I know it,' Romero said. 'I'm never going to die.'

I tapped with my finger-tips on the table. Romero saw it. He shook his head.

'No. Don't do that. The bulls are my best friends.'

I translated to Brett.

'You kill your friends?' she asked.

150

'Always,' he said in English, and laughed. 'So they don't kill me.' He looked at her across the table.

'You know English well.'

'Yes,' he said. 'Pretty well, sometimes. But I must not let anybody know. It would be very bad, a torero who speaks English.'

'Why?' asked Brett.

'It would be bad. The people would not like it. Not yet.'

'Why not?'

'They would not like it. Bull-fighters are not like that.'

'What are bull-fighters like?'

He laughed and tipped his hat down over his eyes and changed the angle of his cigar and the expression of his face.

'Like at the table,' he said. I glanced over. He had mimicked exactly the expression of Nacional. He smiled, his face natural again. 'No. I must forget English.'

'Don't forget it, yet,' Brett said.

'No?'

'No.'

'All right.'

He laughed again.

'I would like a hat like that,' Brett said.

'Good. I'll get you one.'

'Right. See that you do.'

'I will. I'll get you one tonight.'

I stood up. Romero rose, too.

'Sit down,' I said. 'I must go and find our friends and bring them here.'

He looked at me. It was a final look to ask if it were understood. It was understood all right.

'Sit down,' Brett said to him. 'You must teach me Spanish.'

He sat down and looked at her across the table. I went out. The hard-eyed people at the bull-fighter table watched me go. It was not pleasant. When I came back and looked in the café, twenty minutes later, Brett and Pedro Romero were gone. The coffee-glasses and our three empty cognac-glasses were on the table. A waiter came with a cloth and picked up the glasses and mopped off the table.

Chapter 17

Outside the Bar Milano I found Bill and Mike and Edna. Edna was the girl's name.

'We've been thrown out,' Edna said.

'By the police,' said Mike. 'There's some people in there that don't like me.'

'I've kept them out of four fights,' Edna said. 'You've got to help me.'

Bill's face was red.

'Come back in, Edna,' he said. 'Go on in there and dance with Mike.'

'It's silly,' Edna said. 'There'll just be another row.'

'Damned Biarritz swine,' Bill said.

'Come on,' Mike said. 'After all, it's a pub. They can't occupy a whole pub.'

'Good old Mike,' Bill said. 'Damned English swine come here and insult Mike and try and spoil the fiesta.'

'They're so bloody,' Mike said. 'I hate the English.'

'They can't insult Mike,' Bill said. 'Mike is a swell fellow. They can't insult Mike. I won't stand it. Who cares if he is a damn bankrupt?' His voice broke.

'Who cares?' Mike said. 'I don't care. Jake doesn't care. Do *you* care?'

'No,' Edna said. 'Are you a bankrupt?'

'Of course I am. You don't care, do you, Bill?'

Bill put his arm around Mike's shoulder.

'I wish to hell I was a bankrupt. I'd show those bastards.'

'They're just English,' Mike said. 'It never makes any difference what the English say.'

'The dirty swine,' Bill said. 'I'm going to clean them out.'

'Bill,' Edna looked at me. 'Please don't go in again, Bill. They're so stupid.'

'That's it,' said Mike. 'They're stupid. I knew that was what it was.'

'They can't say things like that about Mike,' Bill said.

'Do you know them?' I asked Mike.

'No. I never saw them. They say they know me.'

'I won't stand it,' Bill said.

'Come on. Let's go over to the Suizo,' I said.

'They're a bunch of Edna's friends from Biarritz,' Bill said.

'They're simply stupid,' Edna said.

'One of them's Charley Blackman from Chicago,' Bill said.

'I was never in Chicago,' Mike said.

Edna started to laugh and could not stop.

'Take me away from here,' she said, 'you bankrupts.'

'What kind of a row was it?' I asked Edna. We were walking across the square to the Suizo. Bill was gone.

'I don't know what happened, but someone had the police called to keep Mike out of the back room. There were some people that had known Mike at Cannes. What's the matter with Mike?'

'Probably he owes them money,' I said. 'That's what people usually get bitter about.'

In front of the ticket-booths out in the square there were two lines of people waiting. They were sitting on chairs or crouched on the ground with blankets and newspapers around them. They were waiting for the wickets to open in the morning to buy tickets for the bull-fight. The night was clearing and the moon was out. Some of the people in the line were sleeping.

At the Café Suizo we had just sat down and ordered Fundador when Robert Cohn came up.

'Where's Brett?' he asked.

'I don't know.'

'She was with you.'

'She must have gone to bed.'

'She's not.'

'I don't know where she is.'

His face was sallow under the light. He was standing up.

'Tell me where she is.'

'Sit down,' I said. 'I don't know where she is.'

'The hell you don't!'

'You can shut your face.'

'Tell me where Brett is.'

'I'll not tell you a damn thing.'

'You know where she is.'

'If I did I wouldn't tell you.'

'Oh, go to hell, Cohn,' Mike called from the table. 'Brett's gone off with the bull-fighter chap. They're on their honeymoon.'

'You shut up.'

'Oh, go to hell!' Mike said languidly.

'Is that where she is?' Cohn turned to me.

'Go to hell!'

'She was with you. Is that where she is?'

'Go to hell!'

'I'll make you tell me' – he stepped forward – 'you damned pimp.'

I swung at him and he ducked. I saw his face duck sideways in the light. He hit me and I sat down on the pavement. As I started to get on my feet he hit me twice. I went down backward under a table. I tried to get up and felt I did not have any legs. I felt I must get on my feet and try and hit him. Mike helped me up. Some one poured a carafe of water on my head. Mike had an arm around me, and I found I was sitting on a chair. Mike was pulling at my ears.

'I say, you were cold,' Mike said.

'Where the hell were you?'

'Oh, I was around.'

'You didn't want to mix in it?'

'He knocked Mike down, too,' Edna said.

'He didn't knock me out,' Mike said. 'I just lay there.'

'Does this happen every night at your fiestas?' Edna asked. 'Wasn't that Mr Cohn?'

'I'm all right,' I said. 'My head's a little wobbly.'

There were several waiters and a crowd of people standing around.

'Vaya!' said Mike. 'Get away. Go on.'

The waiters moved the people away.

'It was quite a thing to watch,' Edna said. 'He must be a boxer.'

'He is.'

'I wish Bill had been here,' Edna said. 'I'd like to have seen Bill knocked down, too. I've always wanted to see Bill knocked down. He's so big.'

'I was hoping he would knock down a waiter,' Mike said, 'and get arrested. I'd like to see Mr Robert Cohn in jail.'

'No,' I said.

'Oh, no,' said Edna. 'You don't mean that.'

'I do, though,' Mike said. 'I'm not one of these chaps likes being knocked about. I never play games, even.'

Mike took a drink.

'I never liked to hunt, you know. There was always the danger of having a horse fall on you. How do you feel, Jake?'

'All right.'

'You're nice,' Edna said to Mike. 'Are you really a bankrupt?'

'I'm a tremendous bankrupt,' Mike said. 'I owe money to everybody. Don't you owe any money?'

'Tons.'

'I owe everybody money,' Mike said. 'I borrowed a hundred pesetas from Montoya to-night.'

'The hell you did,' I said.

'I'll pay it back,' Mike said. 'I always pay everything back.'

'That's why you're a bankrupt, isn't it?' Edna said.

I stood up. I had heard them talking from a long way away. It all seemed like some bad play.

'I'm going over to the hotel,' I said. Then I heard them talking about me.

'Is he all right?' Edna asked.

'We'd better walk with him.'

'I'm all right,' I said. 'Don't come. I'll see you all later.'

I walked away from the café. They were sitting at the table. I looked back at them and at the empty tables. There was a waiter sitting at one of the tables with his head in his hands.

Walking across the square to the hotel everything looked new and changed. I had never seen the trees before. I had never seen the flagpoles before, nor the front of the theatre. It was all different. I felt as I felt once coming home from an out-of-town football game. I was carrying a suitcase with my football things in it, and I walked up the street from the station in the town I had lived in all my life and it was all new. They were raking the lawns and burning leaves in the road, and I stopped for a long time and watched. It was all strange. Then I went on, and my feet seemed to be a long way off, and everything seemed to come from a long way off, and I could hear my feet walking a great distance away. I had been kicked in the head early in the game. It was like that crossing the square. It was like that going up the stairs in the hotel. Going up the stairs took a long time, and I had the feeling that I was carrying my suitcase. There was a light in the room. Bill came out and met me in the hall.

'Say,' he said, 'go up and see Cohn. He's been in a jam, and he's asking for you.'

'The hell with him.'

'Go on. Go on up and see him.'

I did not want to climb another flight of stairs.

'What are you looking at me that way for?'

'I'm not looking at you. Go on up and see Cohn. He's in bad shape.'

'You were drunk a little while ago,' I said.

'I'm drunk now,' Bill said. 'But you go up and see Cohn. He wants to see you.'

'All right,' I said. It was just a matter of climbing more stairs. I went on up the stairs carrying my phantom suitcase. I walked down the hall to Cohn's room. The door was shut and I knocked.

'Who is it?'

'Barnes.'

'Come in, Jake.'

I opened the door and went in, and set down my suitcase. There was no light in the room. Cohn was lying, face down, on the bed in the dark.

'Hello, Jake.'

'Don't call me Jake.'

I stood by the door. It was just like this that I had come home. Now it was a hot bath that I needed. A deep, hot bath, to lie back in.

'Where's the bathroom?' I asked.

Cohn was crying. There he was, face down on the bed, crying. He had on a white polo shirt, the kind he'd worn at Princeton.

'I'm sorry, Jake. Please forgive me.'

'Forgive you, hell.'

'Please forgive me, Jake.'

I did not say anything. I stood there by the door.

'I was crazy. You must see how it was.'

'Oh, that's all right.'

'I couldn't stand it about Brett.'

'You called me a pimp.'

I did not care. I wanted a hot bath. I wanted a hot bath in deep water.

'I know. Please don't remember it. I was crazy.'

'That's all right.'

He was crying. His voice was funny. He lay there in his white shirt on the bed in the dark. His polo shirt.

'I'm going away in the morning.'

He was crying without making any noise.

'I just couldn't stand it about Brett. I've been through hell, Jake. It's been simply hell. When I met her down here Brett treated me as though I were a perfect stranger. I just couldn't stand it. We lived together at San Sebastian. I suppose you know it. I can't stand it any more.'

He lay there on the bed.

'Well,' I said, 'I'm going to take a bath.'

'You were the only friend I had, and I loved Brett so.'

'Well,' I said, 'so long.'

'I guess it isn't any use,' he said. 'I guess it isn't any damn use.'

'What?'

'Everything. Please say you forgive me, Jake.'

'Sure,' I said. 'It's all right.'

'I felt so terribly. I've been through such hell, Jake. Now everything's gone. Everything.'

'Well,' I said, 'so long. I've got to go.'

He rolled over, sat on the edge of the bed, and then stood up.

'So long, Jake,' he said. 'You'll shake hands, won't you?'

157

'Sure. Why not?'

We shook hands. In the dark I could not see his face very well.

'Well,' I said, 'see you in the morning.'

'I'm going away in the morning.'

'Oh, yes,' I said.

I went out. Cohn was standing in the door of the room.

'Are you all right, Jake?' he asked.

'Oh, yes,' I said. 'I'm all right.'

I could not find the bathroom. After a while I found it. There was a deep stone tub. I turned on the taps and the water would not run. I sat down on the edge of the bath-tub. When I got up to go I found I had taken off my shoes. I hunted for them and found them and carried them downstairs. I found my room and went inside and undressed and got into bed.

I woke with a headache and the noise of the bands going by in the street. I remembered I had promised to take Bill's friend Edna to see the bulls go through the street and into the ring. I dressed and went downstairs and out into the cold early morning. People were crossing the square, hurrying toward the bull-ring. Across the square were the two lines of men in front of the ticket-booths. They were still waiting for the tickets to go on sale at seven o'clock. I hurried across the street to the café. The waiter told me that my friends had been there and gone.

'How many were they?'

'Two gentlemen and a lady.'

That was all right. Bill and Mike were with Edna. She had been afraid last night they would pass out. That was why I was to be sure to take her. I drank the coffee and hurried with the other people toward the bull-ring. I was not groggy now. There was only a bad headache. Everything looked sharp and clear, and the town smelt of the early morning.

The stretch of ground from the edge of the town to the bull-ring was muddy. There was a crowd all along the fence that led to the ring, and the outside balconies and the top of the bull-ring were solid with people. I heard the rocket and I knew I could not get into the ring in time to see the bulls come in, so

I shoved through the crowd to the fence. I was pushed close against the planks of the fence. Between the two fences of the runway the police were clearing the crowd along. They walked or trotted on into the bull-ring. Then people commenced to come running. A drunk slipped and fell. Two policemen grabbed him and rushed him over to the fence. The crowd were running fast now. There was a great shout from the crowd, and putting my head through between the boards I saw the bulls just coming out of the street into the long running pen. They were going fast and gaining on the crowd. Just then another drunk started out from the fence with a blouse in his hands. He wanted to do capework with the bulls. The two policemen tore out, collared him, one hit him with a club, and they dragged him against the fence and stood flattened out against the fence as the last of the crowd and the bulls went by. There were so many people running ahead of the bulls that the mass thickened and slowed up going through the gate into the ring, and as the bulls passed, galloping together, heavy, muddy-sided, horns swinging, one shot ahead, caught a man in the running crowd in the back and lifted him in the air. Both the man's arms were by his sides, his head went back as the horn went in, and the bull lifted him and then dropped him. The bull picked another man running in front, but the man disappeared into the crowd, and the crowd was through the gate and into the ring with the bulls behind them. The red door of the ring went shut, the crowd on the outside balconies of the bull-ring were pressing through to the inside, there was a shout, then another shout.

The man who had been gored lay face down in the trampled mud. People climbed over the fence, and I could not see the man because the crowd was so thick around him. From inside the ring came the shouts. Each shout meant a charge by some bull into the crowd. You could tell by the degree of intensity in the shout how bad a thing it was that was happening. Then the rocket went up that meant the steers had gotten the bulls out of the ring and into the corrals. I left the fence and started back towards the town.

Back in the town I went to the café to have a second coffee and some buttered toast. The waiters were sweeping out the café and mopping off the tables. One came over and took my order.

'Anything happen at the encierro?'

'I didn't see it all. One man was badly cogido.'

'Where?'

'Here.' I put one hand on the small of my back and the other on my chest, where it looked as though the horn must have come through. The waiter nodded his head and swept the crumbs from the table with his cloth.

'Badly cogido,' he said. 'All for sport. All for pleasure.'

He went away and came back with the long-handled coffee and milk pots. He poured the milk and coffee. It came out of the long spouts in two streams into the big cup. The waiter nodded his head.

'Badly cogido through the back,' he said. He put the pots down on the table and sat down in the chair at the table. 'A big horn wound. All for fun. Just for fun. What do you think of that?'

'I don't know.'

'That's it. All for fun. Fun, you understand.'

'You're not an aficionado?'

'Me? What are bulls? Animals. Brute animals.' He stood up and put his hand on the small of his back. 'Right through the back. A cornada right through the back. For fun – you understand.'

He shook his head and walked away, carrying the coffee-pots. Two men were going by in the street. The waiter shouted to them. They were grave-looking. One shook his head. 'Muerto!' he called.

The waiter nodded his head. The two men went on. They were on some errand. The waiter came over to my table.

'You hear? Muerto. Dead. He's dead. With a horn through him. All for morning fun. Es muy flamenco.'

'It's bad.'

'Not for me,' the waiter said. 'No fun in that for me.'

Later in the day we learned that the man who was killed was named Vicente Girones, and came from near Tafalla. The next day in the paper we read that he was twenty-eight years old, and had a farm, a wife, and two children. He had continued to

160

come to the fiesta each year after he was married. The next day his wife came in from Tafalla to be with the body, and the day after there was a service in the chapel of San Fermin, and the coffin was carried to the railway-station by members of the dancing and drinking society of Tafalla. The drums marched ahead, and there was music on the fifes, and behind the men who carried the coffin walked the wife and two children. . . . Behind them marched all the members of the dancing and drinking societies of Pamplona, Estella, Tafalla, and Sanguesa who could stay over for the funeral. The coffin was loaded into the baggage-car of the train, and the widow and the two children rode, sitting all three together, in an open third-class railway-carriage. The train started with a jerk, and then ran smoothly, going down grade around the edge of the plateau and out into the fields of grain that blew in the wind on the plain on the way to Tafalla.

The bull who killed Vicente Girones was named Bocanegra, was Number 118 of the bull-breeding establishment of Sanchez Taberno, and was killed by Pedro Romero as the third bull of that same afternoon. His ear was cut by popular acclamation and given to Pedro Romero, who, in turn, gave it to Brett, who wrapped it in a handkerchief belonging to myself, and left both ear and handkerchief, along with a number of Muratti cigarette-stubs, shoved far back in the drawer of the bed-table that stood beside her bed in the Hotel Montoya, in Pamplona.

Back in the hotel, the night watchman was sitting on a bench inside the door. He had been there all night and was very sleepy. He stood up as I came in. Three of the waitresses came in at the same time. They had been to the morning show at the bull-ring. They went upstairs laughing. I followed them upstairs and went into my room. I took off my shoes and lay down on the bed. The window was open onto the balcony and the sunlight was bright in the room. I did not feel sleepy. It must have been half past three o'clock when I had gone to bed and the bands had waked me at six. My jaw was sore on both sides. I felt it with my thumb and fingers. That damn Cohn. He should have hit somebody the first time he was insulted, and then gone away. He was so sure that Brett loved him. He was going to stay, and true love would conquer all. Some one knocked on the door.

'Come in.'

It was Bill and Mike. They sat down on the bed.

'Some encierro,' Bill said. 'Some encierro.'

'I say, weren't you there?' Mike asked. 'Ring for some beer, Bill.'

'What a morning!' Bill said. He mopped off his face. 'My God! what a morning! And here's old Jake. Old Jake, the human punching-bag.'

'What happened inside?'

'Good God!' Bill said, 'what happened, Mike?'

'There were these bulls coming in,' Mike said. 'Just ahead of them was the crowd, and some chap tripped and brought the whole lot of them down.'

'And the bulls all came in right over them,' Bill said. 'I heard them yell.'

'That was Edna,' Bill said.

'Chaps kept coming out and waving their shirts.'

'One bull went along the barrera and hooked everybody over.'

'They took about twenty chaps to the infirmary,' Mike said.

'What a morning!' Bill said. 'The damn police kept arresting chaps that wanted to go and commit suicide with the bulls.'

'The steers took them in, in the end,' Mike said.

'It took about an hour.'

'It was really about a quarter of an hour,' Mike objected.

'Oh, go to hell,' Bill said. 'You've been in the war. It was two hours and a half for me.'

'Where's that beer?' Mike asked.

'What did you do with the lovely Edna?'

'We took her home just now. She's gone to bed.'

'How did she like it?'

'Fine. We told her it was just like that every morning.'

'She was impressed,' Mike said.

'She wanted us to go down in the ring, too,' Bill said. 'She likes action.'

'I said it wouldn't be fair to my creditors,' Mike said.

'What a morning,' Bill said. 'And what a night!'

'How's your jaw, Jake?' Mike asked.

'Sore,' I said.

Bill laughed.

'Why didn't you hit him with a chair?'

'You can talk,' Mike said. 'He'd have knocked you out, too. I never saw him hit me. I rather think I saw him just before, and then quite suddenly I was sitting down in the street, and Jake was lying under a table.'

'Where did he go afterward?' I asked.

'Here she is,' Mike said. 'Here's the beautiful lady with the beer.'

The chambermaid put the tray with the beer-bottles and glasses down on the table.

'Now bring up three more bottles,' Mike said.

'Where did Cohn go after he hit me?' I asked Bill.

'Don't you know about that?' Mike was opening a beer-bottle. He poured the beer into one of the glasses, holding close to the bottle.

'Really?' Bill asked.

'Why he went in and found Brett and the bull-fighter chap in the bull-fighter's room, and then he massacred the poor, bloody bull-fighter.'

'No.'

'Yes.'

'What a night!' Bill said.

'He nearly killed the poor, bloody bull-fighter. Then Cohn wanted to take Brett away. Wanted to make an honest woman of her, I imagine. Damned touching scene.'

He took a long drink of the beer.

'He is an ass.'

'What happened?'

'Brett gave him what for. She told him off. I think she was rather good.'

'I'll bet she was,' Bill said.

'Then Cohn broke down and cried, and wanted to shake hands with the bull-fighter fellow. He wanted to shake hands with Brett, too.'

'I know. He shook hands with me.'

'Did he? Well, they weren't having any of it. The bull-fighter fellow was rather good. He didn't say much, but he kept getting up and getting knocked down again. Cohn couldn't knock him out. It must have been damned funny.'

'Where did you hear all this?'

'Brett. I saw her this morning.'

'What happened finally?'

'It seems the bull-fighter fellow was sitting on the bed. He'd been knocked down about fifteen times, and he wanted to fight some more. Brett held him and wouldn't let him get up. He was weak, but Brett couldn't hold him, and he got up. Then Cohn said he wouldn't hit him again. Said he couldn't do it. Said it would be wicked. So the bull-fighter chap sort of rather staggered over to him. Cohn went back against the wall.

'"So you won't hit me?"

'"No," said Cohn. "I'd be ashamed to."

'So the bull-fighter fellow hit him just as hard as he could in the face, and then sat down on the floor. He couldn't get up, Brett said. Cohn wanted to pick him up and carry him to the bed. He said if Cohn helped him he'd kill him, and he'd kill him anyway this morning if Cohn wasn't out of town. Cohn was crying, and Brett had told him off, and he wanted to shake hands. I've told you that before.'

'Tell the rest,' Bill said.

'It seems the bull-fighter chap was sitting on the floor. He was waiting to get strength enough to get up and hit Cohn again. Brett wasn't having any shaking hands, and Cohn was crying and telling her how much he loved her, and she was telling him not to be a ruddy ass. Then Cohn leaned down to shake hands with the bull-fighter fellow. No hard feelings, you know. All for forgiveness. And the bull-fighter chap hit him in the face again.'

'That's quite a kid,' Bill said.

'He ruined Cohn,' Mike said. 'You know I don't think Cohn will ever want to knock people about again.'

'When did you see Brett?'

'This morning. She came in to get some things. She's looking after this Romero lad.'

He poured out another bottle of beer.

'Brett's rather cut up. But she loves looking after people. That's how we came to go off together. She was looking after me.'

'I know,' I said.

'I'm rather drunk,' Mike said. 'I think I'll *stay* rather drunk. This is all awfully amusing, but it's not too pleasant. It's not too pleasant for me.'

He drank off the beer.

'I gave Brett what for, you know. I said if she would go about with Jews and bull-fighters and such people, she must expect trouble.' He leaned forward. 'I say, Jake, do you mind if I drink that bottle of yours? She'll bring you another one.'

'Please,' I said. 'I wasn't drinking it, anyway.'

Mike started to open the bottle. 'Would you mind opening it?' I pressed up the wire fastener and poured it for him.

'You know,' Mike went on, 'Brett was rather good. She's always rather good. I gave her a fearful hiding about Jews and bull-fighters, and all those sort of people, and do you know what she said: "Yes. I've had such a hell of a happy life with the British aristocracy!"'

He took a drink.

'That was rather good. Ashley, chap she got the title from, was a sailor, you know. Ninth baronet. When he came home he wouldn't sleep in a bed. Always made Brett sleep on the floor. Finally, when he got really bad, he used to tell her he'd kill her. Always slept with a loaded service revolver. Brett used to take the shells out when he'd gone to sleep. She hasn't had an absolutely happy life, Brett. Damned shame, too. She enjoys things so.'

He stood up. His hand was shaky.

'I'm going in the room. Try and get a little sleep.'

He smiled.

'We go too long without sleep in these fiestas. I'm going to start now and get plenty of sleep. Damn bad thing not to get sleep. Makes you frightfully nervy.'

'We'll see you at noon at the Iruña,' Bill said.

Mike went out the door. We heard him in the next room. He rang the bell and the chambermaid came and knocked at the door.

'Bring up half a dozen bottles of beer and a bottle of Fundador,' Mike told her.

'Si, Señorito.'

'I'm going to bed,' Bill said. 'Poor old Mike. I had a hell of a row about him last night.'

'Where? At that Milano place?'

'Yes. There was a fellow there that had helped pay Brett and Mike out of Cannes, once. He was damned nasty.'

'I know the story.'

'I didn't. Nobody ought to have a right to say things about Mike.'

'That's what makes it bad.'

'They oughtn't to have any right. I wish to hell they didn't have any right. I'm going to bed.'

'Was anybody killed in the ring?'

'I don't think so. Just badly hurt.'

'A man was killed outside in the runway.'

'Was there?' said Bill.

Chapter 18

At noon we were all at the café. It was crowded. We were eating shrimps and drinking beer. The town was crowded. Every street was full. Big motor-cars from Biarritz and San Sebastian kept driving up and parking around the square. They brought people for the bull-fight. Sight-seeing cars came up, too. There was one with twenty-five Englishwomen in it. They sat in the big, white car and looked through their glasses at the fiesta. The dancers were all quite drunk. It was the last day of the fiesta.

The fiesta was solid and unbroken, but the motor-cars and tourist-cars made little islands of onlookers. When the cars emptied, the onlookers were absorbed into the crowd. You did not see them again except as sport clothes, odd-looking at a table among the closely packed peasants in black smocks. The fiesta absorbed even the Biarritz English so that you did not see them unless you passed close to a table. All the time there was music in the street. The drums kept on pounding and the pipes were going. Inside the cafés men with their hands gripping the table, or on each other's shoulders, were singing the hard-voiced singing.

'Here comes Brett,' Bill said.

I looked and saw her coming through the crowd in the square, walking, her head up, as though the fiesta were being staged in her honour, and she found it pleasant and amusing.

'Hello, you chaps!' she said. 'I say, I *have* a thirst.'

'Get another big beer,' Bill said to the waiter.

'Shrimps?'

'Is Cohn gone?' Brett asked.

'Yes,' Bill said. 'He hired a car.'

The beer came. Brett started to lift the glass mug and her hand shook. She saw it and smiled, and leaned forward and took a long sip.

'Good beer.'

'Very good,' I said. I was nervous about Mike. I did not think he had slept. He must have been drinking all the time, but he seemed to be under control.

'I heard Cohn had hurt you, Jake,' Brett said.

'No. Knocked me out. That was all.'

'I say, he did hurt Pedro Romero,' Brett said. 'He hurt him most badly.'

'How is he?'

'He'll be all right. He won't go out of the room.'

'Does he look badly?'

'Very. He was really hurt. I told him I wanted to pop out and see you chaps for a minute.'

'Is he going to fight?'

'Rather. I'm going with you, if you don't mind.'

'How's your boy friend?' Mike asked. He had not listened to anything that Brett had said.

'Brett's got a bull-fighter,' he said. 'She had a Jew named Cohn, but he turned out badly.'

Brett stood up.

'I am not going to listen to that sort of rot from you, Michael.'

'How's your boy friend?'

'Damned well,' Brett said. 'Watch him this afternoon.'

'Brett's got a bull-fighter,' Mike said. 'A beautiful, bloody bull-fighter.'

'Would you mind walking over with me? I want to talk to you, Jake.'

'Tell him all about your bull-fighter,' Mike said. 'Oh, to hell with your bull-fighter!' He tipped the table so that all the beers and the dish of shrimps went over in a crash.

'Come on,' Brett said. 'Let's get out of this.'

In the crowd crossing the square I said: 'How is it?'

'I'm not going to see him after lunch until the fight. His people come in and dress him. They're very angry about me, he says.'

Brett was radiant. She was happy. The sun was out and the day was bright.

'I feel altogether changed,' Brett said. 'You've no idea, Jake.'

'Anything you want me to do?'

'No, just go to the fight with me.'

'We'll see you at lunch?'

'No. I'm eating with him.'

We were standing under the arcade at the door of the hotel. They were carrying tables out and setting them up under the arcade.

'Want to take a turn out to the park?' Brett asked. 'I don't want to go up yet. I fancy he's sleeping.'

We walked along past the theatre and out of the square and along through the barracks of the fair, moving with the crowd between the lines of booths. We came out on a cross-street that led to the Paseo de Sarasate. We could see the crowd walking there, all the fashionably dressed people. They were making the turn at the upper end of the park.

'Don't let's go there,' Brett said. 'I don't want staring at just now.'

We stood in the sunlight. It was hot and good after the rain and the clouds from the sea.

'I hope the wind goes down,' Brett said. 'It's very bad for him.'

'So do I.'

'He says the bulls are all right.'

'They're good.'

'Is that San Fermin's?'

Brett looked at the yellow wall of the chapel.

'Yes. Where the show started on Sunday.'

'Let's go in. Do you mind? I'd rather like to pray a little for him or something.'

We went in through the heavy leather door that moved very lightly. It was dark inside. Many people were praying. You saw them as your eyes adjusted themselves to the half-light. We knelt at one of the long wooden benches. After a little I felt Brett stiffen beside me, and saw she was looking straight ahead.

'Come on,' she whispered throatily. 'Let's get out of here. Makes me damned nervous.'

Outside in the hot brightness of the street Brett looked up at the tree-tops in the wind. The praying had not been much of a success.

'Don't know why I get so nervy in church,' Brett said. 'Never does me any good.'

We walked along.

'I'm damned bad for a religious atmosphere,' Brett said. 'I've the wrong type of face.'

'You know,' Brett said, 'I'm not worried about him at all. I just feel happy about him.'

'Good.'

'I wish the wind would drop, though.'

'It's liable to go down by five o'clock.'

'Let's hope.'

'You might pray,' I laughed.

'Never does me any good. I've never gotten anything I prayed for. Have you?'

'Oh, yes.'

'Oh, rot,' said Brett. 'Maybe it works for some people, though. You don't look very religious, Jake.'

'I'm pretty religious.'

'Oh, rot,' said Brett. 'Don't start proselyting today. Today's going to be bad enough as it is.'

It was the first time I had seen her in the old happy, careless

169

way since before she went off with Cohn. We were back again in front of the hotel. All the tables were set now, and already several were filled with people eating.

'Do look after Mike,' Brett said. 'Don't let him get too bad.'

'Your frients haff gone upstairs,' the German maitre d'hôtel said in English. He was a continual eavesdropper. Brett turned to him:

'Thank you, so much. Have you anything else to say?'

'No, *ma'am.*'

'Good,' said Brett.

'Save us a table for three,' I said to the German. He smiled his dirty little pink-and-white smile.

'Iss madam eating here?'

'No,' Brett said.

'Den I think a tabul for two will be enuff.'

'Don't talk to him,' Brett said. 'Mike must have been in bad shape,' she said on the stairs. We passed Montoya on the stairs. He bowed and did not smile.

'I'll see you at the café,' Brett said. 'Thank you, so much, Jake.'

We had stopped at the floor our rooms were on. She went straight down the hall and into Romero's room. She did not knock. She simply opened the door, went in, and closed it behind her.

I stood in front of the door of Mike's room and knocked. There was no answer. I tried the knob and it opened. Inside the room was in great disorder. All the bags were opened and clothing was strewn around. There were empty bottles beside the bed. Mike lay on the bed looking like a death mask of himself. He opened his eyes and looked at me.

'Hello, Jake,' he said very slowly. 'I'm getting a lit tle sleep. I've wan ted a lit tle sleep for a long time.'

'Let me cover you over.'

'No. I'm quite warm.'

'Don't go. I have n't got ten to sleep yet.'

'You'll sleep, Mike. Don't worry, boy.'

'Brett's got a bull-fighter,' Mike said. 'But her Jew has gone away.'

He turned his head and looked at me.

'Damned good thing, what?'

'Yes. Now go to sleep, Mike. You ought to get some sleep.'

'I'm just start ing. I'm go ing to get a lit tle sleep.'

He shut his eyes. I went out of the room and turned the door to quietly. Bill was in my room reading the paper.

'See Mike?'

'Yes.'

'Let's go and eat.'

'I won't eat downstairs with that German head-waiter. He was damned snotty when I was getting Mike upstairs.'

'He was snotty to us, too.'

'Let's go out and eat in the town.'

We went down the stairs. On the stairs we passed a girl coming up with a covered tray.

'There goes Brett's lunch,' Bill said.

'And the kid's,' I said.

Outside on the terrace under the arcade the German head-waiter came up. His red cheeks were shiny. He was being polite.

'I haff a tabul for two for you gentlemen,' he said.

'Go sit at it,' Bill said. We went on out across the street.

We ate at a restaurant in a side street off the square. They were all men eating in the restaurant. It was full of smoke and drinking and singing. The food was good and so was the wine. We did not talk much. Afterward we went to the café and watched the fiesta come to the boiling point. Brett came over soon after lunch. She said she had looked in the room and that Mike was asleep.

When the fiesta boiled over and toward the bull-ring we went with the crowd. Brett sat at the ringside between Bill and me. Directly below us was the callejon, the passageway between the stands and the red fence of the barrera. Behind us the concrete stands filled solidly. Out in front, beyond the red fence, the sand of the ring was smooth-rolled and yellow. It looked a little heavy from the rain, but it was dry in the sun and firm and smooth. The sword-handlers and bull-ring servants came down the callejon carrying on their shoulders the wicker baskets of fighting capes and muletas. They were blood-stained and compactly folded and packed in the baskets. The sword-handlers opened the heavy leather sword-cases so the red wrapped hilts of the sheaf of swords showed as the leather case leaned against the fence. They unfolded the dark-stained red flannel of the muletas and fixed batons in them to spread the stuff and give the matador something to hold. Brett watched it all. She was absorbed in the professional details.

'He's his name stencilled on all the capes and muletas,' she said. 'Why do they call them muletas?'

'I don't know.'

'I wonder if they ever launder them.'

'I don't think so. It might spoil the colour.'

'The blood must stiffen them,' Bill said.

'Funny,' Brett said. 'How one doesn't mind the blood.'

Below in the narrow passage of the callejon the sword-handlers arranged everything. All the seats were full. Above, all the boxes were full. There was not an empty seat except in the President's box. When he came in the fight would start. Across the smooth sand, in the high doorway that led into the corrals, the bull-fighters were standing, their arms furled in their capes, talking, waiting for the signal to march in across the arena. Brett was watching them with the glasses.

'Here, would you like to look?'

I looked through the glasses and saw the three matadors. Romero was in the centre, Belmonte on his left, Marcial on his right. Back of them were their people, and behind the banderilleros, back in the passageway and in the open space of the corral I saw the picadors. Romero was wearing a black suit. His tricornered hat was low down over his eyes. I could not see his face clearly under the hat, but it looked badly marked. He was looking straight ahead. Marcial was smoking a cigarette guardedly, holding it in his hand. Belmonte looked ahead, his face wan and yellow, his long wolf jaw out. He was looking at nothing. Neither he nor Romero seemed to have anything in common with the others. They were all alone. The President came in; there was handclapping above us in the grand stand, and I handed the glasses to Brett. There was applause. The music started. Brett looked through the glasses.

'Here, take them,' she said.

Through the glasses I saw Belmonte speak to Romero.

172

Marcial straightened up and dropped his cigarette, and, looking straight ahead, their heads back, their free arms swinging, the three matadors walked out. Behind them came all the procession, opening out, all striding in step, all the capes furled, everybody with free arms swinging, and behind rode the picadors, their pics rising like lances. Behind all came the two trains of mules and the bull-ring servants. The matadors bowed, holding their hats on, before the President's box, and then came over to the barrera below us. Pedro Romero took off his heavy gold-brocaded cape and handed it over the fence to his sword-handler. He said something to the sword-handler. Close below us we saw Romero's lips were puffed, both eyes were discoloured. His face was discoloured and swollen. The sword-handler took the cape, looked up at Brett, and came over to us and handed up the cape.

'Spread it out in front of you,' I said.

Brett leaned forward. The cape was heavy and smoothly stiff with gold. The sword-handler looked back, shook his head, and said something. A man beside me leaned over toward Brett.

'He doesn't want you to spread it,' he said. 'You should fold it and keep it in your lap.'

Brett folded the heavy cape.

Romero did not look up at us. He was speaking to Belmonte. Belmonte had sent his formal cape over to some friends. He looked across at them and smiled, his wolf smile that was only with the mouth. Romero leaned over the barrera and asked for the water-jug. The sword-handler brought it and Romero poured water over the percale of his fighting-cape, and then scuffed the lower folds in the sand with his slippered foot.

'What's that for?' Brett asked.

'To give it weight in the wind.'

'His face looks bad,' Bill said.

'He feels very badly,' Brett said. 'He should be in bed.'

The first bull was Belmonte's. Belmonte was very good. But because he got thirty thousand pesetas and people had stayed in line all night to buy tickets to see him, the crowd demanded that he should be more than very good. Belmonte's great

173

attraction is working close to the bull. In bull-fighting they speak of the terrain of the bull and the terrain of the bull-fighter. As long as a bull-fighter stays in his own terrain he is comparatively safe. Each time he enters into the terrain of the bull he is in great danger. Belmonte, in his best days, worked always in the terrain of the bull. This way he gave the sensation of coming tragedy. People went to the corrida to see Belmonte, to be given tragic sensations, and perhaps to see the death of Belmonte. Fifteen years ago they said if you wanted to see Belmonte you should go quickly, while he was still alive. Since then he has killed more than a thousand bulls. When he retired the legend grew up about how his bull-fighting had been, and when he came out of retirement the public were disappointed because no real man could work as close to the bulls as Belmonte was supposed to have done, not, of course, even Belmonte.

Also Belmonte imposed conditions and insisted that his bulls should not be too large, nor too dangerously armed with horns, and so the element that was necessary to give the sensation of tragedy was not there, and the public, who wanted three times as much from Belmonte, who was sick with a fistula, as Belmonte had ever been able to give, felt defrauded and cheated, and Belmonte's jaw came further out in contempt, and his face turned yellower, and he moved with greater difficulty as his pain increased, and finally the crowd were actively against him, and he was utterly contemptuous and indifferent. He had meant to have a great afternoon, and instead it was an afternoon of sneers, shouted insults, and finally a volley of cushions and pieces of bread and vegetables, thrown down at him in the plaza where he had had his greatest triumphs. His jaw only went further out. Sometimes he turned to smile that toothed, long-jawed, lipless smile when he was called something particularly insulting, and always the pain that any movement produced grew stronger and stronger, until finally his yellow face was parchment colour, and after his second bull was dead and the throwing of bread and cushions was over, after he had saluted the President with the same wolf-jawed smile and contemptuous eyes, and handed his sword over the barrera to be wiped, and put back in its case, he passed through into the callejon and leaned on the barrera below us, his head on his arms, not seeing, not hearing anything, only going through his pain. When he looked up, finally, he asked for a drink of water. He swallowed a little, rinsed his mouth, spat the water, took his cape, and went back into the ring.

Because they were against Belmonte the public were for Romero. From the moment he left the barrera and went toward the bull they applauded him. Belmonte watched Romero, too, watched him always without seeming to. He paid no attention to Marcial. Marcial was the sort of thing he knew all about. He had come out of retirement to compete with Marcial, knowing it was a competition gained in advance. He had expected to compete with Marcial and the other stars of the decadence of bull-fighting, and he knew that the sincerity of his own bull-fighting would be so set off by the false aesthetics of the bull-fighters of the decadent period that he would only have to be in the ring. His return from retirement had been spoiled by Romero. Romero did always, smoothly, calmly, and beautifully, what he, Belmonte, could only bring himself to do now sometimes. The crowd felt it, even the people from Biarritz, even the American ambassador saw it, finally. It was a competition that Belmonte would not enter because it would lead only to a bad horn wound or death. Belmonte was no longer well enough. He no longer had his greatest moments in the bull-ring. He was not sure that there were any great moments. Things were not the same and now life only came in flashes. He had flashes of the old greatness with his bulls, but they were not of value because he had discounted them in advance when he had picked the bulls out for their safety, getting out of a motor and leaning on a fence, looking over at the herd on the ranch of his friend the bull-breeder. So he had two small, manageable bulls without much horns, and when he felt the greatness again coming, just a little of it through the pain that was always with him, it had been discounted and sold in advance, and it did not give him a good feeling. It was the greatness, but it did not make bull-fighting wonderful to him any more.

Pedro Romero had the greatness. He loved bull-fighting, and I think he loved the bulls, and I think he loved Brett.

Everything of which he could control the locality he did in front of her all that afternoon. Never once did he look up. He made it stronger that way, and did it for himself, too, as well as for her. Because he did not look up to ask if it pleased he did it all for himself inside, and it strengthened him, and yet he did it for her, too. But he did not do it for her at any loss to himself. He gained by it all through the afternoon.

His first 'quite' was directly below us. The three matadors take the bull in turn after each charge he makes at a picador. Belmonte was the first. Marcial was the second. Then came Romero. The three of them were standing at the left of the horse. The picador, his hat down over his eyes, the shaft of his pic angling sharply toward the bull, kicked in the spurs and held them and with the reins in his left hand walked the horse forward toward the bull. The bull was watching. Seemingly he watched the white horse, but really he watched the triangular steel point of the pic. Romero, watching, saw the bull start to turn his head. He did not want to charge. Romero flicked his cape so the colour caught the bull's eye. The bull charged with the reflex, charged, and found not the flash of colour but a white horse, and a man leaned far over the horse, shot the steel point of the long hickory shaft into the hump of muscle on the bull's shoulder, and pulled his horse sideways as he pivoted on the pic, making a wound, enforcing the iron into the bull's shoulder, making him bleed for Belmonte.

The bull did not insist under the iron. He did not really want to get at the horse. He turned and the group broke apart and Romero was taking him out with his cape. He took him out softly and smoothly, and then stopped and, standing squarely in front of the bull, offered him the cape. The bull's tail went up and he charged, and Romero moved his arms ahead of the bull, wheeling, his feet firmed. The dampened, mud-weighted cape swung open and full as a sail fills, and Romero pivoted with it just ahead of the bull. At the end of the pass they were facing each other again. Romero smiled. The bull wanted it again, and Romero's cape filled again, this time on the other side. Each time he let the bull pass so close that the man and the bull and the cape that filled and pivoted ahead of the bull were all one sharply etched mass. It was all so slow and so controlled. It was as though he were rocking the bull to sleep. He made four veronicas like that, and finished with a half-veronica that turned his back on the bull and came away toward the applause, his hand on his hip, his cape on his arm, and the bull watching his back going away.

In his own bulls he was perfect. His first bull did not see well. After the first two passes with the cape Romero knew exactly how bad the vision was impaired. He worked accordingly. It was not brilliant bull-fighting. It was only perfect bull-fighting. The crowd wanted the bull changed. They made a great row. Nothing very fine could happen with a bull that could not see the lures, but the President would not order him replaced.

'Why don't they change him?' Brett asked.

'They've paid for him. They don't want to lose their money.'

'It's hardly fair to Romero.'

'Watch how he handles a bull that can't see the colour.'

'It's the sort of thing I don't like to see.'

It was not nice to watch if you cared anything about the person who was doing it. With the bull who could not see the colours of the capes, or the scarlet flannel of the muleta, Romero had to make the bull consent with his body. He had to get so close that the bull saw his body, and would start for it, and then shift the bull's charge to the flannel and finish out the pass in the classic manner. The Biarritz crowd did not like it. They thought Romero was afraid, and that was why he gave that little sidestep each time as he transferred the bull's charge from his own body to the flannel. They preferred Belmonte's imitation of himself or Marcial's imitation of Belmonte. There were three of them in the row behind us.

'What's he afraid of the bull for? The bull's so dumb he only goes after the cloth.'

'He's just a young bullfighter. He hasn't learned it yet.'

'But I thought he was fine with the cape before.'

'Probably he's nervous now.'

Out in the centre of the ring, all alone, Romero was going on with the same thing, getting so close that the bull could see him plainly, offering the body, offering it again a little closer, the bull watching dully, then so close that the bull thought he had him, offering again and finally drawing the charge and then, just before the horns came, giving the bull the red cloth to follow with that little, imperceptible, jerk that so offended the critical judgment of the Biarritz bull-fight experts.

'He's going to kill now,' I said to Brett. 'The bull's still strong. He wouldn't wear himself out.'

Out in the centre of the ring Romero profiled in front of the bull, drew the sword out from the folds of the muleta, rose on his toes, and sighted along the blade. The bull charged as Romero charged. Romero's left hand dropped the muleta over the bull's muzzle to blind him, his left shoulder went forward between the horns as the sword went in, and for just an instant he and the bull were one, Romero way out over the bull, the right arm extended high up to where the hilt of the sword had gone in between the bull's shoulders. Then the figure was broken. There was a little jolt as Romero came clear, and then he was standing, one hand up, facing the bull, his shirt ripped out from under his sleeve, the white blowing in the wind, and the bull, the red sword hilt tight between his shoulders, his head going down and his legs settling.

'There he goes,' Bill said.

Romero was close enough so the bull could see him. His hand still up, he spoke to the bull. The bull gathered himself, then his head went forward and he went over slowly, then all over, suddenly, four feet in the air.

They handed the sword to Romero, and carrying it blade down, the muleta in his other hand, he walked over to in front of the President's box, bowed, straightened, and came over to the barrera and handed over the sword and muleta.

'Bad one,' said the sword-handler.

'He made me sweat,' said Romero. He wiped off his face. The sword-handler handed him the water-jug. Romero wiped his lips. It hurt him to drink out of the jug. He did not look up at us.

Marcial had a big day. They were still applauding him when Romero's last bull came in. It was the bull that had sprinted out and killed the man in the morning running.

During Romero's first bull his hurt face had been very noticeable. Everything he did showed it. All the concentration of the awkwardly delicate working with the bull that could not see well brought it out. The fight with Cohn had not touched his spirit but his face had been smashed and his body hurt. He was wiping all that out now. Each thing that he did with the bull wiped that out a little cleaner. It was a good bull, a big bull, and with horns, and it turned and recharged easily and surely. He was what Romero wanted in bulls.

When he had finished his work with the muleta and was ready to kill, the crowd made him go on. They did not want the bull killed yet, they did not want it to be over. Romero went on. It was like a course in bull-fighting. All the passes he linked up, all completed, all slow, templed and smooth. There were no tricks and no mystifications. There was no brusqueness. And each pass as it reached the summit gave you a sudden ache inside. The crowd did not want it ever to be finished.

The bull was squared on all four feet to be killed, and Romero killed directly below us. He killed not as he had been forced to by the last bull, but as he wanted to. He profiled directly in front of the bull, drew the sword out of the folds of the muleta and sighted along the blade. The bull watched him, Romero spoke to the bull and tapped one of his feet. The bull charged and Romero waited for the charge, the muleta held low, sighting along the blade, his feet firm. Then without taking a step forward, he became one with the bull, the sword was in high between the shoulders, the bull had followed the low-swung flannel, that disappeared as Romero lurched clear to the left, and it was over. The bull tried to go forward, his legs commenced to settle, he swung from side to side, hesitated, then went down on his knees, and Romero's older brother leaned forward behind him and drove a short knife into the bull's neck at the base of the horns. The first time he missed. He drove the knife in again, and the bull went over, twitching and rigid. Romero's brother holding the bull's horn in one hand, the knife in the other, looked up at the President's box. Handkerchiefs were waving all over the bull-ring. The President looked down from the box and waved his handkerchief. The brother cut the notched black ear from the dead bull and trotted over with it to Romero. The bull lay heavy and black on the sand, his tongue out. Boys were running toward him from all parts of the arena, making a little circle around him. They were starting to dance around the bull.

Romero took the ear from his brother and held it up toward the President. The President bowed and Romero, running to get ahead of the crowd, came toward us. He leaned up against the barrera and gave the ear to Brett. He nodded his head and smiled. The crowd were all about him. Brett held down the cape.

'You liked it?' Romero called.

Brett did not say anything. They looked at each other and smiled. Brett had the ear in her hand.

'Don't get bloody,' Romero said, and grinned. The crowd wanted him. Several boys shouted at Brett. The crowd was the boys, the dancers, and the drunks. Romero turned and tried to get through the crowd. They were all around him trying to lift him and put him on their shoulders. He fought and twisted away, and started running, in the midst of them, toward the exit. He did not want to be carried on people's shoulders. But they held him and lifted him. It was uncomfortable and his legs were straddled and his body was very sore. They were lifting him and all running toward the gate. He had his hand on somebody's shoulder. He looked around at us apologetically. The crowd, running, went out the gate with him.

We all three went back to the hotel. Brett went upstairs. Bill and I sat in the downstairs dining-room and ate some hard-boiled eggs and drank several bottles of beer. Belmonte came down in his street clothes with his manager and two other men. They sat at the next table and ate. Belmonte ate very little. They were leaving on the seven o'clock train for Barcelona. Belmonte wore a blue-striped shirt and a dark suit, and ate soft-boiled eggs. The others ate a big meal. Belmonte did not talk. He only answered questions.

Bill was tired after the bull-fight. So was I. We both took a bull-fight very hard. We sat and ate eggs and I watched Belmonte and the people at his table. The men with him were tough-looking and businesslike.

'Come on over to the café,' Bill said. 'I want an absinthe.'

It was the last day of the fiesta. Outside it was beginning to be cloudy again. The square was full of people and the fireworks experts were making up their set pieces for the night and covering them over with beech branches. Boys were watching. We passed stands of rockets with long bamboo stems. Outside the café there was a great crowd. The music and the dancing were going on. The giants and the dwarfs were passing.

'Where's Edna?' I asked Bill.

'I don't know.'

We watched the beginning of the evening of the last night of the fiesta. The absinthe made everything seem better. I drank it without sugar in the dripping glass, and it was pleasantly bitter.

'I feel sorry about Cohn,' Bill said. 'He had an awful time.'

'Oh, to hell with Cohn,' I said.

'Where do you suppose he went?'

'Up to Paris.'

'What do you suppose he'll do?'

'Oh, to hell with him.'

'What do you suppose he'll do?'

'Pick up with his old girl, probably.'

'Who was his old girl?'

'Somebody named Frances.'

We had another absinthe.

'When do you go back?' I asked.

'Tomorrow.'

After a little while Bill said: 'Well, it was a swell fiesta.'

'Yes,' I said; 'something doing all the time.'

'You wouldn't believe it. It's like a wonderful nightmare.'

'Sure,' I said. 'I'd believe anything. Including nightmares.'

'What's the matter? Feel low?'

'Low as hell.'

'Have another absinthe. Here, waiter! Another absinthe for this señor.'

'I feel like hell,' I said.

'Drink that,' said Bill. 'Drink it slow.'

It was beginning to get dark. The fiesta was going on. I

began to feel drunk but I did not feel any better.

'How do you feel?'

'I feel like hell.'

'Have another?'

'It won't do any good.'

'Try it. You can't tell; maybe this is the one that gets it. Hey, waiter! Another absinthe for this señor!'

I poured the water directly into it and stirred it instead of letting it drip. Bill put in a lump of ice. I stirred the ice around with a spoon in the brownish cloudy mixture.

'How is it?'

'Fine.'

'Don't drink it fast that way. It will make you sick.'

I set down the glass. I had not meant to drink it fast.

'I feel tight.'

'You ought to.'

'That's what you wanted, wasn't it?'

'Sure. Get tight. Get over your damn depression.'

'Well, I'm tight. Is that what you want?'

'Sit down.'

'I won't sit down,' I said. 'I'm going over to the hotel.'

I was very drunk. I was drunker than I ever remembered having been. At the hotel I went upstairs. Brett's door was open. I put my head in the room. Mike was sitting on the bed. He waved a bottle.

'Jake,' he said. 'Come in, Jake.'

I went in and sat down. The room was unstable unless I looked at some fixed point.

'Brett, you know. She's gone off with the bull-fighter chap.'

'No.'

'Yes. She looked for you to say good-bye. They went on the seven o'clock train.'

'Did they?'

'Bad thing to do,' Mike said. 'She shouldn't have done it.'

'No.'

'Have a drink? Wait while I ring for some beer.'

'I'm drunk,' I said. 'I'm going in and lie down.'

'Are you blind? I was blind myself.'

'Yes,' I said, I'm blind.'

182

'Well, bung-o,' Mike said. 'Get some sleep, old Jake.'

I went out the door and into my own room and lay on the bed. The bed went sailing off and I sat up in bed and looked at the wall to make it stop. Outside in the square the fiesta was going on. It did not mean anything. Later Bill and Mike came in to get me to go down and eat with them. I pretended to be asleep.

'He's asleep. Better let him alone.'

'He's blind as a tick,' Mike said. They went out.

I got up and went to the balcony and looked out at the dancing in the square. The world was not wheeling any more. It was just very clear and bright, and inclined to blur at the edges. I washed, brushed my hair. I looked strange to myself in the glass, and went downstairs to the dining-room.

'Here he is!' said Bill. 'Good old Jake! I knew you wouldn't pass out.'

'Hello, you old drunk,' Mike said.

'I got hungry and woke up.'

'Eat some soup,' Bill said.

The three of us sat at the table, and it seemed as though about six people were missing.

BOOK THREE

Chapter 19

In the morning it was all over. The fiesta was finished. I woke about nine o'clock, had a bath, dressed, and went downstairs. The square was empty and there were no people on the streets. A few children were picking up rocket-sticks in the square. The cafés were just opening and the waiters were carrying out the comfortable white wicker chairs and arranging them around the marble-topped tables in the shade of the arcade. They were sweeping the streets and sprinkling them with a hose.

I sat in one of the wicker chairs and leaned back comfortably. The waiter was in no hurry to come. The white-paper announcements of the unloading of the bulls and the big schedules of special trains were still up on the pillars of the arcade. A waiter wearing a blue apron came out with a bucket of water and a cloth, and commenced to tear down the notices, pulling the paper off in strips and washing and rubbing away the paper that stuck to the stone. The fiesta was over.

I drank a coffee and after a while Bill came over. I watched him come walking across the square. He sat down at the table and ordered a coffee.

'Well,' he said, 'it's all over.'

'Yes,' I said. 'When do you go?'

'I don't know. We better get a car, I think. Aren't you going back to Paris?'

185

'No. I can stay away another week. I think I'll go to San Sebastian.'

'I want to get back.'

'What's Mike going to do?'

'He's going to Saint Jean de Luz.'

'Let's get a car and all go as far as Bayonne. You can get the train up from there tonight.'

'Good. Let's go after lunch.'

'All right. I'll get the car.'

We had lunch and paid the bill. Montoya did not come near us. One of the maids brought the bill. The car was outside. The chauffeur piled and strapped the bags on top of the car and put them in beside him in the front seat and we got in. The car went out of the square, along through the side streets, out under the trees and down the hill and away from Pamplona. It did not seem like a very long ride. Mike had a bottle of Fundador. I only took a couple of drinks. We came over the mountains and out of Spain and down the white roads and through the overfoliaged, wet, green, Basque country, and finally into Bayonne. We left Bill's baggage at the station, and he bought a ticket to Paris. His train left at seven-ten. We came out of the station. The car was standing out in front.

'What shall we do about the car?' Bill asked.

'Oh, bother the car,' Mike said. 'Let's just keep the car with us.'

'All right,' Bill said. 'Where shall we go?'

'Let's go to Biarritz and have a drink.'

'Old Mike the spender,' Bill said.

We drove in to Biarritz and left the car outside a very Ritz place. We went into the bar and sat on high stools and drank a whisky and soda.

'That drink's mine,' Mike said.

'Let's roll for it.'

So we rolled poker dice out of a deep leather dice-cup. Bill was out first roll. Mike lost to me and handed the bartender a hundred-franc note. The whiskies were twelve francs apiece. We had another round and Mike lost again. Each time he gave the bartender a good tip. In a room off the bar there was a good jazz band playing. It was a pleasant bar. We had another

186

round. I went out on the first roll with four kings. Bill and Mike rolled. Mike won the first roll with four jacks. Bill won the second. On the final roll Mike had three kings and let them stay. He handed the dice-cup to Bill. Bill rattled them and rolled, and there were three kings, an ace, and a queen.

'It's yours, Mike,' Bill said. 'Old Mike, the gambler.'

'I'm so sorry,' Mike said. 'I can't get it.'

'What's the matter?'

'I've no money,' Mike said. 'I'm stony. I've just twenty francs. Here, take twenty francs.'

Bill's face sort of changed.

'I just had enough to pay Montoya. Damned lucky to have it, too.'

'I'll cash you a cheque,' Bill said.

'That's damned nice of you, but you see I can't write cheques.'

'What are you going to do for money?'

'Oh, some will come through. I've two weeks' allowance should be here. I can live on tick at this pub in Saint Jean.'

'What do you want to do about the car?' Bill asked me. 'Do you want to keep it on?'

'It doesn't make any difference. Seems sort of idiotic.'

'Come on, let's have another drink,' Mike said.

'Fine. This one is on me,' Bill said. 'Has Brett any money?' He turned to Mike.

'I shouldn't think so. She put up most of what I gave to old Montoya.'

'She hasn't any money with her?' I asked.

'I shouldn't think so. She never has any money. She gets five hundred quid a year and pays three hundred and fifty of it in interest to Jews.'

'I suppose they get it at the source,' said Bill.

'Quite. They're not really Jews. We just call them Jews. They're Scotsmen, I believe.'

'Hasn't she any at all with her?' I asked.

'I hardly think so. She gave it all to me when she left.'

'Well,' Bill said, 'we might as well have another drink.'

'Damned good idea,' Mike said. 'One never gets anywhere by discussing finances.'

'No,' said Bill. Bill and I rolled for the next two rounds. Bill lost and paid. We went out to the car.

'Anywhere you'd like to go, Mike?' Bill asked.

'Let's take a drive. It might do my credit good. Let's drive about a little.'

'Fine. I'd like to see the coast. Let's drive down toward Hendaye.'

'I haven't any credit along the coast.'

'You can't ever tell,' said Bill.

We drove out along the coast road. There was the green of the headlands, the white, red-roofed villas, patches of forest, and the ocean very blue with the tide out and the water curling far out along the beach. We drove through Saint Jean de Luz and passed through villages farther down the coast. Back of the rolling country we were going through we saw the mountains we had come over from Pamplona. The road went on ahead. Bill looked at his watch. It was time for us to go back. He knocked on the glass and told the driver to turn around. The driver backed the car out into the grass to turn it. In back of us were the woods, below a stretch of meadow, then the sea.

At the hotel where Mike was going to stay in Saint Jean we stopped the car and he got out. The chauffeur carried in his bags. Mike stood by the side of the car.

'Good-bye, you chaps,' Mike said. 'It was a damned fine fiesta.'

'So long, Mike,' Bill said.

'I'll see you around,' I said.

'Don't worry about money,' Mike said. 'You can pay for the car, Jake, and I'll send you my share.'

'So long, Mike.'

'So long, you chaps. You've been damned nice.'

We all shook hands. We waved from the car to Mike. He stood in the road watching. We got to Bayonne just before the train left. A porter carried Bill's bags in from the consigne. I went as far as the inner gate to the tracks.

'So long, fella,' Bill said.

'So long, kid!'

'It was swell. I've had a swell time.'

'Will you be in Paris?'

'No, I have to sail on the 17th. So long, fella!'

'So long, old kid!'

He went in through the gate to the train. The porter went ahead with the bags. I watched the train pull out. Bill was at one of the windows. The window passed, the rest of the train passed, and the tracks were empty. I went outside to the car.

'How much do we owe you?' I asked the driver. The price to Bayonne had been fixed at a hundred and fifty pesetas.

'Two hundred pesetas.'

'How much more will it be if you drive me to San Sebastian on your way back?'

'Fifty pesetas.'

'Don't kid me.'

'Thirty-five pesetas.'

'It's not worth it,' I said. 'Drive me to the Hotel Panier Fleuri.'

At the hotel I paid the driver and gave him a tip. The car was powdered with dust. I rubbed the rod-case through the dust. It seemed the last thing that connected me with Spain and the fiesta. The driver put the car in gear and went down the street. I watched it turn off to take the road to Spain. I went into the hotel and they gave me a room. It was the same room I had slept in when Bill and Cohn and I were in Bayonne. That seemed a very long time ago. I washed, changed my shirt, and went out in the town.

At a newspaper kiosk I bought a copy of the New York *Herald* and sat in a café to read it. It felt strange to be in France again. There was a safe, suburban feeling. I wished I had gone up to Paris with Bill, except that Paris would have meant more fiesta-ing. I was through with fiestas for a while. It would be quiet in San Sebastian. The season does not open there until August. I could get a good hotel room and read and swim. There was a fine beach there. There were wonderful trees along the promenade above the beach, and there were many children sent down with their nurses before the season opened. In the evening there would be band concerts under the trees across from the Café Marinas. I could sit in the Marinas and listen.

'How does one eat inside?' I asked the waiter. Inside the café was a restaurant.

'Well. Very well. One eats very well.'

'Good.'

I went in and ate dinner. It was a big meal for France but it seemed very carefully apportioned after Spain. I drank a bottle of wine for company. It was a Château Margaux. It was pleasant to be drinking slowly and to be tasting the wine and to be drinking alone. A bottle of wine was good company. Afterward I had coffee. The waiter recommended a Basque liqueur called Izzarra. He brought in the bottle and poured a liqueur-glass full. He said Izzarra was made of the flowers of the Pyrenees. The veritable flowers of the Pyrenees. It looked like hair-oil and smelled like Italian *strega*. I told him to take the flowers of the Pyrenees away and bring me a *vieux marc*. The *marc* was good. I had a second *marc* after the coffee.

The waiter seemed a little offended about the flowers of the Pyrenees, so I overtipped him. That made him happy. It felt comfortable to be in a country where it is so simple to make people happy. You can never tell whether a Spanish waiter will thank you. Everything is on such a clear financial basis in France. It is the simplest country to live in. No one makes things complicated by becoming your friend for any obscure reason. If you want people to like you you have only to spend a little money. I spent a little money and the waiter liked me. He appreciated my valuable qualities. He would be glad to see me back. I would dine there again some time and he would be glad to see me, and would want me at this table. It would be a sincere liking because it would have a sound basis. I was back in France.

Next morning I tipped every one a little too much at the hotel to make more friends, and left on the morning train for San Sebastian. At the station I did not tip the porter more than I should because I did not think I would ever see him again. I only wanted a few good French friends in Bayonne to make me welcome in case I should come back there again. I knew that if they remembered me their friendship would be loyal.

At Irun we had to change and show passports. I hated to leave France. Life was so simple in France. I felt I was a fool to be going back into Spain. In Spain you could not tell about anything. I felt like a fool to be going back into it but I stood

190

in line with my passport, opened my bags for the customs, bought a ticket, went through a gate, climbed onto the train, and after forty minutes and eight tunnels I was at San Sebastian.

Even on a hot day San Sebastian has a certain early-morning quality. The trees seem as though their leaves were never quite dry. The streets feel as though they had just been sprinkled. It is always cool and shady on certain streets on the hottest day. I went to a hotel in the town where I had stopped before, and they gave me a room with a balcony that opened out above the roofs of the town. There was a green mountainside beyond the roofs.

I unpacked my bags and stacked my books on the table beside the head of the bed, put out my shaving things, hung up some clothes in the big armoire, and made up a bundle for the laundry. Then I took a shower in the bathroom and went down to lunch. Spain had not changed to summer-time, so I was early. I set my watch again. I had recovered an hour by coming to San Sebastian.

As I went into the dining-room the concierge brought me a police bulletin to fill out. I signed it and asked him for two telegraph forms, and wrote a message to the Hotel Montoya, telling them to forward all mail and telegrams for me to this address. I calculated how many days I would be in San Sebastian and then wrote out a wire to the office asking them to hold mail, but forward all wires for me to San Sebastian for six days. Then I went in and had lunch.

After lunch I went up to my room, read a while, and went to sleep. When I woke it was half past four. I found my swimming-suit, wrapped it with a comb in a towel, and went downstairs and walked up the street to the Concha. The tide was about half-way out. The beach was smooth and firm, and the sand yellow. I went into a bathing-cabin, undressed, put on my suit, and walked across the smooth sand to the sea. The sand was warm under bare feet. There were quite a few people in the water and on the beach. Out beyond where the headlands of the Concha almost meet to form the harbour there was a white line of breakers and the open sea. Although the tide was going out, there were a few slow rollers. They came in like undulations in the water, gathered weight of water, and then broke smoothly on the warm sand. I waded out. The water was cold. As a roller came I dived, swam out under water, and came to the surface with all the chill gone. I swam out to the raft, pulled myself up, and lay on the hot planks. A boy and girl were at the other end. The girl had undone the top strap of her bathing-suit and was browning her back. The boy lay face downward on the raft and talked to her. She laughed at things he said, and turned her brown back in the sun. I lay on the raft in the sun until I was dry. Then I tried several dives. I dived deep once, swimming down to the bottom. I swam with my eyes open and it was green and dark. The raft made a dark shadow. I came out of water beside the raft, pulled up, dived once more, holding it for length, and then swam ashore. I lay on the beach until I was dry, then went into the bathing-cabin, took off my suit, sloshed myself with fresh water, and rubbed dry.

I walked around the harbour under the trees to the casino, and then up one of the cool streets to the Café Marinas. There was an orchestra playing inside the café and I sat out on the terrace and enjoyed the fresh coolness in the hot day, and had a glass of lemon-juice and shaved ice and then a long whisky and soda. I sat in front of the Marinas for a long time and read and watched the people, and listened to the music.

Later when it began to get dark, I walked around the harbour and out along the promenade, and finally back to the hotel for supper. There was a bicycle-race on, the Tour du Pays Basque, and the riders were stopping that night in San Sebastian. In the dining-room, at one side, there was a long table of bicycle-riders, eating with their trainers and managers. They were all French and Belgians, and paid close attention to their meal, but they were having a good time. At the head of the table were two good-looking French girls, with much Rue du Faubourg Montmartre chic. I could not make out whom they belonged to. They all spoke in slang at the long table and there were many private jokes and some jokes at the far end that were not repeated when the girls asked to hear them. The next morning at five o'clock the race resumed with the last lap, San Sebastian–Bilbao. The bicycle-riders drank much wine, and were burned and browned by the sun. They did not take the race seriously except among themselves. They had raced among themselves so often that it did not make much difference who won. Especially in a foreign country. The money could be arranged.

The man who had a matter of two minutes lead in the race had an attack of boils, which were very painful. He sat on the small of his back. His neck was very red and the blond hairs were sunburned. The other riders joked him about his boils. He tapped on the table with his fork.

'Listen,' he said, 'to-morrow my nose is so tight on the handle-bars that the only thing touches those boils is a lovely breeze.'

One of the girls looked at him down the table, and he grinned and turned red. The Spaniards, they said, did not know how to pedal.

I had coffee out on the terrasse with the team manager of one of the big bicycle manufacturers. He said it had been a very pleasant race, and would have been worth watching if Bottechia had not abandoned it at Pamplona. The dust had been bad, but in Spain the roads were better than in France. Bicycle road-racing was the only sport in the world, he said. Had I ever followed the Tour de France? Only in the papers. The Tour de France was the greatest sporting event in the world. Following and organizing the road races had made him know France. Few people know France. All spring and all summer and all fall he spent on the road with bicycle road-racers. Look at the number of motor-cars now that followed the riders from town to town in a road race. It was a rich country and more *sportif* every year. It would be the most *sportif* country in the world. It was bicycle road-racing that did it. That and football. He knew France. *La France Sportive.* He knew road-racing. We had a cognac. After all, though, it wasn't bad to get back to Paris. There is only one Paname. In all the world, that is. Paris is the town the most *sportif* in the world. Did I know the *Chope de Nègre*? Did I not. I would see him there some time. I certainly would. We would drink another *fine* together. We certainly would. They started at six o'clock less a quarter in the morning. Would I be up for the depart? I would certainly try to. Would I like him to call me? It was very interesting. I would leave a call at the desk. He would not mind calling me. I could not let him take the trouble. I would leave a call at the desk. We said good-bye until the next morning.

In the morning when I awoke the bicycle-riders and their following cars had been on the road for three hours. I had coffee and the papers in bed and then dressed and took my bathing-suit down to the beach. Everything was fresh and cool and damp in the early morning. Nurses in uniform and in peasant costume walked under the trees with children. The Spanish children were beautiful. Some bootblacks sat together under a tree talking to a soldier. The soldier had only one arm. The tide was in and there was a good breeze and a surf on the beach.

I undressed in one of the bath-cabins, crossed the narrow line of beach and went into the water. I swam out, trying to swim through the rollers, but having to dive sometimes. Then in the quiet water I turned and floated. Floating I saw only the sky, and felt the drop and lift of the swells. I swam back to the surf and coasted in, face down, on a big roller, then turned and swam, trying to keep in the trough and not have a wave break over me. It made me tired, swimming in the trough, and I turned and swam out to the raft. The water was buoyant and cold. It felt as though you could never sink. I swam slowly, it seemed like a long swim with the high tide, and then pulled up on the raft and sat, dripping, on the boards that were becoming hot in the sun. I looked around at the bay, the old town, the casino, the line of trees along the promenade, and the big hotels with their white porches and gold-lettered names. Off on the right, almost closing the harbour, was a green hill with a castle. The raft rocked with the motion of the water. On the other side of the narrow gap that led into the open sea was another high headland. I thought I would like to swim across the bay but I was afraid of cramp.

I sat in the sun and watched the bathers on the beach. They looked very small. After a while I stood up, gripped with my toes on the edge of the raft as it tipped with my weight, and dived cleanly and deeply, to come up through the lightening water, blew the salt water out of my head, and swam slowly and steadily in to shore.

After I was dressed and had paid for the bath-cabin, I walked back to the hotel. The bicycle-racers had left several copies of *L'Auto* around, and I gathered them up in the reading-room and took them out and sat in an easy chair in the sun to read about and catch up on French sporting life. While I was sitting there the concierge came out with a blue envelope in his hand.

'A telegram for you, sir.'

I poked my finger along under the fold that was fastened down, spread it open, and read it. It had been forwarded from Paris:

> COULD YOU COME HOTEL MONTANA MADRID
> AM RATHER IN TROUBLE BRETT.

I tipped the concierge and read the message again. A postman was coming along the sidewalk. He turned in the hotel. He had a big moustache and looked very military. He came out of the hotel again. The concierge was just behind him.

'Here's another telegram for you, sir.'

'Thank you,' I said.

I opened it. It was forwarded from Pamplona.

> COULD YOU COME HOTEL MONTANA MADRID
> AM RATHER IN TROUBLE BRETT.

The concierge stood there waiting for another tip, probably.

'What time is there a train for Madrid?'

'It left at nine this morning. There is a slow train at eleven, and the Sud Express at ten tonight.'

'Get me a berth on the Sud Express. Do you want the money now?'

'Just as you wish,' he said. 'I will have it put on the bill.'

'Do that.'

Well, that meant San Sebastian all shot to hell. I suppose, vaguely, I had expected something of the sort. I saw the concierge standing in the doorway.

'Bring me a telegram form, please.'

He brought it and I took out my fountain-pen and printed:

> LADY ASHLEY HOTEL MONTANA MADRID
> ARRIVING SUD EXPRESS TOMORROW LOVE JAKE.

That seemed to handle it. That was it. Send a girl off with one man. Introduce her to another to go off with him. Now go and bring her back. And sign the wire with love. That was it all right. I went in to lunch.

I did not sleep much that night on the Sud Express. In the morning I had breakfast in the dining-car and watched the rock and pine country between Avila and Escorial. I saw the Escorial out of the window, gray and long and cold in the sun, and did not give a damn about it. I saw Madrid come up over the plain, a compact white sky-line on the top of a little cliff away off across the sun-hardened country.

The Norte station in Madrid is the end of the line. All trains finish there. They don't go on anywhere. Outside were cabs and taxis and a line of hotel runners. It was like a country town. I took a taxi and we climbed up through the gardens, by the empty palace and the unfinished church on the edge of the cliff, and on up until we were in the high, hot, modern town. The taxi coasted down a smooth street to the Puerto del Sol, and then through the traffic and out into the Carrera San Jeronimo. All the shops had their awnings down against the heat. The windows on the sunny side of the street were shuttered. The taxi stopped at the kerb. I saw the sign HOTEL MONTANA on the second floor. The taxi-driver carried the bags in and left them by the elevator. I could not make the elevator work, so I walked up. On the second floor up was a cut brass sign: HOTEL MONTANA. I rang and no one came to the door. I rang again and a maid with a sullen face opened the door.

'Is Lady Ashley here?' I asked.

She looked at me dully.

'Is an Englishwoman here?'

She turned and called someone inside. A very fat woman came to the door. Her hair was gray and stiffly oiled in scallops around her face. She was short and commanding.

'Muy buenos,' I said. 'Is there an Englishwoman here? I would like to see this English lady.'

'Muy buenos. Yes, there is a female English. Certainly you can see her if she wishes to see you.'

'She wishes to see me.'

'The chica will ask her.'

196

'It is very hot.'

'It is very hot in the summer in Madrid.'

'And how cold in winter.'

'Yes, it is very cold in winter.'

Did I want to stay myself in person in the Hotel Montana?

Of that as yet I was undecided, but it would give me pleasure if my bags were brought from the ground floor in order that they might not be stolen. Nothing was ever stolen in the Hotel Montana. In other fondas, yes. Not here. No. The personages of this establishment were rigidly selectioned. I was happy to hear it. Nevertheless I would welcome the upbringal of my bags.

The maid came in and said that the female English wanted to see the male English now, at once.

'Good,' I said. 'You see. It is as I said.'

'Clearly.'

I followed the maid's back down a long, dark corridor. At the end she knocked on a door.

'Hello,' said Brett. 'Is it you, Jake?'

'It's me.'

'Come in. Come in.'

I opened the door. The maid closed it after me. Brett was in bed. She had just been brushing her hair and held the brush in her hand. The room was in that disorder produced only by those who have always had servants.

'Darling!' Brett said.

I went over to the bed and put my arms around her. She kissed me, and while she kissed me I could feel she was thinking of something else. She was trembling in my arms. She felt very small.

'Darling! I've had such a hell of a time.'

'Tell me about it.'

'Nothing to tell. He only left yesterday. I made him go.'

'Why didn't you keep him?'

'I don't know. It isn't the sort of thing one does. I don't think I hurt him any.'

'You were probably damn good for him.'

'He shouldn't be living with anyone. I realized that right away.'

'No.'

197

'Oh, hell!' she said, 'let's not talk about it. Let's never talk about it.'

'All right.'

'It was rather a knock his being ashamed of me. He was ashamed of me for a while, you know.'

'No.'

'Oh, yes. They ragged him about me at the café, I guess. He wanted me to grow my hair out. Me, with long hair. I'd look so like hell.'

'It's funny.'

'He said it would make me more womanly. I'd look a fright.'

'What happened?'

'Oh, he got over that. He wasn't ashamed of me long.'

'What was it about being in trouble?'

'I didn't know whether I could make him go, and I didn't have a sou to go away and leave him. He tried to give me a lot of money, you know. I told him I had scads of it. He knew that was a lie. I couldn't take his money, you know.'

'No.'

'Oh, let's not talk about it. There were some funny things, though. Do give me a cigarette.'

I lit the cigarette.

'He learned his English as a waiter in Gib.'

'Yes.'

'He wanted to marry me, finally.'

'Really?'

'Of course. I can't even marry Mike.'

'Maybe he thought that would make him Lord Ashley.'

'No. It wasn't that. He really wanted to marry me. So I couldn't go away from him, he said. He wanted to make it sure I could never go away from him. After I'd gotten more womanly, of course.'

'You ought to feel set up.'

'I do. I'm all right again. He's wiped out that damned Cohn.'

'Good.'

'You know I'd have lived with him if I hadn't seen it was bad for him. We got along damned well.'

'Outside of your personal appearance.'

'Oh, he'd have gotten used to that.'

She put out the cigarette.

'I'm thirty-four, you know. I'm not going to be one of these bitches that ruins children.'

'No.'

'I'm not going to be that way. I feel rather good, you know. I feel rather set up.'

'Good.'

She looked away. I thought she was looking for another cigarette. Then I saw she was crying. I could feel her crying. Shaking and crying. She wouldn't look up. I put my arms around her.

'Don't let's ever talk about it. Please don't let's ever talk about it.'

'Dear Brett.'

'I'm going back to Mike.' I could feel her crying as I held her close. 'He's so damned nice and he's so awful. He's my sort of thing.'

She would not look up. I stroked her hair. I could feel her shaking.

'I won't be one of those bitches,' she said. 'But, oh, Jake, please let's never talk about it.'

We left the Hotel Montana. The woman who ran the hotel would not let me pay the bill. The bill had been paid.

'Oh, well. Let it go,' Brett said. 'It doesn't matter now.'

We rode in a taxi down to the Palace Hotel, left the bags, arranged for berths on the Sud Express for the night, and went into the bar of the hotel for a cocktail. We sat on high stools at the bar while the barman shook the Martinis in a large nickelled shaker.

'It's funny what a wonderful gentility you get in the bar of a big hotel,' I said.

'Barmen and jockeys are the only people who are polite any more.'

'No matter how vulgar a hotel is, the bar is always nice.'

'It's odd.'

'Bartenders have always been fine.'

'You know,' Brett said, 'it's quite true. He is only nineteen. Isn't it amazing?'

We touched the two glasses as they stood side by side on the bar. They were coldly beaded. Outside the curtained window was the summer heat of Madrid.

'I like an olive in a Martini,' I said to the barman.

'Right you are, sir. There you are.'

'Thanks.'

'I should have asked, you know.'

The barman went far enough up the bar so that he would not hear our conversation. Brett had sipped from the Martini as it stood, on the wood. Then she picked it up. Her hand was steady enough to lift it after that first sip.

'It's good. Isn't it a nice bar?'

'They're all nice bars.'

'You know I didn't believe it at first. He was born in 1905. I was in school in Paris, then. Think of that.'

'Anything you want me to think about it?'

'Don't be an ass. *Would* you buy a lady a drink?'

'We'll have two more Martinis.'

'As they were before, sir?'

'They were very good.' Brett smiled at him.

'Thank you, ma'am.'

'Well, bung-o,' Brett said.

'Bung-o!'

'You know,' Brett said, 'he'd only been with two women before. He never cared about anything but bull-fighting.'

'He's got plenty of time.'

'I don't know. He thinks it was me. Not the show in general.'

'Well, it was you.'

'Yes. It was me.'

'I thought you weren't going to ever talk about it.'

'How can I help it?'

'You'll lose it if you talk about it.'

'I just talk around it. You know I feel rather damned good, Jake.'

'You should.'

'You know it makes me feel rather good deciding not to be a bitch.'

'Yes.'

200

'It's sort of what we have instead of God.'

'Some people have God,' I said. 'Quite a lot.'

'He never worked very well with me.'

'Should we have another Martini?'

The barman shook up two more Martinis and poured them out into fresh glasses.

'Where will we have lunch?' I asked Brett. The bar was cool. You could feel the heat outside through the window.

'Here?' asked Brett.

'It's rotten here in the hotel. Do you know a place called Botin's?' I asked the barman.

'Yes, sir. Would you like to have me write out the address?'

'Thank you.'

We lunched upstairs at Botin's. It is one of the best restaurants in the world. We had roast young suckling pig and drank *rioja alta*. Brett did not eat much. She never ate much. I ate a very big meal and drank three bottles of *rioja alta*.

'How do you feel, Jake?' Brett asked. 'My God! what a meal you've eaten.'

'I feel fine. Do you want a dessert?'

'Lord, no.'

Brett was smoking.

'You like to eat, don't you?' she said.

'Yes.' I said. 'I like to do a lot of things.'

'What do you like to do?'

'Oh,' I said, 'I like to do a lot of things. Don't you want a dessert?'

'You asked me that once,' Brett said.

'Yes,' I said. 'So I did. Let's have another bottle of *rioja alta*.'

'It's very good.'

'You haven't drunk much of it,' I said.

'I have. You haven't seen.'

'Let's get two bottles,' I said. The bottles came. I poured a little in my glass, then a glass for Brett, then filled my glass. We touched glasses.

'Bung-o!' Brett said. I drank my glass and poured out another. Brett put her hand on my arm.

'Don't get drunk, Jake,' she said. 'You don't have to.'

201

'How do you know?'

'Don't,' she said. 'You'll be all right.'

'I'm not getting drunk,' I said. 'I'm just drinking a little wine. I like to drink wine.'

'Don't get drunk,' she said. 'Jake, don't get drunk.'

'Want to go for a ride?' I said. 'Want to ride through the town?'

'Right,' Brett said. 'I haven't seen Madrid. I should see Madrid.'

'I'll finish this,' I said.

Downstairs we came through the first-floor dining-room to the street. A waiter went for a taxi. It was hot and bright. Up the street was a little square with trees and grass where there were taxis parked. A taxi came up the street, the waiter hanging out at the side. I tipped him and told the driver where to drive, and got in beside Brett. The driver started up the street. I settled back. Brett moved close to me. We sat close against each other. I put my arm around her and she rested against me comfortably. It was very hot and bright, and the houses looked sharply white. We turned out onto the Gran Via.

'Oh, Jake,' Brett said, 'we could have had such a damned good time together.'

Ahead was a mounted policeman in khaki directing traffic. He raised his baton. The car slowed suddenly pressing Brett against me.

'Yes.' I said. 'Isn't it pretty to think so?'

A FAREWELL TO ARMS
CAPORETTO

Chapter I

Now in the fall the trees were all bare and the roads were muddy. I rode to Gorizia from Udine on a camion. We passed other camions on the road and I looked at the country. The mulberry trees were bare and the fields were brown. There were wet dead leaves on the road from the rows of bare trees and men were working on the road, tamping stone in the ruts from piles of crushed stone along the side of the road between the trees. We saw the town with a mist over it that cut off the mountains. We crossed the river and I saw that it was running high. It had been raining in the mountains. We came into the town past the factories and then the houses and villas and I saw that many more houses had been hit. On a narrow street we passed a British Red Cross ambulance. The driver wore a cap and his face was thin and very tanned. I did not know him. I got down from the camion in the big square in front of the Town Major's house, the driver handed down my rucksack and I put it on and swung on the two musettes and walked to our villa. It did not feel like a homecoming.

I walked down the damp gravel driveway looking at the villa through the trees. The windows were all shut but the door was open. I went in and found the major sitting at a table in the bare room with maps and typed sheets of paper on the wall.

'Hello,' he said. 'How are you?' He looked older and drier.

'I'm good,' I said. 'How is everything?'

'It's all over,' he said. 'Take off your kit and sit down.' I put my pack and the two musettes on the floor and my cap on the pack. I brought the other chair over from the wall and sat down by the desk.

'It's been a bad summer,' the major said. 'Are you strong now?'

'Yes.'

'Did you ever get the decorations?'

'Yes. I got them fine. Thank you very much.'

'Let's see them.'

I opened my cape so he could see the two ribbons.

'Did you get the boxes with the medals?'

'No. Just the papers.'

'The boxes will come later. That takes more time.'

'What do you want me to do?'

'The cars are all away. There are six up north at Caporetto. You know Caporetto?'

'Yes,' I said. I remembered it as a little white town with a campanile in a valley. It was a clean little town and there was a fine fountain in the square.

'They are working from there. There are many sick now. The fighting is over.'

'Where are the others?'

'There are two up in the mountains and four still on the Bainsizza. The other two ambulance sections are in the Carso with the third army.'

'What do you wish me to do?'

'You can go and take over the four cars on the Bainsizza if you like. Gino has been up there a long time. You haven't seen it up there, have you?'

'No.'

'It was very bad. We lost three cars.'

'I heard about it.'

'Yes, Rinaldi wrote you.'

'Where is Rinaldi?'

'He is here at the hospital. He has had a summer and fall of it.'

'I believe it.'

'It has been bad,' the major said. 'You couldn't believe how bad it's been. I've often thought you were lucky to be hit when you were.'

'I know I was.'

'Next year will be worse,' the major said. 'Perhaps they will attack now. They say they are to attack but I can't believe it. It is too late. You saw the river?'

'Yes. It's high already.'

'I don't believe they will attack now that the rains have started. We will have the snow soon. What about your countrymen? Will there be other Americans besides yourself?'

'They are training an army of ten million.'

'I hope we get some of them. But the French will hog them all. We'll never get any down here. All right. You stay here tonight and go out tomorrow with the little car and send Gino back. I'll send somebody with you that knows the road. Gino will tell you everything. They are shelling quite a little still but it is all over. You will want to see the Bainsizza.'

'I'm glad to see it. I am glad to be back with you again, Signor Maggiore.'

He smiled. 'You are very good to say so. I am very tired of this war. If I was away I do not believe I would come back.'

'Is it so bad?'

'Yes. It is so bad and worse. Go get cleaned up and find your friend Rinaldi.'

I went out and carried my bags up the stairs. Rinaldi was not in the room but his things were there and I sat down on the bed and unwrapped my puttees and took the shoe off my right foot. Then I lay back on the bed. I was tired and my right foot hurt. It seemed silly to lie on the bed with one shoe off, so I sat up and unlaced the other shoe and dropped it on the floor, then lay back on the blanket again. The room was stuffy with the window closed but I was too tired to get up and open it. I saw my things were all in one corner of the room. Outside it was getting dark. I lay on the bed and thought about Catherine and waited for Rinaldi. I was going to try not to think about Catherine except at night before I went to sleep. But now I was tired and there was nothing to do, so I lay and thought about her. I was thinking about her when Rinaldi came in. He looked just the same. Perhaps he was a little thinner.

'Well, baby,' he said. I sat up on the bed. He came over, sat down and put his arm around me. 'Good old baby.' He whacked me on the back and I held both his arms.

'Old baby,' he said. 'Let me see your knee.'

'I'll have to take off my pants.'

'Take off your pants, baby. We're all friends here. I want to see what kind of a job they did.' I stood up, took off the breeches and pulled off the knee-brace. Rinaldi sat on the floor and bent the knee gently back and forth. He ran his finger along the scar; put his thumbs together over the kneecap and rocked the knee gently with his fingers.

'Is that all the articulation you have?'

'Yes.'

'It's a crime to send you back. They ought to get complete articulation.'

'It's a lot better than it was. It was stiff as a board.'

Rinaldi bent it more. I watched his hands. He had fine surgeon's hands. I looked at the top of his head, his hair shiny and parted smoothly. He bent the knee too far.

'Ouch!' I said.

'You ought to have more treatment on it with the machines,' Rinaldi said.

'It's better than it was.'

'I see that, baby. This is something I know more about than you.' He stood up and sat down on the bed. 'The knee itself is a good job.' He was through with the knee. 'Tell me all about everything.'

'There's nothing to tell,' I said. 'I've led a quiet life.'

'You act like a married man,' he said. 'What's the matter with you?'

'Nothing,' I said. 'What's the matter with you?'

'This war is killing me,' Rinaldi said, 'I am very depressed by it.' He folded his hands over his knee.

'Oh,' I said.

'What's the matter? Can't I even have human impulses?'

'No. I can see you've been having a fine time. Tell me.'

'All summer and all fall I've operated. I work all the time. I do everybody's work. All the hard ones they leave to me. By God, baby, I am becoming a lovely surgeon.'

'That sounds better.'

'I never think. No, by God, I don't think; I operate.'

'That's right.'

'But now, baby, it's all over. I don't operate now and I feel like hell. This is a terrible war, baby. You believe me when I say it. Now you cheer me up. Did you bring the phonograph records?'

'Yes.'

They were wrapped in paper in a cardboard box in my rucksack. I was too tired to get them out.

'Don't you feel good yourself, baby?'

'I feel like hell.'

'This war is terrible,' Rinaldi said. 'Come on. We'll both get drunk and be cheerful. Then we'll go get the ashes dragged. Then we'll feel fine.'

'I've had the jaundice,' I said, 'and I can't get drunk.'

'Oh, baby, how you've come back to me. You come back serious and with a liver. I tell you this war is a bad thing. Why did we make it anyway?'

'We'll have a drink. I don't want to get drunk but we'll have a drink.'

Rinaldi went across the room to the washstand and brought back two glasses and a bottle of cognac.

'It's Austrian cognac,' he said. 'Seven stars. It's all they captured on San Gabriele.'

'Were you up there?'

'No. I haven't been anywhere. I've been here all the time operating. Look, baby, this is your old tooth-brushing glass. I kept it all the time to remind me of you.'

'To remind you to brush your teeth.'

'No. I have my own too. I kept this to remind me of you trying to brush away the Villa Rossa from your teeth in the morning, swearing and eating aspirin and cursing harlots. Every time I see that glass I think of you trying to clean your conscience with a toothbrush.' He came over to the bed. 'Kiss me once and tell me you're not serious.'

'I never kiss you. You're an ape.'

'I know, you are the fine good Anglo-Saxon boy. I know. You are the remorse boy, I know. I will wait till I see the Anglo-Saxon brushing away harlot with a toothbrush.'

'Put some cognac in the glass.'

207

We touched glasses and drank. Rinaldi laughed at me.

'I will get you drunk and take out your liver and put you in a good Italian liver and make you a man again.'

I held the glass for some more cognac. It was dark outside now. Holding the glass of cognac, I went over and opened the window. The rain had stopped falling. It was colder outside and there was a mist in the trees.

'Don't throw the cognac out the window,' Rinaldi said. 'If you can't drink it give it to me.'

'Go something yourself,' I said. I was glad to see Rinaldi again. He had spent two years teasing me and I had always liked it. We understood each other very well.

'Are you married?' he asked from the bed. I was standing against the wall by the window.

'Not yet.'

'Are you in love?'

'Yes.'

'With that English girl?'

'Yes.'

'Poor baby. Is she good to you?'

'Of course.'

'I mean is she good to you practically speaking?'

'Shut up.'

'I will. You will see I am a man of extreme delicacy. Does she –?'

'Rinin,' I said. 'Please shut up. If you want to be my friend, shut up.'

'I don't *want* to be your friend, baby. I *am* your friend.'

'Then shut up.'

'All right.'

I went over to the bed and sat down beside Rinaldi. He was holding his glass and looking at the floor.

'You see how it is, Rinin?'

'Oh, yes. All my life I encounter sacred subjects. But very few with you. I suppose you must have them too.' He looked at the floor.

'You haven't any?'

'No.'

'Not any?'

208

'No.'

'I can't say this about your mother and that about your sister?'

'And that about *your sister*,' Rinaldi said swiftly. We both laughed.

'The old superman,' I said.

'I am jealous maybe,' Rinaldi said.

'No, you're not.'

'I don't mean like that. I mean something else. Have you any married friends?'

'Yes,' I said.

'I haven't,' Rinaldi said. 'Not if they love each other.'

'Why not?'

'They don't like me.'

'Why not?'

'I am the snake. I am the snake of reason.'

'You're getting it mixed. The apple was reason.'

'No, it was the snake.' He was more cheerful.

'You are better when you don't think so deeply,' I said.

'I love you, baby,' he said. 'You puncture me when I become a great Italian thinker. But I know many things I can't say. I know more than you.'

'Yes. You do.'

'But you will have a better time. Even with remorse you will have a better time.'

'I don't think so.'

'Oh, yes. That is true. Already I am only happy when I am working.' He looked at the floor again.

'You'll get over that.'

'No. I only like two other things; one is bad for my work and the other is over in half an hour or fifteen minutes. Sometimes less.'

'Sometimes a good deal less.'

'Perhaps I have improved, baby. You do not know. But there are only the two things and my work.'

'You'll get other things.'

'No. We never get anything. We are born with all we have and we never learn. We never get anything new. We all start complete. You should be glad not to be a Latin.'

209

'There's no such thing as a Latin. That is "Latin" thinking. You are so proud of your defects.' Rinaldi looked up and laughed.

'We'll stop, baby. I am tired from thinking so much.' He had looked tired when he came in. 'It's nearly time to eat. I'm glad you're back. You are my best friend and my war brother.'

'When do the war brothers eat?' I asked.

'Right away. We'll drink once more for your liver's sake.'

'Like Saint Paul.'

'You are inaccurate. That was wine and the stomach. Take a little wine for your stomach's sake.'

'Whatever you have in the bottle,' I said. 'For any sake you mention.'

'To your girl,' Rinaldi said. He held out his glass.

'All right.'

'I'll never say a dirty thing about her.'

'Don't strain yourself.'

He drank off the cognac. 'I am pure,' he said. 'I am like you, baby. I will get an English girl too. As a matter of fact I knew your girl first but she was a little tall for me. A tall girl for a sister,' he quoted.

'You have a lovely pure mind,' I said.

'Haven't I? That's why they call me Rinaldo Purissimo.'

'Rinaldo Sporchissimo.'

'Come on, baby, we'll go down to eat while my mind is still pure.'

I washed, combed my hair and we went down the stairs. Rinaldi was a little drunk. In the room where we ate, the meal was not quite ready.

'I'll go get the bottle,' Rinaldi said. He went off up the stairs, I sat at the table and he came back with the bottle and poured us each half a tumbler of cognac.

'Too much,' I said and held up the glass and sighted at the lamp on the table.

'Not for an empty stomach. It is a wonderful thing. It burns out the stomach completely. Nothing is worse for you.'

'All right.'

'Self-destruction day by day,' Rinaldi said. 'It ruins the

stomach and makes the hand shake. Just the thing for a surgeon.'

'You recommend it?'

'Heartily. I use no other. Drink it down, baby, and look forward to being sick.'

I drank half the glass. In the hall I could hear the orderly calling. 'Soup! Soup is ready!'

The major came in, nodded to us and sat down. He seemed very small at table.

'Is this all we are?' he asked. The orderly put the soup bowl down and he ladled out a plate full.

'We are all,' Rinaldi said. 'Unless the priest comes. If he knew Federico was here he would be here.'

'Where is he?' I asked.

'He's at 307,' the major said. He was busy with his soup. He wiped his mouth, wiping his upturned grey moustache carefully. 'He will come I think. I called them and left word to tell him you were here.'

'I miss the noise of the mess,' I said.

'Yes, it's quiet,' the major said.

'I will be noisy,' said Rinaldi.

'Drink some wine, Enrico,' said the major. He filled my glass. The spaghetti came in and we were all busy. We were finishing the spaghetti when the priest came in. He was the same as ever, small and brown and compact looking. I stood up and we shook hands. He put his hand on my shoulder.

'I came as soon as I heard,' he said.

'Sit down,' the major said. 'You're late.'

'Good evening, priest,' Rinaldo said, using the English word. They had taken that up from the priest-baiting captain, who spoke a little English. 'Good evening, Rinaldo,' the priest said. The orderly brought him soup but he said he would start with the spaghetti.

'How are you?' he asked me.

'Fine,' I said. 'How have things been?'

'Drink some wine, priest,' Rinaldi said. 'Take a little wine for your stomach's sake. That's Saint Paul, you know.'

'Yes I know,' said the priest politely. Rinaldi filled his glass.

'That Saint Paul,' said Rinaldi. 'He's the one who makes all the trouble.' The priest looked at me and smiled. I could see that the baiting did not touch him now.

'That Saint Paul,' Rinaldi said. 'He was a rounder and a chaser and then when he was no longer hot he said it was no good. When he was finished he made the rules for us who are still hot. Isn't it true, Federico?'

The major smiled. We were eating meat stew now.

'I never discuss a Saint after dark,' I said. The priest looked up from the stew and smiled at me.

'There he is, gone over with the priest,' Rinaldi said. 'Where are all the good old priest-baiters? Where is Cavalcanti? Where is Brundi? Where is Cesare? Do I have to bait this priest alone without support?'

'He is a good priest,' said the major.

'He is a good priest,' said Rinaldi. 'But still a priest. I try to make the mess like the old days. I want to make Federico happy. To hell with you, priest!'

I saw the major look at him and notice that he was drunk. His thin face was white. The line of his hair was very black against the white of his forehead.

'It's all right, Rinaldo,' said the priest. 'It's all right.'

'To hell with you,' said Rinaldi. 'To hell with the whole damn business.' He sat back in his chair.

'He's been under a strain and he's tired,' the major said to me. He finished his meat and wiped up the gravy with a piece of bread.

'I don't give a damn,' Rinaldi said to the table. 'To hell with the whole business.' He looked defiantly around the table, his eyes flat, his face pale.

'All right,' I said. 'To hell with the whole damn business.'

'No, no,' said Rinaldi. 'You can't do it. You can't do it. I say you can't do it. You're dry and you're empty and there's nothing else. There's nothing else I tell you. Not a damned thing. I know, when I stop working.'

The priest shook his head. The orderly took away the stew dish.

'What are you eating meat for?' Rinaldi turned to the priest. 'Don't you know it's Friday?'

'It's Thursday,' the priest said.

'It's a lie. It's Friday. You're eating the body of our Lord. It's God-meat. I know. It's dead Austrian. That's what you're eating.'

'The white meat is from officers,' I said, completing the old joke.

Rinaldi laughed. He filled his glass.

'Don't mind me,' he said. 'I'm just a little crazy.'

'You ought to have a leave,' the priest said.

The major shook his head at him. Rinaldi looked at the priest.

'You think I ought to have a leave?'

The major shook his head at the priest. Rinaldi was looking at the priest.

'Just as you like,' the priest said. 'Not if you don't want.'

'To hell with you,' Rinaldi said. 'They try to get rid of me. Every night they try to get rid of me. I fight them off. What if I have it. Everybody has it. The whole world's got it. First,' he went on, assuming the manner of a lecturer, 'it's a little pimple. Then we notice a rash between the shoulders. Then we notice nothing at all. We put our faith in mercury.'

'Or salvarsan,' the major interrupted quietly.

'A mercurial product,' Rinaldi said. He acted very elated now. 'I know something worth two of that. Good old priest,' he said. 'You'll never get it. Baby will get it. It's an industrial accident. It's a simple industrial accident.'

The orderly brought in the sweet and coffee. The dessert was a sort of black bread pudding with hard sauce. The lamp was smoking; the black smoke going close up inside the chimney.

'Bring two candles and take away the lamp,' the major said. The orderly brought two lighted candles each in a saucer, and took out the lamp blowing it out. Rinaldi was quiet now. He seemed all right. We talked and after the coffee we all went out into the hall.

'You want to talk to the priest. I have to go in the town,' Rinaldi said. 'Good-night, priest.'

'Good-night, Rinaldo,' the priest said.

'I'll see you Fredi,' Rinaldo said.

'Yes,' I said. 'Come in early.' He made a face and went out

213

the door. The major was standing with us. 'He's very tired and over-worked,' he said. 'He thinks too he has syphilis. I don't believe it but he may have. He is treating himself for it. Good-night. You will leave before daylight, Enrico?'

'Yes.'

'Good-bye then,' he said. 'Good luck. Peduzzi will wake you and go with you.'

'Good-bye, Signor Maggiore.'

'Good-bye. They talk about an Austrian offensive but I don't believe it. I hope not. But anyway it won't be here. Gino will tell you everything. The telephone works well now.'

'I'll call regularly.'

'Please do. Good-night. Don't let Rinaldi drink so much brandy.'

'I'll try not to.'

'Good-night, priest.'

'Good-night, Signor Maggiore.'

He went off into his office.

Chapter II

I went to the door and looked out. It had stopped raining but there was a mist.

'Should we go upstairs?' I asked the priest.

'I can only stay a little while.'

'Come on up.'

We climbed the stairs and went into my room. I lay down on Rinaldi's bed. The priest sat on my cot that the orderly had set up. It was dark in the room.

'Well,' he said, 'how are you really?'

'I'm all right. I'm tired tonight.'

'I'm tired too, but from no cause.'

'What about the war?'

'I think it will be over soon. I don't know why, but I feel it.'

'How do you feel it?'

'You know how your major is? Gentle? Many people are like that now.'

'I feel that way myself,' I said.

'It has been a terrible summer,' said the priest. He was surer of himself now than when I had gone away. 'You cannot believe how it has been. Except that you have been there and you know how it can be. Many people have realized the war this summer. Officers whom I thought could never realize it realize it now.'

'What will happen?' I stroked the blanket with my hand.

'I do not know but I do not think it can go on much longer.'

'What will happen?'

'They will stop fighting.'

'Who?'

'Both sides.'

'I hope so,' I said.

'You don't believe it?'

'I don't believe both sides will stop fighting at once.'

'I suppose not. It is too much to expect. But when I see the changes in men I do not think it can go on.'

'Who won the fighting this summer?'

'No one.'

'The Austrians won,' I said. 'They kept them from taking San Gabriele. They've won. They won't stop fighting.'

'If they feel as we feel they may stop. They have gone through the same thing.'

'No one ever stopped when they were winning.'

'You discourage me.'

'I can only say what I think.'

'Then you think it will go on and on? Nothing will ever happen?'

'I don't know. I only think the Austrians will not stop when they have won a victory. It is in defeat that we become Christian.'

'The Austrians are Christians – except for the Bosnians.'

'I don't mean technically Christian. I mean like Our Lord.'

He said nothing.

'We are all gentler now because we are beaten. How would Our Lord have been if Peter had rescued him in the Garden?'

'He would have been just the same.'

'I don't think so,' I said.

'You discourage me,' he said. 'I believe and I pray that something will happen. I have felt it very close.'

'Something may happen,' I said. 'But it will happen only to us. If they felt the way we do, it would be all right. But they have beaten us. They feel another way.'

'Many of the soldiers have always felt this way. It is not because they were beaten.'

'They were beaten to start with. They were beaten when they took them from their farms and put them in the army. That is why the peasant has wisdom, because he is defeated from the start. Put him in power and see how wise he is.'

He did not say anything. He was thinking.

'Now I am depressed myself,' I said. 'That's why I never think about these things. I never think and yet when I begin to talk I say the things I have found out in my mind without thinking.'

'I had hoped for something.'

'Defeat?'

'No. Something more.'

'There isn't anything more. Except victory. It may be worse.'

'I hoped for a long time for victory.'

'Me too.'

'Now I don't know.'

'It has to be one or the other.'

'I don't believe in victory any more.'

'I don't. But I don't believe in defeat. Though it may be better.'

'What do you believe in?'

'In sleep,' I said. He stood up.

'I am very sorry to have stayed so long. But I like so to talk with you.'

'It is very nice to talk again. I said that about sleeping, meaning nothing.'

We stood up and shook hands in the dark.

'I sleep at 307 now,' he said.

'I go out on post early tomorrow.'

'I'll see you when you come back.'

'We'll have a walk and talk together.' I walked with him to the door.

'Don't go down,' he said. 'It is very nice that you are back. Though not so nice for you.' He put his hand on my shoulder.

'It's all right for me,' I said. 'Good-night.'

'Good-night. Ciaou!'

'Ciaou!' I said. I was deadly sleepy.

Chapter III

I woke when Rinaldi came in but he did not talk and I went back to sleep again. In the morning I was dressed and gone before it was light. Rinaldi did not wake when I left.

I had not seen the Bainsizza before and it was strange to go up the slope where the Austrians had been, beyond the place on the river where I had been wounded. There was a steep new road and many trucks. Beyond, the road flattened out and I saw woods and steep hills in the mist. There were woods that had been taken quickly and not smashed. Then beyond where the road was not protected by the hills it was screened by matting on the sides and over the top. The road ended in a wrecked village. The lines were up beyond. There was much artillery around. The houses were badly smashed but things were very well organized and there were sign-boards every-where. We found Gino and he got us some coffee and later I went with him and met various people and saw the posts. Gino said the British cars were working further down the Bainsizza at Ravne. He had great admiration for the British. There was still a certain amount of shelling, he said, but not many wounded. There would be many sick now the rains had started. The Austrians were supposed to attack but he did not believe it. We were supposed to attack too, but they had not brought up any new troops so he thought that was off too. Food was scarce and he would be glad to get a full meal in

Gorizia. What kind of supper had I had? I told him and he said that would be wonderful. He was especially impressed by the *dolce*. I did not describe it in detail, only said it was a *dolce*, and I think he believed it was something more elaborate than bread pudding.

Did I know where he was going to go? I said I didn't but that some of the other cars were at Caporetto. He hoped he would go up that way. It was a nice little place and he liked the high mountain hauling up beyond. He was a nice boy and everyone seemed to like him. He said where it really had been hell was at San Gabriele and the attack beyond Lom that had gone bad. He said the Austrians had a great amount of artillery in the woods along Ternova right beyond and above us, and shelled the roads badly at night. There was a battery of naval guns that had gotten on his nerves. I would recognize them because of their flat trajectory. You heard the report and then the shriek commenced almost instantly. They usually fired two guns at once, one right after the other, and the fragments from the burst were enormous. He showed me one, a smoothly jagged piece of metal over a foot long. It looked like babbitting metal.

'I don't suppose they are so effective,' Gino said. 'But they scare me. They all sound as though they came directly for you. There is the boom, then instantly the shriek and burst. What's the use of not being wounded if they scare you to death?'

He said there were Croats in the lines opposite us now and some Magyars. Our troops were still in the attacking positions. There was no wire to speak of and no place to fall back to if there should be an Austrian attack. There were fine positions for defence along the low mountains that came up out of the plateau but nothing had been done about organizing them for defence. What did I think about the Bainsizza anyway?

I had expected it to be flatter, more like a plateau. I had not realized it was so broken up.

'Alto piano,' Gino said, 'but no piano.'

We went back to the cellar of the house where he lived. I said I thought a ridge that flattened out on top and had a little depth would be easier and more practical to hold than a succession of small mountains. It was no harder to attack up a

218

mountain than on the level, I argued. 'That depends on the mountains,' he said. 'Look at San Gabriele.'

'Yes,' I said, 'but where they had trouble was at the top where it was flat. They got up to the top easy enough.'

'Not so easy,' he said.

'Yes,' I said, 'but that was a special case because it was a fortress rather than a mountain, anyway. The Austrians had been fortifying it for years.' I meant tactically speaking in a war where there was some movement a succession of mountains were nothing to hold as a line because it was too easy to turn them. You should have possible mobility and a mountain is not very mobile. Also, people always over-shoot down hill. If the flank were turned, the best men would be left on the highest mountains. I did not believe in a war in mountains. I had thought about it a lot, I said. You pinched off one mountain and they pinched off another but when something really started every one had to get down off the mountains.

What were you going to do if you had a mountain frontier? he asked.

I had not worked that out yet, I said, and we both laughed. 'But,' I said, 'in the old days the Austrians were always whipped in the quadrilateral around Verona. They let them come down onto the plain and whipped them there.'

'Yes,' said Gino. 'But those were Frenchmen and you can work out military problems clearly when you are fighting in somebody else's country.'

'Yes,' I agreed, 'when it is your own country you cannot use it so scientifically.'

'The Russians did, to trap Napoleon.'

'Yes, but they had plenty of country. If you tried to retreat to trap Napoleon in Italy you would find yourself in Brindisi.'

'A terrible place,' said Gino. 'Have you ever been there?'

'Not to stay.'

'I am a patriot,' Gino said. 'But I cannot love Brindisi or Taranto.'

'Do you love the Bainsizza?' I asked.

'The soil is sacred,' he said. 'But I wish it grew more potatoes. You know when we came here we found fields of potatoes the Austrians had planted.'

'Has the food really been short?'

'I myself have never had enough to eat but I am a big eater and I have not starved. The mess is average. The regiments in the line get pretty good food but those in support don't get so much. Something is wrong somewhere. There should be plenty of food.'

'The dogfish are selling it somewhere else.'

'Yes, they give the battalions in the front line as much as they can but the ones in back are very short. They have eaten all the Austrians' potatoes and chestnuts from the woods. They ought to feed them better. We are big eaters. I am sure there is plenty of food. It is very bad for the soldiers to be short of food. Have you ever noticed the difference it makes in the way you think?'

'Yes,' I said. 'It can't win a war but it can lose one.'

'We won't talk about losing. There is enough talk about losing. What has been done this summer cannot have been done in vain.'

I did not say anything. I was always embarrassed by the words sacred, glorious, and sacrifice and the expression in vain. We had heard them, sometimes standing in the rain almost out of earshot, so that only the shouted words came through, and had read them, on proclamations that were slapped up by bill posters over other proclamations, now for a long time, and I had seen nothing sacred, and the things that were glorious had no glory and the sacrifices were like the stockyards at Chicago if nothing was done with the meat except to bury it. There were many words that you could not stand to hear and finally only the names of places had dignity. Certain numbers were the same way and certain dates and these with the names of the places were all you could say and have them mean anything. Abstract words such as glory, honour, courage, or hallow were obscene beside the concrete names of villages, the numbers of roads, the names of rivers, the numbers of regiments and the dates. Gino was a patriot, so he said things that separated us sometimes, but he was also a fine boy and I understood his being a patriot. He was born one. He left with Peduzzi in the car to go back to Gorizia.

It stormed all that day. The wind drove down the rain and everywhere there was standing water and mud. The plaster of the broken houses was grey and wet. Late in the afternoon the rain stopped and from out number two post I saw the bare wet autumn country with clouds over the tops of the hills and the straw screening over the roads wet and dripping. The sun came out once before it went down and shone on the bare woods beyond the ridge. There were many Austrian guns in the woods on that ridge but only a few fired. I watched the sudden round puffs of shrapnel smoke in the sky above a broken farmhouse near where the line was; soft puffs with a yellow white flash in the centre. You saw the flash, then heard the crack, then saw the smoke ball distort and thin in the wind. There were many iron shrapnel balls in the rubble of the houses and on the road beside the broken house where the post was, but they did not shell near the post that afternoon. We loaded two cars and drove down the road that was screened with wet mats and the last of the sun came through in the breaks between the strips of mattings. Before we were out on the clear road behind the hill the sun was down. We went on down the clear road and as it turned a corner into the open and went into the square arched tunnel of matting the rain started again.

The wind rose in the night and at three o'clock in the morning with the rain coming in sheets there was a bombardment and the Croatians came over across the mountain meadows and through patches of woods and into the front line. They fought in the dark in the rain and a counter-attack of scared men from the second line drove them back. There was much shelling and many rockets in the rain and machine-gun and rifle fire all along the line. They did not come again and it was quieter and between the gusts of wind and rain we could hear the sound of a great bombardment far to the north.

The wounded were coming into the post, some were carried on stretchers, some walking and some were brought on the backs of men that came across the field. They were wet to the skin and all were scared. We filled two cars with stretcher cases as they came up from the cellar of the post and as I shut the door of the second car and fastened it I felt the rain on my face turn to snow. The flakes were coming heavy and fast in the rain.

When daylight came the storm was still blowing but the snow had stopped. It had melted as it fell on the wet ground and now it was raining again. There was another attack just after daylight but it was unsuccessful. We expected an attack all day but it did not come until the sun was going down. The bombardment started to the south below the long wooded ridge where the Austrian guns were concentrated. We expected a bombardment but it did not come. It was getting dark. Guns were firing from the field behind the village and the shells, going away, had a comfortable sound.

We heard that the attack to the south had been unsuccessful. They did not attack that night but we heard that they had broken through to the north. In the night word came that we were to prepare to retreat. The captain at the post told me this. He had it from the Brigade. A little while later he came from the telephone and said it was a lie. The Brigade had received orders that the line of the Bainsizza should be held no matter what happened. I asked about the break through and he said that he had heard at the Brigade that the Austrians had broken through the twenty-seventh army corps up toward Caporetto. There had been a great battle in the north all day.

'If those bastards let them through we are cooked,' he said.

'It's Germans that are attacking,' one of the medical officers said. The word Germans was something to be frightened of. We did not want to have anything to do with the Germans.

'There are fifteen divisions of Germans,' the medical officer said. 'They have broken through and we will be cut off.'

'At the Brigade, they say this line is to be held. They say they have not broken through badly and that we will hold a line across the mountains from Monte Maggiore.'

'Where do they hear this?'

'From the Division.'

'The word that we were to retreat came from the Division.'

'We work under the Army Corps,' I said. 'But here I work under you. Naturally when you tell me to go I will go. But get the orders straight.'

'The orders are that we stay here. You clear the wounded from here to the clearing station.'

'Sometimes we clear from the clearing station to the field

hospitals too,' I said. 'Tell me, I have never seen a retreat – if there is a retreat how are all the wounded evacuated?'

'They are not. They take as many as they can and leave the rest.'

'What will I take in the cars?'

'Hospital equipment.'

'All right,' I said.

The next night the retreat started. We heard that Germans and Austrians had broken through in the north and were coming down the mountain valleys toward Cividale and Udine. The retreat was orderly, wet and sullen. In the night, going slowly along the crowded roads we passed troops marching under the rain, guns, horses pulling wagons, mules, motor trucks, all moving away from the front. There was no more disorder than in an advance.

That night we helped empty the field hospitals that had been set up in the least ruined villages of the plateau, taking the wounded down to Plava on the river-bed: and the next day hauled all day in the rain to evacuate the hospitals and clearing station at Plava. It rained steadily and the army of the Bainsizza moved down off the plateau in the October rain and across the river where the great victories had commenced in the spring of that year. We came into Gorizia in the middle of the next day. The rain had stopped and the town was nearly empty. As we came up the street they were loading the girls from the soldiers' whorehouse into a truck. There were seven girls and they had on their hats and coats and carried small suitcases. Two of them were crying. Of the others one smiled at us and put out her tongue and fluttered it up and down. She had thick full lips and black eyes.

I stopped the car and went over and spoke to the matron. The girls from the officers' house had left early that morning, she said. Where were they going? To Conegliano, she said. The truck started. The girl with thick lips put out her tongue again at us. The matron waved. The two girls kept on crying. The others looked interestedly out at the town. I got back in the car.

'We ought to go with them,' Bonello said. 'That would be a good trip.'

'We'll have a good trip,' I said.

'We'll have a hell of a trip.'

'That's what I mean,' I said. We came up the drive to the villa.

'I'd like to be there when some of those tough babies climb in and try and hop them.'

'You think they will?'

'Sure. Everybody in the Second Army knows that matron.'

We were outside the villa.

'They call her the Mother Superior,' Bonello said. 'The girls are new but everybody knows her. They must have brought them up just before the retreat.'

'They'll have a time.'

'I'll say they'll have a time. I'd like to have a crack at them for nothing. They charge too much at that house anyway. The government gyps us.'

'Take the car out and have the mechanics go over it,' I said. 'Change the oil and check the differential. Fill it up and then get some sleep.'

'Yes, Signor Tenente.'

The villa was empty. Rinaldi was gone with the hospital. The major was gone taking hospital personnel in the staff car. There was a note on the window for me to fill the cars with the material piled in the hall and to proceed to Pordenone. The mechanics were gone already. I went out back to the garage. The other two cars came in while I was there and their drivers got down. It was starting to rain again.

'I'm so — sleepy I went to sleep three times coming here from Plava,' Piani said. 'What are we going to do, Tenente?'

'We'll change the oil, grease them, fill them up, then take them around in front and load up the junk they've left.'

'Then do we start?'

'No, we'll sleep for three hours.'

'Christ I'm glad to sleep,' Bonello said. 'I couldn't keep awake driving.'

'How's your car, Aymo?' I asked.

'It's all right.'

'Get me a monkey suit and I'll help you with the oil.'

'Don't you do that, Tenente,' Aymo said. 'It's nothing to do. You go and pack your things.'

224

'My things are all packed,' I said. 'I'll go and carry out the stuff that they left for us. Bring the cars around as soon as they're ready.'

They brought the cars around to the front of the villa and we loaded them with the hospital equipment which was piled in the hallway. When it was all in, the three cars stood in line down the driveway under the trees in the rain. We went inside.

'Make a fire in the kitchen and dry your things' I said.

'I don't care about dry clothes,' Piani said. 'I want to sleep.'

'I'm going to sleep on the major's bed,' Bonello said. 'I'm going to sleep where the old man corks off.'

'I don't care where I sleep,' Piani said.

'There are two beds in here.' I opened the door.

'I never knew what was in that room,' Bonello said.

'That was old fish-face's room,' Piani said.

'You two sleep in there,' I said. 'I'll wake you.'

'The Austrians will wake us if you sleep too long, Tenente,' Bonello said.

'I won't oversleep,' I said. 'Where's Aymo?'

'He went out in the kitchen.'

'Get to sleep,' I said.

'I'll sleep,' Piani said. 'I've been asleep sitting up all day. The whole top of my head kept coming down over my eyes.'

'Take your boots off,' Bonello said. 'That's old fish-face's bed.'

'Fish-face is nothing to me.' Piani lay on the bed, his muddy boots straight out, his head on his arm. I went out to the kitchen. Aymo had a fire in the stove and a kettle of water on.

'I thought I'd start some *pasta asciutta*,' he said. 'We'll be hungry when we wake up.'

'Aren't you sleepy, Bartolomeo?'

'Not so sleepy. When the water boils I'll leave it. The fire will go down.'

'You'd better get some sleep,' I said. 'We can eat cheese and monkey meat.'

'This is better,' he said. 'Something hot will be good for those two anarchists. You go to sleep, Tenente.'

'There's a bed in the major's room.'

'You sleep there.'

225

'No, I'm going up to my old room. Do you want a drink, Bartolomeo?'

'When we go, Tenente. Now it wouldn't do me any good.'

'If you wake in three hours and I haven't called you, wake me, will you?'

'I haven't any watch, Tenente.'

'There's a clock on the wall in the major's room.'

'All right.'

I went out then through the dining-room and the hall and up the marble stairs to the room where I had lived with Rinaldi. It was raining outside. I went to the window and looked out. It was getting dark and I saw the three cars standing in line under the trees. The trees were dripping in the rain. It was cold and the drops hung to the branches. I went back to Rinaldi's bed and lay down and let sleep take me.

We ate in the kitchen before we started. Aymo had a basin of spaghetti with onions and tinned meat chopped up in it. We sat around the table and drank two bottles of the wine that had been left in the cellar of the villa. It was dark outside and still raining. Piani sat at the table very sleepy.

'I like a retreat better than an advance,' Bonello said. 'On a retreat we drink barbera.'

'We drink it now. Tomorrow maybe we drink rainwater,' Aymo said.

'Tomorrow we'll be in Udine. We'll drink champagne. That's where the slackers live. Wake up, Piani! We'll drink champagne tomorrow in Udine!'

'I'm awake,' Piani said. He filled his plate with the spaghetti and meat. 'Couldn't you find tomato sauce, Barto?'

'There wasn't any,' Aymo said.

'We'll drink champagne in Udine,' Bonello said. He filled his glass with the clear red barbera.

'Have you eaten enough, Tenente?' Aymo asked. 'I've got plenty. Give me the bottle, Bartolomeo.'

'I have a bottle apiece to take in the cars,' Aymo said.

'Did you sleep at all?'

'I don't need much sleep. I slept a little.'

'Tomorrow we'll sleep in the king's bed,' Bonello said. He was feeling very good.

'I'll sleep with the queen,' Bonello said. He looked to see how I took the joke.

'Shut up,' I said. 'You get too funny with a little wine.' Outside it was raining hard. I looked at my watch. It was half past nine.

'It's time to roll,' I said and stood up.

'Who are you going to ride with, Tenente?' Bonello asked.

'With Aymo. Then you come. Then Piani. We'll start out on the road for Cormons.'

'I'm afraid I'll go to sleep,' Piani said.

'All right. I'll ride with you. Then Bonello. Then Aymo.'

'That's the best way,' Piani said. 'Because I'm so sleepy.'

'I'll drive and you sleep awhile.'

'No. I can drive just so long as I know somebody will wake me up if I go to sleep.'

'I'll wake you up. Put out the lights, Barto.'

'You might as well leave them,' Bonello said. 'We've got no more use for this place.'

'I have a small locker trunk in my room,' I said. 'Will you help take it down, Piani?'

'We'll take it,' Piani said. 'Come on, Aldo.' He went off into the hall with Bonello. I heard them going upstairs.

'This was a fine place,' Bartolomeo Aymo said. He put two bottles of wine and half a cheese into his haversack. 'There won't be a place like this again. Where will they retreat to, Tenente?'

'Beyond the Tagliamento, they say. The hospital and the sector are to be at Pordenone.'

'This is a better town than Pordenone.'

'I don't know Pordenone,' I said. 'I've just been through there.'

'It's not much of a place,' Aymo said.

Chapter IV

As we moved out through the town it was empty in the rain and the dark except for columns of troops and guns that were going through the main street. There were many trucks too and some carts going through on other streets and converging on the main road. When we were out past the tanneries onto the main road the troops, the motor trucks, the horse-drawn carts and the guns were in one wide slow-moving column. We moved slowly but steadily in the rain, the radiator cap of our car almost against the tailboard of a truck that was loaded high, the load covered with wet canvas. Then the truck stopped. The whole column was stopped. It started again and we went a little farther, then stopped. I got out and walked ahead, going between the trucks and carts and under the wet necks of the horses. The block was farther ahead. I left the road, crossed the ditch on a footboard and walked along the field beyond the ditch. I could see the stalled column between the trees in the rain as I went forward across from it in the field. I went about a mile. The column did not move, although, on the other side beyond the stalled vehicles, I could see the troops moving. I went back to the cars. This block might extend as far as Udine. Piani was asleep over the wheel. I climbed up beside him and went to sleep too. Several hours later I heard the truck ahead of us grinding into gear. I woke Piani and we started, moving a few yards, then stopping, then going on again. It was still raining.

The column stalled again in the night and did not start. I got down and went back to see Aymo and Bonello. Bonello had two sergeants of engineers on the seat of his car with him. They stiffened when I came up.

'They were left to do something to a bridge,' Bonello said. 'They can't find their unit so I gave them a ride.'

'With the Sir Lieutenant's permission.'

'With permission,' I said.

228

'The lieutenant is an American,' Bonello said. 'He'll give anybody a ride.'

One of the sergeants smiled. The other asked Bonello if I was an Italian from North or South America.

'He's not an Italian. He's North American English.'

The sergeants were polite but did not believe it. I left them and went back to Aymo. He had two girls on the seat with him and was sitting back in the corner and smoking.

'Barto, Barto,' I said. He laughed.

'Talk to them, Tenente,' he said. 'I can't understand them. Hey!' he put his hand on the girl's thigh and squeezed it in a friendly way. The girl drew her shawl tight around her and pushed his hand away. 'Hey!' he said. 'Tell the Tenente your name and what you're doing here.'

The girl looked at me fiercely. The other girl kept her eyes down. The girl who looked at me said something in a dialect I could not understand a word of. She was plump and dark and looked about sixteen.

'Sorella?' I asked and pointed at the other girl.

She nodded her head and smiled.

'All right,' I said and patted her knee. I felt her stiffen away when I touched her. The sister never looked up. She looked perhaps a year younger. Aymo put his hand on the elder girl's thigh and she pushed it away. He laughed at her.

'Good man,' he pointed at himself. 'Good man,' he pointed at me. 'Don't you worry.' The girl looked at him fiercely. The pair of them were like two wild birds.

'What does she ride with me for if she doesn't like me?' Aymo asked. 'They got right up in the car the minute I motioned to them.' He turned to the girl. 'Don't worry,' he said. 'No danger of—,' using the vulgar word. 'No place for—.' I could see she understood the word and that was all. Her eyes looked at him very scared. She pulled the shawl tight. 'Car all full,' Aymo said. 'No danger of—. No place for—.' Every time he said the word the girl stiffened a little. Then sitting stiffly and looking at him she began to cry. I saw her lips working and then tears came down her plump cheeks. Her sister, not looking up, took her hand and they sat together. The older one, who had been so fierce, began to sob.

229

'I guess I scared her,' Aymo said. 'I didn't mean to scare her.'

Bartolomeo brought out his knapsack and cut off two pieces of cheese. 'Here,' he said. 'Stop crying.'

The older girl shook her head and still cried, but the younger girl took the cheese and commenced to eat. After a while the younger girl gave her sister the second piece of cheese and they both ate. The older sister still sobbed a little.

'She'll be all right after a while,' Aymo said.

An idea came to him. 'Virgin?' he asked the girl next to him. She nodded her head vigorously. 'Virgin too?' he pointed to the sister. Both girls nodded their heads and the elder said something in dialect.

Both the girls seemed cheered.

I left them sitting together with Aymo sitting back in the corner and went back to Piani's car. The column of vehicles did not move but the troops kept passing alongside. It was still raining hard and I thought some of the stops in the movement of the column might be from cars with wet wiring. More likely they were from horses or men going to sleep. Still, traffic could tie up in cities when everyone was awake. It was the combination of horse and motor vehicles. They did not help each other any. The peasants' carts did not help much either. Those were a couple of fine girls with Barto. A retreat was no place for two virgins. Real virgins. Probably very religious. If there were no war we would probably all be in bed. In bed I lay me down my head. Bed and board. Stiff as a board in bed. Catherine was in bed now between two sheets, over her and under her. Which side did she sleep on? Maybe she wasn't asleep. Maybe she was lying thinking about me. Blow, blow, ye western wind. Well, it blew and it wasn't the small rain but the big rain down that rained. It rained all night. You knew it rained down that rained. Look at it, Christ, that my love were in my arms and I in bed again. That my love Catherine. That my sweet love Catherine down might rain. Blow her again to me. Well, we were in it. Everyone was caught in it and the small rain would not quiet it. 'Good-night, Catherine,' I said out loud. 'I hope you sleep well. If it's too uncomfortable, darling, lie on the other side,' I said. 'I'll get you some cold water. In a little while it will be morning and then it won't be so bad. I'm sorry he makes you so uncomfortable. Try and go to sleep, sweet.'

I was asleep all the time, she said. You've been talking in your sleep. Are you all right?

Are you really there?

Of course I'm here. I wouldn't go away. This doesn't make any difference between us.

You're so lovely and sweet. You wouldn't go away in the night, would you?

Of course I wouldn't go away. I'm always here. I come whenever you want me.

'—,' Piani said 'They've started again.'

'I was dopey,' I said. I looked at my watch. It was three o'clock in the morning. I reached back behind the seat for a bottle of the barbera.

'You talked out loud,' Piani said.

'I was having a dream in English,' I said.

The rain was slacking and we were moving along. Before daylight we were stalled again and when it was light we were at a little rise in the ground and I saw the road of the retreat stretched out far ahead, everything stationary except for the infantry filtering through. We started to move again but seeing the rate of progress in the daylight, I knew we were going to have to get off that main road some way and go across country if we ever hoped to reach Udine.

In the night peasants had joined the column from the roads of the country and in the column there were carts loaded with household goods; there were mirrors projecting up between mattresses, and chickens and ducks tied to carts. There was a sewing-machine on the cart ahead of us in the rain. They had saved the most valuable things. On some carts the women sat huddled from the rain and others walked beside the carts keeping as close to them as they could. There were dogs now in the column, keeping under the wagons as they moved. along. The road was muddy, the ditches at the side were high with water and beyond the trees that lined the road the fields looked too wet and too soggy to try to cross. I got down from the car and worked up the road a way, looking for a place where I could

231

see ahead to find a side-road we could take across country. I knew there were many side-roads but did not want one that would lead to nothing. I could not remember them because we had always passed them bowling along in the car on the main road and they all looked much alike. Now I knew we must find one if we hoped to get through. No one knew where the Austrians were nor how things were going but I was certain that if the rain should stop and planes come over and get to work on that column that it would be all over. All that was needed was for a few men to leave their trucks or a few horses be killed to tie up completely the movement on the road.

The rain was not falling so heavily now and I thought it might clear. I went ahead along the edge of the road and when there was a small road that led off to the north between two fields with a hedge of trees on both sides, I thought that we had better take it and hurried back to the cars. I told Piani to turn off and went back to tell Bonello and Aymo.

'If it leads nowhere we can turn around and cut back in,' I said.

'What about these?' Bonello asked. His two sergeants were beside him on the seat. They were unshaven but still military looking in the early morning.

'They'll be good to push,' I said. I went back to Aymo and told him we were going to try it across country.

'What about my virgin family?' Aymo asked. The two girls were asleep.

'They won't be very useful,' I said. 'You ought to have someone that could push.'

'They could go back in the car,' Aymo said. 'There's room in the car.'

'All right if you want them,' I said. 'Pick up somebody with a wide back to push.'

'Bersaglieri,' Aymo smiled. 'They have the widest backs. They measure them. How do you feel, Tenente?'

'Fine. How are you?'

'Fine. But very hungry.'

'There ought to be something up that road and we will stop and eat.'

'How's your leg, Tenente?'

232

'Fine,' I said. Standing on the step and looking up ahead I could see Piani's car pulling out on to the little side-road and starting up it, his car showing through the hedge of bare branches. Bonello turned off and followed him and then Piani worked his way out and we followed the two ambulances ahead along the narrow road between hedges. It led to a farmhouse. We found Piani and Bonello stopped in the farmyard. The house was low and long with a trellis with a grape-vine over the door. There was a well in the yard and Piani was getting up water to fill his radiator. So much going in low gear had boiled it out. The farmhouse was deserted. I looked back down the road, the farmhouse was on a slight elevation above the plain, and we could see over the country, and saw the road, the hedges, the fields and the line of trees along the main road where the retreat was passing. The two sergeants were looking through the house. The girls were awake and looking at the courtyard, the well and the two big ambulances in front of the farmhouse, with three drivers at the well. One of the sergeants came out with a clock in his hand.

'Put it back,' I said. He looked at me, went in the house and came back without the clock.

'Where's your partner?' I asked.

'He's gone to the latrine.' He got up on the seat of the ambulance. He was afraid we would leave him.

'What about breakfast, Tenente?' Bonello asked. 'We could eat something. It wouldn't take very long.'

'Do you think this road going down on the other side will lead to anything?'

'Sure.'

'All right. Let's eat.' Piani and Bonello went in the house.

'Come on,' Aymo said to the girls. He held his hand to help them down. The older sister shook her head. They were not going into any deserted house. They looked after us.

'They are difficult,' Aymo said. We went into the farmhouse together. It was large and dark, an abandoned feeling. Bonello and Piani were in the kitchen.

'There's not much to eat,' Piani said. 'They've cleaned it out.'

Bonello sliced a big white cheese on the heavy kitchen table.

233

'Where was the cheese?'

'In the cellar. Piani found wine too and apples.'

'That's a good breakfast.'

Piani was taking the wooden cork out of a big wicker-covered wine jug. He tipped it and poured a copper pan full.

'It smells all right,' he said. 'Find some beakers, Barto.'

The two sergeants came in.

'Have some cheese, sergeants,' Bonello said.

'We should go,' one of the sergeants said, eating his cheese and drinking a cup of wine.

'We'll go. Don't worry,' Bonello said.

'An army travels on its stomach,' I said.

'What?' asked the sergeant.

'It's better to eat.'

'Yes. But time is precious.'

'I believe the bastards have eaten already,' Piani said. The sergeants looked at him. They hated the lot of us.

'You know the road?' one of them asked me.

'No,' I said. They looked at each other.

'We would do best to start,' the first one said.

'We are starting,' I said. I drank another cup of the red wine. It tasted very good after the cheese and apple.

'Bring the cheese,' I said and went out. Bonello came out carrying the great jug of wine.

'That's too big,' I said. He looked at it regretfully.

'I guess it is,' he said. 'Give me the canteens to fill.' He filled the canteens and some of the wine ran out on the stone paving of the courtyard. Then he picked up the wine jug and put it just inside the door.

'The Austrians can find it without breaking the door down,' he said.

'We'll roll,' I said. 'Piani and I will go ahead.' The two engineers were already on the seat beside Bonello. The girls were eating cheese and apples. Aymo was smoking. We started off down the narrow road. I looked back at the two cars coming and the farmhouse. It was a fine, low, solid stone house and the ironwork of the well was very good. Ahead of us the road was narrow and muddy and there was a high hedge on either side. Behind, the cars were following closely.

Chapter V

At noon we were stuck in a muddy road about, as nearly as we could figure, ten kilometres from Udine. The rain had stopped during the forenoon and three times we had heard planes coming, seen them pass overhead, watched them go far to the left and heard them bombing on the main highroad. We had worked through a network of secondary roads and had taken many roads that were blind, but had always, by backing up and finding another road, gotten closer to Udine. Now Aymo's car, in backing so that we might get out of a blind road, had gotten into the soft earth at the side and the wheels, spinning, had dug deeper and deeper until the car rested on its differential. The thing to do now was to dig out in front of the wheels, put in brush so that the chains could grip, and then push until the car was on the road. We were all down on the road around the car. The two sergeants looked at the car and examined the wheels. Then they started off down the road without a word. I went after them.

'Come on,' I said. 'Cut some brush.'

'We have to go,' one said.

'Get busy,' I said, 'and cut brush.'

'We have to go,' one said. The other said nothing. They were in a hurry to start. They would not look at me. 'I order you to come back to the car and cut brush,' I said.

The one sergeant turned. 'We have to go on. In a little while you will be cut off. You can't order us. You're not our officer.'

'I order you to cut brush,' I said. They turned and started down the road.

'Halt,' I said. They kept on down the muddy road, the hedge on either side. 'I order you to halt,' I called. They went a little faster. I opened up my holster, took the pistol, aimed at the one who had talked the most, and fired. I missed and they both started to run. I shot three times and dropped one. The

235

other went through the hedge and was out of sight. I fired at him through the hedge as he ran across the field. The pistol clicked empty and I put in another clip. I saw it was too far to shoot at the second sergeant. He was far across the field, running, his head held low. I commenced to reload the empty clip. Bonello came up.

'Let me go finish him,' he said. I handed him the pistol and he walked down to where the sergeant of engineers lay face down across the road. Bonello leaned over, put the pistol against the man's head and pulled the trigger. The pistol did not fire.

'You have to cock it,' I said. He cocked it and fired twice. He took hold of the sergeant's legs and pulled him to the side of the road so he lay beside the hedge. He came back and handed me the pistol.

'The son of a bitch,' he said. He looked toward the sergeant. 'You see me shoot him, Tenente?'

'We've got to get the brush quickly,' I said. 'Did I hit the other one at all?'

'I don't think so,' Aymo said. 'He was too far away to hit with a pistol.'

'The dirty scum,' Piani said. We were all cutting twigs and branches. Everything had been taken out of the car. Bonello was digging out in front of the wheels. When we were ready Aymo started the car and put it into gear. The wheels spun round throwing brush and mud. Bonello and I pushed until we could feel our joints crack. The car would not move.

'Rock her back and forth, Barto,' I said.

He drove the engine in reverse, then forward. The wheels only dug in deeper. Then the car was resting on the differential again and the wheels spun freely in holes they had dug. I straightened up.

'We'll try her with a rope,' I said.

'I don't think it's any use, Tenente. You can't get a straight pull.'

'We have to try it,' I said. 'She won't come out any other way.'

Piani's and Bonello's cars could only move straight ahead down the narrow road. We roped both cars together and pulled. The wheels only pulled sideways against the ruts.

'It's no good,' I shouted. 'Stop it.'

Piani and Bonello got down from their cars and came back. Aymo got down. The girls were up the road about forty yards sitting on a stone wall.

'What do you say, Tenente?' Bonello asked.

'We'll dig out and try once more with the brush,' I said. I looked down the road. It was my fault. I had led them up here. The sun was almost out from behind the clouds and the body of the sergeant lay beside the hedge.

'We'll put his coat and cape under,' I said. Bonello went to get them. I cut brush and Aymo and Piani dug out in front and between the wheels. I cut the cape, then ripped it in two, and laid it under the wheel in the mud, then piled brush for the wheels to catch. We were ready to start and Aymo got up on the seat and started the car. The wheels spun and we pushed and pushed. But it wasn't any use.

'It's finished,' I said. 'Is there anything you want in the car, Barto?'

Aymo climbed up with Bonello, carrying the cheese and two bottles of wine and his cape. Bonello, sitting behind the wheel, was looking through the pockets of the sergeant's coat.

'Better throw the coat away,' I said. 'What about Barto's virgins?'

'They can get in the back,' Piani said. 'I don't think we are going far.'

I opened the back door of the ambulance.

'Come on,' I said. 'Get in.' The two girls climbed in and sat in the corner. They seemed to have taken no notice of the shooting. I looked back up the road. The sergeant lay in his dirty long-sleeved underwear. I got up with Piani and we started. We were going to try to cross the field. When the road entered the field I got down and walked ahead. If we could get across, there was a road on the other side. We could not get across. It was too soft and muddy for the cars. When they were finally and completely stalled, the wheels dug in to the hubs, we left them in the field and started on foot for Udine.

When we came to the road which led back toward the main highway I pointed down it to the girls.

'Go down there,' I said. 'You'll meet people.' They looked at me. I took out my pocket-book and gave them each a ten-lira note. 'Go down there,' I said, pointing. 'Friends! Family!'

They did not understand but they held the money tightly and started down the road. They looked back as though they were afraid I might take the money back. I watched them go down the road, their shawls close around them, looking back apprehensively at us. The three drivers were laughing.

'How much will you give me to go in that direction, Tenente?' Bonello asked.

'They're better off in a bunch of people than alone if they catch them,' I said.

'Give me two hundred lire and I'll walk straight back towards Austria,' Bonello said.

'They'd take it away from you,' Piani said.

'Maybe the war will be over,' Aymo said. We were going up the road as fast as we could. The sun was trying to come through. Beside the road were mulberry trees. Through the trees I could see our two big moving-vans of cars stuck in the field. Piani looked back too.

'They'll have to build a road to get them out,' he said.

'I wish to Christ we had bicycles,' Bonello said.

'Do they ride bicycles in America?' Aymo asked.

'They used to.'

'Here it is a great thing,' Aymo said. 'A bicycle is a splendid thing.'

'I wish to Christ we had bicycles,' Bonello said. 'I'm no walker.'

'Is that firing?' I asked. I thought I could hear firing a long way away.

'I don't know,' Aymo said. He listened.

'I think so,' I said.

'The first thing we will see will be the cavalry,' Piani said.

'I don't think they've got any cavalry.'

'I hope to Christ not,' Bonello said. 'I don't want to be stuck on a lance by any cavalry.'

'You certainly shot that sergeant, Tenente,' Piani said. We were walking fast.

'I killed him,' Bonello said. 'I never killed anybody in this war, and all my life I've wanted to kill a sergeant.'

'You killed him on the sit all right,' Piani said. 'He wasn't flying very fast when you killed him.'

'Never mind. That's one thing I can always remember. I killed that — of a sergeant.'

'What will you say in confession?' Aymo asked.

'I'll say, "Bless me, father, I killed a sergeant".' They all laughed.

'He's an anarchist,' Piani said. 'He doesn't go to church.'

'Piani's an anarchist too,' Bonello said.

'Are you really anarchists?' I asked.

'No, Tenente. We're socialists. We come from Imola.'

'Haven't you ever been there?'

'No.'

'By Christ it's a fine place, Tenente. You come there after the war and we'll show you something.'

'Are you all socialists?'

'Everybody.'

'Is it a fine town?'

'Wonderful. You never saw a town like that.'

'How did you get to be socialists?'

'We're all socialists. Everybody is a socialist. We've always been socialists.'

'You come, Tenente. We'll make you a socialist too.'

Ahead the road turned off to the left and there was a little hill and, beyond a stone wall, an apple orchard. As the road went uphill they ceased talking. We walked along together all going fast against time.

Chapter VI

Later we were on a road that led to a river. There was a long line of abandoned trucks and carts on the road leading up to the bridge. No one was in sight. The river was high and the bridge had been blown up in the centre; the stone arch was fallen into the river and the brown water was going over it. We went on up the bank looking for a place to cross. Up ahead I knew there was a railway bridge and I thought we might be able to get across there. The path was wet and muddy. We did not see any troops; only abandoned trucks and stores. Along the river bank there was nothing and no one but the wet brush and muddy ground. We went up to the bank and finally we saw the railway bridge.

'What a beautiful bridge,' Aymo said. It was a long plain iron bridge across what was usually a dry river-bed.

'We better hurry and get across before they blow it up,' I said.

'There's nobody to blow it up,' Piani said. 'They're all gone.'

'It's probably mined,' Bonello said. 'You cross first, Tenente.'

'Listen to the anarchist,' Aymo said. 'Make him go first.'

'I'll go,' I said. 'It won't be mined to blow up with one man.'

'You see,' Piani said. 'That is brains. Why haven't you brains, anarchist?'

'If I had brains I wouldn't be here,' Bonello said.

'That's pretty good, Tenente,' Aymo said.

'That's pretty good,' I said. We were close to the bridge now. The sky had clouded over again and it was raining a little. The bridge looked long and solid. We climbed up the embankment.

'Come one at a time,' I said and started across the bridge. I watched the ties and the rails for any trip-wires or signs of explosive but I saw nothing. Down below the gaps in the ties the river ran muddy and fast. Ahead across the wet country-side I could see Udine in the rain. Across the bridge I looked back. Just up the river was another bridge. As I watched, a yellow mud-coloured motor car crossed it. The sides of the bridge were high and the body of the car, once on, was out of sight. But I saw the heads of the driver, the man on the seat with him, and the two men on the rear seat. They all wore German helmets. Then the car was over the bridge and out of sight behind the trees and the abandoned vehicles on the road.

I waved to Aymo who was crossing and to the others to come on. I climbed down and crouched beside the railway embankment. Aymo came down with me.

'Did you see the car?' I asked.

'No. We were watching you.'

'A German staff car crossed on the upper bridge.'

'A staff car?'

'Yes.'

'Holy Mary.'

The others came and we all crouched in the mud behind the embankment, looking across the rails at the bridge, the line of trees, the ditch and the road.

'Do you think we're cut off then, Tenente?'

'I don't know. All I know is a German staff car went along that road.'

'You don't feel funny, Tenente? You haven't got strange feelings in the head?'

'Don't be funny, Bonello.'

'What about a drink?' Piani asked. 'If we're cut off we might as well have a drink.' He unhooked his canteen and uncorked it.

'Look! Look!' Aymo said and pointed toward the road. Along the top of the stone bridge we could see German helmets moving. They were bent forward and moved smoothly, almost supernaturally, along. As they came off the bridge we saw them. They were bicycle troops. I saw the faces of the first two. They were ruddy and healthy-looking. Their helmets came low down over their foreheads and the side of their faces. Their carbines were clipped to the frame of the bicycles. Stick bombs hung handle down from their belts. Their helmets and their grey uniforms were wet and they rode easily, looking ahead and to both sides. There were two – then four in line, then two, then almost a dozen; then another dozen – then one alone. They did not talk but we could not have heard them because of the noise from the river. They were gone out of sight up the road.

'Holy Mary,' Aymo said.

'They were Germans,' Piani said. 'Those weren't Austrians.'

'Why isn't there somebody here to stop them?' I said. 'Why

241

haven't they blown the bridge up? Why aren't there machine-guns along this embankment?'

'You tell us, Tenente,' Bonello said.

I was very angry.

'The whole bloody thing is crazy. Down below they blow up a little bridge. Here they leave a bridge on the main road. Where is everybody? Don't they try and stop them at all?'

'You tell us, Tenente,' Bonello said. I shut up. It was none of my business; all I had to do was to get to Pordenone with three ambulances. I had failed at that. All I had to do now was get to Pordenone. I probably could not even get to Udine. The hell I couldn't. The thing to do was to be calm and not get shot or captured.

'Didn't you have a canteen open?' I asked Piani. He handed it to me. I took a long drink. 'We might as well start,' I said. 'There's no hurry though. Do you want to eat something?'

'This is no place to stay,' Bonello said.

'All right. We'll start.'

'Should we keep on this side – out of sight?'

'We'd be better off on top. They may come along this bridge too. We don't want them on top of us before we see them.'

We walked along the railroad track. On both sides of us stretched the wet plain. Ahead across the plain was the hill of Udine. The roofs fell away from the castle on the hill. We could see the campanile and the clock-tower. There were many mulberry trees in the fields. Ahead I saw a place where the rails were torn up. The ties had been dug out too and thrown down the embankment.

'Down! down!' Aymo said. We dropped down beside the embankment. There was another group of bicyclists passing along the road. I looked over the edge and saw them go on.

'They saw us but they went on,' Aymo said.

'We'll get killed up there, Tenente,' Bonello said.

'They don't want us,' I said. 'They're after something else. We're in more danger if they should come on us suddenly.'

'I'd rather walk here out of sight,' Bonello said.

'All right. We'll walk along the tracks.'

'Do you think we can get through?' Aymo asked.

'Sure. There aren't very many of them yet. We'll go through in the dark.'

'What was that staff car doing?'

'Christ knows,' I said. We kept on up the tracks. Bonello tired of walking in the mud of the embankment and came up with the rest of us. The railway moved south away from the highway now and we could not see what passed along the road. A short bridge over a canal was blown up but we climbed across on what was left of the span. We heard firing ahead of us.

We came up on the railway beyond the canal. It went on straight toward the town across the low fields. We could see the line of the other railway ahead of us. To the north was the main road where we had seen the cyclists; to the south there was a small branch-road across the fields with thick trees on each side. I thought we had better cut to the south and work around the town that way and across country toward Campoformio and the main road to the Tagliamento. We could avoid the main line of the retreat by keeping to the secondary roads beyond Udine. I knew there were plenty of side-roads across the plain. I started down the embankment.

'Come on,' I said. We would make for the side-road and work to the south of the town. We all started down the embankment. A shot was fired at us from the side-road. The bullet went into the mud of the embankment.

'Go on back,' I shouted. I started up the embankment, slipping in the mud. The drivers were ahead of me. I went up the embankment as fast as I could go. Two more shots came from the thick brush and Aymo, as he was crossing the tracks, lurched, tripped and fell face down. We pulled him down on the other side and turned him over. 'His head ought to be uphill,' I said. Piani moved him around. He lay in the mud on the side of the embankment, his feet pointing downhill, breathing blood irregularly. The three of us squatted over him in the rain. He was hit low in the back of the neck and the bullet had ranged upward and come out under the right eye. He died while I was stopping up the two holes. Piani laid his head down, wiped at his face, with a piece of the emergency dressing, then let it alone.

'The bastards,' he said.

'They weren't Germans,' I said. 'There can't be any Germans over there.'

'Italians,' Piani said, using the word as an epithet, 'Italiani!' Bonello said nothing. He was sitting beside Aymo, not looking at him. Piani picked up Aymo's cap where it had rolled down the embankment and put it over his face. He took out his canteen.

'Do you want a drink?' Piani handed Bonello the canteen.

'No,' Bonello said. He turned to me. 'That might have happened to us any time on the railway tracks.'

'No,' I said. 'It was because we started across the field.'

Bonello shook his head. 'Aymo's dead,' he said. 'Who's dead next, Tenente? Where do we go now?'

'Those were Italians that shot,' I said. 'They weren't Germans.'

'I suppose if they were Germans they'd have killed all of us,' Bonello said.

'We are in more danger from Italians than Germans,' I said. 'The rear guard are afraid of everything. The Germans know what they're after.'

'You reason it out, Tenente,' Bonello said.

'Where do we go now?' Piani asked.

'We better lie up some place till it's dark. If we could get south we'd be all right.'

'They'd have to shoot us all to prove they were right the first time,' Bonello said. 'I'm not going to try them.'

'We'll find a place to lie up as near to Udine as we can get and then go through when it's dark.'

'Let's go then,' Bonello said. We went down the north side of the embankment. I looked back. Aymo lay in the mud with the angle of the embankment. He was quite small and his arms were by his side, his puttee-wrapped legs and muddy boots together, his cap over his face. He looked very dead. It was raining. I had liked him as well as anyone I ever knew. I had his papers in my pocket and would write to his family. Ahead across the fields was a farmhouse. There were trees around it and the farm buildings were built against the house. There was a balcony along the second floor held up by columns.

'We better keep a little way apart,' I said. 'I'll go ahead.' I started toward the farmhouse. There was a path across the field.

Crossing the field, I did not know but that someone would fire on us from the trees near the farmhouse or from the farmhouse itself. I walked toward it, seeing it very clearly. The balcony of the second floor merged into the barn and there was hay coming out between the columns. The courtyard was of stone blocks and all the trees were dripping with the rain. There was a big empty two-wheeled cart, the shafts tipped high up in the rain. I came to the courtyard, crossed it, and stood under the shelter of the balcony. The door of the house was open and I went in. Bonello and Piani came in after me. It was dark inside. I went back to the kitchen. There were ashes of a fire on the big open hearth. The pots hung over the ashes, but they were empty. I looked around but I could not find anything to eat.

'We ought to lie up in the barn,' I said. 'Do you think you could find anything to eat, Piani, and bring it up there?'

'I'll look,' Piani said.

'I'll look too,' Bonello said.

'All right,' I said. 'I'll go up and look at the barn.' I found a stone stairway that went up from the stable underneath. The stable smelt dry and pleasant in the rain. The cattle were all gone, probably driven off when they left. The barn was half full of hay. There were two windows in the roof, one was blocked with boards, the other was a narrow dormer window on the north side. There was a chute so that hay might be pitched down to the cattle. Beams crossed the opening down into the main floor where the haycarts drove in when the hay was hauled in to be pitched up. I heard the rain on the roof and smelled the hay and, when I went down, the clean smell of dried dung in the stable. We could prise a board loose and see out of the south window down into the courtyard. The other window looked out on the field toward the north. We could get out of either window onto the roof and down, or go down the hay chute if the stairs were impractical. It was a big barn and we could hide in the hay if we heard anyone. It seemed like a good place. I was sure we could have gotten through to the south if they had not fired on us. It was impossible that there were Germans there. They were coming from the north and down the road from Cividale. They could not have come through from the south. The Italians were even more dangerous. They were frightened and firing on anything they saw. Last night on the retreat we had heard that there had been many Germans in Italian uniforms mixing with the retreat in the north. I did not believe it. That was one of those things you always heard in the war. It was one of the things the enemy always did to you. You did not know anyone who went over in German uniform to confuse them. Maybe they did but it sounded difficult. I did not believe the Germans did it. I did not believe they had to. There was no need to confuse our retreat. The size of the army and the fewness of the roads did that. Nobody gave any orders, let alone Germans. Still, they would shoot us for Germans. They shot Aymo. The hay smelled good and lying in a barn in the hay took away all the years in between. We had lain in hay and talked and shot sparrows with an air-rifle when they perched in the triangle cut high up in the wall of the barn. The barn was gone now and one year they had cut the hemlock woods and there were only stumps, dried tree-tops, branches and fire-weed where the woods had been. You could not go back. If you did not go forward what happened? You never got back to Milan. And if you got back to Milan what happened? I listened to the firing to the north toward Udine. I could hear machine-gun firing. There was no shelling. That was something. They must have gotten some troops along the road. I looked down in the half-light of the hay-barn and saw Piani standing on the hauling floor. He had a long sausage, a jar of something and two bottles of wine under his arm.

'Come up,' I said. 'There is the ladder.' Then I realized that I should help him with the things and went down. I was vague in the head from lying in the hay. I had been nearly asleep.

'Where's Bonello?' I asked.

'I'll tell you,' Piani said. We went up the ladder. Up on the hay we set the things down. Piani took out his knife with the corkscrew and drew the cork on a wine bottle.

'They have sealing-wax on it,' he said. 'It must be good.' He smiled.

'Where's Bonello?' I asked.

Piani looked at me.

'He went away, Tenente,' he said. 'He wanted to be a prisoner.'

I did not say anything.

'He was afraid we would get killed.'

I held the bottle of wine and did not say anything.

'You see we don't believe in the war anyway, Tenente.'

'Why didn't you go?' I asked.

'I did not want to leave you.'

'Where did he go?'

'I don't know, Tenente. He went away.'

'All right,' I said. 'Will you cut the sausage?'

Piani looked at me in the half-light.

'I cut it while we were talking,' he said. We sat in the hay and ate the sausage and drank the wine. It must have been wine they had saved for a wedding. It was so old that it was losing its colour.

'You look out of this window, Luigi,' I said. 'I'll go look out the other window.'

We had each been drinking out of one of the bottles and I took my bottle with me and went over and lay flat on the hay and looked out the narrow window at the wet country. I do not know what I expected to see but I did not see anything except the fields and the bare mulberry trees and the rain falling. I drank the wine and it did not make me feel good. They had kept it too long and it had gone to pieces and lost its quality and colour. I watched it get dark outside; the darkness came very quickly. It would be a black night with the rain. When it was dark there was no use watching any more, so I went over to Piani. He was lying asleep and I did not wake him but sat down beside him for a while. He was a big man and he slept heavily. After a while I woke him and we started.

That was a very strange night. I do not know what I had expected, death perhaps and shooting in the dark and running, but nothing happened. We waited, lying flat beyond the ditch along the main road while a German battalion passed, then when they were gone we crossed the road and went on to the north. We were very close to Germans twice in the rain but they did not see us. We got past the town to the north without seeing any Italians, then after a while came on the main channels of the retreat and walked all night toward the Tagliamento. I had not realized how gigantic the retreat was. The whole country was moving, as well as the army. We walked all night, making better time than the vehicles. My leg ached and I was tired but we made good time. It seemed so silly for Bonello to have decided to be taken prisoner. There was no danger. We had walked through two armies without incident. If Aymo had not been killed there would never have seemed to be any danger. No one had bothered us when we were in plain sight along the railway. The killing came suddenly and unreasonably. I wondered where Bonello was.

'How do you feel, Tenente?' Piani asked. We were going along the side of a road crowded with vehicles and troops.

'Fine.'

'I'm tired of this walking.'

'Bonello was a fool.'

'He was a fool all right.'

'What will you do about him, Tenente?'

'I don't know.'

'Can't you just put him down as taken prisoner?'

'I don't know.'

'You see if the war went on they would make bad trouble for his family.'

'The war won't go on,' a soldier said. 'We're going home. The war is over.'

'Everybody's going home.'

'We're all going home.'

'Come on, Tenente,' Piani said. He wanted to get past them.

'Tenente? Who's a Tenente? *A basso gli ufficiali!* Down with the officers!'

Piani took me by the arm. 'I better call you by your name,' he said. 'They might try and make trouble. They've shot some officers.' We worked up past them.

'I won't make a report that will make trouble for his family.' I went on with our conversation.

'If the war is over it makes no difference,' Piani said. 'But I don't believe it's over. It's too good that it should be over.'

'We'll know pretty soon,' I said.

'I don't believe it's over. They all think it's over but I don't believe it.'

'*Evviva la Pace!*' a soldier shouted out. 'We're going home!'

'It would be fine if we all went home,' Piani said. 'Wouldn't you like to go home?'

'Yes.'

'We'll never go. I don't think it's over.'

'*Andiamo a casa!*' a soldier shouted.

'They throw away their rifles,' Piani said. 'They take them off and drop them down while they're marching. Then they shout.'

'They ought to keep their rifles.'

'They think if they throw away their rifles they can't make them fight.'

In the dark and the rain, making our way along the side of the road I could see that many of the troops still had their rifles. They stuck up above the capes.

'What brigade are you?' an officer called out.

'*Brigata di Pace*,' someone shouted. 'Peace Brigade!' The officer said nothing.

'What does he say? What does the officer say?'

'Down with the officer. *Evviva la Pace!*'

'Come on,' Piani said. We passed two British ambulances, abandoned in the block of vehicles.

'They're from Gorizia,' Piani said. 'I know the cars.'

'They got farther than we did.'

'I wonder where the drivers are?'

'The Germans have stopped outside Udine,' I said. 'These people will all get across the river.'

'Yes,' Piani said. 'That's why I think the war will go on.'

'The Germans could come on,' I said. 'I wonder why they don't come on.'

'I don't know. I don't know anything about this kind of war.'

'They have to wait for their transport I suppose.'

'I don't know,' Piani said. Alone he was much gentler. When he was with the others he was a very rough talker.

'Are you married, Luigi?'

'You know I am married.'

'Is that why you did not want to be a prisoner?'

'That is one reason. Are you married, Tenente?'

'No.'

'Neither is Bonello.'

'You can't tell anything by a man's being married. But I should think a married man would want to get back to his wife,' I said. I would be glad to talk about wives.

'Yes.'

'How are your feet?'

'They're sore enough.'

Before daylight we reached the bank of the Tagliamento and followed down along the flooded river to the bridge where all the traffic was crossing.

'They ought to be able to hold at this river,' Piani said. In the dark the flood looked high. The water swirled and it was wide. The wooden bridge was nearly three-quarters of a mile across, and the river, that usually ran in narrow channels in the wide stony bed far below the bridge, was close under the wooden planking. We went along the bank and then worked our way into the crowd that were crossing the bridge. Crossing slowly in the rain a few feet above the flood, pressed tight in the crowd, the box of an artillery caisson just ahead, I looked over the side and watched the river. Now that we could go our own pace I felt very tired. There was no exhilaration in crossing the bridge. I wondered what it would be like if a plane bombed it in the daytime.

'Piani,' I said.

'Here I am, Tenente.' He was a little ahead in the jam. No one was talking. They were all trying to get across as soon as they could: thinking only of that. We were almost across. At the far end of the bridge there were officers and carabinieri standing on both sides flashing lights. I saw them silhouetted against the sky-line. As we came close to them I saw one of the officers point to a man in the column. A carabiniere went in after him and came out holding the man by the arm. He took him away from the road. We came almost opposite them. The officers were scrutinizing everyone in the column, sometimes speaking to each other, going forward to flash a light in some one's face. They took someone else out just before we came opposite. I saw the man. He was a lieutenant-colonel. I saw the stars in the box on his sleeve as they flashed a light on him. His hair was grey and he was short and fat. The carabiniere pulled him in behind the line of officers. As we came opposite I saw one or two of them look at me. Then one pointed at me and spoke to a carabiniere. I saw the carabiniere start for me, come through the edge of the column toward me, then felt him take me by the collar.

'What's the matter with you?' I said and hit him in the face. I saw the face under the hat, upturned moustaches and blood coming down his cheek. Another one dove in toward us.

'What's the matter with you?' I said. He did not answer. He was watching a chance to grab me. I put my arm behind me to loosen my pistol.

'Don't you know you can't touch an officer?'

The other one grabbed me from behind and pulled my arm up so that it twisted in the socket. I turned with him and the other one grabbed me around the neck. I kicked his shins and got my left knee into his groin.

'Shoot him if he resists,' I heard someone say.

'What's the meaning of this?' I tried to shout but my voice was not very loud. They had me at the side of the road now.

'Shoot him if he resists,' an officer said. 'Take him over back.'

'Who are you?'

'You'll find out.'

'Who are you?'

'Battle police,' another officer said.

'Why don't you ask me to step over instead of having one of these airplanes grab me?'

They did not answer. They did not have to answer. They were battle police.

'Take him back there with the others,' the first officer said. 'You see. He speaks Italian with an accent.'

'So do you, you bastard,' I said.

'Take him back with the others,' the first officer said. They took me down behind the line of officers below the road toward a group of people in a field by the river bank. As we walked toward them shots were fired. I saw flashes of the rifles and heard the reports. We came up to the group. There were four officers standing together, with a man in front of them with a carabiniere on each side of him. A group of men were standing guarded by carabinieri. Four other carabinieri stood near the questioning officers, leaning on their carbines. They were wide-hatted carabinieri. The two who had me shoved me in with the group waiting to be questioned. I looked at the man the officers were questioning. He was the fat grey-haired little lieutenant-colonel they had taken out of the column. The questioners had all the efficiency, coldness and command of themselves of Italians who are firing and are not being fired on.

'Your brigade?'

He told them.

'Regiment?'

He told them.

'Do you not know that an officer should be with his troops?'

He did.

That was all. Another officer spoke.

'It is you and such as you that have let the barbarians onto the sacred soil of the fatherland.'

'I beg your pardon,' said the lieutenant-colonel.

'It is because of treachery such as yours that we have lost the fruits of victory.'

'Have you ever been in a retreat?' the lieutenant-colonel asked.

'Italy should never retreat.'

We stood there in the rain and listened to this. We were facing the officers and the prisoner stood in front and a little to one side of us.

'If you are going to shoot me,' the lieutenant-colonel said, 'please shoot me at once without further questioning. The questioning is stupid.' He made the sign of the cross. The officers spoke together. One wrote something on a pad of paper.

'Abandoned his troops, ordered to be shot,' he said.

Two carabinieri took the lieutenant-colonel to the river bank. He walked in the rain, an old man with his hat off, a carabiniere on either side. I did not watch them shoot him but

I heard the shots. They were questioning some one else. This officer too was separated from his troops. He was not allowed to make an explanation. He cried when they read the sentence from the pad of paper, and they were questioning another when they shot him. They made a point of being intent on questioning the next man while the man who had been questioned before was being shot. In this way there was obviously nothing they could do about it. I did not know whether I should wait to be questioned or make a break now. I was obviously a German in Italian uniform. I saw how their minds worked; if they had minds and if they worked. They were all young men and they were saving their country. The second army was being re-formed beyond the Tagliamento. They were executing officers of the rank of major and above who were separated from their troops. They were also dealing summarily with German agitators in Italian uniform. They wore steel helmets. Only two of us had steel helmets. Some of the carabinieri had them. The other carabinieri wore the wide hat. Airplanes we called them. We stood in the rain and were taken out one at a time to be questioned and shot. So far they had shot everyone they had questioned. The questioners had that beautiful detachment and devotion to stern justice of men dealing in death without being in any danger of it. They were questioning a full colonel of a line regiment. Three more officers had just been put in with us.

'Where was his regiment?'

I looked at the carabinieri. They were looking at the newcomers. The others were looking at the colonel. I ducked down, pushed between two men, and ran for the river, my head down, I tripped at the edge and went in with a splash. The water was very cold and I stayed under as long as I could. I could feel the current swirl me and I stayed under until I thought I could never come up. The minute I came up I took a breath and went down again. It was easy to stay under with so much clothing and my boots. When I came up the second time I saw a piece of timber ahead of me and reached it and held on with one hand. I kept my head behind it and did not even look over it. I did not want to see the bank. There were shots when I ran and shots when I came up the first time. I heard them when I was almost above water. There were no shots now. The piece of timber swung in the current and I held it with one hand. I looked at the bank. It seemed to be going by very fast. There was much wood in the stream. The water was very cold. We passed the brush of an island above the water. I held onto the timber with both hands and let it take me along. The shore was out of sight now.

Chapter VII

You do not know how long you are in a river when the current moves swiftly. It seems a long time and it may be very short. The water was cold and in flood and many things passed that had been floated off the banks when the river rose. I was lucky to have a heavy timber to hold on to, and I lay in the icy water with my chin on the wood, holding as easily as I could with both hands. I was afraid of cramps and I hoped we would move toward the shore. We went down the river in a long curve. It was beginning to be light enough so I could see the bushes along the shore-line. There was a brush island ahead and the current moved toward the shore. I wondered if I should take off my boots and clothes and try to swim ashore, but decided not to. I had never thought of anything but that I would reach the shore some way, and I would be in a bad position if I landed barefoot. I had to get to Mestre some way.

I watched the shore come close, then swing away, then come closer again. We were floating more slowly. The shore was very close now. I could see twigs on the willow bush. The timber swung slowly so that the bank was behind me and I knew we were in an eddy. We went slowly around. As I saw the bank again, very close now, I tried holding with one arm and kicking and swimming the timber toward the bank with the other, but I did not bring it any closer. I was afraid we would move out of the eddy and, holding with one hand, I drew up my feet so they were against the side of the timber and shoved hard toward the bank. I could see the brush, but even with my momentum and swimming as hard as I could, the current was taking me away. I thought then I would drown because of my boots, but I thrashed and fought through the water, and when I looked up the bank was coming toward me, and I kept thrashing and swimming in a heavy-footed panic until I reached it. I hung to the willow branch and did not have strength to pull myself up but I knew I would not drown now. It had never occurred to me on the timber that I might drown. I felt hollow and sick in my stomach and chest from the effort, and I held to the branches and waited. When the sick feeling was gone I pulled into the willow bushes and rested again, my arms around some brush, holding tight with my hands to the branches. Then I crawled out, pushed on through the willows and onto the bank. It was half-daylight and I saw no one. I lay flat on the bank and heard the river and the rain.

After a while I got up and started along the bank. I knew there was no bridge across the river until Latisana. I thought I might be opposite San Vito. I began to think out what I should do. Ahead there was a ditch running into the river. I went toward it. So far I had seen no one and I sat down by some bushes along the bank of the ditch and took off my shoes and emptied them of water. I took off my coat, took my wallet with my papers and my money all wet in it out of the inside pocket and then wrung the coat out. I took off my trousers and wrung them too, then my shirt and underclothing. I slapped and rubbed myself and then dressed again. I had lost my cap.

Before I put on my coat I cut the cloth stars off my sleeves and put them in the inside pocket with my money. My money was wet but was all right. I counted it. There was three thousand and some lire. My clothes felt wet and clammy and I slapped my arms to keep the circulation going. I had woven underwear and I did not think I would catch cold if I kept moving. They had taken my pistol at the road and I put the holster under my coat. I had no cape and it was cold in the rain. I started up the bank of the canal. It was daylight and the country was wet, low and dismal looking. The fields were bare and wet; a long way away I could see a campanile rising out of the plain. I came up onto a road. Ahead I saw some troops coming down the road. I limped along the side of the road and they passed me and paid no attention to me. They were a machine-gun detachment going up toward the river. I went on down the road.

That day I crossed the Venetian plain. It is a low level country and under the rain it is even flatter. Toward the sea there are salt marshes and very few roads. The roads all go along the river mouths to the sea and to cross the country you must go along the paths beside the canals. I was working across the country from the north to the south and had crossed two railway lines and many roads and finally I came out at the end of a path onto a railway line where it ran beside a marsh. It was the main line from Venice to Trieste, with a high solid embankment, a solid roadbed and double track. Down the tracks a way was a flag-station and I could see soldiers on guard. Up the line there was a bridge over a stream that flowed into the marsh. I could see a guard too at the bridge. Crossing the fields to the north I had seen a train pass on this railroad, visible a long way across the flat plain, and I thought a train might come from Portogruaro. I watched the guards and lay down on the embankment so that I could see both ways along the track. The guard at the bridge walked a way up the line toward where I lay, then turned and went back toward the bridge. I lay, and was hungry, and waited for the train. The one I had seen was so long that the engine moved it slowly and I was sure I could get aboard it. After I had almost given up hoping for one I saw a train coming. The engine, coming straight on, grew larger slowly. I looked at the guard at the bridge. He was walking on the near side of the bridge but on the other side of the tracks. That would put him out of sight when the train passed. I watched the engine come nearer. It was working hard. I could see there were many cars. I knew there would be guards on the train, and I tried to see where they were, but, keeping out of sight, I could not. The engine was almost to where I was lying. When it came opposite, working and puffing even on the level, and I saw the engineer pass, I stood up and stepped up close to the passing cars. If the guards were watching I was a less suspicious object standing beside the track. Several closed freight-cars passed. Then I saw a low open car of the sort they call gondolas coming, covered

256

with canvas. I stood until it had almost passed, then jumped and caught the rear hand-rods and pulled up. I crawled down between the gondola and the shelter of the high freight-car behind. I did not think anyone had seen me. I was holding to the hand-rods and crouching low, my feet on the coupling. We were almost opposite the bridge. I remembered the guard. As we passed him he looked at me. He was a boy and his helmet was too big for him. I stared at him contemptuously and he looked away. He thought I had something to do with the train.

We were past. I saw him still looking uncomfortable, watching the other cars pass and I stooped to see how the canvas was fastened. It had grummets and was laced down at the edge with cord. I took out my knife, cut the cord and put my arm under. There were hard bulges under the canvas that tightened in the rain. I looked up and ahead. There was a guard on the freight-car ahead but he was looking forward. I let go of the hand-rails and ducked under the canvas. My forehead hit something that gave me a violent bump and I felt blood on my face but I crawled on in and lay flat. Then I turned around and fastened down the canvas.

I was in under the canvas with guns. They smelled cleanly of oil and grease. I lay and listened to the rain on the canvas and the clicking of the car over the rails. There was a little light came through and I lay and looked at the guns. They had their canvas jackets on. I thought they must have been sent ahead from the third army. The bump on my forehead was swollen and I stopped the bleeding by lying still and letting it coagulate, then picked away the dried blood except over the cut. It was nothing. I had no handkerchief, but feeling with my fingers I washed away where the dried blood had been, with rainwater that dripped from the canvas, and wiped it clean with the sleeve of my coat. I did not want to look conspicuous. I knew I would have to get out before they got to Mestre because they would be taking care of these guns. They had no guns to lose or forget about. I was terrifically hungry.

Chapter VIII

Lying on the floor of the flat-car with the guns beside me under the canvas I was wet, cold and very hungry. Finally I rolled over and lay flat on my stomach with my head on my arms. My knee was stiff, but it had been very satisfactory. Valentini had done a fine job. I had done half the retreat on foot and swum part of the Tagliamento with his knee. It was his knee all right. The other knee was mine. Doctors did things to you and then it was not your body any more. The head was mine, and the inside of the belly. It was very hungry in there. I could feel it turn over on itself. The head was mine, but not to use, not to think with; only to remember and not too much remember.

I could remember Catherine but I knew I would get crazy if I thought about her when I was not sure yet I would see her, so I would not think about her, only about her a little, only about her with the car going slowly and clickingly, and some light through the canvas and my lying with Catherine on the floor of the car. Hard as the floor of the car to lie not thinking only feeling, having been away too long, the clothes wet and the floor moving only a little each time and lonesome inside and alone with wet clothing and hard floor for a wife.

You did not love the floor of a flat-car nor guns with canvas jackets and the smell of vaselined metal or a canvas that rain leaked through, although it is very fine under a canvas and pleasant with guns; but you loved someone else whom now you knew was not even to be pretended there; you seeing now very clearly and coldly – not so coldly as clearly and emptily. You saw emptily, lying on your stomach, having been present when one army moved back and another came forward. You had lost your cars and your men as a floorwalker loses the stock of his department in a fire. There was, however, no insurance. You were out of it now. You had no more obligation. If they

258

shot floorwalkers after a fire in the department store because they spoke with an accent they had always had, then certainly the floorwalkers would not be expected to return when the store opened again for business. They might seek other employment; if there was any other employment and the police did not get them.

Anger was washed away in the river along with any obligation. Although that ceased when the carabiniere put his hand on my collar. I would like to have had the uniform off although I did not care much about the outward forms. I had taken off the stars, but that was for convenience. It was no point of honour. I was not against them. I was through. I wished them all the luck. There were the good ones, and the brave ones, and the calm ones and the sensible ones, and they deserved it. But it was not my show any more and I wished this bloody train would get to Mestre and I would eat and stop thinking. I would have to stop.

Piani would tell them they had shot me. They went through the pockets and took the papers of the people they shot. They would not have my papers. They might call me drowned. I wondered what they would hear in the States. Dead from wounds and other causes. Good Christ I was hungry. I wondered what had become of the priest at the mess. And Rinaldi. He was probably at Pordenone. If they had not gone further back. Well, I would never see him now. I would never see any of them now. That life was over. I did not think he had syphilis. It was not a serious disease anyway if you took it in time, they said. But he would worry. I would worry too if I had it. Anyone would worry.

I was not made to think. I was made to eat. My God, yes. Eat and drink and sleep with Catherine. Tonight maybe. No that was impossible. But tomorrow night, and a good meal and sheets and never going away again except together. Probably have to go damned quickly. She would go. I knew she would go. When would we go? That was something to think about. It was getting dark. I lay and thought where we would go. There were many places.

TO HAVE AND HAVE NOT

A Boatload for Cuba

Albert was on board the boat and the gas was loaded.

'I'll start her up and try how those two cylinders hit,' Harry said. 'You got the things stowed?'

'Yes.'

'Cut some baits then.'

'You want a wide bait?'

'That's right. For tarpon.'

Albert was on the stern cutting baits and Harry was at the wheel warming up the motors when he heard a noise like a motor back-firing. He looked down the street and saw a man come out of the bank. He had a gun in his hand and he came running. Then he was out of sight. Two men came out carrying leather brief-cases and guns in their hands and ran in the same direction. Harry looked at Albert busy cutting baits. The fourth man, the big one, came out of the bank door as he watched, holding a Thompson gun in front of him, and as he backed out of the door the siren in the bank rose in a long breath-holding shriek and Harry saw the gun muzzle jump-jump-jump and heard the bop-bop-bop-bop, small and hollow sounding in the wail of the siren. The man turned and ran, stopping to fire once more at the bank door, and as Albert stood up in the stern saying, 'Christ, they're robbing the bank. Christ, what can we do?' Harry heard the Ford taxi coming out of the side street and saw it careening up on to the dock.

There were three Cubans in the back and one beside the driver.

'Where's the boat?' yelled one in Spanish.

'There, you fool,' said another.

'That's not the boat.'

261

'That's the captain.'

'Come on. Come on for Christ sake.'

'Get out,' said the Cuban to the driver. 'Get your hands up.'

As the driver stood beside the car he put a knife inside his belt and ripping it toward him cut the belt and slit his pants almost to the knee. He yanked the trousers down. 'Stand still,' he said. The two Cubans with the valises tossed them into the cockpit of the launch and they all came tumbling aboard.

'Geta going,' said one. The big one with the machine-gun poked it into Harry's back.

'Come on, Cappie,' he said. 'Let's go.'

'Take it easy,' said Harry. 'Point that some place else.'

'Cast off those lines,' the big one said. 'You!' to Albert.

'Wait a minute,' Albert said. 'Don't start her. These are the bank robbers.'

The biggest Cuban turned and swung the Thompson gun and held it on Albert. 'Hey, don't! Don't!' Albert said. 'Don't!'

The burst was so close to his chest that the bullets whocked like three slaps. Albert slid down on his knees, his eyes wide, his mouth open. He looked like he was still trying to say, 'Don't!'

'You don't need no mate,' the big Cuban said. 'You one-armed son of a bitch.' Then in Spanish, 'Cut those lines with that fish knife.' And in English, 'Come on. Let's go.'

Then in Spanish, 'Put a gun against his back!' and in English, 'Come on. Let's go. I'll blow your head off.'

'We'll go,' said Harry.

One of the Indian-looking Cubans was holding a pistol against the side his bad arm was on. The muzzle almost touched the hook.

As he swung her out, spinning the wheel with his good arm, he looked astern to watch the clearance past the piling, and saw Albert on his knees in the stern, his head slipped sideways now, in a pool of it. On the dock was the Ford taxi, and the fat driver in his underdrawers, his trousers around his ankles, his hands above his head, his mouth as open wide as Albert's. There was still no one coming down the street.

The pilings of the dock went past as she came out of the

262

basin and then he was in the channel passing the lighthouse dock.

'Come on. Hook her up,' the big Cuban said. 'Make some time.'

'Take that gun away,' Harry said. He was thinking, I could run her on Crawfish bar, but sure as hell that Cuban would plug me.

'Make her go,' said the big Cuban. Then, in Spanish, 'Lie down flat, everybody. Keep the captain covered.' He lay down himself in the stern, pulling Albert flat down into the cockpit. The other three all lay flat in the cockpit now. Harry sat on the steering seat. He was looking ahead steering out the channel, past the opening into the sub-base now, with the notice board to yachts and the green blinker, out away from the jetty, past the fort now, past the red blinker; he looked back. The big Cuban had a green box of shells out of his pocket and was filling clips. The gun lay by his side, and he was filling clips without looking at them, filling by feel, looking back over the stern. The others were all looking astern except the one that was watching him. This one, one of the two Indian-looking ones, motioned with his pistol for him to look ahead. No boat had started after them yet. The engines were running smoothly and they were going with the tide. He noticed the heavy slant seawards of the buoy he passed, with the current swirling at its base.

There are two speedboats that could catch us, Harry was thinking. One, Ray's, is running the mail from Matecumbe. Where is the other? I saw her a couple of days ago on Ed. Taylor's ways, he checked. That was the one I thought of having Bee-lips hire. There's two more, he remembered now. One the State Road Department has up along the quays. The other's laid up in the Garrison Bight. How far are we now? He looked back to where the fort was well astern, the red-brick building of the old Post Office starting to show up above the Navy yard buildings and the yellow hotel building now dominating the short skyline of the town. There was the cove at the Fort, and the lighthouse showed above the houses that strung out toward the big winter hotel. Four miles anyway, he thought. There they come, he thought. Two white fishing boats were rounding the breakwater and heading out toward him. They can't do ten, he thought. It's pitiful.

The Cubans were chattering in Spanish.

'How fast you going, Cappie?' the big one said, looking back from the stern.

'About twelve,' Harry said.

'What can those boats do?'

'Maybe ten.'

They were all watching them now, even the one who was supposed to keep him, Harry, covered. But what can I do? He thought. Nothing to do yet.

The two white boats got no larger.

'Look at that, Roberto,' said the nice-speaking one.

'Where?'

'Look!'

A long way back, so far you could hardly see it, a little spout rose in the water.

'They're shooting at us,' the pleasant-speaking one said. 'It's silly.'

'For Christ's sake,' the big-faced one said. 'At three miles.'

'Four,' thought Harry. 'All of four.'

Harry could see the tiny spouts rise on the calm surface but he could not hear the shots.

'Those Conchs are pitiful,' he thought. 'They're worse. They're comical.'

'What government boat is there, Cappie?' asked the big-faced one looking away from the stern.

'Coast-guard.'

'What can she make?'

'Maybe twelve.'

'Then we're O.K. now.'

Harry did not answer.

'Aren't we O.K. then?'

Harry said nothing. He was keeping the rising, widening spire of Sand Key on his left and the stake on little Sand Key shoals showed almost abeam to starboard. In ten more minutes they would be past the reef.

'What's the matter with you? Can't you talk?'

'What did you ask me?'

'Is there anything can catch us now?'

'Coast-guard plane,' said Harry.

'We cut the telephone wire before we came in town,' the pleasant-speaking one said.

'You didn't cut the wireless, did you?' Harry asked.

'You think the plane can get here?'

'You got a chance of her until dark,' Harry said.

'What do you think, Cappie?' asked Roberto, the big-faced one.

Harry did not answer.

'Come on, what do you think?'

'What did you let that son of a bitch kill my mate for?' Harry said to the pleasant-speaking one who was standing beside him now looking at the compass course.

'Shut up,' said Roberto. 'Kill you, too.'

'How much money you get?' Harry asked the pleasant-speaking one.

'We don't know. We haven't counted it yet. It isn't ours anyway.'

'I guess not,' said Harry. He was past the light now and he put her on 225°, his regular course for Havana.

'I mean we do it not for ourselves. For a revolutionary organization.'

'You kill my mate for that, too?'

'I am very sorry,' said the boy. 'I cannot tell you how badly I feel about that.'

'Don't try,' said Harry.

'You see,' the boy said, speaking quietly, 'this man Roberto is bad. He is a good revolutionary but a bad man. He kills so much in the time of Machado he gets to like it. He thinks it is funny to kill. He kills in a good cause, of course. The best cause.' He looked back at Roberto who sat now in one of the fishing chairs in the stern, the Thompson gun across his lap, looking back at the white boats which were, Harry saw, much smaller now.

'What you got to drink?' Roberto called from the stern.

'Nothing,' Harry said.

'I drink my own then,' Roberto said. One of the other Cubans lay on one of the seats built over the gas tanks. He looked seasick already. The other was obviously seasick too, but still sitting up.

Looking back, Harry saw a lead-coloured boat, now clear of the Fort, coming up on the two white boats.

'There's the coast-guard boat,' he thought. 'She's pitiful too.'

'You think the seaplane will come?' the pleasant-spoken boy asked.

'Be dark in half an hour,' Harry said. He settled on the steering seat. 'What you figure on doing? Killing me?'

'I don't want to,' the boy said. 'I hate killing.'

'What you doing?' Roberto, who sat now with a pint of whisky in his hand, asked. 'Making friends with the captain? What you want to do? Eat at the captain's table?'

'Take the wheel,' Harry said to the boy. 'See the course? Two twenty-five.' He straightened up from the stool and went aft.

'Let me have a drink,' Harry said to Roberto. 'There's your coast-guard boat but she can't catch us.'

He had abandoned anger, hatred and any dignity as luxuries, now, and had started to plan.

'Sure,' said Roberto. 'She can't catch us. Look at those seasick babies. What you say? You want a drink? You got any other last wishes, Cappie?'

'You're some kidder,' Harry said. He took a long drink.

'Go easy!' Roberto protested. 'That's all there is.'

'I got some more,' Harry told him. 'I was just kidding you.'

'Don't kid me,' said Roberto suspiciously.

'Why should I try?'

'What you got?'

'Bacardi.'

'Bring it out.'

'Take it easy,' Harry said. 'Why do you get so tough?'

He stepped over Albert's body as he walked forward. As he came to the wheel he looked at the compass. The boy was about twenty-five degrees off and the compass dial was swinging. He's no sailor, Harry thought. That gives me more time. Look at the wake.

The wake ran in two bubbling curves toward where the

266

light, astern now, showed brown, conical and thinly latticed on the horizon. The boats were almost out of sight. He could just see a blur where the wireless masts of the town were. The engines were running smoothly. Harry put his head below and reached for one of the bottles of Bacardi. He went aft with it. At the stern he took a drink, then handed the bottle to Roberto. Standing, he looked down at Albert and felt sick inside. The poor hungry bastard, he thought.

'What's the matter? He scare you?' the big-faced Cuban asked.

'What you say we put him over?' Harry said. 'No sense to carry him.'

'O.K.,' said Roberto. 'You got good sense.'

'Take him under the arms,' said Harry. 'I'll take the legs.' Roberto laid the Thompson gun down on the wide stern and leaning down lifted the body by the shoulders.

'You know the heaviest thing in the world is a dead man,' he said. 'You ever lift a dead man before, Cappie?'

'No,' said Harry. 'You ever lift a big dead woman?'

Roberto pulled the body up on to the stern. 'You're a tough fellow,' he said. 'What do you say we have a drink?'

'Go ahead,' said Harry.

'Listen, I'm sorry I killed him,' Roberto said. 'When I kill you I feel worse.'

'Cut out talking that way,' Harry said. 'What do you want to talk that way for?'

'Come on,' said Roberto. 'Over he goes.'

As they leaned over and slid the body up and over the stern, Harry kicked the machine gun over the edge. It splashed at the same time Albert did, but while Albert turned over twice in the white, churned, bubbling back-suction of the propeller wash before sinking, the gun went straight down.

'That's better, eh?' Roberto said. 'Make it shipshape.' Then as he saw the gun was gone, 'Where is it? What did you do with it?'

'With what?'

'The *ametralladora*!' going into Spanish in excitement.

'The what?'

'You know what.'

'I didn't see it.'

267

'You knocked it off the stern. Now I'll kill you, *now*.'

'Take it easy,' said Harry. 'What the hell you going to kill me about?'

'Give me a gun,' Roberto said to one of the seasick Cubans in Spanish. 'Give me a gun quick!'

Harry stood there, never having felt so tall, never having felt so wide, feeling the sweat trickle from under his armpits, feeling it go down his flanks.

'You kill too much,' he heard the seasick Cuban say in Spanish. 'You kill the mate. Now you want to kill the captain. Who's going to get us across?'

'Leave him alone,' said the other. 'Kill him when we get over.'

'He knocked the machine gun overboard,' Roberto said.

'We got the money. What you want a machine gun for now? There's plenty of machine guns in Cuba.'

'I tell you, you make a mistake if you don't kill him now, I tell you. Give me a gun.'

'Oh, shut up. You're drunk. Every time you're drunk you want to kill somebody.'

'Have a drink,' said Harry looking out across the grey swell of the Gulf Stream where the round red sun was just touching the water. 'Watch that. When she goes all the way under it'll turn bright green.'

'The hell with that,' said the big-faced Cuban. 'You think you got away with something.'

'I'll get you another gun,' said Harry. 'They only cost forty-five dollars in Cuba. Take it easy. You're all right now. There ain't any coast-guard plane going to come now.'

'I'm going to kill you,' Roberto said, looking him over. 'You did that on purpose. That's why you got me to lift on that.'

'You don't want to kill me,' Harry said. 'Who's going to take you across?'

'I ought to kill you now.'

'Take it easy,' said Harry. 'I'm going to look at the engines.'

He opened the hatch, got down in, screwed down the grease cups on the two stuffing boxes, felt the motors, and with his hand touched the butt of the Thompson gun. Not yet, he thought. No, better not yet. Christ, that was lucky. What the

268

hell difference does it make to Albert when he's dead? Saves his old woman to bury him. That big-faced bastard. That big-faced murdering bastard. Christ, I'd like to take him now. But I better wait.

He stood up, climbed out and shut the hatch.

'How you doing?' he said to Roberto. He put his hand on the fat shoulder. The big-faced Cuban looked at him and did not say anything.

'Did you see it turn green?' Harry asked.

'The hell with you,' Roberto said. He was drunk but he was suspicious and, like an animal, he knew how wrong something had gone.

'Let me take her a while,' Harry said to the boy at the wheel. 'What's your name?'

'You can call me Emilio,' said the boy.

'Go below and you'll find something to eat.' Harry said. 'There's bread and corn beef. Make coffee if you want.'

'I don't want any.'

'I'll make some later,' Harry said. He sat at the wheel, the binnacle light on now, holding her on the point easily in the light following sea, looking out at the night coming on the water. He had no running lights on.

It would be a pretty night to cross, he thought, a pretty night. Soon as the last of that afterglow is gone I've got to work her east. If I don't, we'll sight the glare of Havana in another hour. In two, anyway. Soon as he sees the glare it may occur to that son of a bitch to kill me. That was lucky getting rid of that gun. Damn, that was lucky. Wonder what that Marie's having for supper. I guess she's plenty worried. I guess she's too worried to eat. Wonder how much money these bastards have got. Funny they don't count it. If that ain't a hell of a way to raise money for a revolution. Cubans are a hell of a people.

That's a mean boy, that Roberto. I'll get him tonight. I get him no matter how the rest of it comes out. That won't help that poor damned Albert though. It made me feel bad to dump him like that. I don't know what made me think of it.

He lit a cigarette and smoked in the dark.

I'm doing all right, he thought. I'm doing better than I

expected. The kid is a nice kind of kid. I wish I could get those other two on the same side. I wish there was some way to bunch them. Well, I'll have to do the best I can. Easier I can make them take it before-hand the better. Smoother everything goes the better.

'Do you want a sandwich?' the boy asked.

'Thanks,' said Harry 'You give one to your partner?'

'He's drinking. He won't eat,' the boy said.

'What about the others?'

'Seasick,' the boy said.

'It's a nice night to cross.' Harry said. He noticed the boy did not watch the compass so he kept letting her go off to the east.

'I'd enjoy it,' the boy said. 'If it wasn't for your mate.'

'He was a good fellow,' said Harry. 'Did anyone get hurt at the bank?'

'The lawyer. What was his name? Simmons.'

'Get killed?'

'I think so.'

So, thought Harry, Mr Bee-lips. What the hell did he expect? How could he have thought he wouldn't get it? That comes from playing at being tough. That comes from being too smart too often. Mr Bee-lips. Good-bye, Mr Bee-lips.

'How he come to get killed?'

'I guess you can imagine,' the boy said. 'That's very different from your mate. I feel badly about that. You know he doesn't mean to do wrong. It's just what that phase of the revolution has done to him.'

'I guess he's probably a good fellow,' Harry said, and thought, Listen to what my mouth says. God damn it, my mouth will say anything. But I got to try to make a friend of this boy in case –

'What kind of revolution do you make now?' he asked.

'We are the only true revolutionary party,' the boy said. 'We want to do away with all the old politicians, with all the American imperialism that strangles us, with the tyranny of the army. We want to start clean and give every man a chance. We want to end the slavery of the *guajiros,* you know, the peasants, and divide the big sugar estates among the people that work them. But we are not Communists.'

Harry looked up from the compass card at him.

'How you coming on?' he asked.

'We just raise money now for the fight,' the boy said. 'To do that we have to use means that later we would never use. Also we have to use people we would not employ later. But the end is worth the means. They had to do the same thing in Russia. Stalin was a sort of brigand for many years before the revolution.'

He's a radical, Harry thought. That's what he is, a radical.

'I guess you've got a good programme,' he said, 'if you're out to help the working man. I was out on strike plenty times in the old days when we had the cigar factories in Key West. I'd have been glad to do whatever I could if I'd known what kind of outfit you were.'

'Lots of people would help us,' the boy said. 'But because of the state the movement is in at present we can't trust people. I regret the necessity for the present phase very much. I hate terrorism. I also feel very badly about the methods for raising the necessary money. But there is no choice. You do not know how bad things are in Cuba.'

'I guess they're plenty bad,' Harry said.

'You can't know how bad they are. There is an absolutely murderous tyranny that extends over every little village in the country. Three people cannot be together on the street. Cuba has no foreign enemies and doesn't need any army, but she has an army of twenty-five thousand now, and the army, from the corporals up, suck the blood from the nation. Everyone, even the private soldiers, are out to make their fortunes. Now they have a military reserve with every kind of crook, bully and informer of the old days of Machado in it, and they take anything the army does not bother with. We have to get rid of the army before anything can start. Before we were ruled by clubs. Now we are ruled by rifles, pistols, machine guns and bayonets.'

'It sounds bad,' Harry said, steering, and letting her go off to the eastward.

'You cannot realize how bad it is,' the boy said. 'I love my poor country and I would do anything, anything to free it from this tyranny we have now. I do things I hate. But I would do things I hate a thousand times more.'

271

I want a drink, Harry was thinking. What the hell do I care about his revolution. F — his revolution. To help the working man he robs a bank and kills a fellow works with him and then kills that poor damned Albert that never did any harm. That's a working man he kills. He never thinks of that. With a family. It's the Cubans run Cuba. They all double-cross each other. They sell each other out. They get what they deserve. The hell with their revolutions. All I got to do is make a living for my family and I can't do that. Then he tells me about his revolution. The hell with his revolution.

'It must be bad, all right,' he said to the boy. 'Take the wheel a minute, will you? I want to get a drink.'

'Sure,' said the boy. 'How should I steer?'

'Two twenty-five,' Harry said.

It was dark now and there was quite a swell this far out in the Gulf Stream. He passed the two seasick Cubans lying out on the seats and went aft to where Roberto sat in the fishing chair. The water was racing past the boat in the dark. Roberto sat with his feet in the other fishing chair that was turned toward him.

'Let me have some of that,' Harry said to him.

'Go to hell,' said the big-faced man thickly. 'This is mine.'

'All right,' said Harry, and went forward to get the other bottle. Below in the dark, with the bottle under the flap of his right arm, he pulled the cork that Freddy had drawn and re-inserted and took a drink.

Now's as good as any time, he said to himself. No sense waiting now. Little boy's spoke his piece. The big-faced bastard drunk. The other two seasick. It might as well be now.

He took another drink and the Bacardi warmed and helped him but he felt cold and hollow all around his stomach still. His whole insides were cold.

'Want a drink?' he asked the boy at the wheel.

'No, thanks,' the boy said. 'I don't drink.' Harry could see him smile in the binnacle light. He was a nice-looking boy all right. Pleasant talking, too.

'I'll take one,' he said. He swallowed a big one but it could not warm the dank cold part that had spread from his stomach to all over the inside of his chest now. He put the bottle down on the cockpit floor.

272

'Keep her on that course,' he said to the boy. 'I'm going to have a look at the motors.'

He opened the hatch and stepped down. Then locked the hatch up with a long hook that set into a hole in the flooring. He stooped over the motors, with his one hand felt the water manifold, the cylinders, and put his hand on the stuffing boxes. He tightened the two grease cups a turn and a half each. Quit stalling, he said to himself. Come on, quit stalling. Where're your balls now? Under my chin, I guess, he thought.

He looked out of the hatch. He could almost touch the two seats over the gas tanks where the seasick men lay. The boy's back was toward him, sitting on the high stool, outlined clearly by the binnacle light. Turning, he could see Roberto sprawled in the chair in the stern, silhouetted against the dark water.

Twenty-one to a clip is four bursts of five at the most, he thought. I got to be light-fingered. All right. Come on. Quit stalling, you gutless wonder. Christ, what I'd give for another one. Well, there isn't any other one now. He reached his left hand up, unhooked the length of belting, put his hand around the trigger guard, pushed the safety all the way over with his thumb and pulled the gun out. Squatting in the engine pit he sighted carefully on the base of the back of the boy's head where it outlined against the light from the binnacle.

The gun made a big flame in the dark and the shells rattled against the lifted hatch and on to the engine. Before the slump of the boy's body fell from the stool he had turned and shot into the figure on the left bunk, holding the jerking, flame-stabbing gun almost against the man, so close he could smell it burn his coat; then swung to put a burst into the other bunk where the man was sitting up, tugging at his pistol. He crouched low now and looked astern. The big-faced man was gone out of the chair. He could see both chairs silhouetted. Behind him the boy lay still. There wasn't any doubt about him. On one bunk a man was flopping. On the other, he could see with the corner of his eye, a man lay half over the gunwale, fallen over on his face.

Harry was trying to locate the big-faced man in the dark. The boat was going in a circle now and the cockpit lightened a little. He held his breath and looked. That must be him

273

where it was a little darker on the floor in the corner. He watched it and it moved a little. That was him.

The man was crawling toward him. No, toward the man who lay half overboard. He was after his gun. Crouching low, Harry watched him move until he was absolutely sure. Then he gave him a burst. The gun lighted him on hands and knees, and, as the flame and the bot-bot-bot-bot stopped, he heard him flopping heavily.

'You son of a bitch,' said Harry. 'You big-faced murdering bastard.'

All the cold was gone from around his heart now and he had the old hollow, singing feeling and he crouched low down and felt under the square, wood-crated gas tank for another clip to put in the gun. He got the clip, but his hand was cold-drying wet.

Hit the tank, he said to himself. I've got to cut the engines. I don't know where that tank cuts.

He pressed the curved lever, dropped the empty clip, shoved in the fresh one, and climbed up and out of the cockpit.

As he stood up, holding the Thompson gun in his left hand, looking around before shutting the hatch with the hook on his right arm, the Cuban who had lain on the port bunk and had been shot three times through the left shoulder, two shots going into the gas tank, sat up, took careful aim, and shot him in the belly.

Harry sat down in a backward lurch. He felt as though he had been struck in the abdomen with a club. His back was against one of the iron-pipe supports of the fishing chairs and while the Cuban shot at him again and splintered the fishing chair above his head, he reached down, found the Thompson gun, raised it carefully, holding the forward grip with the hook and rattled half of the fresh clip into the man who sat leaning forward, calmly shooting at him from the seat. The man was down on the seat in a heap and Harry felt around on the cockpit floor until he could find the big-faced man, who lay face down, felt for his head with the hook on his bad arm, hooked it around, then put the muzzle of the gun against the head and touched the trigger. Touching the head, the gun made a noise like hitting a pumpkin with a club. Harry put down the gun and lay on his side on the cockpit floor.

'I'm a son of a bitch,' he said, his lips against the planking. I'm a gone son of a bitch now. I got to cut the engines or we'll all burn up, he thought. I got a chance still. I got a kind of a chance. Jesus Christ. One thing to spoil it. One thing to go wrong. God damn it. Oh, God *damn* that Cuban bastard. Who'd have thought I hadn't got him?

He got on his hands and knees and letting one side of the hatch over the engines slam down, crawled over it forward to where the steering stool was. He pulled up on it, surprised to find how well he could move, then suddenly feeling faint and weak as he stood erect, he leaned forward with his bad arm resting on the compass and cut the two switches. The engines were quiet and he could hear the water against her sides. There was no other sound. She swung into the trough of the little sea the north wind had raised and began to roll.

He hung against the wheel, then eased himself on to the steering stool, leaning against the chart table. He could feel the strength drain out of him in a steady faint nausea. He opened his shirt with his good hand and felt the hole with the base of the palm of his hand, then fingered it. There was very little bleeding. All inside, he thought. I better lie down and give it a chance to quiet.

The moon was up now and he could see what was in the cockpit.

Some mess, he thought, some hell of a mess.

Better get down before I fall down, he thought and he lowered himself down to the cockpit floor.

He lay on his side and then, as the boat rolled, the moonlight came in and he could see everything in the cockpit clearly.

It's crowded, he thought. That's what it is, it's crowded. Then, he thought, I wonder what she'll do? I wonder what Marie will do? Maybe they'll pay her the rewards. God damn that Cuban. She'll get along, I guess. She's a smart woman. I guess we would all have gotten along. I guess it was nuts all right. I guess I bit off too much more than I could chew. I shouldn't have tried it. I had it all right up to the end. Nobody'll know how it happened. I wish I could do something about Marie. Plenty money on this boat. I don't even know how much. Anybody be O.K. with that money. I wonder if the coast-guard will pinch it. Some of it, I guess. I wish I could let the old woman know what happened. I wonder what she'll do? I don't know. I guess I should have got a job in a filling station or something. I should have quit trying to go in boats. There's no honest money going in boats any more. If the bitch wouldn't only roll. If she'd only quit rolling. I can feel all that slopping back and forth inside. Me, Mr Bee-lips and Albert. Everybody that had to do with it. These bastards too. It must be an unlucky business. Some unlucky business. I guess what a man like me ought to do is run something like a filling station. Hell, I couldn't run no filling station. Marie, she'll run something. She's too old to peddle her hips now. I wish this bitch wouldn't roll. I'll just have to take it easy. I got to take it as easy as I can. They say if you don't drink water and lay still. They say especially if you don't drink water.

He looked at what the moonlight showed in the cockpit.

Well, I don't have to clean her up, he thought. Take it easy. That's what I got to do. Take it easy. I've got to take it as easy as I can. I've got sort of a chance. If you lay still and don't drink any water.

He lay on his back and tried to breathe steadily. The launch rolled in the Gulf Stream swell and Harry Morgan lay on his back in the cockpit. At first he tried to brace himself against the roll with his good hand. Then he lay quietly and took it.

FOR WHOM THE BELL TOLLS

El Sordo on the Hilltop

El Sordo was making his fight on a hilltop. He did not like this hill and when he saw it he thought it had the shape of a chancre. But he had had no choice except this hill and he had picked it as far away as he could see it and galloped for it, the automatic rifle heavy on his back, the horse labouring, barrel heaving between his thighs, the sack of grenades swinging against one side, the sack of automatic rifle pans banging against the other, and Joaquín and Ignacio halting and firing, halting and firing to give him time to get the gun in place.

There had still been snow then, the snow that had ruined them, and when his horse was hit so that he wheezed in a slow, jerking, climbing stagger up the last part of the crest, splattering the snow with a bright, pulsing jet, Sordo had hauled him along by the bridle, the reins over his shoulder as he climbed. He climbed as hard as he could with the bullets spatting on the rocks, with the two sacks heavy on his shoulders, and then holding the horse by the mane, had shot him quickly, expertly, and tenderly just where he had needed him, so that the horse pitched, head forward down to plug a gap between two rocks. He had gotten the gun to firing over the horse's back and he fired two pans, the gun clattering, the empty shells pitching into the snow, the smell of burnt hair from the burnt hide where the hot muzzle rested, him firing at what came up to the hill, forcing them to scatter for cover, while all the time there was a chill in his back from not knowing what was behind him. Once the last of the five men had reached the hilltop the chill went out of his back and he had saved the pans he had left until he would need them.

There were two more horses dead along the slope and three

more were dead here on the hilltop. He had only succeeded in stealing three horses last night and one had bolted when they tried to mount him bareback in the corral at the camp when the first shooting had started.

Of the five men who had reached the hilltop three were wounded. Sordo was wounded in the calf of his leg and in two places in his left arm. He was very thirsty, his wounds had stiffened, and one of the wounds in his left arm was very painful. He also had a bad headache and as he lay waiting for the planes to come he thought of a joke in Spanish. It was, '*Hay que tomar la muerte como si fuera aspirin*', which means, 'You will have to take death as an aspirin.' But he did not make the joke aloud. He grinned somewhere inside the pain in his head and inside the nausea that came whenever he moved his arm and looked around at what there was left of his band.

The five men were spread out like the points of a five-pointed star. They had dug with their knees and hands and made mounds in front of their heads and shoulders with the dirt and piles of stones. Using this cover, they were linking the individual mounds up with stones and dirt. Joaquín, who was eighteen years old, had a steel helmet that he dug with and he passed dirt in it.

He had gotten this helmet at the blowing up of the train. It had a bullet hole through it and everyone had always joked at him for keeping it. But he had hammered the jagged edges of the bullet hole smooth and driven a wooden plug into it and then cut the plug off and smoothed it even with the metal inside the helmet.

When the shooting started he had clapped this helmet on his head so hard it banged his head as though he had been hit with a casserole and, in the last lung-aching, leg-dead, mouth-dry, bullet-spatting, bullet-cracking, bullet-singing run up the final slope of the hill after his horse was killed, the helmet had seemed to weigh a great amount and to ring his bursting forehead with an iron band. But he had kept it. Now he dug with it in a steady, almost machine-like desperation. He had not yet been hit.

'It serves for something finally,' Sordo said to him in his deep, throaty voice.

'*Resistir y fortificar es vencer*,' Joaquín said, his mouth stiff with the dryness of fear which surpassed the normal thirst of battle. It was one of the slogans of the Communist party and it meant, 'Hold out and fortify, and you will win'.

Sordo looked away and down the slope at where a cavalryman was sniping from behind a boulder. He was very fond of this boy and he was in no mood for slogans.

'What did you say?'

One of the men turned from the building that he was doing. This man was lying flat on his face, reaching carefully up with his hands to put a rock in place while keeping his chin flat against the ground.

Joaquín repeated the slogan in his dried-up boy's voice without checking his digging for a moment.

'What was the last word?' the man with his chin on the ground asked.

'*Vencer*,' the boy said. 'Win.'

'*Mierda*,' the man with his chin on the ground said.

'There is another that applies to here,' Joaquín said, bringing them out as though they were talismans, 'Pasionaria says it is better to die on your feet than to live on your knees.'

'*Mierda* again,' the man said and another man said, over his shoulder, 'We're on our bellies, not our knees.'

'Thou. Communist. Do you know your Pasionaria has a son thy age in Russia since the start of the movement?'

'It's a lie,' Joaquín said.

'*Qué va* it's a lie,' the other said. 'The dynamiter with the rare name told me. He was of thy party too. Why should he lie?'

'It's a lie,' Joaquín said. 'She would not do such a thing as keep a son hidden in Russia out of the war.'

'I wish I were in Russia,' another of Sordo's men said. 'Will not thy Pasionaria send me now from here to Russia, Communist?'

'If thou believest so much in thy Pasionaria, get her to get us off this hill,' one of the men who had a bandaged thigh said.

'The fascists will do that,' the man with his chin in the dirt said.

'Do not speak thus,' Joaquin said to him.

279

'Wipe the pap of your mother's breast off thy lips and give me a hatful of that dirt,' the man with his chin on the ground said. 'No one of us will see the sun go down this night.'

El Sordo was thinking: It is shaped like a chancre. Or the breast of a young girl with no nipple. Or the top cone of a volcano. You have never seen a volcano, he thought. Nor will you ever see one. And this hill is like a chancre. Let the volcanoes alone. It's late now for the volcanoes.

He looked very carefully around the withers of the dead horse and there was a quick hammering of firing from behind a boulder well down the slope and he heard the bullets from the sub-machine-gun thud into the horse. He crawled along behind the horse and looked out of the angle between the horse's hindquarters and the rock. There were three bodies on the slope just below him where they had fallen when the fascists had rushed the crest under cover of the automatic rifle and sub-machine-gun fire and he and the others had broken down the attack by throwing and rolling down hand grenades. There were other bodies that he could not see on the other side of the hill crest. There was no dead ground by which attackers could approach the summit and Sordo knew that as long as the ammunition and grenades held out and he had as many as four men they could not get him out of there unless they brought up a trench mortar. He did not know whether they had sent to La Granja for a trench mortar. Perhaps they had not, because surely, soon, the planes would come. It had been four hours since the observation plane had flown over them.

This hill is truly like a chancre, Sordo thought, and we are the very pus of it. But we killed many when they made that stupidness. How could they think that they would take us thus? They have such modern armament that they lose all their sense with over-confidence. He had killed the young officer who had led the assault with a grenade that had gone bouncing and rolling down the slope as they came up it, running, bent half over. In the yellow flash and grey roar of smoke he had seen the officer dive forward to where he lay now like a heavy, broken bundle of old clothing marking the farthest point that the assault had reached. Sordo looked at this body and then, down the hill, at the others.

They are brave but stupid people, he thought. But they have sense enough now not to attack us again until the planes come. Unless, of course, they have a mortar coming. It would be easy with a mortar. The mortar was the normal thing and he knew that they would die as soon as a mortar came up, but when he thought of the planes coming up he felt naked on that hilltop as though all of his clothing and even his skin had been removed. There is no nakeder thing than I feel, he thought. A flayed rabbit is as well covered as a bear in comparison. But why should they bring planes? They could get us out of here with a trench mortar easily. They are proud of their planes, though, and they will probably bring them. Just as they were so proud of their automatic weapons that they made that stupidness. But undoubtedly they must have sent for a mortar, too.

One of the men fired. Then jerked the bolt and fired again, quickly.

'Save thy cartridges,' Sordo said.

'One of the sons of the great whore tried to reach that boulder,' the man pointed.

'Did you hit him?' Sordo asked, turning his head with difficulty.

'Nay,' the man said. 'The fornicator ducked back.'

'Who is a whore of whores is Pilar,' the man with his chin in the dirt said. 'That whore knows we are dying here.'

'She could do no good,' Sordo said. The man had spoken on the side of his good ear and he had heard him without turning his head. 'What could she do?'

'Take these sluts from the rear.'

'*Qué va*,' Sordo said. 'They are spread around a hillside. How would she come on them? There are a hundred and fifty of them. Maybe more now.'

'But if we hold out until dark,' Joaquín said.

'And if Christmas comes on Easter,' the man with his chin on the ground said.

'And if thy aunt had *cojones* she would be thy uncle,' another said to him. 'Send for thy Pasionaria. She alone can help us.'

'I do not believe that about the son,' Joaquín said. 'Or if he is there he is training to be an aviator or something of that sort.'

281

'He is hidden there for safety,' the man told him.

'He is studying dialectics. Thy Pasionaria has been there. So have Lister and Modesto and others. The one with the rare name told me.'

'That they should go to study and return to aid us,' Joaquín said.

'That they should aid us now,' another man said. 'That all the cruts of Russian sucking swindlers should aid us now.' He fired and said, '*Me cago en tal;* I missed him again.'

'Save thy cartridges and do not talk so much or thou wilt be very thirsty,' Sordo said. 'There is no water on this hill.'

'Take this,' the man said and rolling on his side he pulled a wine-skin that he wore slung from his shoulder over his head and handed it to Sordo. 'Wash thy mouth out, old one. Thou must have much thirst with thy wounds.'

'Let all take it,' Sordo said.

'Then I will have some first,' the owner said and squirted a long stream into his mouth before he handed the leather bottle around.

'Sordo, when thinkest thou the planes will come?' the man with his chin in the dirt asked.

'Any time,' said Sordo. 'They should have come before.'

'Do you think these sons of the great whore will attack again?'

'Only if the planes do not come.'

He did not think there was any need to speak about the mortar. They would know it soon enough when the mortar came.

'God knows they've enough planes with what we saw yesterday.'

'Too many,' Sordo said.

His head hurt very much and his arm was stiffening so that the pain of moving it was almost unbearable. He looked up at the bright, high, blue, early summer sky as he raised the leather wine bottle with his good arm. He was fifty-two years old and he was sure this was the last time he would see that sky.

He was not at all afraid of dying but he was angry at being trapped on this hill which was only utilizable as a place to die. If we could have gotten clear, he thought. If we could have made them come up the long valley or if we could have broken loose across the road it would have been all right. But this chancre of a hill. We must use it as well as we can and we have used it very well so far.

If he had known how many men in history have had to use a hill to die on it would not have cheered him any for, in the moment he was passing through, men are not impressed by what has happened to other men in similar circumstances any more than a widow of one day is helped by the knowledge that other loved husbands have died. Whether one has fear of it or not, one's death is difficult to accept. Sordo had accepted it but there was no sweetness in its acceptance even at fifty-two, with three wounds and him surrounded on a hill.

He joked about it to himself but he looked at the sky and at the far mountains and he swallowed the wine and he did not want it. If one must die, he thought, and clearly one must, I can die. But I hate it.

Dying was nothing and he had no picture of it nor fear of it in his mind. But living was a field of grain blowing in the wind on the side of a hill. Living was a hawk in the sky. Living was an earthen jar of water in the dust of the threshing with the grain flailed out and the chaff blowing. Living was a horse between your legs and a carbine under one leg and a hill and a valley and a stream with trees along it and the far side of the valley and the hills beyond.

Sordo passed the wine bottle back and nodded his head in thanks. He leaned forward and patted the dead horse on the shoulder where the muzzle of the automatic rifle had burned the hide. He could still smell the burnt hair. He thought how he had held the horse there, trembling, with the fire around them, whispering and crackling, over and around them like a curtain, and had carefully shot him just at the intersection of the cross-line between the two eyes and the ears. Then as the horse pitched down he had dropped down behind his warm, wet back to get the gun going as they came up the hill.

'*Eras mucho caballo*,' he said, meaning. 'Thou wert plenty of horse.'

El Sordo lay now on his good side and looked up at the sky. He was lying on a heap of empty cartridge hulls but his head was protected by the rock and his body lay in the lee of the horse. His wounds had stiffened badly and he had much pain and he felt too tired to move.

'What passes with thee, old one?' the man next to him asked.

'Nothing. I am taking a little rest.'

'Sleep,' the other said. '*They* will wake us when they come.'

Just then someone shouted from down the slope.

'Listen, bandits!' the voice came from behind the rocks where the closest automatic rifle was placed. 'Surrender now before the planes blow you to pieces.'

'What is it he says?' Sordo asked.

Joaquín told him. Sordo rolled to one side and pulled himself up so that he was crouched behind the gun again.

'Maybe the planes aren't coming,' he said. 'Don't answer them and do not fire. Maybe we can get them to attack again.'

'If we should insult them a little?' the man who had spoken to Joaquín about La Pasionaria's son in Russia asked.

'No,' Sordo said. 'Give me thy big pistol. Who has a big pistol?'

'Here.'

'Give it to me.' Crouched on his knees he took the big 9 mm. Star and fired one shot into the ground beside the dead horse, waited, then fired again four times at irregular intervals. Then he waited while he counted sixty and then fired a final shot directly into the body of the dead horse. He grinned and handed back the pistol.

'Reload it,' he whispered, 'and that everyone should keep his mouth shut and no one shoot.'

'*Bandidos*!' the voice shouted from behind the rocks.

No one spoke on the hill.

'*Bandidos*! Surrender now before we blow thee to little pieces.'

'They're biting,' Sordo whispered happily.

As he watched, a man showed his head over the top of the rocks. There was no shot from the hilltop and the head went down again. El Sordo waited, watching, but nothing more happened. He turned his head and looked at the others who were all watching down their sectors of the slope. As he looked at them the others shook their heads.

'Let no one move,' he whispered.

'Sons of the great whore,' the voice came now from behind the rocks again.

'Red swine. Mother rapers. Eaters of the milk of thy fathers.'

Sordo grinned. He could just hear the bellowed insults by turning his good ear. This is better than the aspirin, he thought. How many will we get? Can they be that foolish?

The voice had stopped again and for three minutes they heard nothing and saw no movement. Then the sniper behind the boulder a hundred yards down the slope exposed himself and fired. The bullet hit a rock and ricocheted with a sharp whine. Then Sordo saw a man, bent double, run from the shelter of the rocks where the automatic rifle was across the open ground to the big boulder behind which the sniper was hidden. He almost dived behind the boulder.

Sordo looked around. They signalled to him that there was no movement on the other slopes. El Sordo grinned happily and shook his head. This is ten times better than the aspirin, he thought, and he waited, as happy as only a hunter can be happy.

Below on the slope the man who had run from the pile of stones to the shelter of the boulder was speaking to the sniper.

'Do you believe it?'

'I don't know,' the sniper said.

'It would be logical,' the man, who was the officer in command, said. 'They are surrounded. They have nothing to expect but to die.'

The sniper said nothing.

'What do you think?' the officer asked.

'Nothing,' the sniper said.

'Have you seen any movement since the shots?'

'None at all.'

The officer looked at his wristwatch. It was ten minutes to three o'clock.

'The planes should have come an hour ago,' he said. Just then another officer flopped in behind the boulder. The sniper moved over to make room for him.

'Thou, Paco,' the first officer said. 'How does it seem to thee?'

The second officer was breathing heavily from his sprint up and across the hillside from the automatic rifle position.

'For me it is a trick,' he said.

'But if it is not? What a ridicule we make waiting here and laying siege to dead men.'

'We have done something worse than ridiculous already,' the second officer said. 'Look at that slope.'

He looked up the slope to where the dead were scattered close to the top. From where he looked the line of the hilltop showed the scattered rocks, the belly, projecting legs, shod hooves jutting out, of Sordo's horse, and the fresh dirt thrown up by the digging.

'What about the mortars?' asked the second officer.

'They should be here in an hour. If not before.'

'Then wait for them. There has been enough stupidity already.'

'*Bandidos!*' the first officer shouted suddenly, getting to his feet and putting his head well up above the boulder so that the crest of the hill looked much closer as he stood upright. 'Red swine! Cowards!'

The second officer looked at the sniper and shook his head. The sniper looked away but his lips tightened.

The first officer stood there, his head all clear of the rock and with his hand on his pistol butt. He cursed and vilified the hilltop. Nothing happened. Then he stepped clear of the boulder and stood there looking up the hill.

'Fire, cowards, if you are alive,' he shouted. 'Fire on one who has no fear of any Red that ever came out of the belly of the great whore.'

This last was quite a long sentence to shout and the officer's face was red and congested as he finished.

The second officer, who was a thin sunburned man with quiet eyes, a thin, long-lipped mouth and a stubble of beard over his hollow cheeks, shook his head again. It was this officer who was shouting who had ordered the first assault. The young lieutenant who was named Paco Berrendo was listening to the shouting of the captain, who was obviously in a state of exaltation.

'Those are the swine who shot my sister and my mother,' the

captain said. He had a red face and a blond, British-looking moustache and there was something wrong about his eyes. They were a light blue and the lashes were light, too. As you looked at them they seemed to focus slowly. Then 'Reds', he shouted. 'Cowards!' and commenced cursing again.

He stood absolutely clear now and, sighting carefully, fired his pistol at the only target that the hilltop presented: the dead horse that had belonged to Sordo. The bullet threw up a puff of dirt fifteen yards below the horse. The captain fired again. The bullet hit a rock and sung off.

The captain stood there looking at the hilltop. The Lieutenant Berrendo was looking at the body of the other lieutenant just below the summit. The sniper was looking at the ground under his eyes. Then he looked up at the captain.

'There is no one alive up there,' the captain said. 'Thou,' he said to the sniper, 'go up there and see.'

The sniper looked down. He said nothing.

'Don't you hear me?' the captain shouted at him.

'Yes, my captain,' the sniper said, not looking at him.

'Then get up and go.' The captain still had his pistol out. 'Do you hear me?'

'Yes, my captain.'

'Why don't you go, then?'

'I don't want to, my captain.'

'You don't *want* to?' The captain pushed the pistol against the small of the man's back. 'You don't *want* to?'

'I am afraid, my captain,' the soldier said with dignity.

Lieutenant Berrendo, watching the captain's face and his odd eyes, thought he was going to shoot the man then.

'Captain Mora,' he said.

'Lietenant Berrendo?'

'It is possible the soldier is right.'

'That he is right to say he is afraid? That he is right to say he does not *want* to obey an order?'

'No. That he is right that it is a trick.'

'They are all dead,' the captain said. 'Don't you hear me say they are all dead?'

'You mean our comrades on the slope?' Berrendo asked him. 'I agree with you.'

287

'Paco,' the captain said, 'don't be a fool. Do you think you are the only one who cared for Julián? I tell you the Reds are dead. Look!'

He stood up, then put both hands on top of the boulder and pulled himself up, kneeing-up awkwardly, then getting on his feet.

'Shoot,' he shouted, standing on the grey granite boulder and waved both his arms. 'Shoot me! Kill me!'

On the hilltop El Sordo lay behind the dead horse and grinned.

What a people, he thought. He laughed, trying to hold it in because the shaking hurt his arm.

'Reds,' came the shout from below. 'Red canaille. Shoot me! Kill me!'

Sordo, his chest shaking, barely peeped past the horse's crupper and saw the captain on top of the boulder waving his arms. Another officer stood by the boulder. The sniper was standing at the other side. Sordo kept his eye where it was and shook his head happily.

'Shoot me,' he said softly to himself. 'Kill me!' Then his shoulders shook again. The laughing hurt his arm and each time he laughed his head felt as though it would burst. But the laughter shook him again like a spasm.

Captain Mora got down from the boulder.

'Now do you believe me, Paco?' he questioned Lieutenant Berrendo.

'No,' said Lieutenant Berrendo.

'*Cojones!*' the captain said. 'Here there is nothing but idiots and cowards.'

The sniper had gotten carefully behind the boulder again and Lieutenant Berrendo was squatting beside him.

The captain, standing in the open beside the boulder, commenced to shout filth at the hilltop. There is no language so filthy as Spanish. There are words for all the vile words in English and there are other words and expressions that are used in countries where blasphemy keeps pace with the austerity of religion. Lieutenant Berrendo was a very devout Catholic. So was the sniper. They were Carlists from Navarra and while both of them cursed and blasphemed when they

288

were angry they regarded it as a sin which they regularly confessed.

As they crouched now behind the boulder watching the captain and listening to what he was shouting, they both disassociated themselves from him and what he was saying. They did not want to have that sort of talk on their consciences on a day in which they might die. Talking thus will not bring luck, the sniper thought. Speaking thus of the *Virgen is* bad luck. This one speaks worse than the Reds.

Julián is dead, Lieutenant Berrendo was thinking. Dead there on the slope on such a day as this is. And this foul mouth stands there bringing more ill fortune with his blasphemies.

Now the captain stopped shouting and turned to Lieutenant Berrendo. His eyes looked stranger than ever.

'Paco,' he said happily, 'you and I will go up there.'

'Not me.'

'What?' The captain had his pistol out again.

I hate these pistol brandishers, Berrendo was thinking. They cannot give an order without jerking a gun out. They probably pull out their pistols when they go to the toilet and order the move they will make.

'I will go if you order me to. But under protest,' Lieutenant Berrendo told the captain.

'Then I will go alone,' the captain said. 'The smell of cowardice is too strong here.'

Holding his pistol in his right hand, he strode steadily up the slope. Berrendo and the sniper watched him. He was making no attempt to take any cover and he was looking straight ahead of him at the rocks, the dead horse, and the fresh-dug dirt of the hilltop.

El Sordo lay behind the horse at the corner of the rock, watching the captain come striding up the hill.

Only one, he thought. We get only one. But from his manner of speaking he is *caza mayor*. Look at him walking. Look what an animal. Look at him stride forward. This one is for me. This one I take with me on the trip. This one coming now makes the same voyage I do. Come on, Comrade Voyager. Come striding. Come right along. Come along to meet it. Come on. Keep on walking. Don't slow up. Come right along. Come as thou art coming. Don't stop and look at those. That's right. Don't even look down. Keep on coming with your eyes forward. Look, he has a moustache. What do you think of that? He runs to a moustache, the Comrade Voyager. He is a captain. Look at his sleeves. I said he was *caza mayor*. He has the face of an *Inglés*. Look. With a red face and blond hair and blue eyes. With no cap on and his moustache is yellow. With blue eyes. With pale blue eyes. With pale blue eyes with something wrong with them. With pale blue eyes that don't focus. Close enough. Too close. Yes, Comrade Voyager. Take it, Comrade Voyager.

He squeezed the trigger of the automatic rifle gently and it pounded back three times against his shoulder with the slippery jolt the recoil of a tripoded automatic weapon gives.

The captain lay on his face on the hillside. His left arm was under him. His right arm that had held the pistol was stretched forward of his head. From all down the slope they were firing on the hill crest again.

Crouched behind the boulder, thinking that now he would have to sprint across that open space under fire, Lieutenant Berrendo heard the deep hoarse voice of Sordo from the hilltop.

'*Bandidos!*' the voice came. '*Bandidos!* Shoot me! Kill me!'

On the top of the hill El Sordo lay behind the automatic rifle laughing so that his chest ached, so that he thought the top of his head would burst.

'*Bandidos*,' he shouted again happily. 'Kill me, *bandidos*!' then he shook his head happily. We have lots of company for the Voyage, he thought.

He was going to try for the other officer with the automatic rifle when he would leave the shelter of the boulder. Sooner or later he would have to leave it. Sordo knew that he could never command from there and he thought he had a very good chance to get him.

Just then the others on the hill heard the first sound of the coming of the planes.

El Sordo did not hear them. He was covering the down-slope edge of the boulder with his automatic rifle and he was

290

thinking: when I see him he will be running already and I will miss him if I am not careful. I could shoot behind him all across that stretch. I should swing the gun with him and ahead of him. Or let him start and then get on him and ahead of him. I will try to pick them up there at the edge of the rock and swing just ahead of him. Then he felt a touch on his shoulder and he turned and saw the grey, fear-drained face of Joaquín and he looked where the boy was pointing and saw three planes coming.

At this moment Lieutenant Berrendo broke from behind the boulder and, with his head bent and his legs plunging, ran down and across the slope to the shelter of the rocks where the automatic rifle was placed.

Watching the planes, Sordo never saw him go.

'Help me to pull this out,' he said to Joaquín and the boy dragged the automatic rifle clear from between the horse and the rock.

The planes were coming on steadily. They were in echelon and each second they grew larger and their noise was greater.

'Lie on your backs to fire at them,' Sordo said. 'Fire ahead of them as they come.'

He was watching them all the time. '*Cabrones! Hijos de puta*!' he said rapidly.

'Ignacio!' he said. 'Put the gun on the shoulder of the boy. Thou!' to Joaquín, 'sit there and do not move. Crouch over. More. No. More.'

He lay back and sighted with the automatic rifle as the planes came on steadily.

'Thou, Ignacio, hold me the three legs of that tripod.' They were dangling down the boy's back and the muzzle of the gun was shaking from the jerking of his body that Joaquín could not control as he crouched with bent head hearing the droning roar of their coming.

Lying flat on his belly and looking up into the sky watching them come, Ignacio gathered the legs of the tripod into his two hands and steadied the gun.

'Keep thy head down,' he said to Joaquín. 'Keep thy head forward.'

'Pasionaria says "Better to die on the –"' Joaquín was saying

291

to himself as the drone came nearer them. Then he shifted suddenly into 'Hail Mary, full of grace, the Lord is with thee; Blessed art thou among women and Blessed is the fruit of thy womb, Jesus. Holy Mary, Mother of God, pray for us sinners now and at the hour of our death. Amen. Holy Mary, Mother of God,' he started, then he remembered quickly as the roar came now unbearably and started an act of contrition racing in it, 'Oh my God, I am heartily sorry for having offended thee who art worthy of all my love –'

Then there were the hammering explosions past his ears and the gun barrel hot against his shoulder. It was hammering now again and his ears were deafened by the muzzle blast. Ignacio was pulling down hard on the tripod and the barrel was burning his back. It was hammering now in the roar and he could not remember the act of contrition.

All he could remember was at the hour of our death. Amen. At the hour of our death. Amen. At the hour. At the hour. Amen. The others all were firing. Now and at the hour of our death. Amen.

Then, through the hammering of the gun, there was the whistle of the air splitting apart and then in the red black roar the earth rolled under his knees and then waved up to hit him in the face and then dirt and bits of rock were falling all over and Ignacio was lying on him and the gun was lying on him. But he was not dead because the whistle came again and the earth rolled under him with the roar. Then it came again and the earth lurched under his belly and one side of the hilltop rose into the air and then fell slowly over them where they lay.

The planes came back three times and bombed the hilltop but no one on the hilltop knew it. Then the planes machine-gunned the hilltop and went away. As they dived on the hill for the last time with their machine guns hammering, the first plane pulled up and winged over and then each plane did the same and they moved from echelon to V-formation and went away into the sky in the direction of Segovia.

Keeping a heavy fire on the hilltop, Lieutenant Berrendo pushed a patrol up to one of the bomb craters from where they could throw grenades on to the crest. He was taking no chances of anyone being alive and waiting for them in the mess that was up there and he threw four grenades into the confusion of dead horses, broken and split rocks, and torn yellow-stained explosive-stinking earth before he climbed out of the bomb crater and walked over to have a look.

No one was alive on the hilltop except the boy Joaquín who was unconscious under the dead body of Ignacio. Joaquín was bleeding from the nose and from the ears. He had known nothing and had no feeling since he had suddenly been in the very heart of the thunder and the breath had been wrenched from his body when the one bomb struck so close and Lieutenant Berrendo made the sign of the cross and then shot him in the back of the head, as quickly and as gently, if such an abrupt movement can be gentle, as Sordo had shot the wounded horse.

Lieutenant Berrendo stood on the hilltop and looked down the slope at his own dead and then across the country seeing where they had galloped before Sordo had turned at bay here. He noticed all the dispositions that had been made of the troops and then he ordered the dead men's horses to be brought up and the bodies tied across the saddles so that they might be packed in to La Granja.

'Take that one, too,' he said. 'The one with his hands on the automatic rifle. That should be Sordo. He is the oldest and it was he with the gun. No. Cut the head off and wrap it in a poncho.' He considered a minute. 'You might as well take all the heads. And of the others below on the slope and where we first found them. Collect the rifles and pistols and pack that gun on a horse.'

Then he walked down to where the lieutenant lay who had been killed in the first assault. He looked down at him but did not touch him.

'*Qué cosa más mala es la guerra,*' he said to himself, which meant, 'What a bad thing war is.'

Then he made the sign of the cross again and as he walked down the hill he said five Our Fathers and five Hail Marys for the repose of the soul of his dead comrade. He did not wish to stay to see his orders being carried out.

The Stories

IN OUR TIME

Everybody was drunk. The whole battery was drunk going along the road in the dark. We were going to the Champagne. The lieutenant kept riding his horse out into the fields, and saying to him, 'I'm drunk, I tell you, mon vieux. Oh, I am so soused.' We went along the road all night in the dark and the adjutant kept riding up alongside my kitchen and saying, 'You must put it out. It is dangerous. It will be observed.' We were fifty kilometres from the front, but the adjutant worried about the fire in my kitchen. It was funny going along that road. That was when I was a kitchen corporal.

Indian Camp

At the lake shore there was another rowboat drawn up. The two Indians stood waiting.

Nick and his father got in the stern of the boat and the Indians shoved it off and one of them got in to row. Uncle George sat in the stern of the camp rowboat. The young Indian shoved the camp boat off and got in to row Uncle George.

The two boats started off in the dark. Nick heard the oarlocks of the other boat quite a way ahead of them in the mist. The Indians rowed with quick choppy strokes. Nick lay back with his father's arm around him. It was cold on the water. The Indian who was rowing them was working very hard, but the other boat moved further ahead in the mist all the time.

'Where are we going, Dad?' Nick asked.

'Over to the Indian camp. There is an Indian lady very sick.'

'Oh,' said Nick.

Across the bay they found the other boat beached. Uncle George was smoking a cigar in the dark. The young Indian pulled the boat way up the beach. Uncle George gave both the Indians cigars.

They walked up from the beach through a meadow that was soaking wet with dew, following the young Indian who carried a lantern. Then they went into the woods and followed a trail that led to the logging road that ran back into the hills. It was much lighter on the logging road as the timber was cut away on both sides. The young Indian stopped and blew out his lantern and they all walked on along the road.

They came around a bend and a dog came out barking. Ahead were the lights of the shanties where the Indian bark-peelers lived. More dogs rushed out at them. The two Indians sent them back to the shanties. In the shanty nearest the road there was a light in the window. An old woman stood in the doorway holding a lamp.

Inside on a wooden bunk lay a young Indian woman. She had been trying to have her baby for two days. All the old women in the camp had been helping her. The men had moved off up the road to sit in the dark and smoke out of range of the noise she made. She screamed just as Nick and the two Indians followed his father and Uncle George into the shanty. She lay in the lower bunk, very big under a quilt. Her head was turned to one side. In the upper bunk was her husband. He had cut his foot very badly with an axe three days before. He was smoking a pipe. The room smelled very bad.

Nick's father ordered some water to be put on the stove, and while it was heating he spoke to Nick.

'This lady is going to have a baby, Nick,' he said.

'I know,' said Nick.

'You don't know,' said his father. 'Listen to me. What she is going through is called being in labour. The baby wants to be born and she wants it to be born. All her muscles are trying to get the baby born. That is what is happening when she screams.'

'I see,' Nick said.

Just then the woman cried out.

'Oh, Daddy, can't you give her something to make her stop screaming?' asked Nick.

'No. I haven't any anaesthetic,' his father said. 'But her screams are not important. I don't hear them because they are not important.'

The husband in the upper bunk rolled over against the wall.

The woman in the kitchen motioned to the doctor that the water was hot. Nick's father went into the kitchen and poured about half of the water out of the big kettle into a basin. Into the water left in the kettle he put several things he unwrapped from a handkerchief.

'Those must boil,' he said, and began to scrub his hands in the basin of hot water with a cake of soap he had brought from the camp. Nick watched his father's hands scrubbing each other with the soap. While his father washed his hands very carefully and thoroughly, he talked.

'You see, Nick, babies are supposed to be born head first but sometimes they're not. When they're not they make a lot of trouble for everybody. Maybe I'll have to operate on this lady. We'll know in a little while.'

When he was satisfied with his hands he went in and went to work.

'Pull back that quilt, will you, George?' he said. 'I'd rather not touch it.'

Later when he started to operate Uncle George and three Indian men held the woman still. She bit Uncle George on the arm and Uncle George said, 'Damn squaw bitch!' and the young Indian who had rowed Uncle George over laughed at him. Nick held the basin for his father. It all took a long time.

His father picked the baby up and slapped it to make it breathe and handed it to the old woman.

'See, it's a boy, Nick,' he said. 'How do you like being an interne?'

Nick said, 'All right.' He was looking away so as not to see what his father was doing.

'There. That gets it,' said his father and put something into the basin.

Nick didn't look at it.

'Now,' his father said, 'there's some stitches to put in. You can watch this or not, Nick, just as you like. I'm going to sew up the incision I made.'

Nick did not watch. His curiosity had been gone for a long time.

His father finished and stood up. Uncle George and the three Indian men stood up. Nick put the basin out in the kitchen.

Uncle George looked at his arm. The young Indian smiled reminiscently.

'I'll put some peroxide on that, George,' the doctor said.

He bent over the Indian woman. She was quiet now and her eyes were closed. She looked very pale. She did not know what had become of the baby or anything.

'I'll be back in the morning,' the doctor said, standing up. 'The nurse should be here from St Ignace by noon and she'll bring everything we need.'

He was feeling exalted and talkative as football players are in the dressing-room after a game.

'That's one for the medical journal, George,' he said. 'Doing a Caesarean with a jack-knife and sewing it up with nine-foot, tapered gut leaders.'

Uncle George was standing against the wall, looking at his arm.

'Oh, you're a great man, all right,' he said.

'Ought to have a look at the proud father. They're usually the worst sufferers in these little affairs,' the doctor said. 'I must say he took it all pretty quietly.'

He pulled back the blanket from the Indian's head. His hand came away wet. He mounted on the edge of the lower bunk with the lamp in one hand and looked in. The Indian lay with his face toward the wall. His throat had been cut from ear to ear. The blood had flowed down into a pool where his body sagged the bunk. His head rested on his left arm. The open razor lay, edge up, in the blankets.

'Take Nick out of the shanty, George,' the doctor said.

There was no need of that. Nick, standing in the door of the kitchen, had a good view of the upper bunk when his father, the lamp in one hand, tipped the Indian's head back.

It was just beginning to be daylight when they walked along the logging road back toward the lake.

'I'm terribly sorry I brought you along, Nickie,' said his

father, all his post-operative exhilaration gone. 'It was an awful mess to put you through.'

'Do ladies always have such a hard time having babies?' Nick asked.

'No, that was very, very exceptional.'

'Why did he kill himself, Daddy?'

'I don't know, Nick. He couldn't stand things, I guess.'

'Do many men kill themselves, Daddy?'

'Not very many, Nick.'

'Do many women?'

'Hardly ever.'

'Don't they ever?'

'Oh, yes. They do sometimes.'

'Daddy?'

'Yes.'

'Where did Uncle George go?'

'He'll turn up all right.'

'Is dying hard, Daddy?'

'No, I think it's pretty easy. Nick. It all depends.'

They were seated in the boat, Nick in the stern, his father rowing.

The sun was coming up over the hills. A bass jumped, making a circle in the water. Nick trailed his hand in the water. It felt warm in the sharp chill of the morning.

In the early morning on the lake sitting in the stern of the boat with his father rowing, he felt quite sure that he would never die.

Minarets stuck up in the rain out of Adrianople across the mud flats. The carts were jammed for thirty miles along the Karagatch road. Water buffalo and cattle were hauling carts through the mud. There was no end and no beginning. Just carts loaded with everything they owned. The old men and women, soaked through, walked along keeping the cattle moving. The Maritza was running yellow almost up to the bridge. Carts were jammed solid on the bridge with camels bobbing along through them. Greek cavalry herded along the procession. The women and children were in the carts, crouched with mattresses, mirrors, sewing machines, bundles. There was

301

a woman having a baby with a young girl holding a blanket over her and crying. Scared sick looking at it. It rained all through the evacuation.

The Doctor and the Doctor's Wife

Dick Boulton came from the Indian camp to cut up logs for Nick's father. He brought his son Eddy, and another Indian named Billy Tabeshaw with him. They came in through the back gate out of the woods, Eddy carrying the long cross-cut saw. It flopped over his shoulder and made a musical sound as he walked. Billy Tabeshaw carried two big cant-hooks. Dick had three axes under his arm.

He turned and shut the gate. The others went on ahead of him down to the lake shore where the logs were buried in the sand.

The logs had been lost from the big log booms that were towed down the lake to the mill by the steamer *Magic*. They had drifted up on to the beach and if nothing were done about them sooner or later the crew of the *Magic* would come along the shore in a rowboat, spot the logs, drive an iron spike with a ring on it into the end of each one and then tow them out into the lake to make a new boom. But the lumbermen might never come for them because a few logs were not worth the price of a crew to gather them. If no one came for them they would be left to waterlog and rot on the beach.

Nick's father always assumed that this was what would happen, and hired the Indians to come down from the camp and cut the logs up with the cross-cut saw and split them with a wedge to make cordwood and chunks for the open fireplace. Dick Boulton walked around past the cottage down to the lake. There were four big beech logs lying almost buried in the sand. Eddy hung the saw up by one of its handles in the crotch of a tree. Dick put the three axes down on the little dock. Dick was a half-breed and many of the farmers around the lake

302

believed he was really a white man. He was very lazy but a great worker once he was started. He took a plug of tobacco out of his pocket, bit off a chew and spoke in Ojibway to Eddy and Billy Tabeshaw.

They sunk the ends of their cant-hooks into one of the logs and swung against it to loosen it in the sand. They swung their weight against the shafts of the cant-hooks. The log moved in the sand. Dick Boulton turned to Nick's father.

'Well, Doc,' he said, 'that's a nice lot of timber you've stolen.'

'Don't talk that way, Dick,' the doctor said. 'It's driftwood.'

Eddy and Billy Tabeshaw had rocked the log out of the wet sand and rolled it toward the water.

'Put it right in,' Dick Boulton shouted.

'What are you doing that for?' asked the doctor.

'Wash it off. Clean off the sand on account of the saw. I want to see who it belongs to,' Dick said.

The log was just awash in the lake. Eddy and Billy Tabeshaw leaned on their cant-hooks sweating in the sun. Dick kneeled down in the sand and looked at the mark of the scaler's hammer in the wood at the end of the log.

'It belongs to White and McNally,' he said, standing up and brushing off his trousers knees.

The doctor was very uncomfortable.

'You'd better not saw it up, then, Dick,' he said, shortly.

'Don't get huffy, Doc,' said Dick. 'Don't get huffy. I don't care who you steal from. It's none of my business.'

'If you think the logs are stolen, leave them alone and take your tools back to the camp,' the doctor said. His face was red.

'Don't go off at half cock, Doc,' Dick said. He spat tobacco juice on the log. It slid off, thinning in the water. 'You know they're stolen as well as I do. It don't make any difference to me.'

'All right. If you think the logs are stolen, take your stuff and get out.'

'Now, Doc –'

'Take your stuff and get out.'

'Listen, Doc.'

'If you call me Doc once again, I'll knock your eye teeth down your throat.'

'Oh, no, you won't, Doc.'

Dick Boulton looked at the doctor. Dick was a big man. He knew how big a man he was. He liked to get into fights. He was happy. Eddy and Billy Tabeshaw leaned on their cant-hooks and looked at the doctor. The doctor chewed the beard on his lower lip and looked at Dick Boulton. Then he turned away and walked up the hill to the cottage. They could see from his back how angry he was. They all watched him walk up the hill and go inside the cottage.

Dick said something in Ojibway. Eddy laughed but Billy Tabeshaw looked very serious. He did not understand English but he had sweat all the time the row was going on. He was fat with only a few hairs of moustache like a Chinaman. He picked up the two cant-hooks. Dick picked up the axes and Eddy took the saw down from the tree. They started off and walked up past the cottage and out the back gate into the woods. Dick left the gate open. Billy Tabeshaw went back and fastened it. They were gone through the woods.

In the cottage the doctor, sitting on the bed in his room, saw a pile of medical journals on the floor by the bureau. They were still in their wrappers unopened. It irritated him.

'Aren't you going back to work, dear?' asked the doctor's wife from the room where she was lying with the blinds drawn.

'No!'

'Was anything the matter?'

'I had a row with Dick Boulton.'

'Oh,' said his wife. 'I hope you didn't lose your temper, Henry.'

'No,' said the doctor.

'Remember, that he who ruleth his spirit is greater than he that taketh a city,' said his wife. She was a Christian Scientist. Her Bible, her copy of *Science and Health* and her *Quarterly* were on a table beside her bed in the darkened room.

Her husband did not answer. He was sitting on his bed now, cleaning a shotgun. He pushed the magazine full of the heavy yellow shells and pumped them out again. They were scattered on the bed.

'Henry,' his wife called. Then paused a moment. 'Henry!'

'Yes,' the doctor said.

'You didn't say anything to Boulton to anger him, did you?'

'No,' said the doctor.

'What was the trouble about, dear?'

'Nothing much.'

'Tell me, Henry. Please don't try and keep anything from me. What was the trouble about?'

'Well, Dick owes me a lot of money for pulling his squaw through pneumonia and I guess he wanted a row so he wouldn't have to take it out in work.'

His wife was silent. The doctor wiped his gun carefully with a rag. He pushed the shells back in against the spring of the magazine. He sat with the gun on his knees. He was very fond of it. Then he heard his wife's voice from the darkened room.

'Dear, I don't think, I really don't think that anyone would really do a thing like that.'

'No?' said the doctor.

'No. I can't believe that anyone would do a thing of that sort intentionally.'

The doctor stood up and put the shotgun in the corner behind the dresser.

'Are you going out, dear?' his wife said.

'I think I'll go for a walk,' the doctor said.

'If you see Nick, dear, will you tell him his mother wants to see him?' his wife said.

The doctor went out on the porch. The screen door slammed behind him. He heard his wife catch her breath when the door slammed.

'Sorry,' he said, outside her window with the blinds drawn.

'It's all right, dear,' she said.

He walked in the heat out the gate and along the path into the hemlock woods. It was cool in the woods even on such a hot day. He found Nick sitting with his back against a tree, reading.

'Your mother wants you to come and see her,' the doctor said.

'I want to go with you,' Nick said.

His father looked down at him.

'All right. Come on, then,' his father said. 'Give me the book, I'll put it in my pocket.'

305

'I know where there's black squirrels, Daddy,' Nick said.

'All right,' said his father. 'Let's go there.'

We were in a garden in Mons. Young Buckley came in with his patrol from across the river. The first German I saw climbed over up the garden wall. We waited till he got one leg over and then potted him. He had so much equipment on and looked awfully surprised and fell down into the garden. Then three more came over further down the wall. We shot them. They all came just like that.

The End of Something

In the old days Hortons Bay was a lumbering town. No one who lived in it was out of sound of the big saws in the mill by the lake. Then one year there were no more logs to make lumber. The lumber schooners came into the bay and were loaded with the cut of the mill that stood stacked in the yard. All the piles of lumber were carried away. The big mill building had all its machinery that was removable taken out and hoisted on board one of the schooners by the men who had worked in the mill. The schooner moved out of the bay toward the open lake carrying the two great saws, the travelling carriage that hurled the logs against the revolving, circular saws and all the rollers, wheels, belts and iron piled on a hull-deep load of lumber. Its open hold covered with canvas and lashed tight, the sails of the schooner filled and it moved out into the open lake, carrying with it everything that had made the mill a mill and Hortons Bay, a town.

The one-storey bunk houses, the eating-house, the company store, the mill offices, and the big mill itself stood deserted in the acres of sawdust that covered the swampy meadow by the shore of the bay.

Then years later there was nothing of the mill left except the broken white limestone of its foundations showing through the swampy second growth as Nick and Marjorie rowed along the shore. They were trolling along the edge of the channel-bank where the bottom dropped off suddenly from sandy shallows to twelve feet of dark water. They were trolling on their way to the point to set night lines for rainbow trout.

'There's our old ruin, Nick,' Marjorie said.

Nick, rowing, looked at the white stone in the green trees.

'There it is,' he said.

'Can you remember when it was a mill?' Marjorie asked.

'I can just remember,' Nick said.

'It seems more like a castle,' Marjorie said.

Nick said nothing. They rowed on out of sight of the mill, following the shore line. Then Nick cut across the bay.

'They aren't striking,' he said.

'No,' Marjorie said. She was intent on the rod all the time they trolled, even when she talked. She loved to fish. She loved to fish with Nick.

Close beside the boat a big trout broke the surface of the water. Nick pulled hard on one oar so the boat would turn and the bait spinning far behind would pass where the trout was feeding. As the trout's back came up out of the water the minnows jumped wildly. They sprinkled the surface like a handful of shot thrown into the water. Another trout broke water, feeding on the other side of the boat.

'They're feeding,' Marjorie said.

'But they won't strike,' Nick said.

He rowed the boat around to troll past both the feeding fish, then headed it for the point. Marjorie did not reel in until the boat touched the shore.

They pulled the boat up the beach and Nick lifted out a pail of live perch. The perch swam in the water in the pail. Nick caught three of them with his hands and cut their heads off and skinned them while Marjorie chased with her hands in the bucket, finally caught a perch, cut its head off and skinned it. Nick looked at her fish.

'You don't want to take the ventral fin out,' he said. 'It'll be all right for bait but it's better with the ventral fin in.'

He hooked each of the skinned perch through the tail. There were two hooks attached to a leader on each rod. Then

Marjorie rowed the boat out over the channel-bank, holding the line in her teeth, and looking toward Nick, who stood on the shore holding the rod and letting the line run out from the reel.

'That's about right,' he called.

'Should I let it drop?' Marjorie called back, holding the line in her hand.

'Sure. Let it go.' Marjorie dropped the line overboard and watched the baits go down through the water.

She came in with the boat and ran the second line out the same way. Each time Nick set a heavy slab of driftwood across the butt of the rod to hold it solid and propped it up at an angle with a small slab. He reeled in the slack line so the line ran taut out to where the bait rested on the sandy floor of the channel and set the click on the reel. When a trout, feeding on the bottom, took the bait it would run with it, taking line out of the reel in a rush and making the reel sing with the click on.

Marjorie rowed up the point a little way so she would not disturb the line. She pulled hard on the oars and the boat went way up the beach. Little waves came in with it. Marjorie stepped out of the boat and Nick pulled the boat high up the beach.

'What's the matter, Nick?' Marjorie asked.

'I don't know,' Nick said, getting wood for a fire.

They made a fire with driftwood. Marjorie went to the boat and brought a blanket. The evening breeze blew the smoke toward the point, so Marjorie spread the blanket out between the fire and the lake.

Marjorie sat on the blanket with her back to the fire and waited for Nick. He came over and sat down beside her on the blanket. In back of them was the close second-growth timber of the point and in front was the bay with the mouth of Hortons Creek. It was not quite dark. The firelight went as far as the water. They could both see the two steel rods at an angle over the dark water. The fire glinted on the reels.

Marjorie unpacked the basket of supper.

'I don't feel like eating,' said Nick.

'Come on and eat, Nick.'

'All right.'

They ate without talking, and watched the two rods and the firelight in the water.

'There's going to be a moon tonight,' said Nick. He looked across the bay to the hills that were beginning to sharpen against the sky. Beyond the hills he knew the moon was coming up.

'I know it,' Marjorie said happily.

'You know everything,' Nick said.

'Oh, Nick, please cut it out! Please, please don't be that way!'

'I can't help it,' Nick said. 'You do. You know everything. That's the trouble. You know you do.'

Marjorie did not say anything.

'I've taught you everything. You know you do. What don't you know, anyway?'

'Oh, shut up,' Marjorie said. 'There comes the moon.'

They sat on the blanket without touching each other and watched the moon rise.

'You don't have to talk silly,' Marjorie said; 'what's really the matter?'

'I don't know.'

'Of course you know.'

'No I don't.'

'Go on and say it.'

Nick looked on at the moon, coming up over the hills.

'It isn't fun any more.'

He was afraid to look at Marjorie. Then he looked at her. She sat there with her back toward him. He looked at her back. 'It isn't fun any more. Not any of it.'

She didn't say anything. He went on, 'I feel as though everything was gone to hell inside of me. I don't know, Marge. I don't know what to say.'

He looked at her back.

'Isn't love any fun?' Marjorie said.

'No,' Nick said. Marjorie stood up. Nick sat there, his head in his hands.

'I'm going to take the boat,' Marjorie called to him. 'You can walk back around the point.'

'All right,' Nick said. 'I'll push the boat off for you.'

'You don't need to,' she said. She was afloat in the boat on the water with the moonlight on it. Nick went back and lay down with his face in the blanket by the fire. He could hear Marjorie rowing on the water.

He lay there for a long time. He lay there while he heard Bill come into the clearing, walking around through the woods. He felt Bill coming up to the fire. Bill didn't touch him, either.

'Did she go all right?' Bill said.

'Oh, yes,' Nick said, lying, his face on the blankets.

'Have a scene?'

'No, there wasn't any scene.'

'How do you feel?'

'Oh, go away, Bill! Go away for a while.'

Bill selected a sandwich from the lunch basket and walked over to have a look at the rods.

It was a frightfully hot day. We'd jammed an absolutely perfect barricade across the bridge. It was simply priceless. A big old wrought-iron grating from the front of a house. Too heavy to lift and you could shoot through it and they would have to climb over it. It was absolutely topping. They tried to get over it, and we potted them from forty yards. They rushed it, and officers came out alone and worked on it. It was an absolutely perfect obstacle. Their officers were very fine. We were frightfully put out when we heard the flank had gone, and we had to fall back.

The Three-Day Blow

The rain stopped as Nick turned into the road that went up through the orchard. The fruit had been picked and the fall wind blew through the bare trees. Nick stopped and picked up a Wagner apple from beside the road, shiny in the brown grass from the rain. He put the apple in the pocket of his Mackinaw coat.

The road came out of the orchard on to the top of the hill.

There was the cottage, the porch bare, smoke coming from the chimney. In back was the garage, the chicken coop and the second-growth timber like a hedge against the woods behind. The big trees swayed far over in the wind as he watched. It was the first of the autumn storms.

As Nick crossed the open field above the orchard the door of the cottage opened and Bill came out. He stood on the porch looking out.

'Well, Wemedge,' he said.

'Hey, Bill,' Nick said, coming up the steps.

They stood together looking out across the country, down over the orchard, beyond the road, across the lower fields and the woods of the point to the lake. The wind was blowing straight down the lake. They could see the surf along the Ten Mile point.

'She's blowing,' Nick said.

'She'll blow like that for three days,' Bill said.

'Is your dad in?' Nick asked.

'No. He's out with the gun. Come on in.'

Nick went inside the cottage. There was a big fire in the fireplace. The wind made it roar. Bill shut the door.

'Have a drink?' he said.

He went out to the kitchen and came back with two glasses and a pitcher of water. Nick reached the whisky bottle from the shelf above the fireplace.

'All right?' he said.

'Good,' said Bill.

They sat in front of the fire and drank the Irish whisky and water.

'It's got a swell, smoky taste,' Nick said, and looked at the fire through the glass.

'That's the peat,' Bill said.

'You can't get peat into liquor,' Nick said.

'That doesn't make any difference,' Bill said.

'You ever seen any peat?' Nick asked.

'No,' said Bill.

'Neither have I,' Nick said.

His shoes, stretched out on the hearth, began to steam in front of the fire.

'Better take your shoes off,' Bill said.

'I haven't got any socks on.'

'Take them off and dry them and I'll get you some,' Bill said. He went upstairs into the loft and Nick heard him walking about overhead. Upstairs was open under the roof and was where Bill and his father and he, Nick, sometimes slept. In back was a dressing-room. They moved the cots back out of the rain and covered them with rubber blankets.

Bill came down with a pair of heavy wool socks.

'It's getting too late to go around without socks,' he said.

'I hate to start them again,' Nick said. He pulled the socks on and slumped back in the chair, putting his feet up on the screen in front of the fire.

'You'll dent in the screen,' Bill said. Nick swung his feet over to the side of the fireplace.

'Got anything to read?' he asked.

'Only the paper.'

'What did the Cards do?'

'Dropped a double header to the Giants.'

'That ought to cinch it for them.'

'It's a gift,' Bill said. 'As long as McGraw can buy every good player in the league there's nothing to it.'

'He can't buy them all,' Nick said.

'He buys all the ones he wants,' Bill said. 'Or he makes them discontented so they have to trade them to him.'

'Like Heinie Zim,' Nick agreed.

'That bonehead will do him a lot of good.'

Bill stood up.

'He can hit,' Nick offered. The heat from the fire was baking his legs.

'He's a sweet fielder, too,' Bill said. 'But he loses ball games.'

'Maybe that's what McGraw wants him for,' Nick suggested.

'Maybe,' Bill agreed.

'There's always more to it than we know about,' Nick said.

'Of course. But we've got pretty good dope for being so far away.'

'Like how much better you can pick them if you don't

see the horses.'

'That's it.'

Bill reached down the whisky bottle. His big hand went all the way around it. He poured the whisky into the glass Nick held out.

'How much water?'

'Just the same.'

He sat down on the floor beside Nick's chair.

'It's good when the fall storms come, isn't it?' Nick said.

'It's swell.'

'It's the best time of year,' Nick said.

'Wouldn't it be hell to be in town?' Bill said.

'I'd like to see the World Series,' Nick said.

'Well, they're always in New York or Philadelphia now,' Bill said. 'That doesn't do us any good.'

'I wonder if the Cards will ever win a pennant?'

'Not in our lifetime,' Bill said.

'Gee, they'd go crazy,' Nick said.

'Do you remember when they got going that once before they had the train wreck?'

'Boy!' Nick said, remembering.

Bill reached over to the table under the window for the book that lay there, face down, where he had put it when he went to the door. He held his glass in one hand and the book in the other, leaning back against Nick's chair.

'What are you reading?'

'*Richard Feverel.*'

'I couldn't get into it.'

'It's all right,' Bill said. 'It ain't a bad book, Wemedge.'

'What else have you got I haven't read?' Nick asked.

'Did you read the *Forest Lovers*?'

'Yup. That's the one where they go to bed every night with the naked sword between them.'

'That's a good book, Wemedge.'

'It's a swell book. What I couldn't ever understand was what good the sword would do. It would have to stay edge up all the time because if it went over flat you could roll right over it and it wouldn't make any trouble.'

'It's a symbol,' Bill said.

313

'Sure,' said Nick, 'but it isn't practical.'

'Did you ever read *Fortitude?*'

'It's fine,' Nick said. 'That's a real book. That's where his old man is after him all the time. Have you got any more by Walpole?'

'*The Dark Forest,*' Bill said. 'It's about Russia.'

'What does he know about Russia?' Nick asked.

'I don't know. You can't ever tell about those guys. Maybe he was there when he was a boy. He's got a lot of dope on it.'

'I'd like to meet him,' Nick said.

'I'd like to meet Chesterton,' Bill said.

'I wish he was here now,' Nick said. 'We'd take him fishing to the 'Voix tomorrow.'

'I wonder if he'd like to go fishing,' Bill said.

'Sure,' said Nick. 'He must be about the best guy there is. Do you remember the *Flying Inn?*'

> 'If an angel out of heaven
> Gives you something else to drink,
> Thank him for his kind intentions;
> Go and pour them down the sink!'

'That's right,' said Nick. 'I guess he's a better guy than Walpole.'

'Oh, he's a better guy, all right,' Bill said.

'But Walpole's a better writer.'

'I don't know,' Nick said. 'Chesterton's a classic.'

'Walpole's a classic, too,' Bill insisted.

'I wish we had them both here,' Nick said. 'We'd take them both fishing to the 'Voix tomorrow.'

'Let's get drunk,' Bill said.

'All right,' Nick agreed.

'My old man won't care,' Bill said.

'Are you sure?' said Nick.

'I know it,' Bill said.

'I'm a little drunk now,' Nick said.

'You aren't drunk,' Bill said.

He got up from the floor and reached for the whisky bottle. Nick held out his glass. His eyes fixed on it while Bill poured.

Bill poured the glass half-full of whisky.

'Put in your own water,' he said. 'There's just one more shot.'

'Got any more?' Nick asked.

'There's plenty more but dad only likes me to drink what's open.'

'Sure,' said Nick.

'He says opening bottles is what makes drunkards,' Bill explained.

'That's right,' said Nick. He was impressed. He had never thought of that before. He had always thought it was solitary drinking that made drunkards.

'How is your dad?' he asked respectfully.

'He's all right,' Bill said. 'He gets a little wild sometimes.'

'He's a swell guy,' Nick said. He poured water into his glass out of the pitcher. It mixed slowly with the whisky. There was more whisky than water.

'You bet your life he is,' Bill said.

'My old man's all right,' Nick said.

'You're damn right he is,' said Bill.

'He claims he's never taken a drink in his life,' Nick said, as though announcing a scientific fact.

'Well, he's a doctor. My old man's a painter. That's different.'

'He's missed a lot,' Nick said sadly.

'You can't tell,' Bill said. 'Everything's got its compensations.'

'He says he's missed a lot himself,' Nick confessed.

'Well, Dad's had a tough time,' Bill said.

'It all evens up,' Nick said.

They sat looking into the fire and thinking of this profound truth.

'I'll get a chunk from the back porch,' Nick said. He had noticed while looking into the fire that the fire was dying down. Also he wished to show he could hold his liquor and be practical. Even if his father had never touched a drop Bill was not going to get him drunk before he himself was drunk.

'Bring one of the big beech chunks,' Bill said. He was also being consciously practical.

Nick came in with the log through the kitchen and in

passing knocked a pan off the kitchen table. He laid the log down and picked up the pan. It had contained dried apricots, soaking in water. He carefully picked up all the dried apricots off the floor, some of them had gone under the stove, and put them back in the pan. He dipped some more water on to them from the pail by the table. He felt quite proud of himself. He had been thoroughly practical.

He came in carrying the log and Bill got up from the chair and helped him put it on the fire.

'That's a swell log,' Nick said.

'I'd been saving it for the bad weather,' Bill said. 'A log like that will burn all night.'

'There'll be coals left to start the fire in the morning,' Nick said.

'That's right,' Bill agreed. They were conducting the conversation on a high plane.

'Let's have another drink,' Nick said.

'I think there's another bottle open in the locker,' Bill said.

He kneeled down in the corner in front of the locker and brought out a square-faced bottle.

'It's Scotch,' he said.

'I'll get some more water,' Nick said. He went out into the kitchen again. He filled the pitcher with the dipper, dipping cold spring water from the pail. On his way back to the living-room he passed a mirror in the dining-room and looked in it. His face looked strange. He smiled at the face in the mirror and it grinned back at him. He winked at it and went on. It was not his face but it didn't make any difference.

Bill had poured out the drinks.

'That's an awfully big shot,' Nick said.

'Not for us, Wemedge,' Bill said.

'What'll we drink to?' Nick asked, holding up the glass.

'Let's drink to fishing,' Bill said.

'All right,' Nick said. 'Gentlemen, I give you fishing.'

'All fishing,' Bill said. 'Everywhere.'

'Fishing,' Nick said. 'That's what we drink to.'

'It's better than baseball,' Bill said.

'There isn't any comparison,' said Nick. 'How did we ever get talking about baseball?'

'It was a mistake,' Bill said. 'Baseball is a game for louts.'

They drank all that was in their glasses.

'Now let's drink to Chesterton.'

'And Walpole,' Nick interposed.

Nick poured out the liquor. Bill poured in the water. They looked at each other. They felt very fine.

'Gentlemen,' Bill said, 'I give you Chesterton and Walpole.'

'Exactly, gentlemen,' Nick said.

They drank. Bill filled up the glasses. They sat down in the big chairs in front of the fire.

'You were very wise, Wemedge,' Bill said.

'What do you mean?' asked Nick.

'To bust off that Marge business,' Bill said.

'I guess so,' said Nick.

'It was the only thing to do. If you hadn't, by now you'd be back home working trying to get enough money to get married.'

Nick said nothing.

'Once a man's married he's absolutely bitched,' Bill went on. 'He hasn't got anything more. Nothing. Not a damn thing. He's done for. You've seen the guys that get married.'

Nick said nothing.

'You can tell them,' Bill said, 'They get this sort of fat married look. They're done for.'

'Sure,' said Nick.

'It was probably bad busting it off,' Bill said. 'But you always fall for somebody else and then it's all right. Fall for them but don't let them ruin you.'

'Yes,' said Nick.

'If you'd have married her you would have had to marry the whole family. Remember her mother and that guy she married.'

Nick nodded.

'Imagine having them around the house all the time and going to Sunday dinners at their house, and having them over to dinner and telling Marge all the time what to do and how to act.'

Nick sat quiet.

'You came out of it damned well,' Bill said. 'Now she can

marry somebody of her own sort and settle down and be happy. You can't mix oil and water and you can't mix that sort of thing any more than if I'd marry Ida that works for Strattons. She'd probably like it, too.'

Nick said nothing. The liquor had all died out of him and left him alone. Bill wasn't there. He wasn't sitting in front of the fire or going fishing tomorrow with Bill and his dad or anything. He wasn't drunk. It was all gone. All he knew was that he had once had Marjorie and that he had lost her. She was gone and he had sent her away. That was all that mattered. He might never see her again. Probably he never would. It was all gone, finished.

'Let's have another drink,' Nick said.

Bill poured it out. Nick splashed in a little water.

'If you'd gone on that way we wouldn't be here now,' Bill said.

That was true. His original plan had been to go down home and get a job. Then he had planned to stay in Charlevoix all winter so he could be near Marge. Now he did not know what he was going to do.

'Probably we wouldn't even be going fishing tomorrow,' Bill said. 'You had the right dope, all right.'

'I couldn't help it,' Nick said.

'I know. That's the way it works out,' Bill said.

'All of a sudden everything was over,' Nick said. 'I don't know why it was. I couldn't help it. Just like when the three-day blows come now and rip all the leaves off the trees.'

'Well, it's over. That's the point,' Bill said.

'It was my fault,' Nick said.

'It doesn't make any difference whose fault it was,' Bill said.

'No, I suppose not,' Nick said.

The big thing was that Marjorie was gone and that probably he would never see her again. He had talked to her about how they would go to Italy together and the fun they would have. Places they would be together. It was all gone now.

'So long as it's over that's all that matters,' Bill said. 'I tell you, Wemedge, I was worried while it was going on. You played it right. I understand her mother is sore as hell. She told a lot of people you were engaged.'

'We weren't engaged,' Nick said.

'It was all around that you were.'

'I can't help it,' Nick said. 'We weren't.'

'Weren't you going to get married?' Bill asked.

'Yes. But we weren't engaged,' Nick said.

'What's the difference?' Bill asked judicially.

'I don't know. There's a difference.'

'I don't see it,' said Bill.

'All right,' said Nick. 'Let's get drunk.'

'All right,' Bill said. 'Let's get really drunk.'

'Let's get drunk and then go swimming,' Nick said.

He drank off his glass.

'I'm sorry as hell about her but what could I do?' he said. 'You know what her mother was like!'

'She was terrible,' Bill said.

'All of a sudden it was over,' Nick said. 'I oughtn't to talk about it.'

'You aren't,' Bill said. 'I talked about it and now I'm through. We won't ever speak about it again. You don't want to think about it. You might get back into it again.'

Nick had not thought about that. It had seemed so absolute. That was a thought. That made him feel better.

'Sure,' he said. 'There's always that danger.'

He felt happy now. There was not anything that was irrevocable. He might go into town Saturday night. Today was Thursday.

'There's always a chance,' he said.

'You'll have to watch yourself,' Bill said.

'I'll watch myself,' he said.

He felt happy. Nothing was finished. Nothing was ever lost. He would go into town on Saturday. He felt lighter, as he had felt before Bill started to talk about it. There was always a way out.

'Let's take the guns and go down to the point and look for your dad,' Nick said.

'All right.'

Bill took down the two shotguns from the rack on the wall. He opened a box of shells. Nick put on his Mackinaw coat and his shoes. His shoes were stiff from the drying. He was still quite drunk but his head was clear.

'How do you feel?' Nick asked.

'Swell, I've just got a good edge on.' Bill was buttoning up his sweater.

'There's no use getting drunk.'

'No. We ought to get outdoors.'

They stepped out the door. The wind was blowing a gale.

'The birds will lie right down in the grass with this,' Nick said.

They struck down toward the orchard.

'I saw a woodcock this morning,' Bill said.

'Maybe we'll jump him,' Nick said.

'You can't shoot in this wind,' Bill said.

Outside now the Marge business was no longer so tragic. It was not even very important. The wind blew everything like that away.

'It's coming right off the big lake,' Nick said.

Against the wind they heard the thud of a shotgun.

'That's Dad,' Bill said. 'He's down in the swamp.'

'Let's cut down that way,' Nick said.

'Let's cut across the lower meadow and see if we jump anything,' Bill said.

'All right,' Nick said.

None of it was important now. The wind blew it out of his head. Still, he could always go into town Saturday night. It was a good thing to have in reserve.

They shot the six cabinet ministers at half past six in the morning against the wall of the hospital. There were pools of water in the courtyard. There were wet dead leaves on the paving of the courtyard. It rained hard. All the shutters of the hospital were nailed shut. One of the ministers was sick with typhoid. Two soldiers carried him downstairs and out into the rain. They tried to hold him up against the wall but he sat down in a puddle of water. The other five stood quietly against the wall. Finally the officer told the soldiers it was no good trying to make him stand up. When they fired the first volley he was sitting down in the water with his head on his knees.

The Battler

Nick stood up. He was all right. He looked up the track at the lights of the caboose going out of sight around a curve. There was water on both sides of the track, then tamarack swamp.

He felt his knee. The pants were torn and the skin was barked. His hands were scraped and there were sand and cinders driven up under his nails. He went over to the edge of the track, down the little slope to the water and washed his hands. He washed them carefully in the cold water, getting the dirt out from the nails. He squatted down and bathed his knee.

That lousy crut of a brakeman. He would get him some day. He would know him again. That was a fine way to act.

'Come here, kid,' he said. 'I got something for you.'

He had fallen for it. What a lousy kid thing to have done. They would never suck him in that way again.

'Come here, kid, I got something for you.' Then *wham* and he lit on his hands and knees beside the track.

Nick rubbed his eye. There was a big bump coming up. He would have a black eye, all right. It ached already. That son of a crutting brakeman.

He touched the bump over his eye with his fingers. Oh, well, it was only a black eye. That was all that he had gotten out of it. Cheap at the price. He wished he could see it. Could not see it looking into the water, though. It was dark and he was a long way off from anywhere. He wiped his hands on his trousers and stood up, then climbed the embankment to the rails.

He started up the track. It was well ballasted and made easy walking, sand and gravel packed between the ties, solid walking. The smooth roadbed like a causeway went on ahead through the swamp. Nick walked along. He must get to somewhere.

Nick had swung on to the freight train when it slowed down for the yards outside of Walton Junction. The train, with Nick

321

on it, had passed through Kalkaska as it started to get dark. Now he must be nearly to Mancelona. Three or four miles of swamp. He stepped along the track, walking so he kept on the ballast between the ties, the swamp ghostly in the rising mist. His eye ached and he was hungry. He kept on hiking, putting the miles of track back of him. The swamp was all the same on both sides of the track.

Ahead there was a bridge. Nick crossed it, his boots ringing hollow on the iron. Down below the water showed black between the splits of ties. Nick kicked a loose spike and it dropped into the water. Beyond the bridge were hills. It was high and dark on both sides of the track. Up the track Nick saw a fire.

He came up the track toward the fire carefully. It was off to one side of the track, below the railway embankment. He had only seen the light from it. The track came out through a cut and where the fire was burning the country opened out and fell away into woods. Nick dropped carefully down the embankment and cut into the woods to come up to the fire through the trees. It was a beechwood forest and the fallen beechnut burrs were under his shoes as he walked between the trees. The fire was bright now, just at the edge of the trees. There was a man sitting by it. Nick waited behind the tree and watched. The man looked to be alone. He was sitting there with his head in his hands looking at the fire. Nick stepped out and walked into the firelight.

The man sat there looking into the fire. When Nick stopped quite close to him he did not move.

'Hello!' Nick said.

The man looked up.

'Where did you get the shiner?' he said.

'A brakeman busted me.'

'Off the through freight?'

'Yes.'

'I saw the bastard,' the man said. 'He went through here 'bout an hour and a half ago. He was walking the top of the cars slapping his arms and singing.'

'The bastard!'

'It must have made him feel good to bust you,' the man said seriously.

'I'll bust him.'

'Get him with a rock some time when he's going through,' the man advised.

'I'll get him.'

'You're a tough one, aren't you?'

'No,' Nick answered.

'All you kids are tough.'

'You got to be tough,' Nick said.

'That's what I said.'

The man looked at Nick and smiled. In the firelight Nick saw that his face was misshapen. His nose was sunken, his eyes were slits, he had queer shaped lips. Nick did not perceive all this at once, he only saw the man's face was queerly formed and mutilated. It was like putty in colour. Dead looking in the firelight.

'Don't you like my pan?' the man asked.

Nick was embarrassed.

'Sure,' he said.

'Look here!' the man took off his cap.

He had only one ear. It was thickened and tight against the side of his head. Where the other ear should have been there was a stump.

'Ever see one like that?'

'No,' said Nick. It made him a little sick.

'I could take it,' the man said. 'Don't you think I could take it, kid?'

'You bet!'

'They all bust their hands on me,' the little man said. 'They couldn't hurt me.'

He looked at Nick. 'Sit down,' he said. 'Want to eat?'

'Don't bother,' Nick said. 'I'm going on to the town.'

'Listen!' the man said. 'Call me Ad.'

'Sure!'

'Listen,' the little man said. 'I'm not quite right.'

'What's the matter?'

'I'm crazy.'

He put on his cap. Nick felt like laughing.

'You're all right,' he said.

'No, I'm not. I'm crazy. Listen, you ever been crazy?'

323

'No,' Nick said. 'How does it get you?'

'I don't know,' Ad said. 'When you got it you don't know about it. You know me, don't you?'

'No.'

'I'm Ad Francis.'

'Honest to God?'

'Don't you believe it?'

'Yes.'

Nick knew it must be true.

'You know how I beat them?'

'No.' Nick said.

'My heart's slow. It only beats forty a minute. Feel it.'

Nick hesitated.

'Come on,' the man took hold of his hand. 'Take hold of my wrist. Put your fingers there.'

The little man's wrist was thick and the muscles bulged above the bone. Nick felt the slow pumping under his fingers.

'Got a watch?'

'No.'

'Neither have I,' Ad said. 'It ain't any good if you haven't got a watch.'

Nick dropped his wrist.

'Listen,' Ad Francis said. 'Take ahold again. You count and I'll count up to sixty.'

Feeling the slow hard throb under his fingers Nick started to count. He heard the little man counting slowly, one, two, three, four, five, and on – aloud.

'Sixty,' Ad finished. 'That's a minute. What did you make it?'

'Forty,' Nick said.

'That's right,' Ad said happily. 'She never speeds up.'

A man dropped down the railroad embankment and came across the clearing to the fire.

'Hello, Bugs!' Ad said.

'Hello!' Bugs answered. It was a Negro's voice. Nick knew from the way he walked that he was a Negro. He stood with his back to them bending over the fire. He straightened up.

'This is my pal Bugs,' Ad said. 'He's crazy, too.'

'Glad to meet you,' Bugs said. 'Where you say you're from?'

'Chicago,' Nick said.

'That's a fine town,' the Negro said. 'I didn't catch your name.'

'Adams. Nick Adams.'

'He says he's never been crazy, Bugs,' Ad said.

'He's got a lot coming to him,' the Negro said. He was unwrapping a package by the fire.

'When are we going to eat, Bugs?' the prize-fighter asked.

'Right away.'

'Are you hungry, Nick?'

'Hungry as hell.'

'Hear that, Bugs?'

'I hear most of what goes on.'

'That ain't what I asked you.'

'Yes. I heard what the gentleman said.'

Into a skillet he was laying slices of ham. As the skillet grew hot the grease sputtered and Bugs, crouching on long nigger legs over the fire, turned the ham and broke eggs into the skillet, tipping it from side to side to baste the eggs with the hot fat.

'Will you cut some bread out of that bag, Mister Adams?' Bugs turned from the fire.

'Sure.'

Nick reached in the bag and brought out a loaf of bread. He cut six slices. Ad watched him and leaned forward. 'Let me take your knife, Nick,' he said.

'No, you don't,' the Negro said. 'Hang on to your knife, Mister Adams.'

The prize-fighter sat back.

'Will you bring me the bread, Mister Adams?' Bugs asked. Nick brought it over.

'Do you like to dip your bread in the ham fat?' the Negro asked.

'You bet!'

'Perhaps we'd better wait until later. It's better at the finish of the meal. Here.'

The Negro picked up a slice of ham and laid it on one of the pieces of bread, then slid an egg on top of it.

'Just close that sandwich, will you, please, and give it to Mister Francis.'

Ad took the sandwich and started eating.

'Watch out how that egg runs,' the Negro warned. 'This is for you, Mister Adams. The remainder for myself.'

Nick bit into the sandwich. The Negro was sitting opposite him beside Ad. The hot fried ham and eggs tasted wonderful.

'Mister Adams is right hungry,' the Negro said. The little man whom Nick knew by name as a former champion fighter was silent. He had said nothing since the Negro had spoken about the knife.

'May I offer you a slice of bread dipped right in the hot ham fat?' Bugs said.

'Thanks a lot.'

The little white man looked at Nick.

'Will you have some, Mister Adolph Francis?' Bugs offered from the skillet.

Ad did not answer. He was looking at Nick.

'Mister Francis?' came the nigger's soft voice.

Ad did not answer. He was looking at Nick.

'I spoke to you, Mister Francis,' the nigger said softly.

Ad kept on looking at Nick. He had his cap down over his eyes. Nick felt nervous.

'How the hell do you get that way?' came out from under the cap sharply at Nick.

'Who the hell do you think you are? You're a snotty bastard. You come in here when nobody asks you and eat a man's food and when he asks to borrow a knife you get snotty.'

He glared at Nick, his face was white and his eyes almost out of sight under his cap.

'You're a hot sketch. Who the hell asked you to butt in here?'

'Nobody.'

'You're damn right nobody did. Nobody asked you to stay either. You come in here and act snotty about my face and smoke my cigars and drink my liquor and then talk snotty. Where the hell do you think you get off?'

Nick said nothing. Ad stood up.

'I'll tell you, you yellow-livered Chicago bastard. You're going to get your can knocked off. Do you get that?'

Nick stepped back. The little man came toward him slowly,

326

stepping flat-footed forward, his left foot stepping forward, his right dragging up to it.

'Hit me,' he moved his head. 'Try and hit me.'

'I don't want to hit you.'

'You won't get out of it that way. You're going to take a beating, see? Come on and lead at me.'

'Cut it out,' Nick said.

'All right, then, you bastard.'

The little man looked down at Nick's feet. As he looked down the Negro, who had followed behind him as he moved away from the fire, set himself and tapped him across the base of the skull. He fell forward and Bugs dropped the cloth-wrapped blackjack on the grass. The little man lay there, his face in the grass. The Negro picked him up, his head hanging, and carried him to the fire. His face looked bad, the eyes open. Bugs laid him down gently.

'Will you bring me the water in the bucket, Mister Adams?' he said. 'I'm afraid I hit him just a little hard.'

The Negro splashed water with his hand on the man's face and pulled his ears gently. The eyes closed.

Bugs stood up.

'He's all right,' he said. 'There's nothing to worry about. I'm sorry, Mister Adams.'

'It's all right.' Nick was looking down at the little man. He saw the blackjack on the grass and picked it up. It had a flexible handle and was limber in his hand. Worn black leather with a handkerchief wrapped around the heavy end.

'That's a whalebone handle,' the Negro smiled. 'They don't make them any more. I didn't know how well you could take care of yourself and, anyway, I didn't want you to hurt him or mark him up no more than he is.'

The Negro smiled again.

'You hurt him yourself.'

'I know how to do it. He won't remember nothing of it. I have to do it to change him when he gets that way.'

Nick was still looking down at the little man, lying, his eyes closed in the firelight. Bugs put some wood on the fire.

'Don't worry about him none, Mister Adams. I seen him like this plenty of times before.'

'What made him crazy?' Nick said.

'Oh, a lot of things,' the Negro answered from the fire. 'Would you like a cup of this coffee, Mister Adams?'

He handed Nick the cup and smoothed the coat he had placed under the unconscious man's head.

'He took too many beatings, for one thing,' the Negro sipped the coffee. 'But that just made him sort of simple. Then his sister was his manager and they was always being written up in the papers all about brothers and sisters and how she loved her brother and how he loved his sister, and then they got married in New York and that made a lot of unpleasantness.'

'I remember about it.'

'Sure. Of course they wasn't brother and sister no more than a rabbit, but there was a lot of people didn't like it either way and they commenced to have disagreements, and one day she just went off and never come back.'

He drank the coffee and wiped his lips with the pink palm of his hand.

'He just went crazy. Will you have some more coffee, Mister Adams?'

'Thanks.'

'I seen her a couple of times,' the Negro went on. 'She was an awful good-looking woman. Looked enough like him to be twins. He wouldn't be bad-looking without his face all busted.'

He stopped. The story seemed to be over.

'Where did you meet him?' asked Nick.

'I met him in jail,' the Negro said. 'He was busting people all the time after she went away and they put him in jail. I was in for cuttin' a man.'

He smiled, and went on, soft-voiced:

'Right away I liked him and when I got out I looked him up. He likes to think I'm crazy and I don't mind. I like to be with him and I like seeing the country and I don't have to commit no larceny to do it. I like living like a gentleman.'

'What do you all do?' Nick asked.

'Oh, nothing. Just move around. He's got money.'

'He must have made a lot of money.'

'Sure. He spent all his money, though. Or they took it away from him. She sends him money.'

He poked up the fire.

'She's a mighty fine woman,' he said. 'She looks enough like him to be his own twin.'

The Negro looked over at the little man, lying breathing heavily. His blond hair was down over his forehead. His mutilated face looked childish in repose.

'I can wake him up any time now, Mister Adams. If you don't mind I wish you'd sort of pull out. I don't like to not be hospitable, but it might disturb him back again to see you. I hate to have to thump him and it's the only thing to do when he gets started. I have to sort of keep him away from people. You don't mind, do you Mister Adams? No, don't thank me, Mister Adams. I'd have warned you about him but he seemed to have taken such a liking to you and I thought things were going to be all right. You'll hit a town about two miles up the track. Mancelona they call it. Good-bye. I wish we could ask you to stay the night but it's just out of the question. Would you like to take some of that ham and some bread with you? No? You better take a sandwich,' all this in a low, smooth, polite nigger voice.

'Good. Well, good-bye, Mister Adams. Good-bye and good luck!'

Nick walked away from the fire across the clearing to the railway tracks. Out off the range of the fire he listened. The low soft voice of the Negro was talking. Nick could not hear the words. Then he heard the little man say, 'I got an awful headache, Bugs.'

'You'll feel better, Mister Francis,' the Negro's voice soothed. 'Just you drink a cup of this hot coffee.'

Nick climbed the embankment and started up the track. He found he had a ham sandwich in his hand and put it in his pocket. Looking back from the mounting grade before the track curved into the hills he could see the firelight in the clearing.

Nick sat against the wall of the church where they had dragged him to be clear of machine-gun fire in the street. Both legs stuck out awkwardly. He had been hit in the spine. His face was sweaty and dirty. The sun shone on his face. The day was very hot.

Rinaldi, big backed, his equipment sprawling, lay face downward against the wall. Nick looked straight ahead brilliantly. The pink wall of the house opposite had fallen out from the roof and an iron bedstead hung twisted toward the street. Two Austrian dead lay in the rubble in the shade of the house. Up the street were other dead. Things were getting forward in the town. It was going well. Stretcher bearers would be along any time now. Nick turned his head and looked down at Rinaldi. 'Senta Rinaldo; Senta. You and me we've made a separate peace.' Rinaldi lay still in the sun, breathing with difficulty. 'We're not patriots.' Nick turned his head away, smiling sweatily. Rinaldi was a disappointing audience.

A Very Short Story

One hot evening in Padua they carried him up on to the roof and he could look out over the top of the town. There were chimney swifts in the sky. After a while it got dark and the searchlights came out. The others went down and took the bottles with them. He and Luz could hear them below on the balcony. Luz sat on the bed. She was cool and fresh in the hot night.

Luz stayed on night duty for three months. They were glad to let her. When they operated on him she prepared him for the operating table; and they had a joke about friend or enema. He went under the anaesthetic holding tight on to himself so he would not blab about anything during the silly, talky time. After he got on crutches he used to take the temperatures so Luz would not have to get up from the bed. There were only a few patients, and they all knew about it. They all liked Luz. As he walked back along the halls he thought of Luz in his bed.

Before he went back to the front they went into the Duomo and prayed. It was dim and quiet, and there were other people praying. They wanted to get married, but there was not enough time for the banns, and neither of them had birth certificates. They felt as though they were married, but they wanted everyone to know about it, and to make it so they could not lose it.

Luz wrote him many letters that he never got until after the armistice. Fifteen came in a bunch to the front and he sorted them by the dates and read them all straight through. They were all about the hospital and how much she loved him and how it was impossible to get along without him and how terrible it was missing him at night.

After the armistice they agreed he should go home to get a job so they might be married. Luz would not come home until he had a good job and could come to New York to meet her. It was understood he would not drink, and he did not want to see his friends or anyone in the States. Only to get a job and be married. On the train from Padua to Milan they quarrelled about her not being willing to come home at once. When they had to say good-bye, in the station at Milan, they kissed good-bye, but were not finished with the quarrel. He felt sick about saying good-bye like that.

He went to America on a boat from Genoa. Luz went back to Pordenone to open a hospital. It was lonely and rainy there, and there was a battalion of arditi quartered in the town. Living in the muddy, rainy town in the winter, the major of the battalion made love to Luz, and she had never known Italians before, and finally wrote to the States that theirs had been only a boy and girl affair. She was sorry, and she knew he would probably not be able to understand, but might some day forgive her, and be grateful to her, and she expected, absolutely unexpectedly, to be married in the spring. She loved him as always, but she realized now it was only a boy and girl love. She hoped he would have a great career, and believed in him absolutely. She knew it was for the best.

The major did not marry her in the spring, or any other time. Luz never got an answer to the letter to Chicago about it. A short time after he contracted gonorrhoea from a sales girl in a Loop department store while riding in a taxicab through Lincoln Park.

While the bombardment was knocking the trench to pieces at Fossalta, he lay very flat and sweated and prayed, 'Oh Jesus

Christ, get me out of here. Dear Jesus, please get me out. Christ, please, please, please, Christ. If you only keep me from getting killed I'll do anything you say. I believe in you and I'll tell everybody in the world that you are the only thing that matters. Please, please, dear Jesus.' The shelling moved further up the line. We went to work on the trench and in the morning the sun came up and the day was hot and muggy and cheerful and quiet. The next night back at Mestre he did not tell the girl he went upstairs with at the Villa Rossa about Jesus. And he never told anybody.

Soldier's Home

Krebs went to the war from a Methodist college in Kansas. There is a picture which shows him among his fraternity brothers, all of them wearing exactly the same height and style collar. He enlisted in the Marines in 1917 and did not return to the United States until the second division returned from the Rhine in the summer of 1919.

There is a picture which shows him on the Rhine with two German girls and another corporal. Krebs and the corporal look too big for their uniforms. The German girls are not beautiful. The Rhine does not show in the picture.

By the time Krebs returned to his home town in Oklahoma the greeting of heroes was over. He came back much too late. The men from the town who had been drafted had all been welcomed elaborately on their return. There had been a great deal of hysteria. Now the reaction had set in. People seemed to think it was rather ridiculous for Krebs to be getting back so late, years after the war was over.

At first Krebs, who had been at Belleau Wood, Soissons, the Champagne, St Mihiel and in the Argonne did not want to talk about the war at all. Later he felt the need to talk but no one wanted to hear about it. His town had heard too many atrocity stories to be thrilled by actualities. Krebs found that to be listened to at all he had to lie, and after he had done this twice he, too, had a reaction against the war and against talking about it. A distaste for everything that happened to him in the war set in because of the lies he had told. All of the times that had been able to make him feel cool and clear inside himself when he thought of them; the times so long back when he had done the one thing, the only thing for a man to do, easily and naturally, when he might have done something else, now lost their cool, valuable quality and then were lost themselves.

His lies were quite unimportant lies and consisted in attributing to himself things other men had seen, done or heard of, and stating as facts certain apocryphal incidents familiar to all soldiers. Even his lies were not sensational at the pool room. His acquaintances, who had heard detailed accounts of German women found chained to machine-guns in the Argonne forest and who could not comprehend, or were barred by their patriotism from interest in, any German machine-gunners who were not chained, were not thrilled by his stories.

Krebs acquired the nausea in regard to experience that is the result of untruth or exaggeration, and when he occasionally met another man who had really been a soldier and they talked a few minutes in the dressing-room at a dance he fell into the easy pose of the old soldier among other soldiers: that he had been badly, sickeningly frightened all the time. In this way he lost everything.

During this time, it was late summer, he was sleeping late in bed, getting up to walk down town to the library to get a book, eating lunch at home, reading on the front porch until he became bored and then walking down through the town to spend the hottest hours of the day in the cool dark of the pool room. He loved to play pool.

In the evening he practised on his clarinet, strolled down town, read and went to bed. He was still a hero to his two young sisters. His mother would have given him breakfast in bed if he had wanted it. She often came in when he was in bed and asked him to tell her about the war, but her attention always wandered. His father was non-committal.

Before Krebs went away to the war he had never been allowed to drive the family motor car. His father was in the real

333

estate business and always wanted the car to be at his command when he required it to take clients out into the country to show them a piece of farm property. The car always stood outside the First National Bank building where his father had an office on the second floor. Now, after the war, it was still the same car.

Nothing was changed in the town except that the young girls had grown up. But they lived in such a complicated world of already defined alliances and shifting feuds that Krebs did not feel the energy or the courage to break into it. He liked to look at them, though. There were so many good-looking young girls. Most of them had their hair cut short. When he went away only little girls wore their hair like that or girls that were fast. They all wore sweaters and shirt waists with round Dutch collars. It was a pattern. He liked to look at them from the front porch as they walked on the other side of the street. He liked to watch them walking under the shade of the trees. He liked the round Dutch collars above their sweaters. He liked their silk stockings and flat shoes. He liked their bobbed hair and the way they walked.

When he was in town their appeal to him was not very strong. He did not like them when he saw them in the Greek's ice cream parlour. He did not want them themselves really. They were too complicated. There was something else. Vaguely he wanted a girl but he did not want to have to work to get her. He would have liked to have a girl but he did not want to have to spend a long time getting her. He did not want to get into the intrigue and the politics. He did not want to have to do any courting. He did not want to tell any more lies. It wasn't worth it.

He did not want any consequences. He did not want any consequences ever again. He wanted to live along without consequences. Besides he did not really need a girl. The army had taught him that. It was all right to pose as though you had to have a girl. Nearly everybody did that. But it wasn't true. You did not need a girl. That was the funny thing. First a fellow boasted how girls mean nothing to him, that he never thought of them, that they could not touch him. Then a fellow boasted that he could not get along without girls, that he had to have them all the time, that he could not go to sleep without them.

That was all a lie. It was all a lie both ways. You did not need a girl unless you thought about them. He learned that in the army. Then sooner or later you always got one. When you were really ripe for a girl you always got one. You did not have to think about it. Sooner or later it would come. He had learned that in the army.

Now he would have liked a girl if she had come to him and not wanted to talk. But here at home it was all too complicated. He knew he could never go through it all again. It was not worth the trouble. That was the thing about French girls and German girls. There was not all this talking. You couldn't talk much and you did not need to talk. It was simple and you were friends. He thought about France and then he began to think about Germany. On the whole he had liked Germany better. He did not want to leave Germany. He did not want to come home. Still, he had come home. He sat on the front porch.

He liked the girls that were walking along the other side of the street. He liked the look of them much better than the French girls or the German girls. But the world they were in was not the world he was in. He would like to have one of them. But it was not worth it. They were such a nice pattern. He liked the pattern. It was exciting. But he would not go through all the talking. He did not want one badly enough. He liked to look at them all, though. It was not worth it. Not now when things were getting good again.

He sat there on the porch reading a book on the war. It was a history and he was reading about all the engagements he had been in. It was the most interesting reading he had ever done. He wished there were more maps. He looked forward with a good feeling to reading all the really good histories when they would come out with good detail maps. Now he was really learning about the war. He had been a good soldier. That made a difference.

One morning after he had been home about a month his mother came into his bedroom and sat on the bed. She smoothed her apron.

'I had a talk with your father last night, Harold,' she said, 'and he is willing for you to take the car out in the evenings.'

335

'Yeah?' said Krebs, who was not fully awake. 'Take the car out? Yeah?'

'Yes. Your father has felt for some time that you should be able to take the car out in the evenings whenever you wished but we only talked it over last night.'

'I'll bet you made him,' Krebs said.

'No. It was your father's suggestion that we talk the matter over.'

'Yeah. I'll bet you made him.' Krebs sat up in bed.

'Will you come down to breakfast, Harold?' his mother said.

'As soon as I get my clothes on,' Krebs said.

His mother went out of the room and he could hear her frying something downstairs while he washed, shaved and dressed to go down into the dining-room for breakfast. While he was eating breakfast his sister brought in the mail.

'Well, Hare,' she said. 'You old sleepy-head. What do you ever get up for?'

Krebs looked at her. He liked her. She was his best sister.

'Have you got the paper?' he asked.

She handed him the Kansas City *Star* and he shucked off its brown wrapper and opened it to the sporting page. He folded the *Star* open and propped it against the water pitcher with his cereal dish to steady it, so he could read while he ate.

'Harold,' his mother stood in the kitchen doorway, 'Harold, please don't muss up the paper. Your father can't read his *Star* if it's been mussed.'

'I won't muss it,' Krebs said.

His sister sat down at the table and watched him while he read.

'We're playing indoor over at school this afternoon,' she said. 'I'm going to pitch.'

'Good,' said Krebs. 'How's the old wing?'

'I can pitch better than lots of the boys. I tell them all you taught me. The other girls aren't much good.'

'Yeah?' said Krebs.

'I tell them all you're my beau. Aren't you my beau, Hare?'

'You bet.'

'Couldn't your brother really be your beau just because he's your brother?'

336

'I don't know.'

'Sure you know. Couldn't you be my beau, Hare, if I was old enough and if you wanted to?'

'Sure. You're my girl now.'

'Am I really your girl?'

'Sure.'

'Do you love me?'

'Uh, huh.'

'Will you love me always?'

'Sure.'

'Will you come over and watch me play indoor?'

'Maybe.'

'Aw, Hare, you don't love me. If you loved me, you'd want to come over and watch me play indoor.'

Krebs's mother came into the dining-room from the kitchen. She carried a plate with two fried eggs and some crisp bacon on it and a plate of buckwheat cakes.

'You run along, Helen,' she said. 'I want to talk to Harold.'

She put the eggs and bacon down in front of him and brought in a jug of maple syrup for the buckwheat cakes. Then she sat down across the table from Krebs.

'I wish you'd put down the paper a minute, Harold,' she said.

Krebs took down the paper and folded it.

'Have you decided what you are going to do yet, Harold?' his mother said, taking off her glasses.

'No,' said Krebs.

'Don't you think it's about time?' His mother did not say this in a mean way. She seemed worried.

'I hadn't thought about it,' Krebs said.

'God has some work for everyone to do,' his mother said. 'There can be no idle hands in His Kingdom.'

'I'm not in His Kingdom,' Krebs said.

'We are all of us in His Kingdom.'

Krebs felt embarrassed and resentful as always.

'I've worried about you so much, Harold,' his mother went on. 'I know the temptations you must have been exposed to. I know how weak men are. I know what your own dear grandfather, my own father, told us about the Civil

War and I have prayed for you. I pray for you all day long, Harold.'

Krebs looked at the bacon fat hardening on his plate.

'Your father is worried, too,' his mother went on. 'He thinks you have lost your ambition, that you haven't got a definite aim in life. Charley Simmons, who is just your age, has a good job and is going to be married. The boys are all settling down; they're all determined to get somewhere; you can see that boys like Charley Simmons are on their way to being really a credit to the community.'

Krebs said nothing.

'Don't look that way, Harold,' his mother said. 'You know we love you and I want to tell you for your own good how matters stand. Your father does not want to hamper your freedom. He thinks you should be allowed to drive the car. If you want to take some of the nice girls out riding with you, we are only too pleased. We want you to enjoy yourself. But you are going to have to settle down to work, Harold. Your father doesn't care what you start in at. All work is honourable as he says. But you've got to make a start at something. He asked me to speak to you this morning and then you can stop in and see him at his office.'

'Is that all?' Krebs said.

'Yes. Don't you love your mother, dear boy?'

'No,' said Krebs.

His mother looked at him across the table. Her eyes were shiny. She started crying.

'I don't love anybody,' Krebs said.

It wasn't any good. He couldn't tell her, he couldn't make her see it. It was silly to have said it. He had only hurt her. He went over and took hold of her arm. She was crying with her head in her hands.

'I didn't mean it,' he said. 'I was just angry at something. I didn't mean I didn't love you.'

His mother went on crying. Krebs put his arm on her shoulder.

'Can't you believe me, Mother?'

His mother shook her head.

'Please, please, Mother. Please believe me.'

'All right,' his mother said chokily. She looked up at him. 'I believe you, Harold.'

Krebs kissed her hair. She put her face up to him.

'I'm your mother,' she said. 'I held you next to my heart when you were a tiny baby.'

Krebs felt sick and vaguely nauseated.

'I know, Mummy,' he said. 'I'll try and be a good boy for you.'

'Would you kneel and pray with me, Harold?' his mother said.

They knelt down beside the dining-room table and Krebs's mother prayed.

'Now, you pray, Harold,' she said.

'I can't,' Krebs said.

'Try, Harold.'

'I can't.'

'Do you want me to pray for you?'

'Yes.'

So his mother prayed for him and then they stood up and Krebs kissed his mother and went out of the house. He had tried so to keep his life from being complicated. Still, none of it had touched him. He had felt sorry for his mother and she had made him lie. He would go to Kansas City and get a job and she would feel all right about it. There would be one more scene maybe before he got away. He would not go down to his father's office. He would miss that one. He wanted his life to go smoothly. It had just gotten going that way. Well, that was all over now, anyway. He would go over to the schoolyard and watch Helen play indoor baseball.

At two o'clock in the morning two Hungarians got into a cigar store at Fifteenth Street and Grand Avenue. Drevitts and Boyle drew up from the Fifteenth Street police station in a Ford. The Hungarians were backing their wagon out of an alley. Boyle shot one off the seat of the wagon and one off the wagon box. Drevitts got frightened when he found they were both dead. Hell, Jimmy,' he said, 'you oughtn't to have done it. There's liable to be a hell of a lot of trouble.'

'They're crooks, ain't they?' said Boyle. 'They're wops, ain't they? Who the hell is going to make any trouble?'

'That's all right maybe this time,' said Drevitts, 'but how did you know they were wops when you bumped them off?'

'Wops,' said Boyle, 'I can tell wops a mile off.'

The Revolutionist

In 1919 he was travelling on the railroads in Italy, carrying a square of oilcloth from the headquarters of the party written in indelible pencil and saying here was a comrade who had suffered very much under the Whites in Budapest and requesting comrades to aid him in any way. He used this instead of a ticket. He was very shy and quite young and the train men passed him on from one crew to another. He had no money, and they fed him behind the counter in railway eating houses.

He was delighted with Italy. It was a beautiful country, he said. The people were all kind. He had been in many towns, walked much, and seen many pictures. Giotto, Masaccio, and Piero della Francesca he bought reproductions of and carried them wrapped in a copy of *Avanti*. Mantegna he did not like.

He reported at Bologna, and I took him with me up to the Romagna where it was necessary I go to see a man. We had a good trip together. It was early September and the country was pleasant. He was a Magyar, a very nice boy and very shy. Horthy's men had done some bad things to him. He talked about it a little. In spite of Hungary, he believed altogether in the world revolution.

'But how is the movement going in Italy?' he asked.

'Very badly,' I said.

'But it will go better,' he said. 'You have everything here. It is the one country that everyone is sure of. It will be the starting-point of everything.'

I did not say anything.

At Bologna he said good-bye to us to go on the train to Milano and then to Aosta to walk over the pass into

Switzerland. I spoke to him about the Mantegnas in Milano. 'No,' he said, very shyly, he did not like Mantegna. I wrote out for him where to eat in Milano and the addresses of comrades. He thanked me very much, but his mind was already looking forward to walking over the pass. He was very eager to walk over the pass while the weather held good. He loved the mountains in the autumn. The last I heard of him the Swiss had him in jail near Sion.

The first matador got the horn through his sword hand and the crowd hooted him out. The second matador slipped, and the bull caught him through the belly and he hung on to the horn with one hand and held the other tight against the place, and the bull rammed him wham against the barrier and the horn came out, and he lay in the sand, and then got up like crazy drunk and tried to slug the men carrying him away and yelled for his sword, but he fainted. The kid came out and had to kill five bulls because you can't have more than three matadors, and the last bull he was so tired he could hardly get the sword in. He could hardly lift his arm. He tried five times and the crowd was quiet because it was a good bull and it looked like him or the bull and then he finally made it. He sat down in the sand and puked and they held a cape over him while the crowd hollered and threw things down into the bull-ring.

Mr and Mrs Elliot

Mr and Mrs Elliot tried very hard to have a baby. They tried as often as Mrs Elliot could stand it. They tried in Boston after they were married and they tried coming over on the boat. They did not try very often on the boat because Mrs Elliot was quite sick. She was sick and when she was sick she was sick as Southern women are sick. That is women from the Southern part of the United States. Like all Southern women Mrs Elliot disintegrated very quickly under sea sickness, travelling at night, and getting up too early in the morning. Many of the people on the boat took her for Elliot's mother. Other people who knew they were married believed she was going to have a baby. In reality she was forty years old. Her years had been precipitated suddenly when she started travelling.

She had seemed much younger, in fact she had seemed not to have any age at all, when Elliot had married her after several weeks of making love to her after knowing her for a long time in her tea-shop before he had kissed her one evening.

Hubert Elliot was taking postgraduate work in law at Harvard when he was married. He was a poet with an income of nearly ten thousand dollars a year. He wrote very long poems very rapidly. He was twenty-five years old and had never gone to bed with a woman until he married Mrs Elliot. He wanted to keep himself pure so that he could bring to his wife the same purity of mind and body that he expected of her. He called it to himself living straight. He had been in love with various girls before he kissed Mrs Elliot and always told them sooner or later that he had led a clean life. Nearly all the girls lost interest in him. He was shocked and really horrified at the way girls would become engaged to and marry men whom they must know had dragged themselves through the gutter. He once tried to warn a girl he knew against a man of whom he had almost proof that he had been a rotter at college and a very unpleasant incident had resulted.

Mrs Elliot's name was Cornelia. She had taught him to call her Calutina, which was her family nickname in the South. His mother cried when he brought Cornelia home after their marriage but brightened very much when she learned they were going to live abroad.

Cornelia had said, 'You dear sweet boy,' and held him closer than ever when he told her how he had kept himself clean for her. Cornelia was pure too. 'Kiss me again like that,' she said.

Hubert explained to her that he had learned that way of kissing from hearing a fellow tell a story once. He was delighted with his experiment and they developed it as far as possible. Sometimes when they had been kissing together a long time, Cornelia would ask him to tell her again that he had kept himself really straight for her. The declaration always set her off again.

At first Hubert had no idea of marrying Cornelia. He had never thought of her that way. She had been such a good friend of his, and then one day in the little back room of the shop they had been dancing to the gramophone while her girl friend was in the front of the shop and she had looked up into his eyes and he had kissed her. He could never remember just when it was decided that they were to be married. But they were married.

They spent the night of the day they were married in a Boston hotel. They were both disappointed but finally Cornelia went to sleep. Hubert could not sleep and several times went out and walked up and down the corridor of the hotel in his new Jaeger bathrobe that he had bought for his wedding trip. As he walked he saw all the pairs of shoes, small shoes and big shoes, outside the doors of the hotel rooms. This set his heart to pounding and he hurried back to his own room but Cornelia was asleep. He did not like to waken her and soon everything was quite all right and he slept peacefully.

The next day they called on his mother and the next day they sailed for Europe. It was possible to try to have a baby but Cornelia could not attempt it very often although they wanted a baby more than anything else in the world. They landed in Cherbourg and came to Paris. They tried to have a baby in Paris. Then they decided to go to Dijon where there was summer school and where a number of people who crossed on the boat with them had gone. They found there was nothing to do in Dijon. Hubert, however, was writing a great number of poems and Cornelia typed them for him. They were all very long poems. He was very severe about mistakes and would make her re-do an entire page if there was one mistake. She cried a good deal and they tried several times to have a baby before they left Dijon.

They came to Paris and most of their friends from the boat came back too. They were tired of Dijon and anyway would now be able to say that after leaving Harvard or Columbia or Wabash they had studied at the University of Dijon down in the Côte d'Or. Many of them would have preferred to go to Languedoc, Montpellier or Perpignan if there are universities there. But all those places are too far away. Dijon is only four and a half hours from Paris and there is a diner on the train.

So they all sat around the Café du Dôme, avoiding the Rotonde across the street because it is always so full of foreigners, for a few days and then the Elliots rented a château in Touraine through an advertisement in the New York *Herald*. Elliot had a number of friends by now all of whom admired his poetry and Mrs Elliot had prevailed upon him to send over to Boston for her girl friend who had been in the tea-shop. Mrs Elliot became much brighter after her girl friend came and they had many good cries together. The girl friend was several years older than Cornelia and called her Honey. She too came from a very old Southern family.

The three of them, with several of Elliot's friends who called him Hubie, went down to the château in Touraine. They found Touraine to be a very flat hot country very much like Kansas. Elliot had nearly enough poems for a book now. He was going to bring it out in Boston and had already sent his cheque to, and made a contract with, a publisher.

In a short time the friends began to drift back to Paris. Touraine had not turned out the way it looked when it started. Soon all the friends had gone off with a rich young and unmarried poet to a seaside resort near Trouville. There they were all very happy.

Elliot kept on at the château in Touraine because he had taken it for all summer. He and Mrs Elliot tried very hard to have a baby in the big hot bedroom on the big, hard bed. Mrs Elliot was learning the touch system on the typewriter, but she found that while it increased the speed it made more mistakes. The girl friend was now typing practically all of the manuscripts. She was very neat and efficient and seemed to enjoy it.

Elliot had taken to drinking white wine and lived apart in his own room. He wrote a good deal of poetry during the night and in the morning looked very exhausted. Mrs Elliot and the girl friend now slept together in the big medieval bed. They had many a good cry together. In the evening they all sat at dinner together in the garden under a plane tree and the hot evening wind blew and Elliot drank white wine and Mrs Elliot and the girl friend made conversation and they were all quite happy.

They whack-whacked the white horse on the legs and he kneed himself up. The picador twisted the stirrups straight and pulled and hauled up into the saddle. The horse's entrails hung down in a blue bunch and swung backward and forward as he began to canter, the monos *whacking him on the back of his legs with the rods. He cantered jerkily along the barrera. He stopped stiff and one of the* monos *held his bridle and walked him forward. The picador kicked in his spurs, leaned forward and shook his lance at the bull. Blood pumped regularly from between the horse's front legs. He was nervously unsteady. The bull could not make up his mind to charge.*

Cat in the Rain

There were only two Americans stopping at the hotel. They did not know any of the people they passed on the stairs on their way to and from their room. Their room was on the second floor facing the sea. It also faced the public garden and the war monument. There were big palms and green benches in the public garden. In the good weather there was always an artist with his easel. Artists liked the way the palms grew and the bright colours of the hotels facing the gardens and the sea. Italians came from a long way off to look up at the war monument. It was made of bronze and glistened in the rain. It was raining. The rain dripped from the palm trees. Water stood in pools on the gravel paths. The sea broke in a long line in the rain and slipped back down the beach to come up and break again in a long line in the rain. The motor cars were gone from the square by the war monument. Across the square in the doorway of the café a waiter stood looking out at the empty square.

The American wife stood at the window looking out. Outside right under their window a cat was crouched under one of the dripping green tables. The cat was trying to make herself so compact that she would not be dripped on.

'I'm going down and get that kitty,' the American wife said.

'I'll do it,' her husband offered from the bed.

'No, I'll get it. The poor kitty out trying to keep dry under a table.'

The husband went on reading, lying propped up with the two pillows at the foot of the bed.

'Don't get wet,' he said.

The wife went downstairs and the hotel owner stood up and bowed to her as she passed the office. His desk was at the far end of the office. He was an old man and very tall.

'Il piove,' the wife said. She liked the hotel-keeper.

'Si, si, Signora, brutto tempo. It is very bad weather.'

He stood behind his desk in the far end of the dim room. The wife liked him. She liked the deadly serious way he received any complaints. She liked his dignity. She liked the way he wanted to serve her. She liked the way he felt about being a hotel-keeper. She liked his old, heavy face and big hands.

Liking him she opened the door and looked out. It was raining harder. A man in a rubber cape was crossing the empty square to the café. The cat would be around to the right. Perhaps she could go along under the eaves. As she stood in the doorway an umbrella opened behind her. It was the maid who looked after their room.

'You must not get wet,' she smiled, speaking Italian. Of course, the hotel-keeper had sent her.

With the maid holding the umbrella over her, she walked along the gravel path until she was under their window. The table was there, washed bright green in the rain, but the cat was gone. She was suddenly disappointed. The maid looked up at her.

'Ha perduto qualque cosa, Signora?'

'There was a cat,' said the American girl.

'A cat?'

'Si, il gatto.'

'A cat?' the maid laughed. 'A cat in the rain?'

'Yes,' she said, 'under the table.' Then, 'Oh, I wanted it so much, I wanted a kitty.'

When she talked English the maid's face tightened.

'Come, Signora,' she said. 'We must get back inside. You will be wet.'

'I suppose so,' said the American girl.

They went back along the gravel path and passed in the door. The maid stayed outside to close the umbrella. As the American girl passed the office, the padrone bowed from his desk. Something felt very small and tight inside the girl. The padrone made her feel very small and at the same time really important. She had a momentary feeling of being of supreme importance. She went on up the stairs. She opened the door of the room. George was on the bed, reading.

'Did you get the cat?' he asked, putting the book down.

'It was gone.'

'Wonder where it went to?' he said, resting his eyes from reading.

She sat down on the bed.

'I wanted it so much,' she said. 'I don't know why I wanted it so much. I wanted that poor kitty. It isn't any fun to be a poor kitty out in the rain.'

George was reading again.

She went over and sat in front of the mirror of the dressing-table, looking at herself with the hand glass. She studied her profile, first one side and then the other. Then she studied the back of her head and her neck.

'Don't you think it would be a good idea if I let my hair grow out?' she asked, looking at her profile again.

George looked up and saw the back of her neck, clipped close like a boy's.

'I like it the way it is.'

'I get so tired of it,' she said. 'I get so tired of looking like a boy.'

George shifted his position in the bed. He hadn't looked away from her since she started to speak.

'You look pretty darn nice,' he said.

She laid the mirror down on the dresser and went over to the window and looked out. It was getting dark.

'I want to pull my hair back tight and smooth and make a big knot at the back that I can feel,' she said. 'I want to have a kitty to sit on my lap and purr when I stroke her.'

'Yeah?' George said from the bed.

'And I want to eat at a table with my own silver and I want candles. And I want it to be spring and I want to brush my hair out in front of a mirror and I want a kitty and I want some new clothes.'

'Oh, shut up and get something to read,' George said. He was reading again.

His wife was looking out of the window. It was quite dark now and still raining in the palm trees.

'Anyway, I want a cat,' she said, 'I want a cat. I want a cat now. If I can't have long hair or any fun, I can have a cat.'

George was not listening. He was reading his book. His wife looked out of the window where the light had come on in the square.

Someone knocked at the door.

'Avanti,' George said. He looked up from his book.

In the doorway stood the maid. She held a big tortoiseshell cat pressed tight against her and swung down against her body.

'Excuse me,' she said, 'the padrone asked me to bring this for the Signora.'

The crowd shouted all the time, and threw pieces of bread down into the bull-ring, then cushions and leather wine bottles, keeping up whistling and yelling. Finally the bull was too tired from so much sticking and folded his knees and lay down and one of the cuadrilla *leaned out over his neck and killed him with the* puntillo. *The crowd came over the barrera and around the torero and two men grabbed him and held him and someone cut off his pigtail and was waving it and a kid grabbed it and ran away with it. Afterwards I saw him at the café. He was very short with a brown face and quite drunk and he said: After all, it has happened before like that. I am not really a good bull-fighter!*

Out of Season

On the four lire Peduzzi had earned by spading the hotel garden he got quite drunk. He saw the young gentleman coming down the path and spoke to him mysteriously. The young gentleman said he had not eaten but would be ready to go as soon as lunch was finished. Forty minutes or an hour.

At the cantina near the bridge they trusted him for three more grappas because he was so confident and mysterious about his job for the afternoon. It was a windy day with the sun coming out from behind clouds and then going under in sprinkles of rain. A wonderful day for trout fishing.

The young gentleman came out of the hotel and asked him about the rods. Should his wife come behind with the rods? 'Yes,' said Peduzzi, 'let her follow us.' The young gentleman went back into the hotel and spoke to his wife. He and Peduzzi started down the road. The young gentleman had a musette over his shoulder. Peduzzi saw the wife, who looked as young as the young gentleman, and was wearing mountain boots and a blue beret, start out to follow them down the road, carrying the fishing rods, unjointed, one in each hand. Peduzzi didn't like her to be way back there. 'Signorina,' he called, winking at the young gentleman, 'come up here and walk with us. Signora, come up here. Let us all walk together.' Peduzzi wanted them all three to walk down the street of Cortina together.

The wife stayed behind, following rather sullenly. 'Signorina,' Peduzzi called tenderly, 'come up here with us.' The young gentleman looked back and shouted something. The wife stopped lagging behind and walked up.

Everyone they met walking through the main street of the town Peduzzi greeted elaborately. Buon' di, Arturo! Tipping his hat. The bank clerk stared at him from the door of the Fascist café. Groups of three and four people standing in front of the shops stared at the three. The workmen in their stone-powdered jackets, working on the foundations of the new hotel looked up as they passed. Nobody spoke or gave any sign to them except the town beggar, lean and old, with a spittle-thickened beard, who lifted his hat as they passed.

Peduzzi stopped in front of a store with the window full of bottles and brought his empty grappa bottle from an inside pocket of his old military coat. 'A little to drink, some marsala for the Signora, something, something to drink.' He gestured with the bottle. It was a wonderful day. 'Marsala, you like marsala, Signorina? A little marsala?'

The wife stood sullenly. 'You'll have to play up to this,' she said. 'I can't understand a word he says. He's drunk, isn't he?'

The young gentleman appeared not to hear Peduzzi. He was thinking, what in hell makes him say marsala? That's what Max Beerbohm drinks.

'Geld,' Peduzzi said finally, taking hold of the young gentleman's sleeve. 'Lire.' He smiled, reluctant to press the subject but needing to bring the young gentleman into action.

The young gentleman took out his pocketbook and gave him a ten-lira note. Peduzzi went up the steps to the door of the Speciality of Domestic and Foreign Wines shop. It was locked.

'It is closed until two,' someone passing in the street said scornfully. Peduzzi came down the steps. He felt hurt. Never mind, he said, we can get it at the Concordia.

They walked down the road to the Concordia three abreast. On the porch of the Concordia, where the rusty bobsleds were stacked, the young gentleman said, 'Was wollen sie?' Peduzzi handed him the ten-lira note folded over and over. 'Nothing,' he said, 'anything.' He was embarrassed. 'Marsala, maybe. I don't know. Marsala?'

The door of the Concordia shut on the young gentleman and the wife. 'Three marsalas,' said the young gentleman to the girl behind the pastry counter. 'Two, you mean?' she asked. 'No,' he said, 'one for a vecchio.' 'Oh,' she said, 'a vecchio,' and laughed, getting down the bottle. She poured out the three muddy-looking drinks into three glasses. The wife was sitting at a table under the line of newspapers on sticks. The young gentleman put one of the marsalas in front of her. 'You might as well drink it,' he said, 'maybe it'll make you feel better.' She sat and looked at the glass. The young gentleman went outside the door with a glass for Peduzzi but could not see him.

'I don't know where he is,' he said, coming back into the pastry room carrying the glass.

'He wanted a quart of it,' said the wife.

'How much is a quarter litre?' the young gentleman asked the girl.

'Of the bianco? One lira.'

'No, of the marsala. Put these two in, too,' he said, giving her his own glass and the one poured for Peduzzi. She filled the quarter litre wine measure with a funnel. 'A bottle to carry it,' said the young gentleman.

She went to hunt for a bottle. It all amused her.

'I'm sorry you feel so rotten, Tiny,' he said. 'I'm sorry I talked the way I did at lunch. We were both getting at the same thing from different angles.'

'It doesn't make any difference,' she said. 'None of it makes any difference.'

'Are you too cold?' he asked. 'I wish you'd worn another sweater.'

'I've got on three sweaters.'

The girl came in with a very slim brown bottle and poured the marsala into it. The young gentleman paid five lire more. They went out the door. The girl was amused. Peduzzi was walking up and down at the other end out of the wind and holding the rods.

'Come on,' he said, 'I will carry the rods. What difference does it make if anybody sees them? No one will trouble us. No one will make any trouble for me in Cortina. I know them at the municipio. I have been a soldier. Everybody in this town likes me. I sell frogs. What if it is forbidden to fish? Not a thing. Nothing. No trouble. Big trout, I tell you. Lots of them.'

They were walking down the hill toward the river. The town was in back of them. The sun had gone under and it was sprinkling rain. 'There,' said Peduzzi, pointing to a girl in the doorway of a house they passed. 'My daughter.'

'His doctor,' the wife said, 'has he got to show us his doctor?'

'He said his daughter,' said the young gentleman.

The girl went into the house as Peduzzi pointed.

They walked down the hill across the fields and then turned to follow the river bank. Peduzzi talked rapidly with much winking and knowingness. As they walked three abreast the wife caught his breath across the wind. Once he nudged her in the ribs. Part of the time he talked in d'Ampezzo dialect and sometimes in Tyroler German dialect. He could not make out which the young gentleman and his wife understood the best so he was being bilingual. But as the young gentleman said, Ja, Ja, Peduzzi decided to talk altogether in Tyroler. The young gentleman and the wife understood nothing.

'Everybody in the town saw us going through with these rods. We're probably being followed by the game police now. I wish we weren't in on this damn thing. This damned old fool is so drunk, too.'

'Of course you haven't got the guts to just go back,' said the wife. 'Of course you have to go on.'

'Why don't you go back? Go on back, Tiny.'

'I'm going to stay with you. If you go to jail we might as well both go.'

They turned sharp down the bank and Peduzzi stood, his coat blowing in the wind, gesturing at the river. It was brown and muddy. Off on the right there was a dump heap.

'Say it to me in Italian,' said the young gentleman.

'Un' mezz' ora. Più d' un' mezz' ora.'

'He says it's at least a half hour more. Go on back, Tiny. You're cold in this wind anyway. It's a rotten day and we aren't going to have any fun, anyway.'

'All right,' she said, and climbed up the grassy bank.

Peduzzi was down at the river and did not notice her till she was almost out of sight over the crest. 'Frau!' he shouted. 'Frau! Fraülein! You're not going.'

She went on over the crest of the hill.

'She's gone!' said Peduzzi. It shocked him.

He took off the rubber bands that held the rod segments together and commenced to joint up one of the rods.

'But you said it was half an hour farther.'

'Oh, yes. It is good half an hour down. It is good here, too.'

'Really?'

'Of course. It is good here and good there, too.'

The young gentleman sat down on the bank and jointed up a rod, put on the reel and threaded the line through the guides. He felt uncomfortable and afraid that any minute a gamekeeper or a posse of citizens would come over the bank from the town. He could see the houses of the town and the campanile over the edge of the hill. He opened his leader box. Peduzzi leaned over and dug his flat, hard thumb and forefinger in and tangled the moistened leaders.

'Have you some lead?'

'No.'

'You must have some lead.' Peduzzi was excited. 'You must have piombo. Piombo. A little piombo. Just here. Just above the hook or your bait will float on the water. You must have it. Just a little piombo.'

'Have you got some?'

'No.' He looked through his pockets desperately. Sifting through the cloth dirt in the linings of his inside military pockets. 'I haven't any. We must have piombo.'

'We can't fish then,' said the young gentleman, and unjointed the rod, reeling the line back through the guides. 'We'll get some piombo and fish tomorrow.'

'But listen, caro, you must have piombo. The line will lie flat on the water.' Peduzzi's day was going to pieces before his eyes. 'You must have piombo. A little is enough. Your stuff is all clean and new but you have no lead. I would have brought some. You said you had everything.'

The young gentleman looked at the stream discoloured by the melting snow. 'I know,' he said, 'we'll get some piombo and fish tomorrow.'

'At what hour in the morning? Tell me that.'

'At seven.'

The sun came out. It was warm and pleasant. The young gentleman felt revived. He was no longer breaking the law. Sitting on the bank he took the bottle of marsala out of his pocket and passed it to Peduzzi. Peduzzi passed it back. The young gentleman took a drink of it and passed it to Peduzzi again. Peduzzi passed it back again. 'Drink,' he said, 'drink. It's your marsala.' After another short drink the young gentleman handed the bottle over. Peduzzi had been watching it closely. He took the bottle very hurriedly and tipped it up. The grey hairs in the folds of his neck oscillated as he drank, his eyes fixed on the end of the narrow brown bottle. He drank it all. The sun shone while he drank. It was wonderful. This was a great day, after all. A wonderful day.

'Senta, caro! In the morning at seven.' He had called the young gentleman caro several times and nothing had happened. It was good marsala. His eyes glistened. Days like this stretched out ahead. It would begin at seven in the morning.

They started to walk up the hill toward the town. The young gentleman went on ahead. He was quite a way up the hill. Peduzzi called to him.

'Listen, caro, can you let me take five lire for a favour?'

'For today?' asked the young gentleman frowning.

'No, not today. Give it to me today for tomorrow. I will provide everything for tomorrow. Pane, salami, formaggio, good stuff for all of us. You and I and the signora. Bait for fishing, minnows, not worms only. Perhaps I can get some marsala. All for five lire. Five lire for a favour.'

The young gentleman looked through his pocketbook and took out a two-lira note and two ones.

'Thank you, caro. Thank you,' said Peduzzi, in the tone of one member of the Carleton Club accepting the *Morning Post* from another. This was living. He was through with the hotel garden, breaking up frozen manure with a dung fork. Life was opening out.

'Until seven o'clock then, caro,' he said, slapping the young gentleman on the back. 'Promptly at seven.'

'I may not be going,' said the young gentleman, putting his purse back in his pocket.

'What,' said Peduzzi, 'I will have minnows, Signor. Salami, everything. You and I and the Signora. The three of us.'

'I may not be going,' said the young gentleman, 'very probably not. I will leave word with the padrone at the hotel office.'

If it happened right down close in front of you, you could see Villalta snarl at the bull and curse him, and when the bull charged he swung back firmly like an oak when the wind hits it, his legs tight together, the muleta trailing and the sword following the curve behind. Then he cursed the bull, flopped the muleta at him, and swung back from the charge, his feet firm, the muleta curving and at each swing the crowd roaring.

When he started to kill it was all in the same rush. The bull looking at him straight in front, hating. He drew out the sword from the folds of the muleta and sighted with the same movement and called to the bull, 'Toro! Toro!' and the bull charged and Villalta charged and just for a moment they became one. Villalta became one with the bull and then it was over. Villalta standing straight and the red hilt of the sword sticking out dully between the bull's shoulders. Villalta, his hand up at the crowd and the bull roaring blood, looking straight at Villalta and his legs caving.

Cross-Country Snow

The funicular car bucked once more and then stopped. It could not go farther, the snow drifted solidly across the track. The gale scouring the exposed surface of the mountain had swept the snow surface into a wind-board crust. Nick, waxing his skis in the baggage car, pushed his boots into the toe irons and shut the clamp tight. He jumped from the car sideways on to the hard wind-board, made a jump turn and crouching and trailing his sticks slipped in a rush down the slope.

On the white below George dipped and rose and dipped out of sight. The rush and the sudden swoop as he dropped down a steep undulation in the mountain side plucked Nick's mind out and left him only the wonderful flying, dropping sensation in his body. He rose to a slight up-run and then the snow seemed to drop out from under him as he went down, down, faster and faster in a rush down the last, long, steep slope.

Crouching so he was almost sitting back on his skis, trying to keep the centre of gravity low, the snow driving like a sandstorm, he knew the pace was too much. But he held it. He would not let go and spill. Then a patch of soft snow, left in a hollow by the wind, spilled him and he went over and over in a clashing of skis, feeling like a shot rabbit, then stuck, his legs crossed, his skis sticking straight up and his nose and ears jammed full of snow.

George stood a little farther down the slope, knocking the snow from his wind jacket with big slaps.

'You took a beauty, Mike,' he called to Nick. 'That's lousy soft snow. It bagged me the same way.'

'What's it like over the khud?' Nick kicked his skis around as he lay on his back and stood up.

'You've got to keep to your left. It's a good fast drop with a Christy at the bottom on account of a fence.'

'Wait a sec and we'll take it together.'

'No, you come on and go first. I like to see you take the khuds.'

Nick Adams came up past George, big back and blond head still faintly snowy, then his skis started slipping at the edge and he swooped down, hissing in the crystalline powder snow and seeming to float up and drop down as he went up and down the billowing khuds. He held to his left and at the end, as he rushed toward the fence, keeping his knees locked tight together and turning his body like tightening a screw brought his skis sharply around to the right in a smother of snow and slowed into a loss of speed parallel to the hillside and the wire fence.

He looked up the hill. George was coming down in telemark position, kneeling; one leg forward and bent, the other trailing; his sticks hanging like some insect's thin legs, kicking up puffs of snow as they touched the surface and finally the whole kneeling, trailing figure coming around in a beautiful right curve, crouching, the legs forward and back, the body leaning out against the swing, the sticks accenting the curve like points of light, all in a wild cloud of snow.

'I was afraid to Christy,' George said, 'the snow was too deep. You made a beauty.'

'I can't telemark with my leg,' Nick said.

Nick held down the top strand of the wire fence with his ski and George slid over. Nick followed him down to the road. They thrust bent-kneed along the road into a pine forest. The road became polished ice, stained orange and a tobacco yellow from the teams hauling logs. The skiers kept to the stretch of snow along the side. The road dipped sharply to a stream and then ran straight up-hill. Through the woods they could see a long, low-eaved, weather-beaten building. Through the trees it was a faded yellow. Closer the window frames were painted green. The paint was peeling. Nick knocked his clamps loose with one of his ski sticks and kicked off the skis.

'We might as well carry them up here,' he said.

He climbed the steep road with the skis on his shoulder, kicking his heel nails into the icy footing. He heard George breathing and kicking in his heels just behind him. They stacked the skis against the side of the inn and slapped the snow off each other's trousers, stamped their boots clean, and went in.

Inside it was quite dark. A big porcelain stove shone in the corner of the room. There was a low ceiling. Smooth benches back of dark, wine-stained tables were along each side of the rooms. Two Swiss sat over their pipes and two decies of cloudy new wine next to the stove. The boys took off their jackets and sat against the wall on the other side of the stove. A voice in the next room stopped singing and a girl in a blue apron came in through the door to see what they wanted to drink.

'A bottle of Sion,' Nick said. 'Is that all right, Gidge?'

'Sure,' said George. 'You know more about wine than I do. I like any of it.'

The girl went out.

'There's nothing really can touch ski-ing, is there?' Nick said. 'The way it feels when you first drop off on a long run.'

'Huh,' said George. 'It's too swell to talk about.'

The girl brought the wine in and they had trouble with the cork. Nick finally opened it. The girl went out and they heard her singing in German in the next room.

'Those specks of cork in it don't matter,' said Nick.

'I wonder if she's got any cake.'

'Let's find out.'

The girl came in and Nick noticed that her apron covered swellingly her pregnancy. I wonder why I didn't see that when she first came in, he thought.

'What were you singing?' he asked her.

'Opera, German opera.' She did not care to discuss the subject. 'We have some apple strudel if you want it.'

'She isn't so cordial, is she?' said George.

'Oh, well. She doesn't know us and she thought we were going to kid her about her singing, maybe. She's from up where they speak German probably and she's touchy about being here and then she's got that baby coming without being married and she's touchy.'

'How do you know she isn't married?'

'No ring. Hell, no girls get married around here till they're knocked up.'

The door came open and a gang of woodcutters from up the road came in, stamping their boots and steaming in the room. The waitress brought in three litres of new wine for the gang and they sat at the two tables, smoking and quiet, with their hats off, leaning back against the wall or forward on the table. Outside the horses on the wood sledges made an occasional sharp jangle of bells as they tossed their heads.

George and Nick were happy. They were fond of each other. They knew they had the run back home ahead of them.

'When have you got to go back to school?' Nick asked.

'Tonight,' George answered. 'I've got to get the ten-forty from Montreux.'

'I wish you could stick over and we could do the Dent du Lys tomorrow.'

'I got to get educated,' George said. 'Gee, Nick, don't you wish we could just bum together? Take our skis and go on the train to where there was good running and then go on and put up at pubs and go right across the Oberland and up the Valais and all through the Engadine and just take repair kit and extra sweaters and pyjamas in our rucksacks and not give a damn about school or anything.'

'Yes, and go through the Schwartzwald that way. Gee, the swell places.'

'That's where you went fishing last summer, isn't it?'

'Yes.'

They ate the strudel and drank the rest of the wine.

George leaned back against the wall and shut his eyes.

'Wine always makes me feel this way,' he said.

'Feel bad?' Nick asked.

'No. I feel good, but funny.'

'I know.' Nick said.

'Sure,' said George.

'Should we have another bottle?' Nick asked.

'Not for me,' George said.

They sat there, Nick leaning his elbows on the table, George slumped back against the wall.

'Is Helen going to have a baby?' George said, coming down to the table from the wall.

'Yes.'

'When?'

'Late next summer.'

'Are you glad?'

'Yes. Now.'

'Will you go back to the States?'

'I guess so.'

'Do you want to?'

'No.'

'Does Helen?'

'No.'

George sat silent. He looked at the empty bottle and the empty glasses.

'It's hell, isn't it?' he said.

'No. Not exactly,' Nick said.

'Why not?'

'I don't know,' Nick said.

'Will you ever go ski-ing together in the States?' George said.

'I don't know,' said Nick.

'The mountains aren't much,' George said.

'No,' said Nick. 'They're too rocky. There's too much timber and they're too far away.'

'Yes,' said George, 'that's the way it is in California.'

'Yes,' Nick said, 'that's the way it is everywhere I've ever been.'

'Yes,' said George, 'that's the way it is.'

The Swiss got up and paid and went out.

'I wish we were Swiss,' George said.

'They've all got goitre,' said Nick.

'I don't believe it,' George said.

'Neither do I,' said Nick.

They laughed.

'Maybe we'll never go ski-ing again, Nick,' George said.

'We've got to,' said Nick. 'It isn't worth while if you can't.'

'We'll go, all right,' George said.

'We've got to,' Nick agreed.

'I wish we could make a promise about it,' George said.

Nick stood up. He buckled his wind jacket tight. He leaned over George and picked up the two ski poles from against the wall. He stuck one of the ski poles into the floor.

'There isn't any good in promising,' he said.

They opened the door and went out. It was very cold. The snow had crusted hard. The road ran up the hill into the pine trees.

They took down their skis from where they leaned against the wall in the inn. Nick put on his gloves. George was already started up the road, his skis on his shoulder. Now they would have the run home together.

I heard the drums coming down the street and then the fifes and pipes and then they came around the corner, all dancing. The street full of them. Maera saw him and then I saw him. When they stopped the music for the crouch he hunched down in the street with them all and when they started it again he jumped up and went dancing down the street with them. He was drunk all right.

'You go down after him,' said Maera, 'he hates me.'

So I went down and caught up with them and grabbed him while he was crouched down waiting for the music to break loose and said, 'Come on, Luis. For Christ sake, you've got bulls this afternoon.' He didn't listen to me, he was listening so hard for the music to start.

I said, 'Don't be a damn fool, Luis. Come on back to the hotel.'

360

Then the music started again and he jumped up and twisted away from me and started dancing. I grabbed his arm and he pulled loose and said, 'Oh, leave me alone. You're not my mother.'

I went back to the hotel and Maera was on the balcony looking out to see if I'd be bringing him back. He went inside when he saw me and came downstairs disgusted.

'Well, after all,' I said, 'he's just an ignorant Mexican savage.'

'Yes,' Maera said, 'and who will kill his bulls after he gets cogido?'

'We, I suppose,' I said.

'Yes, we,' said Maera. 'We kill the savages' bulls, and the drunkards' bulls, and the riau-riau dancers' bulls. Yes. We kill them. We kill them all right. Yes. Yes. Yes.'

My Old Man

I guess looking at it, now, my old man was cut out for a fat guy, one of those regular little roly fat guys you see around, but he sure never got that way, except a little toward the last, and then it wasn't his fault, he was riding over the jumps only and he could afford to carry plenty of weight then. I remember the way he'd pull on a rubber shirt over a couple of jerseys and a big sweat shirt over that, and get me to run with him in the forenoon in the hot sun. He'd have, maybe, taken a trial trip with one of Razzo's skins early in the morning after just getting in from Torino at four o'clock in the morning and beating it out to the stables in a cab and then with the dew all over everything and the sun just starting to get going, I'd help him pull off his boots and he'd get into a pair of sneakers and all these sweaters and we'd start out.

'Come on, kid,' he'd say, stepping up and down on his toes in front of the jocks' dressing-room, 'let's get moving.'

Then we'd start off jogging around the infield once, maybe,

with him ahead, running nice, and then turn out the gate and along one of those roads with all the trees along both sides of them that run out from San Siro. I'd go ahead of him when we hit the road and I could run pretty stout and I'd look around and he'd be jogging easy just behind me and after a while I'd look around again and he'd begun to sweat. Sweating heavy and he'd just be dogging it along with his eyes on my back, but when he'd catch me looking at him he'd grin and say, 'Sweating plenty?' When my old man grinned, nobody could help but grin too. We'd keep right on running out towards the mountains and then my old man would yell, 'Hey, Joe!' and I'd look back and he'd be sitting under a tree with a towel he'd had around his waist wrapped around his neck.

I'd come back and sit down beside him and he'd pull a rope out of his pocket and start skipping rope out in the sun with the sweat pouring off his face and him skipping rope out in the white dust with the rope going cloppetty, cloppetty, clop, clop, clop, and the sun hotter, and him working harder up and down a patch of road. Say, it was a treat to see my old man skip rope, too. He could whirr it fast or lop it slow and fancy. Say, you ought to have seen wops look at us sometimes, when they'd come by, going into town walking along with big white steers hauling the cart. They sure looked as though they thought the old man was nuts. He'd start the rope whirring till they'd stop dead still and watch him, then give the steers a cluck and a poke with the goad and get going again.

When I'd sit watching him working out in the hot sun I sure felt fond of him. He sure was fun and he done his work so hard and he'd finish up with a regular whirring that'd drive the sweat out on his face like water and then sling the rope at the tree and come over and sit down with me and lean back against the tree with the towel and a sweater wrapped around his neck.

'Sure is hell keeping it down, Joe,' he'd say and lean back and shut his eyes and breathe long and deep, 'it ain't like when you're a kid.' Then he'd get up before he started to cool and we'd jog along back to the stables. That's the way it was keeping down to weight. He was worried all the time. Most jocks can just about ride off all they want to. A jock loses about a kilo every time he rides, but my old man was sort of

362

dried out and he couldn't keep down his kilos without all that running.

I remember once at San Siro, Regoli, a little wop, that was riding for Buzoni, came out across the paddock going to the bar for something cool; and flicking his boots with his whip, after he'd just weighed in and my old man had just weighed in too, and came out with the saddle under his arm looking red-faced and tired and too big for his silks and he stood there looking at young Regoli standing up to the outdoors bar, cool and kid-looking, and I says, 'What's the matter, Dad?' 'cause I thought maybe Regoli had bumped him or something and he just looked at Regoli and said, 'Oh, to hell with it', and went on to the dressing-room.

Well, it would have been all right, maybe, if we'd stayed in Milan and ridden at Milan and Torino, 'cause if there ever were any easy courses, it's those two. 'Pianola, Joe,' my old man said when he dismounted in the winning stall after what the wops thought was a hell of a steeplechase. I asked him once. 'This course rides itself. It's the pace you're going at, that makes riding the jumps dangerous, Joe. We ain't going any pace here, and they ain't any really bad jumps either. But it's the pace always – not the jumps that makes the trouble.'

San Siro was the swellest course I'd ever seen but the old man said it was a dog's life. Going back and forth between Mirafiore and San Siro and riding just about every day in the week with a train ride every other night.

I was nuts about the horses, too. There's something about it, when they come out and go up the track to the post. Sort of dancy and tight looking with the jock keeping a tight hold on them and maybe easing off a little and letting them run a little going up. Then once they were at the barrier it got me worse than anything. Especially at San Siro with that big green infield and the mountains way off and the fat wop starter with his big whip and the jocks fiddling them around and then the barrier snapping up and that bell going off and them all getting off in a bunch and then commencing to string out. You know the way a bunch of skins gets off. If you're up in the stand with a pair of glasses all you see is them plunging off and then that bell goes off and it seems like it rings for a thousand years and then they come sweeping round the turn. There wasn't ever anything like it for me.

But my old man said one day, in the dressing-room, when he was getting into his street clothes, 'None of these things are horses, Joe. They'd kill that bunch of skates for their hides and hoofs up at Paris.' That was the day he'd won the Premio Commercio with Lantorna shooting her out of the field the last hundred metres like pulling a cork out of a bottle.

It was right after the Premio Commercio that we pulled out and left Italy. My old man and Holbrook and a fat wop in a straw hat that kept wiping his face with a handkerchief were having an argument at a table in the Galleria. They were all talking French and the two of them were after my old man about something. Finally he didn't say anything any more but just sat there and looked at Holbrook, and the two of them kept after him, first one talking and then the other, and the fat wop always butting in on Holbrook.

'You go out and buy me a *Sportsman*, will you, Joe?' my old man said, and handed me a couple of soldi without looking away from Holbrook.

So I went out of the Galleria and walked over to in front of the Scala and bought a paper, and came back and stood a little way away because I didn't want to butt in and my old man was sitting back in his chair looking down at his coffee and fooling with a spoon and Holbrook and the big wop were standing and the big wop was wiping his face and shaking his head. And I came up and my old man acted just as though the two of them weren't standing there and said, 'Want an ice, Joe?' Holbrook looked down at my old man and said slow and careful, 'You son of a bitch', and he and the fat wop went out through the tables.

My old man sat there and sort of smiled at me, but his face was white and he looked sick as hell and I was scared and felt sick inside because I knew something had happened and I didn't see how anybody could call my old man a son of a bitch, and get away with it. My old man opened up the *Sportsman* and studied the handicaps for a while and then he said, 'You got to take a lot of things in this world, Joe.' And three days later we left Milan for good on the Turin train for Paris, after an auction sale out in front of Turner's stables of everything we couldn't get into a trunk and a suit-case.

We got into Paris early in the morning in a long, dirty station the old man told me was the Gare de Lyon. Paris was an awful big town after Milan. Seems like in Milan everybody is going somewhere and all the trams run somewhere and there ain't any sort of mix-up, but Paris is all balled up and they never do straighten it out. I got to like it, though, part of it, anyway, and say, it's got the best racecourses in the world. Seems as though that were the thing that keeps it all going and about the only thing you can figure on is that every day the buses will be going out to whatever track they're running at, going right out through everything to the track. I never really got to know Paris well, because I just came in about once or twice a week with the old man from Maisons and he always sat at the Café de la Paix on the Opéra side with the rest of the gang from Maisons and I guess that's one of the busiest parts of the town. But, say, it is funny that a big town like Paris wouldn't have a Galleria, isn't it?

Well, we went out to live at Maisons-Lafitte, where just about everybody lives except the gang at Chantilly, with a Mrs Meyers that runs a boarding house. Maisons is about the swellest place to live I've ever seen in all my life. The town ain't so much, but there's a lake and a swell forest that we used to go off bumming in all day, a couple of us kids, and my old man made me a sling shot and we got a lot of things with it but the best one was a magpie. Young Dick Atkinson shot a rabbit with it one day and we put it under a tree and were all sitting around and Dick had some cigarettes and all of a sudden the rabbit jumped up and beat it into the brush and we chased it but we couldn't find it. Gee, we had fun at Maisons. Mrs Meyers used to give me lunch in the morning and I'd be gone all day. I learned to talk French quick. It's an easy language.

As soon as we got to Maisons, my old man wrote to Milan for his licence and was pretty worried till it came. He used to sit around the Café de Paris in Maisons with the gang; there were lots of guys he'd known when he rode up at Paris, before the war, lived at Maisons, and there's a lot of time to sit around because the work around a racing stable, for the jocks, that is, is all cleaned up by nine o'clock in the morning. They take the first batch of skins out to gallop them at 5.30 in the morning and they work the second lot at 8 o'clock. That means getting up early all right and going to bed early, too. If a jock's riding for somebody too, he can't go boozing around because the trainer always has an eye on him if he's a kid and if he ain't a kid he's always got an eye on himself. So mostly if a jock ain't working he sits around the Café de Paris with the gang and they can all sit around about two or three hours in front of some drink like a vermouth and seltz and they talk and tell stories and shoot pool and it's sort of like a club or the Galleria in Milan. Only it ain't really like the Galleria because there everybody is going by all the time and there's everybody around at the tables.

Well, my old man got his licence all right. They sent it through to him without a word and he rode a couple of times. Amiens, up country and that sort of thing, but he didn't seem to get any engagement. Everybody liked him and whenever I'd come in to the café in the forenoon I'd find somebody drinking with him because my old man wasn't tight like most of these jockeys that have got the first dollar they made riding at the World's Fair in St Louis in nineteen ought four. That's what my old man would say when he'd kid George Burns. But it seemed like everybody steered clear of giving my old man any mounts.

We went out to wherever they were running every day with the car from Maisons and that was the most fun of all. I was glad when the horses came back from Deauville and the summer. Even though it meant no more bumming in the woods, 'cause then we'd ride to Enghien or Tremblay or St Cloud and watch them from the trainers' and jockeys' stand. I sure learned about racing from going out with that gang and the fun of it was going every day.

I remember once out at St Cloud. It was a big two hundred thousand franc race with seven entries and War Cloud a big favourite. I went around to the paddock to see the horses with my old man and you never saw such horses. This War Cloud is a great big yellow horse that looks like just nothing but run. I never saw such a horse. He was being led around the paddocks with his head down and when he went by me I felt all hollow inside he was so beautiful. There never was such a wonderful, lean, running built horse. And he went around the paddock putting his feet just so and quiet and careful and moving easy like he knew just what he had to do and not jerking and standing up on his legs and getting wild-eyed like you see these selling platers with a shot of dope in them. The crowd was so thick I couldn't see him again except just his legs going by and some yellow and my old man started out through the crowd and I followed him over to the jocks' dressing-room back in the trees and there was a big crowd around there, too, but the man at the door in a derby nodded to my old man and we got in and everybody was sitting around and getting dressed and pulling shirts over their heads and pulling boots on and it all smelled hot and sweaty and linimenty and outside was the crowd looking in.

The old man went over and sat down beside George Gardner that was getting into his pants and said, 'What's the dope, George?' just in an ordinary tone of voice 'cause there ain't any use him feeling around because George either can tell him or he can't tell him.

'He won't win,' George says very low, leaning over and buttoning the bottoms of his pants.

'Who will?' my old man says, leaning over close so nobody can hear.

'Foxless,' George says, 'and if he does, save me a couple of tickets.'

My old man says something in a regular voice to George and George says, 'Don't ever bet on anything, I tell you,' kidding like, and we beat it out and through all the crowd that was looking in over to the 100 franc mutuel machine. But I knew something big was up because George is War Cloud's jockey. On the way he gets one of the yellow odds-sheets with the starting prices on and War Cloud is only paying 5 for 10, Cefisidote is next at 3 to 1 and fifth down the list this Foxless at 8 to 1. My old man bets five thousand on Foxless to win and puts on a thousand to place and we went around back of the grandstand to go up the stairs and get a place to watch the race.

We were jammed in tight and first a man in a long coat with

a grey tall hat and a whip folded up in his hand came out and then one after another the horses, with the jocks up and a stable-boy holding the bridle on each side and walking along, followed the old guy. That big yellow horse War Cloud came first. He didn't look so big when you first looked at him until you saw the length of his legs and the whole way he's built and the way he moves. Gosh, I never saw such a horse. George Gardner was riding him and they moved along slow, back of the old guy in the grey tall hat that walked along like he was the ring master in a circus. Back of War Cloud, moving along smooth and yellow in the sun, was a good-looking black with a nice head with Tommy Archibald riding him; and after the black was a string of five more horses all moving along slow in a procession past the grandstand and the pesage. My old man said the black was Foxless and I took a good look at him and he was a nice-looking horse, all right, but nothing like War Cloud.

Everybody cheered War Cloud when he went by and he sure was one swell-looking horse. The procession of them went around on the other side past the pelouse and then back up to the near end of the course and the circus master had the stable-boys turn them loose one after another so they could gallop by the stands on their way up to the post and let everybody have a good look at them. They weren't at the post hardly any time at all when the gong started and you could see them way off across the infield all in a bunch starting on the first swing like a lot of little toy horses. I was watching them through the glasses and War Cloud was running well back, with one of the bays making the pace. They swept down and around and came pounding past and War Cloud was way back when they passed us and this Foxless horse in front and going smooth. Gee, it's awful when they go by you and then you have to watch them go farther away and get smaller and smaller and then all bunched up on the turns and then come around toward into the stretch and you feel like swearing and god-damning worse and worse. Finally they made the last turn and came into the straight-away with this Foxless way out in front. Everybody was looking funny and saying 'War Cloud' in a sort of sick way and them pounding nearer down the stretch, and then something came out of the pack right into my glasses like a horse-headed yellow streak and everybody began to yell 'War Cloud' as though they were crazy. War Cloud came on faster than I'd ever seen anything in my life and pulled up on Foxless that was going fast as any black horse could go with the jock flogging hell out of him with the gad and they were right dead neck and neck for a second but War Cloud seemed going about twice as fast with those great jumps and that head out – but it was while they were neck and neck that they passed the winning post and when the numbers went up in the slots the first one was 2 and that meant Foxless had won.

I felt all trembly and funny inside, and then we were all jammed in with the people going downstairs to stand in front of the board where they'd post what Foxless paid. Honest, watching the race I'd forgot how much my old man had bet on Foxless. I'd wanted War Cloud to win so damned bad. But now it was all over it was swell to know we had the winner.

'Wasn't it a swell race, Dad?' I said to him.

He looked at me sort of funny with his derby on the back of his head. 'George Gardner's a swell jockey, all right,' he said. 'It sure took a great jock to keept that War Cloud from winning.'

Of course I knew it was funny all the time. But my old man saying that right out like that sure took the kick all out of it for me and I didn't get the real kick back again ever, even when they posted the numbers up on the board and the bell rang to pay off and we saw that Foxless paid 67.50 for 10. All round people were saying, 'Poor War Cloud! Poor War Cloud!' And I thought, I wish I were a jockey and could have rode him instead of that son of a bitch. And that was funny, thinking of George Gardner as a son of a bitch because I'd always liked him and besides he'd given us the winner, but I guess that's what he is, all right.

My old man had a big lot of money after that race and he took to coming into Paris oftener. If they raced at Tremblay he'd have them drop him in town on their way back to Maisons, and he and I'd sit out in front of the Café de la Paix and watch the people go by. It's funny sitting there. There's streams of people going by and all sorts of guys come up and want to sell you things, and I loved to sit there with my old man. That was when we'd have the most fun. Guys would come by selling funny rabbits that jumped if you squeezed a bulb and they'd come up to us and my old man would kid with them. He could talk French just like English and all those kind of guys knew him 'cause you can always tell a jockey – and then we always sat at the same table and they got used to seeing us there. There were guys selling matrimonial papers and girls selling rubber eggs that when you squeezed them a rooster came out of them and one old wormy-looking guy that went by with post cards of Paris, showing them to everybody, and, of course, nobody ever bought any, and then he would come back and show the under side of the pack and they would all be smutty post cards and lots of people would dig down and buy them.

Gee, I remember the funny people that used to go by. Girls around supper time looking for somebody to take them out to eat and they'd speak to my old man and he'd make some joke at them in French and they'd pat me on the head and go on. Once there was an American woman sitting with her kid daughter at the next table to us and they were both eating ices and I kept looking at the girl and she was awfully good-looking and I smiled at her and she smiled at me but that was all that ever came of it because I looked for her mother and her every day and I made up ways that I was going to speak to her and I wondered if I got to know her if her mother would let me take her out to Auteuil or Tremblay but I never saw either of them again. Anyway, I guess it wouldn't have been any good, anyway, because looking back on it I remember the way I thought out would be best to speak to her was to say, 'Pardon me, but perhaps I can give you a winner at Enghien today?' and, after all, maybe she would have thought I was a tout instead of really trying to give her a winner.

We'd sit at the Café de la Paix, my old man and me, and we had a big drag with the waiter because my old man drank whisky and it cost five francs, and that meant a good tip when the saucers were counted up. My old man was drinking more than I'd ever seen him, but he wasn't riding at all now and besides he said that whisky kept his weight down. But I noticed

370

he was putting it on, all right, just the same. He'd busted away from his old gang out at Maisons and seemed to like just sitting around on the boulevard with me. But he was dropping money every day at the track. He'd feel sort of doleful after the last race, if he'd lost on the day, until we'd get to our table and he'd have his first whisky and then he'd be fine.

He'd be reading the *Paris-Sport* and he'd look over at me and say, 'Where's your girl, Joe?' to kid me on account I had told him about the girl that day at the next table. And I'd get red, but I liked being kidded about her. It gave me a good feeling. 'Keep your eye peeled for her, Joe,' he'd say, 'she'll be back.'

He'd ask me questions about things and some of the things I'd say he'd laugh. And then he'd get started talking about things. About riding down in Egypt, or at St Moritz on the ice before my mother died, and about during the war when they had regular races down in the south of France without any purses, or betting or crowd or anything just to keep the breed up. Regular races with the jocks riding hell out of the horses. Gee, I could listen to my old man talk by the hour, especially when he'd had a couple or so of drinks. He'd tell me about when he was a boy in Kentucky and going coon hunting, and the old days in the States before everything went on the bum there. And he'd say, 'Joe, when we've got a decent stake, you're going back to the States and go to school.'

'What've I got to go back there to go to school for when everything's on the bum there?' I'd ask him.

'That's different,' he'd say and get the waiter over and pay the pile of saucers and we'd get a taxi to the Gare St Lazare and get on the train out to Maisons.

One day at Auteuil, after a selling steeplechase, my old man bought in the winner for 30,000 francs. He had to bid a little to get him but the stable let the horse go finally and my old man had his permit and his colours in a week. Gee, I felt proud when my old man was an owner. He fixed it up for stable space with Charles Drake and cut out coming in to Paris, and started his running and sweating out again, and him and I were the whole stable gang. Our horse's name was Gilford; he was Irish bred and a nice, sweet jumper. My old man figured that training him and riding him, himself, he was a good investment. I was proud of everything and I thought Gilford was as good a horse as War Cloud. He was a good, solid jumper, a bay, with plenty of speed on the flat, if you asked him for it, and he was a nice-looking horse, too.

Gee, I was fond of him. The first time he started with my old man up, he finished third in a 2,500 metre hurdle race and when my old man got off him, all sweating and happy in the place stall, and went in to weigh, I felt as proud of him as though it was the first race he'd ever placed in. You see, when a guy ain't been riding for a long time, you can't make yourself really believe that he has ever rode. The whole thing was different now, 'cause down in Milan, even big races never seemed to make any difference to my old man, if he won he wasn't ever excited or anything, and now it was so I couldn't hardly sleep the night before a race and I knew my old man was excited, too, even if he didn't show it. Riding for yourself makes an awful difference.

Second time Gilford and my old man started, was a rainy Sunday at Auteuil, in the Prix du Marat, a 4,500 metre steeplechase. As soon as he'd gone out I beat it up in the stand with the new glasses my old man had bought for me to watch them. They started way over at the far end of the course and there was some trouble at the barrier. Something with goggle blinders on was making a great fuss and rearing around and busted the barrier once, but I could see my old man in our black jacket, with a white cross and a black cap, sitting up on Gilford, and patting him with his hand. Then they were off in a jump and out of sight behind the trees and the gong going for dear life and the pari-mutuel wickets rattling down. Gosh, I was so excited, I was afraid to look at them, but I fixed the glasses on the place where they would come out back of the trees and then out they came with the old black jacket going third and they all sailing over the jump like birds. Then they went out of sight again and then they came pounding out and down the hill and all going nice and sweet and easy and taking the fence smooth in a bunch, and moving away from us all solid. Looked as though you could walk across on their backs they were all so bunched and going so smooth. Then they bellied over the big double Bullfinch and something came down. I couldn't see who it was, but in a minute the horse was up and galloping free and the field, all bunched still, sweeping around the long left turn into the straight-away. They jumped the stone wall and came jammed down the stretch toward the big water-jump right in front of the stands. I saw them coming and hollered at my old man as he went by, and he was leading by about a length and riding way out, and light as a monkey, and they were racing for the water-jump. They took off over the big hedge of the water-jump in a pack and then there was a crash, and two horses pulled sideways out off it, and kept on going, and three others were piled up. I couldn't see my old man anywhere. One horse kneed himself up and the jock had hold of the bridle and mounted and went slamming on after the place money. The other horse was up and away by himself, jerking his head and galloping with the bridle rein hanging and the jock staggered over to one side of the track against the fence. Then Gilford rolled over to one side off my old man and got up and started to run on three legs with his off hoof dangling and there was my old man laying there on the grass flat out with his face up and blood all over the side of his head. I ran down the stand and bumped into a jam of people and got to the rail and a cop grabbed me and held me and two big stretcher-bearers were going out after my old man and around on the other side of the course I saw three horses, strung way out, coming out of the trees and taking the jump.

My old man was dead when they brought him in and while a doctor was listening to his heart with a thing plugged in his ears, I heard a shot up the track that mean't they'd killed Gilford. I lay down beside my old man, when they carried the stretcher into the hospital room, and hung on to the stretcher and cried and cried, and he looked so white and gone and so awfully dead, and I couldn't help feeling that if my old man was dead maybe they didn't need to have shot Gilford. His hoof might have got well. I don't know. I loved my old man so much.

Then a couple of guys came in and one of them patted me on the back and then went over and looked at my old man and then pulled a sheet off the cot and spread it over him; and the other was telephoning in French for them to send the ambulance to take him out to Maisons. And I couldn't stop crying, crying and choking, sort of, and George Gardner came in and sat down beside me on the floor and put his arm around me and says, 'Come on, Joe, old boy. Get up and we'll go out and wait for the ambulance.'

George and I went out to the gate and I was trying to stop bawling and George wiped off my face with his handkerchief and we were standing back a little ways while the crowd was going out of the gate and a couple of guys stopped near us while we were waiting for the crowd to get through the gate and one of them was counting a bunch of mutuel tickets and he said, 'Well, Butler got his, all right.'

The other guy said, 'I don't give a good goddam if he did, the crook. He had it coming to him on the stuff he's pulled.'

'I'll say he had,' said the other guy, and tore the bunch of tickets in two.

And George Gardner looked at me to see if I'd heard and I had all right and he said, 'Don't you listen to what those bums said, Joe. Your old man was one swell guy.'

But I don't know. Seems like when they get started they don't leave a guy nothing.

Maera lay still, his head on his arms, his face in the sand. He felt warm and sticky from the bleeding. Each time he felt the horn coming. Sometimes the bull only bumped him with his head. Once the horn went all the way through him and he felt it go into the sand. Someone had the bull by the tail. They were swearing at him and flopping the cape in his face. Then the bull was gone. Some men picked Maera up and started to run with him toward the barriers through the gate out the passage way around under the grandstand to the infirmary. They laid Maera down on a cot and one of the men went for the doctor. The doctor came running from the corral, where he had been sewing up picador horses. He had to stop and wash his hands. There was a great shouting going on in the grandstand overhead. Maera wanted to say something and found he could not talk. Maera felt everything getting larger and larger and then smaller and smaller. Then it got larger and larger and then smaller and smaller. Then everything commenced to run faster and faster as when they speed up a cinematograph film. Then he was dead.

Big Two-Hearted River: I

The train went on up the track out of sight, around one of the hills of burnt timber. Nick sat down on the bundle of canvas and bedding the baggage man had pitched out of the door of the baggage car. There was no town, nothing but the rails and the burned-over country. The thirteen saloons that had lined the one street of Seney had not left a trace. The foundations of the Mansion House hotel stuck up above the ground. The stone was chipped and split by the fire. It was all that was left of the town of Seney. Even the surface had been burned off the ground.

Nick looked at the burned-over stretch of hillside, where he had expected to find the scattered houses of the town and then walked down the railroad track to the bridge over the river. The river was there. It swirled against the log piles of the bridge. Nick looked down into the clear, brown water, coloured from the pebbly bottom, and watched the trout keeping themselves steady in the current with wavering fins. As he watched them they changed their positions by quick angles, only to hold steady in the fast water again. Nick watched them a long time.

He watched them holding themselves with their noses into the current, many trout in deep, fast moving water, slightly distorted as he watched far down through the glassy convex surface of the pool, its surface pushing and swelling smooth against the resistance of the log driven piles of the bridge. At the bottom of the pool were the big trout. Nick did not see them at first. Then he saw them at the bottom of the pool, big trout looking to hold themselves on the gravel bottom in a varying mist of gravel and sand, raised in spurts by the current.

Nick looked down into the pool from the bridge. It was a hot day. A kingfisher flew up the stream. It was a long time since Nick had looked into a stream and seen trout. They were very satisfactory. As the shadow of the kingfisher moved up the stream, a big trout shot upstream in a long angle, only his shadow marking the angle, then lost his shadow as he came through the surface of the water, caught the sun, and then, as he went back into the stream under the surface, his shadow seemed to float down the stream with the current, unresisting, to his post under the bridge where he tightened facing up into the current.

Nick's heart tightened as the trout moved. He felt all the old feeling.

He turned and looked down the stream. It stretched away, pebbly-bottomed with shallows and big boulders and a deep pool as it curved away around the foot of a bluff.

Nick walked back up the ties to where his pack lay in the cinders beside the railway track. He was happy. He adjusted the pack harness around the bundle, pulling straps tight, slung the pack on his back, got his arms through the shoulder straps and took some of the pull off his shoulders by leaning his forehead against the wide band of the tump-line. Still, it was too heavy. It was much too heavy. He had his leather rod-case in his hand and leaning forward to keep the weight of the pack high on his shoulders he walked along the road that paralleled the railway track, leaving the burned town behind in the heat, and then turned off around a hill with a high, fire-scarred hill on either side on to a road that went back into the country. He walked along the road feeling the ache from the pull of the heavy pack. The road climbed steadily. It was hard work walking up-hill. His muscles ached and the day was hot, but Nick felt happy. He felt he had left everything behind, the need for thinking, the need to write, other needs. It was all back of him.

From the time he had gotten down off the train and the baggage man had thrown his pack out of the open car door things had been different. Seney was burned, the country was burned over and changed, but it did not matter. It could not all be burned. He knew that. He hiked along the road, sweating in the sun, climbing to cross the range of hills that separated the railway from the pine plains.

The road ran on, dipping occasionally, but always climbing.

Nick went on up. Finally the road after going parallel to the burnt hillside reached the top. Nick leaned back against a stump and slipped out of the pack harness. Ahead of him, as far as he could see, was the pine plain. The burned country stopped off at the left with the range of hills. On ahead islands of dark pine trees rose out of the plain. Far off to the left was the line of the river. Nick followed it with his eye and caught glints of the water in the sun.

There was nothing but the pine plain ahead of him, until the far blue hills that marked the Lake Superior height of land. He could hardly see them, faint and far away in the heat-light over the plain. If he looked too steadily they were gone. But if he only half-looked they were there, the far off hills of the height of land.

Nick sat down against the charred stump and smoked a cigarette. His pack balanced on the top of the stump, harness holding ready, a hollow moulded in it from his back. Nick sat smoking, looking out over the country. He did not need to get his map out. He knew where he was from the position of the river.

As he smoked, his legs stretched out in front of him, he noticed a grasshopper walk along the ground and up on to his woollen sock. The grasshopper was black. As he walked along the road, climbing, he had started many grasshoppers from the dust. They were all black. They were not the big grasshoppers with yellow and black or red and black wings whirring out from their black wing sheathing as they fly up. These were just ordinary hoppers, but all a sooty black in colour. Nick had wondered about them as he walked, without really thinking about them. Now, as he watched the black hopper that was nibbling at the wool of his sock with its fourway lip, he realized that they had all turned black from living in the burned-over land. He realized that the fire must have come the year before, but the grasshoppers were all black now. He wondered how long they would stay that way.

Carefully he reached his hand down and took hold of the hopper by the wings. He turned him up, all his legs walking in the air; and looked at his jointed belly. Yes, it was black too, iridescent where the back and head were dusty.

'Go on, hopper,' Nick said, speaking out loud for the first time, 'fly away somewhere.'

He tossed the grasshopper up into the air and watched him sail away to a charcoal stump across the road.

Nick stood up. He leaned his back against the weight of his pack where it rested upright on the stump and got his arms through the shoulder straps. He stood with the pack on his back on the brow of the hill looking out across the country, toward the distant river and then struck down the hillside away from the road. Underfoot the ground was good walking. Two hundred yards down the hillside the fire line stopped. Then it was sweet fern, growing ankle high, to walk through, and clumps of jack-pines; a long undulating country with frequent rises and descents, sandy underfoot and the country alive again.

Nick kept his direction by the sun. He knew where he wanted to strike the river and he kept on through the pine plain, mounting small rises to see other rises ahead of him and sometimes from the top of a rise a great solid island of pines off to his right or his left. He broke off some sprigs of the heathery sweet fern, and put them under his pack straps. The chafing crushed it and he smelled it as he walked.

He was tired and very hot, walking across the uneven, shadeless pine plain. At any time he knew he could strike the river by turning off to his left. It could not be more than a mile away. But he kept on toward the north to hit the river as far upstream as he could go in one day's walking.

For some time as he walked Nick had been in sight of one of the big islands of pine standing out above the rolling high ground he was crossing. He dipped down and then as he came slowly up to the crest of the ridge he turned and made toward the pine trees.

There was no underbrush in the island of pine trees. The trunks of the trees went straight up or slanted toward each other. The trunks were straight and brown without branches. The branches were high above. Some interlocked to make a solid shadow on the brown forest floor. Around the grove of trees was a bare space. It was brown and soft underfoot as Nick walked on it. This was the overlapping of the pine needle floor, extending out beyond the width of the high branches. The trees had grown tall and the branches moved high, leaving in the sun this bare space they had once covered with shadow. Sharp at the edge of this extension of the forest floor commenced the sweet fern.

Nick slipped off his pack and lay down in the shade. He lay on his back and looked up into the pine trees. His neck and back and the small of his back rested as he stretched. The earth felt good against his back. He looked up at the sky, through the branches, and then shut his eyes. He opened them and looked up again. There was a wind high up in the branches. He shut his eyes again and went to sleep.

Nick woke stiff and cramped. The sun was nearly down. His pack was heavy and the straps painful as he lifted it on. He leaned over with the pack on and picked up the leather rod-case and started out from the pine trees across the sweet fern swale, toward the river. He knew it could not be more than a mile.

He came down a hill-side covered with stumps into a meadow. At the edge of the meadow flowed the river. Nick was glad to get to the river. He walked upstream through the meadow. His trousers were soaked with the dew as he walked. After the hot day, the dew had come quickly and heavily. The river made no sound. It was too fast and smooth. At the edge of the meadow, before he mounted to a piece of high ground to make camp, Nick looked down the river at the trout rising. They were rising to insects come from the swamp on the other side of the stream when the sun went down. The trout jumped out of the water to take them. While Nick walked through the little stretch of meadow alongside the stream, trout had jumped high out of the water. Now as he looked down the river, the insects must be settling on the surface, for the trout were feeding steadily all down the stream. As far down the long stretch as he could see, the trout were rising, making circles all down the surface of the water, as though it were starting to rain.

The ground rose, wooded and sandy, to overlook the meadow, the stretch of river and the swamp. Nick dropped his pack and rod-case and looked for a level piece of ground. He

379

was very hungry and he wanted to make his camp before he cooked. Between two jack-pines, the ground was quite level. He took the axe out of the pack and chopped out two projecting roots. That levelled a piece of ground large enough to sleep on. He smoothed out the sandy soil with his hand and pulled all the sweet fern bushes by their roots. His hands smelled good from the sweet fern. He smoothed the uprooted earth. He did not want anything making lumps under the blankets. When he had the ground smooth, he spread his three blankets. One he folded double, next to the ground. The other two he spread on top.

With the axe he slit off a bright slab of pine from one of the stumps and split it into pegs for the tent. He wanted them long and solid to hold in the ground. With the tent unpacked and spread on the ground, the pack, leaning against a jack-pine, looked much smaller. Nick tied the rope that served the tent for a ridge-pole to the trunk of one of the pine trees and pulled the tent up off the ground with the other end of the rope and tied it to the other pine. The tent hung on the rope like a canvas blanket on a clothes line. Nick poked a pole he had cut up under the back peak of the canvas and then made it a tent by pegging out the sides. He pegged the sides out taut and drove the pegs, hitting them down into the ground with the flat of the axe until the rope loops were buried and the canvas was drum tight.

Across the open mouth of the tent Nick fixed cheese cloth to keep out mosquitoes. He crawled inside under the mosquito bar with various things from the pack to put at the head of the bed under the slant of the canvas. Inside the tent the light came through the brown canvas. It smelled pleasantly of canvas. Already there was something mysterious and homelike. Nick was happy as he crawled inside the tent. He had not been unhappy all day. This was different though. Now things were done. There had been this to do. Now it was done. It had been a hard trip. He was very tired. That was done. He had made his camp. He was settled. Nothing could touch him. It was a good place to camp. He was there, in the good place. He was in his home where he had made it. Now he was hungry.

He came out, crawling under the cheese cloth. It was quite dark outside. It was lighter in the tent.

Nick went over to the pack and found, with his fingers, a long nail in a paper sack of nails, in the bottom of the pack. He drove it into the pine tree, holding it close and hitting it gently with the flat of the axe. He hung the pack up on the nail. All his supplies were in the pack. They were off the ground and sheltered now.

Nick was hungry. He did not believe he had ever been hungrier. He opened and emptied a can of pork and beans and a can of spaghetti into the frying-pan.

'I've got a right to eat this kind of stuff, if I'm willing to carry it,' Nick said. His voice sounded strange in the darkening woods. He did not speak again.

He started a fire with some chunks of pine he got with the axe from a stump. Over the fire he stuck a wire grill, pushing the four legs down into the ground with his boot. Nick put the frying-pan on the grill over flames. He was hungrier. The beans and spaghetti warmed. Nick stirred them and mixed them together. They began to bubble, making little bubbles that rose with difficulty to the surface. There was a good smell. Nick got out a bottle of tomato ketchup and cut four slices of bread. The little bubbles were coming faster now. Nick sat down beside the fire and lifted the frying-pan off. He poured about half the contents out into the tin plate. It spread slowly on the plate. Nick knew it was too hot. He poured on some tomato ketchup. He knew the beans and spaghetti were still too hot. He looked at the fire, then at the tent, he was not going to spoil it all by burning his tongue. For years he had never enjoyed fried bananas because he had never been able to wait for them to cool. His tongue was very sensitive. He was very hungry. Across the river in the swamp, in the almost dark, he saw a mist rising. He looked at the tent once more. All right. He took a full spoonful from the plate.

'Chrise,' Nick said, 'Geezus Chrise,' he said happily.

He ate the whole plateful before he remembered the bread. Nick finished the second plateful with the bread, mopping the plate shiny. He had not eaten since a cup of coffee and a ham sandwich in the station restaurant at St Ignace. It had been a very fine experience. He had been hungry before, but had not been able to satisfy it. He could have made camp hours before if he had wanted to. There were plenty of good places to camp on the river. But this was good.

Nick tucked two big chips of pine under the grill. The fire flared up. He had forgotten to get water for the coffee. Out of the pack he got a folding canvas bucket and walked down the hill, across the edge of the meadow, to the stream. The other bank was in the white mist. The grass was wet and cold as he knelt on the bank and dipped the canvas bucket into the stream. It bellied and pulled hard in the current. The water was ice cold. Nick rinsed the bucket and carried it full up to the camp. Up away from the stream it was not so cold.

Nick drove another big nail and hung up the bucket full of water. He dipped the coffee pot half full, put some more chips under the grill on to the fire and put the pot on. He could not remember which way he made coffee. He could remember an argument about it with Hopkins, but not which side he had taken. He decided to bring it to a boil. He remembered now that was Hopkins's way. He had once argued about everything with Hopkins. While he waited for the coffee to boil, he opened a small can of apricots. He liked to open cans. He emptied the can of apricots out into a tin cup. While he watched the coffee on the fire, he drank the juice syrup of the apricots, carefully at first to keep from spilling, then meditatively, sucking the apricots down. They were better than fresh apricots.

The coffee boiled as he watched. The lid came up and coffee and grounds ran down the side of the pot. Nick took it off the grill. It was a triumph for Hopkins. He put sugar in the empty apricot cup and poured some of the coffee out to cool. It was too hot to pour and he used his hat to hold the handle of the coffee pot. He would not let it steep in the pot at all. Not the first cup. It should be straight Hopkins all the way. Hop deserved that. He was a very serious coffee maker. He was the most serious man Nick had ever known. Not heavy, serious. That was a long time ago. Hopkins spoke without moving his lips. He had played polo. He made millions of dollars in Texas. He had borrowed car fare to go to Chicago, when the wire came that his first big well had come in. He could have wired for money. That would have been too slow. They called Hop's girl the Blonde Venus. Hop did not mind because she was not his real girl. Hopkins said very confidently that none of them would make fun of his real girl. He was right. Hopkins went away when the telegram came. That was on the Black River. It took eight days for the telegram to reach him. Hopkins gave away his .22 calibre Colt automatic pistol to Nick. He gave his camera to Bill. It was to remember him always by. They were all going fishing again next summer. The Hop Head was rich. He would get a yacht and they would all cruise along the north shore of Lake Superior. He was excited but serious. They said good-bye and all felt bad. It broke up the trip. They never saw Hopkins again. That was a long time ago on the Black River.

Nick drank his coffee according to Hopkins. The coffee was bitter. Nick laughed. It made a good ending to the story. His mind was starting to work. He knew he could choke it because he was tired enough. He spilled the coffee out of the pot and shook the grounds loose into the fire. He lit a cigarette and went inside the tent. He took off his shoes and trousers, sitting on the blankets, rolled the shoes up inside the trousers for a pillow and got in between the blankets.

Out through the front of the tent he watched the glow of the fire, when the night wind blew on it. It was a quiet night. The swamp was perfectly quiet. Nick stretched under the blanket comfortably. A mosquito hummed close to his ear. Nick sat up and lit a match. The mosquito was on the canvas, over his head. Nick moved the match quickly up to it. The mosquito made a satisfactory hiss in the flame. The match went out. Nick lay down again under the blankets. He turned on his side and shut his eyes. He was sleepy. He felt sleep coming. He curled up under the blanket and went to sleep.

They hanged Sam Cardinella at six o'clock in the morning in the corridor of the county jail. The corridor was high and narrow with tiers of cells on either side. All the cells were occupied. The prisoners had been brought in for the hanging. Five men sentenced to be hanged were in the five top cells. Three of the men to be hanged were negroes. They were very frightened. One of the white men sat on his cot with his head in his hands. The other lay flat on his cot with a blanket wrapped around his head.

They came out on to the gallows through a door in the wall. There were six or seven of them including two priests. They were carrying Sam Cardinella. He had been like that since about four o'clock in the morning.

While they were strapping his legs together two guards held him up and the two priests were whispering to him. 'Be a man, my son,' said one priest. When they came toward him with the cap to go over his head Sam Cardinella lost control of his sphincter muscles. The guards who had been holding him up dropped him. They were both disgusted. 'How about a chair, Will?' asked one of the guards. 'Better get one,' said a man in a derby hat.

When they all stepped back on the scaffolding back of the drop, which was very heavy, built of oak and steel and swung on ball bearings, Sam Cardinella was left sitting there strapped tight with the rope around his neck, the younger of the two priests kneeling beside the chair holding up a little crucifix. The priest skipped back on to the scaffolding just before the drop fell.

Big Two-Hearted River: II

In the morning the sun was up and the tent was starting to get hot. Nick crawled out under the mosquito netting stretched across the mouth of the tent, to look at the morning. The grass was wet on his hands as he came out. He held his trousers and his shoes in his hands. The sun was just up over the hill. There was the meadow, the river and the swamp. There were birch trees in the green of the swamp on the other side of the river.

The river was clear and smoothly fast in the early morning. Down about two hundred yards were three logs all the way across the stream. They made the water smooth and deep above them. As Nick watched, a mink crossed the river on the logs and went into the swamp. Nick was excited. He was excited by the early morning and the river. He was really too hurried to eat breakfast, but he knew he must. He built a little fire and put on the coffee pot.

While the water was heating in the pot he took an empty bottle and went down over the edge of the high ground to the meadow. The meadow was wet with dew and Nick wanted to catch grasshoppers for bait before the sun dried the grass. He found plenty of good grasshoppers. They were at the base of the grass stems. Sometimes they clung to a grass stem. They were cold and wet with the dew, and could not jump until the sun warmed them. Nick picked them up, taking only the medium-sized brown ones, and put them into the bottle. He turned over a log and just under the shelter of the edge were several hundred hoppers. It was a grasshopper lodging house. Nick put about fifty of the medium browns into the bottle. While he was picking up the hoppers the others warmed in the sun and commenced to hop away. They flew when they hopped. At first they made one flight and stayed stiff when they landed, as though they were dead.

Nick knew that by the time he was through with breakfast they would be as lively as ever. Without dew in the grass it would take him all day to catch a bottle full of good grasshoppers and he would have to crush many of them, slamming at them with his hat. He washed his hands at the stream. He was excited to be near it. Then he walked up to the tent. The hopppers were already jumping stiffly in the grass. In the bottle, warmed by the sun, they were jumping in a mass. Nick put in a pine stick as a cork. It plugged the mouth of the bottle enough, so the hoppers could not get out and left plenty of air passage.

He had rolled the log back and knew he could get grass-hoppers there every morning.

Nick laid the bottle full of jumping grasshoppers against a pine trunk. Rapidly he mixed some buckwheat flour with water and stirred it smooth, one cup of flour, one cup of water. He put a handful of coffee in the pot and dipped a lump of grease out of a can and slid it sputtering across the hot skillet. On the smoking skillet he poured smoothly the buckwheat batter. It spread like lava, the grease spitting sharply. Around the edges the buckwheat cake began to firm, then brown, then crisp. The surface was bubbling slowly, to porousness. Nich pushed under the browned under surface with a fresh pine chip. He shook the skillet sideways and the cake was loose on the surface. I won't try to flop it, he thought. He slid the chip of clean wood all the way under the cake, and flopped it over on to its face. It spluttered in the pan.

When it was cooked. Nick regreased the skillet. He used all the batter. It made another big flapjack and one smaller one.

Nick ate a big flapjack and a smaller one, covered with apple butter. He put apple butter on the third cake, folded it over twice, wrapped it in oiled paper and put it in his shirt pocket. He put the apple-butter jar back in the pack and cut bread for two sandwiches.

In the pack he found a big onion. He sliced it in two and peeled the silky outer skin. Then he cut one half into slices and made onion sandwiches. He wrapped them in oiled paper and buttoned them in the other pocket of his khaki shirt. He turned the skillet upside down on the grill, drank the coffee, sweetened and yellow brown with the condensed milk in it, and tidied up the camp. It was a good camp.

Nick took his fly rod out of the leather rod-case, jointed it, and shoved the rod-case back into the tent. He put on the reel and threaded the line through the guides. He had to hold it from hand to hand, as he threaded it, or it would slip back through its own weight. It was a heavy, double tapered fly line. Nick had paid eight dollars for it a long time ago. It was made heavy to lift back in the air and come forward flat and heavy and straight to make it possible to cast a fly which has no weight. Nick opened the aluminium leader box. The leaders were coiled between the damp flannel pads. Nick had wet the pads at the water cooler on the train up to St Ignace. In the damp pads the gut leaders had softened and Nick unrolled one and tied it by a loop at the end to a heavy fly line. He fastened a hook on the end of the leader. It was a small hook; very thin and springy.

Nick took it from his hook book, sitting with the rod across his lap. He tested the knot and the spring of the rod by pulling the line taut. It was a good feeling. He was careful not to let the hook bite into his finger.

He started down to the stream, holding his rod, the bottle of grasshoppers hung from his neck by a thong tied in half hitches around the neck of the bottle. His landing net hung by a hook from his belt. Over his shoulder was a long flour sack tied at each corner into an ear. The cord went over his shoulder. The sack flapped against his legs.

Nick felt awkward and professionally happy with all his equipment hanging from him. The grasshopper bottle swung against his chest. In his shirt the breast pockets bulged against him with the lunch and his fly book.

He stepped into the stream. It was a shock. His trousers clung tight to his legs. His shoes felt the gravel. The water was a rising cold shock.

Rushing, the current sucked against his legs. Where he stepped in, the water was over his knees. He waded with the current. The gravel slid under his shoes. He looked down at the swirl of water below each leg and tipped up the bottle to get a grasshopper.

The first grasshopper gave a jump in the neck of the bottle and went out into the water. He was sucked under in the whirl by Nick's right leg and came to the surface a little way down stream. He floated rapidly, kicking. In a quick circle, breaking the smooth surface of the water, he disappeared. A trout had taken him.

Another hopper poked his head out of the bottle. His antennae wavered. He was getting his front legs out of the bottle to jump. Nick took him by the head and held him while he threaded the slim hook under his chin, down through his thorax and into the last segments of his abdomen. The grasshopper took hold of the hook with his front feet, spitting tobacco juice on it. Nick dropped him into the water.

Holding the rod in his right hand he let out line against the pull of the grasshopper in the current. He stripped off line from the reel with his left hand and let it run free. He could see the hopper in the little waves of the current. It went out of sight.

There was a tug on the line. Nick pulled against the taut line. It was his first strike. Holding the now living rod across the current, he brought in the line with his left hand. The rod bent in jerks, the trout pumping against the current. Nick knew it was a small one. He lifted the rod straight up in the air. It bowed with the pull.

He saw the trout in the water jerking with his head and body against the shifting tangent of the line in the stream. Nick took the line in his left hand and pulled the trout, thumping tiredly against the current, to the surface. His back was mottled the clear, water-over-gravel colour, his side flashing in the sun. The rod under his right arm, Nick stooped, dipping his right hand into the current. He held the trout, never still, with his moist right hand, while he unhooked the barb from his mouth, then dropped him back into the stream.

He hung unsteadily in the current, then settled to the bottom beside a stone. Nick reached down his hand to touch him, his arm to the elbow under water. The trout was steady in the moving stream, resting on the gravel, beside a stone. As Nick's fingers touched him, touched his smooth, cool, underwater feeling he was gone, gone in a shadow across the bottom of the stream.

He's all right, Nick thought. He was only tired.

He had wet his hand before he touched the trout, so he would not disturb the delicate mucus that covered him. If a trout was touched with a dry hand, a white fungus attacked the unprotected spot. Years before when he had fished crowded streams, with fly fishermen ahead of him and behind him, Nick had again and again come on dead trout, furry with white fungus, drifted against a rock, or floating belly up in some pool. Nick did not like to fish with other men on the river. Unless they were of your party, they spoiled it.

He wallowed down the stream, above his knees in the current, through the fifty yards of shallow water above the pile of logs that crossed the stream. He did not rebait his hook and held it in his hand as he waded. He was certain he could catch small trout in the shallows, but he did not want them. There would be no big trout in the shallows this time of day.

Now the water deepened up his thighs sharply and coldly. Ahead was the smooth dammed-back flood of water above the logs. The water was smooth and dark; on the left, the lower edge of the meadow; on the right the swamp.

Nick leaned back against the current and took a hopper from the bottle. He threaded the hopper on the hook and spat on him for good luck. Then he pulled several yards of line from the reel and tossed the hopper out ahead on to the fast, dark water. It floated down toward the logs, then the weight of the line pulled the bait under the surface. Nick held the rod in his right hand, letting the line run out through his fingers.

There was a long tug. Nick struck and the rod came alive and dangerous, bent double, the line tightening, coming out of water, tightening, all in a heavy, dangerous, steady pull. Nick felt the moment when the leader would break if the strain increased and let the line go.

The reel ratcheted into a mechanical shriek as the line went out in a rush. Too fast. Nick could not check it, the line rushing out, the reel note rising as the line ran out.

With the core of the reel showing, his heart feeling stopped with the excitement, leaning back against the current that mounted icily his thighs, Nick thumbed the reel hard with his left hand. It was awkward getting his thumb inside the fly reel frame.

As he put on pressure the line tightened into sudden hardness and beyond the logs a huge trout went high out of water. As he jumped, Nick lowered the tip of the rod. But he felt as he dropped the tip to ease the strain, the moment when the strain was too great; the hardness too tight. Of course, the leader had broken. There was no mistaking the feeling when all spring left the line and it became dry and hard. Then it went slack.

His mouth dry, his heart down, Nick reeled in. He had never seen so big a trout. There was a heaviness, a power not to be held, and then the bulk of him, as he jumped. He looked as broad as a salmon.

Nick's hand was shaky. He reeled in slowly. The thrill had been too much. He felt, vaguely, a little sick, as though it would be better to sit down.

The leader had broken where the hook was tied to it. Nick took it in his hand. He thought of the trout somewhere on the bottom, holding himself steady over the gravel, far down below the light, under the logs, with the hook in his jaw. Nick knew the trout's teeth would cut through the snell of the hook. The hook would embed itself in his jaw. He'd bet the trout was angry. Anything that size would be angry. That was a trout. He had been solidly hooked. Solid as a rock. He felt like a rock, too, before he started off. By God, he was a big one. By God, he was the biggest one I ever heard of.

Nick climbed out on to the meadow and stood, water running down his trousers and out of his shoes, his shoes squelchy. He went over and sat on the logs. He did not want to rush his sensations any.

He wriggled his toes in the water in his shoes, and got out a cigarette from his breast pocket. He lit it and tossed the match into the fast water below the logs. A tiny trout rose at the match, as it swung around in the fast current. Nick laughed. He would finish the cigarette.

He sat on the logs, smoking, drying in the sun, the sun warm on his back, the river shallow ahead entering the woods, curving into the woods, shallows, light glittering, big water-smooth rocks, cedars along the bank and white birches, the logs warm in the sun, smooth to sit on, without bark, grey to the touch; slowly the feeling of disappointment left him. It went away slowly, the feeling of disappointment that came sharply after the thrill that made his shoulders ache. It was all right now. His rod lying out on the logs, Nick tied a new hook on the leader, pulling the gut tight until it grimped itself in a hard knot.

He baited up, then picked up the rod and walked to the far end of the logs to get into the water, where it was not too deep. Under and beyond the logs was a deep pool. Nick walked around the shallow shelf near the swamp shore until he came out on the shallow bed of the stream.

On the left, where the meadow ended and the woods began, a great elm tree was uprooted. Gone over in a storm, it lay back into the woods, its roots clotted with dirt, grass growing in them, rising a solid bank beside the stream. The river cut to the edge of the uprooted tree. From where Nick stood he could see deep channels, like ruts, cut in the shallow bed of the stream by the flow of the current. Pebbly where he stood and pebbly and full of boulders beyond; where it curved near the tree roots, the bed of the stream was marly and between the ruts of deep water green weed fronds swung in the current.

Nick swung the rod back over his shoulder and forward, and the line, curving forward, laid the grasshopper down on one of the deep channels in the weeds. A trout struck and Nick hooked him.

Holding the rod far out toward the uprooted tree and sloshing backward in the current, Nick worked the trout, plunging, the rod bending alive, out of the danger of the weeds into the open river. Holding the rod, pumping alive against the current, Nick brought the trout in. He rushed, but always came, the spring of the rod yielding to the rushes, sometimes jerking under water, but always bringing him in. Nick eased downstream with the rushes. The rod above his head, he led the trout over the net, then lifted.

The trout hung heavy in the net, mottled trout back and silver sides in the meshes. Nick unhooked him; heavy sides, good to hold, big undershot jaw, and slipped him, heaving and big sliding, into the long sack that hung from his shoulders in the water.

Nick spread the mouth of the sack against the current and it filled heavy with water. He held it up, the bottom in the stream, and the water poured out through the sides. Inside at the bottom was the big trout, alive in the water.

Nick moved downstream. The sack out ahead of him, sunk, heavy in the water, pulling from his shoulders.

It was getting hot, the sun hot on the back of his neck.

Nick had one good trout. He did not care about getting many trout. Now the stream was shallow and wide. There were trees along both banks. The trees of the left bank made short shadows on the current in the forenoon sun. Nick knew there were trout in each shadow. In the afternoon, after the sun had crossed toward the hills, the trout would be in the cool shadows on the other side of the stream.

The very biggest ones would lie up close to the bank. You could always pick them up there on the Black. When the sun was down they all moved out into the current. Just when the sun made the water blinding in the glare before it went down, you were liable to strike a big trout anywhere in the current. It was almost impossible to fish then, the surface of the water was blinding as a mirror in the sun. Of course, you could fish upstream, but in a stream like the Black, or this, you had to wallow against the current and in a deep place, the water piled up on you. It was no fun to fish upstream with this much current.

Nick moved along through the shallow stretch watching the banks for deep holes. A beech tree grew close beside the river, so that the branches hung down in the water. The stream went back in under the leaves. There were always trout in a place like that.

Nick did not care about fishing that hole. He was sure he would get hooked in the branches.

It looked deep though. He dropped the grasshopper so the current took it under water, back in under the overhanging branch. The line pulled hard and Nick struck. The trout threshed heavily, half out of water in the leaves and branches. The line was caught. Nick pulled hard and the trout was off. He reeled in and holding the reel in his hand, walked down the stream.

Ahead, close to the left bank, was a big log. Nick saw it was hollow; pointing up river the current entered it smoothly, only a little ripple spread each side of the log. The water was deepening. The top of the hollow log was gray and dry. It was partly in the shadow.

Nick took the cork out of the grasshopper bottle and a hopper clung to it. He picked him off, hooked him and tossed him out. He held the rod far out so that the hopper on the water moved into the current flowing into the hollow log. Nick lowered the rod and the hopper floated in. There was a heavy strike. Nick swung the rod against the pull. It felt as though he were hooked into the log itself, except for the live feeling.

He tried to force the fish out into the current. It came, heavily.

The line went slack and Nick thought the trout was gone. Then he saw him, very near, in the current, shaking his head, trying to get the hook out. His mouth was clamped shut. He was fighting the hook in the clear flowing current.

Looping in the line with his left hand, Nick swung the rod

to make the line taut and tried to lead the trout toward the net, but he was gone, out of sight, the line pumping. Nick fought him against the current, letting him thump in the water against the spring of the rod. He shifted the rod to his left hand, worked the trout upstream, holding his weight, fighting on the rod, and then let him down into the net. He lifted him clear of the water, a heavy half circle in the net, the net dripping, unhooked him and slid him into the sack.

He spread the mouth of the sack and looked down in at the two big trout alive in the water.

Through the deepening water, Nick waded over to the hollow log. He took the sack off, over his head, the trout flopping as it came out of water, and hung it so the trout were deep in the water. Then he pulled himself up on the log and sat, the water from his trousers and boots running down into the stream. He laid his rod down, moved along to the shady end of the log and took the sandwiches out of his pocket. He dipped the sandwiches in the cold water. The current carried away the crumbs. He ate the sandwiches and dipped his hat full of water to drink, the water running out through his hat just ahead of his drinking.

It was cool in the shade, sitting on the log. He took a cigarette out and struck a match to light it. The match sunk into the grey wood, making a tiny furrow. Nick leaned over the side of the log, found a hard place and lit the match. He sat smoking and watching the river.

Ahead the river narrowed and went into a swamp. The river became smooth and deep and the swamp looked solid with cedar trees, their trunks close together, their branches solid. It would not be possible to walk through a swamp like that. The branches grew so low. You would have to keep almost level with the ground to move at all. You could not crash through the branches. That must be why the animals that lived in swamps were built the way they were, Nick thought.

He wished he had brought something to read. He felt like reading. He did not feel like going on into the swamp. He looked down the river. A big cedar slanted all the way across the stream. Beyond that the river went into the swamp.

Nick did not want to go in there now. He felt a reaction against deep wading with the water deepening up under his armpits, to hook big trout in places impossible to land them. In the swamp the banks were bare, the big cedars came together overhead, the sun did not come through, except in patches; in the fast deep water, in the half light, the fishing would be tragic. In the swamp fishing was a tragic adventure. Nick did not want it. He did not want to go down the stream any farther today.

He took out his knife, opened it and stuck it in the log. Then he pulled up the sack, reached into it and brought out one of the trout. Holding him near the tail, hard to hold, alive, in his hand, he whacked him against the log. The trout quivered, rigid. Nick laid him on the log in the shade and broke the neck of the other fish the same way. He laid them side by side on the log. They were fine trout.

Nick cleaned them, slitting them from the vent to the tip of the jaw. All the insides and the gills and tongue came out in one piece. They were both males; long grey-white strips of milt, smooth and clean. All the insides clean and compact, coming out all together. Nick tossed the offal ashore for the minks to find.

He washed the trout in the stream. When he held them back up in the water they looked like live fish. Their colour was not gone yet. He washed his hands and dried them on the log. Then he laid the trout on the sack spread out on the log, rolled them up in it, tied the bundle and put it in the landing net. His knife was still standing, blade stuck in the log. He cleaned it on the wood and put it in his pocket.

Nick stood up on the log, holding his rod, the landing net hanging heavy, then stepped into the water and splashed ashore. He climbed the bank and cut up into the woods, toward the high ground. He was going back to camp. He looked back. The river just showed through the trees. There were plenty of days coming when he could fish the swamp.

L'Envoi

The king was working in the garden. He seemed very glad to see me. We walked through the garden. 'This is the queen,' he said. She was clipping a rose bush. 'Oh, how do you do?' she said. We sat down at a table under a big tree and the king ordered whisky and soda. 'We have good whisky anyway,' he said. The revolutionary committee, he told me, would not allow him to go outside the palace grounds. 'Plastiras is a very good man, I believe,' he said, 'but frightfully difficult. I think he did right, though, shooting those chaps. If Kerensky had shot a few men things might have been altogether different. Of course, the great thing in this sort of an affair is not to be shot oneself.'

It was very jolly. We talked for a long time. Like all Greeks he wanted to go to America.

MEN WITHOUT WOMEN

In Another Country

In the fall the war was always there, but we did not go to it any more. It was cold in the fall in Milan and the dark came very early. Then the electric lights came on, and it was pleasant along the streets looking in the windows. There was much game hanging outside the shops, and snow powdered in the fur of the foxes and the wind blew their tails. The deer hung stiff and heavy and empty, and small birds flew in the wind and the wind turned their feathers. It was a cold fall and the wind came down from the mountains.

We were all at the hospital every afternoon, and there were different ways of walking across the town through the dusk to the hospital. Two of the ways were alongside canals, but they were long. Always, though, you crossed a bridge across a canal to enter the hospital. There was a choice of three bridges. On one of them a woman sold roasted chestnuts. It was warm, standing in front of her charcoal fire, and the chestnuts were warm afterward in your pocket. The hospital was very old and very beautiful, and you entered through a gate and walked across a courtyard and out a gate on the other side. There were usually funerals starting from the courtyard. Beyond the old hospital were the new brick pavilions and there we met every afternoon and were all very polite and interested in what was the matter, and sat in the machines that were to make so much difference.

The doctor came up to the machine where I was sitting and said: 'What did you like best to do before the war? Did you practise a sport?'

I said: 'Yes, football.'

'Good,' he said. 'You will be able to play football again better than ever.'

My knee did not bend and the leg dropped straight from the knee to the ankle without a calf, and the machine was to bend the knee and make it move as in riding a tricycle. But it did not bend yet, and instead the machine lurched when it came to the bending part. The doctor said: 'That will all pass. You are a fortunate young man. You will play football again like a champion.'

In the next machine was a major who had a little hand like a baby's. He winked at me when the doctor examined his hand, which was between two leather straps that bounced up and down and flapped the stiff fingers, and said: 'And will I too play football, captain-doctor?' He had been a very great fencer and, before the war, the greatest fencer in Italy.

The doctor went to his office in a back room and brought a photograph which showed a hand that had been withered almost as small as the major's, before it had taken a machine course, and after was a little larger. The major held the photograph with his good hand and looked at it very carefully. 'A wound?' he asked.

'An industrial accident,' the doctor said.

'Very interesting, very interesting,' the major said, and handed it back to the doctor.

'You have confidence?'

'No,' said the major.

There were three boys who came each day who were about the same age I was. They were all three from Milan, and one of them was to be a lawyer, and one was to be a painter, and one had intended to be a soldier, and after we were finished with the machines, sometimes we walked back together to the Café Cova, which was next door to the Scala. We walked the short way through the communist quarter because we were four together. The people hated us because we were officers, and from a wine-shop someone called out, 'A basso gli ufficiali!' as we passed. Another boy who walked with us sometimes and made us five wore a black silk handkerchief across his face because he had no nose then and his face was to be rebuilt. He

398

had gone out to the front from the military academy and been wounded within an hour after he had gone into the front line for the first time. They rebuilt his face, but he came from a very old family and they could never get the nose exactly right. He went to South America and worked in a bank. But this was a long time ago, and then we did not any of us know how it was going to be afterward. We only knew that there was always the war, but that we were not going to it any more.

We all had the same medals, except the boy with the black silk bandage across his face, and he had not been at the front long enough to get any medals. The tall boy with a very pale face who was to be a lawyer had been a lieutenant of Arditi and had three medals of the sort we each had only one of. He had lived a very long time with death and was a little detached. We were all a little detached, and there was nothing that held us together except that we met every afternoon at the hospital. Although, as we walked to the Cova through the tough part of town, walking in the dark, with light and singing coming out of the wine-shops, and sometimes having to walk into the street when the men and women would crowd together on the sidewalk so that we would have had to jostle them to get by, we felt held together by there being something that had happened that they, the people who disliked us, did not understand.

We ourselves all understood the Cova, where it was rich and warm and not too brightly lighted, and noisy and smoky at certain hours, and there were always girls at the tables and the illustrated papers on a rack on the wall. The girls at the Cova were very patriotic, and I found that the most patriotic people in Italy were the café girls – and I believe they are still patriotic.

The boys at first were very polite about my medals and asked me what I had done to get them. I showed them the papers, which were written in very beautiful language and full of *fratellanza* and *abnegazione,* but which really said, with the adjectives removed, that I had been given the medals because I was an American. After that their manner changed a little toward me, although I was their friend against outsiders. I was a friend, but I was never really one of them after they had read the citations, because it had been different with them and they had done very different things to get their medals. I had been wounded, it was true; but we all knew that being wounded, after all, was really an accident. I was never ashamed of the ribbons, though, and sometimes, after the cocktail hour, I would imagine myself having done all the things they had done to get their medals; but walking home at night through the empty streets with the cold wind and all the shops closed, trying to keep near the street lights, I knew that I would never have done such things, and I was very much afraid to die, and often lay in bed at night by myself, afraid to die and wondering how I would be when I went back to the front again.

The three with the medals were like hunting-hawks; and I was not a hawk, although I might seem a hawk to those who had never hunted; they, the three, knew better and so we drifted apart. But I stayed good friends with the boy who had been wounded his first day at the front, because he would never know how he would have turned out; so he could never be accepted either, and I liked him because I thought perhaps he would not have turned out to be a hawk either.

The major, who had been the great fencer, did not believe in bravery, and spent much time while we sat in the machines correcting my grammar. He had complimented me on how I spoke Italian, and we talked together very easily. One day I had said that Italian seemed such an easy language to me that I could not take a great interest in it; everything was so easy to say. 'Ah, yes,' the major said. 'Why, then, do you not take up the use of grammar?' So we took up the use of grammar, and soon Italian was such a difficult language that I was afraid to talk to him until I had the grammar straight in my mind.

The major came very regularly to the hospital. I do not think he ever missed a day, although I am sure he did not believe in the machines. There was a time when none of us believed in the machines, and one day the major said it was all nonsense. The machines were new then and it was we who were to prove them. It was an idiotic idea, he said, 'a theory, like another.' I had not learned my grammar, and he said I was a stupid impossible disgrace, and he was a fool to have bothered with me. He was a small man and sat straight up in his chair with his right hand thrust into the machine and looked straight ahead at the wall while the straps thumped up and down with his fingers in them.

'What will you do when the war is over, if it is over?' he asked me. 'Speak grammatically!'

'I will go to the States.'

'Are you married?'

'No, but I hope to be.'

'The more of a fool you are,' he said. He seemed very angry. 'A man must not marry.'

'Why, Signor Maggiore?'

'Don't call me "Signor Maggiore".'

'Why must not a man marry?'

'He cannot marry. He cannot marry,' he said angrily. 'If he is to lose everything, he should not place himself in a position to lose that. He should not place himself in a position to lose. He should find things he cannot lose.'

He spoke very angrily and bitterly, and looked straight ahead while he talked.

'But why should he necessarily lose it?'

'He'll lose it,' the major said. He was looking at the wall. Then he looked down at the machine and jerked his little hand out from between the straps and slapped it hard against his thigh. 'He'll lose it,' he almost shouted. 'Don't argue with me!' Then he called to the attendant who ran the machines. 'Come and turn this damned thing off.'

He went back into the other room for the light treatment and the massage. Then I heard him ask the doctor if he might use his telephone and he shut the door. When he came back into the room, I was sitting in another machine. He was wearing his cape and had his cap on, and he came directly towards my machine and put his arm on my shoulder.

'I am so sorry,' he said, and patted me on the shoulder with his good hand. 'I would not be rude. My wife has just died. You must forgive me.'

'Oh –' I said, feeling sick for him. 'I am so sorry.'

He stood there biting his lower lip. 'It is very difficult,' he said. 'I cannot resign myself.'

He looked straight past me and out through the window. Then he began to cry. 'I am utterly unable to resign myself,' he said and choked. And then crying, his head up looking at nothing, carrying himself straight and soldierly, with tears on both his cheeks and biting his lips, he walked past the machines and out of the door.

The doctor told me that the major's wife, who was very young and whom he had not married until he was definitely invalided out of the war, had died of pneumonia. She had been sick only a few days. No one expected her to die. The major did not come to the hospital for three days. Then he came at the usual hour, wearing a black band on the sleeve of his uniform. When he came back, there were large framed photographs around the wall, of all sorts of wounds before and after they had been cured by the machines. In front of the machine the major used were three photographs of hands like his that were completely restored. I do not know where the doctor got them. I always understood we were the first to use the machines. The photographs did not make much difference to the major because he only looked out of the window.

Hills Like White Elephants

The hills across the valley of the Ebro were long and white. On this side there was no shade and no trees and the station was between two lines of rails in the sun. Close against the side of the station there was the warm shadow of the building and a curtain, made of strings of bamboo beads, hung across the open door into the bar, to keep out flies. The American and the girl with him sat at a table in the shade, outside the building. It was very hot and the express from Barcelona would come in forty minutes. It stopped at this junction for two minutes and went on to Madrid.

'What should we drink?' the girl asked. She had taken off her hat and put it on the table.

'It's pretty hot,' the man said.

'Let's drink beer.'

'Dos cervezas,' the man said into the curtain.

'Big ones?' a woman asked from the doorway.

'Yes. Two big ones.'

The woman brought two glasses of beer and two felt pads. She put the felt pads and the beer glasses on the table and looked at the man and the girl. The girl was looking off at the line of hills. They were white in the sun and the country was brown and dry.

'They look like white elephants,' she said.

'I've never seen one.' The man drank his beer.

'No, you wouldn't have.'

'I might have,' the man said. 'Just because you say I wouldn't have doesn't prove anything.'

The girl looked at the bead curtain. 'They've painted something on it,' she said. 'What does it say?'

'Anis del Toro. It's a drink.'

'Could we try it?'

The man called 'Listen' through the curtain. The woman came out from the bar.

'Four reales.'

'He want two Anis del Toro.'

'With water?'

'Do you want it with water?'

'I don't know,' the girl said. 'Is it good with water?'

'It's all right.'

'You want them with water?' asked the woman.

'Yes, with water.'

'It tastes like liquorice,' the girl said and put the glass down.

'That's the way with everything.'

'Yes,' said the girl. 'Everything tastes of liquorice. Especially all the things you've waited so long for, like absinthe.'

'Oh, cut it out.'

'You started it,' the girl said. 'I was being amused. I was having a fine time.'

'Well, let's try and have a fine time.'

'All right. I was trying. I said the mountains looked like white elephants. Wasn't that bright?'

'That was bright.'

'I wanted to try this new drink. That's all we do, isn't it – look at things and try new drinks?'

'I guess so.'

The girl looked across at the hills.

'They're lovely hills,' she said. 'They don't really look like white elephants. I just meant the colouring of their skin through the trees.'

'Should we have another drink?'

'All right.'

The warm wind blew the bead curtain against the table.

'The beer's nice and cool,' the man said.

'It's lovely,' the girl said.

'It's really an awfully simple operation, Jig,' the man said. 'It's not really an operation at all.'

The girl looked at the ground the table legs rested on.

'I know you wouldn't mind it, Jig. It's really not anything. It's just to let the air in.'

The girl did not say anything.

'I'll go with you and I'll stay with you all the time. They just let the air in and then it's all perfectly natural.'

'Then what will we do afterward?'

'We'll be fine afterward. Just like we were before.'

'What makes you think so?'

'That's the only thing that bothers us. It's the only thing that's made us unhappy.'

The girl looked at the bead curtain, put her hand out and took hold of two of the strings of beads.

'And you think then we'll be all right and be happy.'

'I know we will. You don't have to be afraid. I've known lots of people that have done it.'

'So have I,' said the girl. 'And afterward they were all so happy.'

'Well,' the man said, 'if you don't want to you don't have to. I wouldn't have you do it if you didn't want to. But I know it's perfectly simple.'

'And you really want to?'

'I think it's the best thing to do. But I don't want you to do it if you don't really want to.'

'And if I do you'll be happy and things will be like they were and you'll love me?'

'I love you now. You know I love you.'

'I know. But if I do it, then it will be nice again if I say things are like white elephants, and you'll like it?'

'I'll love it. I love it now but I just can't think about it. You know how I get when I worry.'

'If I do it you won't ever worry?'

'I won't worry about that because it's perfectly simple.'

'Then I'll do it. Because I don't care about me.'

'What do you mean?'

'I don't care about me.'

'Well, I care about you.'

'Oh, yes. But I don't care about me. And I'll do it and then everything will be fine.'

'I don't want you to do it if you feel that way.'

The girl stood up and walked to the end of the station. Across, on the other side, were fields of grain and trees along the banks of the Ebro. Far away, beyond the river, were mountains. The shadow of a cloud moved across the field of grain and she saw the river through the trees.

'And we could have all this,' she said. 'And we could have everything and every day we make it more impossible.'

'What did you say?'

'I said we could have everything.'

'We can have everything.'

'No, we can't.'

'We can have the whole world.'

'No, we can't.'

'We can go everywhere.'

'No, we can't. It isn't ours any more.'

'It's ours.'

'No, it isn't. And once they take it away, you never get it back.'

'But they haven't taken it away.'

'We'll wait and see.'

'Come on back in the shade,' he said. 'You mustn't feel that way.'

'I don't feel any way,' the girl said. 'I just know things.'

'I don't want you to do anything that you dont want to do –'

'Nor that isn't good for me,' she said. 'I know. Could we have another beer?'

'All right. But you've got to realize –'

'I realize,' the girl said. 'Can't we maybe stop talking?'

They sat down at the table and the girl looked across at the hills on the dry side of the valley and the man looked at her and at the table.

'You've got to realize,' he said, 'that I don't want you to do it if you don't want to. I'm perfectly willing to go through with it if it means anything to you.'

'Doesn't it mean anything to you? We could get along.'

'Of course it does. But I don't want anybody but you. I don't want anyone else. And I know it's perfectly simple.'

'Yes, you know it's perfectly simple.'

'It's all right for you to say that, but I do know it.'

'Would you do something for me now?'

'I'd do anything for you.'

'Would you please please please please please please please stop talking?'

He did not say anything but looked at the bags against the wall of the station. There were labels on them from all the hotels where they had spent nights.

'But I don't want you to,' he said, 'I don't care anything about it.'

'I'll scream,' the girl said.

The woman came out through the curtains with two glasses of beer and put them down on the damp felt pads. 'The train comes in five minutes,' she said.

'What did she say?' asked the girl.

'That the train is coming in five minutes.'

The girl smiled brightly at the woman, to thank her.

'I'd better take the bags over to the other side of the station,' the man said. She smiled at him.

'All right. Then come back and we'll finish the beer.'

He picked up the two heavy bags and carried them around the station to the other tracks. Coming back, he walked through the bar-room, where people waiting for the train were drinking. He drank an Anis at the bar and looked at the people. They were all waiting reasonably for the train. He went out

406

through the bead curtain. She was sitting at the table and smiled at him.

'Do you feel better?' he asked.

'I feel fine,' she said. 'There's nothing wrong with me. I feel fine.'

The Killers

The door of Henry's lunch-room opened and two men came in. They sat down at the counter.

'What's yours?' George asked them.

'I don't know,' one of the men said. 'What do you want to eat, Al?'

'I don't know,' said Al. 'I don't know what I want to eat.'

Outside it was getting dark. The street-light came on outside the window. The two men at the counter read the menu. From the other end of the counter Nick Adams watched them. He had been talking to George when they came in.

'I'll have a roast pork tenderloin with apple sauce and mashed potatoes,' the first man said.

'It isn't ready yet.'

'What the hell do you put it on the card for?'

'That's the dinner,' George explained. 'You can get that at six o'clock.'

George looked at the clock on the wall behind the counter.

'It's five o'clock.'

'The clock says twenty minutes past five,' the second man said.

'It's twenty minutes fast.'

'Oh, to hell with the clock,' the first man said. 'What have you got to eat?'

'I can give you any kind of sandwiches,' George said. 'You can have ham and eggs, bacon and eggs, liver and bacon, or a steak.'

'Give me chicken croquettes with green peas and cream sauce and mashed potatoes.'

'That's the dinner.'

'Everything we want's the dinner, eh? That's the way you work it.'

'I can give you ham and eggs, bacon and eggs, liver –'

'I'll take ham and eggs,' the man called Al said. He wore a derby hat and a black overcoat buttoned across the chest. His face was small and white and he had tight lips. He wore a silk muffler and gloves.

'Give me bacon and eggs,' said the other man. He was about the same size as Al. Their faces were different, but they were dressed like twins. Both wore overcoats too tight for them. They sat leaning forward, their elbows on the counter.

'Got anything to drink?' Al asked.

'Silver beer, bevo, ginger-ale,' George said.

'I mean you got anything to *drink?*'

'Just those I said.'

'This is a hot town,' said the other. 'What do they call it?'

'Summit.'

'Ever hear of it?' Al asked his friend.

'No,' said the friend.

'What do you do here nights?' Al asked.

'They eat the dinner,' his friend said. 'They all come here and eat the big dinner.'

'That's right,' George said.

'So you think that's right?' Al asked George.

'Sure.'

'You're a pretty bright boy, aren't you?'

'Sure,' said George.

'Well, you're not,' said the other little man. 'Is he, Al?'

'He's dumb,' said Al. He turned to Nick. 'What's your name?'

'Adams.'

'Another bright boy,' Al said. 'Ain't he a bright boy, Max?'

'The town's full of bright boys,' Max said.

George put the two platters, one of ham and eggs, the other of bacon and eggs, on the counter. He set down two side-dishes of fried potatoes and closed the wicket into the kitchen.

'Which is yours?' he asked Al.

'Don't you remember?'

'Ham and eggs.'

'Just a bright boy,' Max said. He leaned forward and took

the ham and eggs. Both men ate with their gloves on. George watched them eat.

'What are *you* looking at?' Max looked at George.

'Nothing.'

'The hell you were. You were looking at me.'

'Maybe the boy meant it for a joke, Max,' Al said.

George laughed.

'*You* don't have to laugh,' Max said to him. '*You* don't have to laugh at all, see?'

'All right,' said George.

'So he thinks it's all right.' Max turned to Al. 'He thinks it's all right. That's a good one.'

'Oh, he's a thinker,' Al said. They went on eating.

'What's the bright boy's name down the counter?' Al asked Max.

'Hey, bright boy,' Max said to Nick. 'You go around on the other side of the counter with your boy friend.'

'What's the idea?' Nick asked.

'There isn't any idea.'

'You better go around, bright boy,' Al said. Nick went around behind the counter.

'What's the idea?' George asked.

'None of your damn business,' Al said. 'Who's out in the kitchen?'

'The nigger.'

'What do you mean the nigger?'

'The nigger that cooks.'

'Tell him to come in.'

'What's the idea?'

'Tell him to come in.'

'Where do you think you are?'

'We know damn well where we are,' the man called Max said. 'Do we look silly?'

'You talk silly,' Al said to him. 'What the hell do you argue with this kid for? Listen,' he said to George, 'tell the nigger to come out here.'

'What are you going to do to him?'

'Nothing. Use your head, bright boy. What would we do to a nigger?'

George opened the slit that opened back into the kitchen. 'Sam,' he called. 'Come in here a minute.'

The door to the kitchen opened and the nigger came in. 'What was it?' he asked. The two men at the counter took a look at him.

'All right, nigger. You stand right there,' Al said.

Sam, the nigger, standing in his apron, looked at the two men sitting at the counter. 'Yes, sir,' he said. Al got down from his stool.

'I'm going back to the kitchen with the nigger and bright boy,' he said. 'Go on back to the kitchen, nigger. You go with him, bright boy.' The little man walked after Nick and Sam, the cook, back into the kitchen. The door shut after them. The man called Max sat at the counter opposite George. He didn't look at George but looked in the mirror that ran along back of the counter. Henry's had been made over from a saloon into a lunch-counter.

'Well, bright boy,' Max said, looking into the mirror, 'why don't you say something?'

'What's it all about?'

'Hey, Al,' Max called, 'bright boy wants to know what it's all about.'

'Why don't you tell him?' Al's voice came from the kitchen.

'What do you think it's all about?'

'I don't know.'

'What do you think?'

Max looked into the mirror all the time he was talking.

'I wouldn't say.'

'Hey, Al, bright boy says he wouldn't say what he thinks it's all about.'

'I can hear you, all right,' Al said from the kitchen. He had propped open the slit that dishes passed through into the kitchen with a catsup bottle. 'Listen, bright boy,' he said from the kitchen to George. 'Stand a little farther along the bar. You move a little to the left, Max.' He was like a photographer arranging for a group picture.

'Talk to me, bright boy.' Max said. What do you think's going to happen?'

George did not say anything.

'I'll tell you,' Max said. 'We're going to kill a Swede. Do you know a big Swede named Ole Andreson?'

'Yes.'

'He comes here to eat every night, don't he?'

'Sometimes he comes here.'

'He comes here at six o'clock, don't he?'

'If he comes.'

'We know all that, bright boy,' Max said. 'Talk about something else. Ever go to the movies?'

'Once in a while.'

'You ought to go to the movies more. The movies are fine for a bright boy like you.'

'What are you going to kill Ole Andreson for? What did he ever do to you?'

'He never had a chance to do anything to us. He never even seen us.'

'And he's only going to see us once,' Al said from the kitchen.

'What are you going to kill him for, then?' George asked.

'We're killing him for a friend. Just to oblige a friend, bright boy.'

'Shut up,' said Al from the kitchen. 'You talk too goddam much.'

'Well, I got to keep bright boy amused. Don't I, bright boy?'

'You talk too damn much,' Al said. 'The nigger and my bright boy are amused by themselves. I got them tied up like a couple of girl friends in the convent.'

'I suppose you were in a convent.'

'You never know.'

'You were in a kosher convent. That's where you were.'

George looked up at the clock.

'If anybody comes in you tell them the cook is off, and if they keep after it, you tell them you'll go back and cook yourself. Do you get that, bright boy?'

'All right,' George said. 'What you going to do with us afterward?'

'That'll depend,' Max said. 'That's one of those things you never know at the time.'

George looked up at the clock. It was a quarter past six. The door from the street opened. A street-car motorman came in.

'Hello, George,' he said. 'Can I get supper?'

'Sam's gone out,' George said. 'He'll be back in about half an hour.'

'I'd better go up the street,' the motorman said. George looked at the clock. It was twenty minutes past six.

'That was nice, bright boy,' Max said. 'You're a regular little gentleman.'

'He knew I'd blow his head off,' Al said from the kitchen.

'No,' said Max. 'It ain't that. Bright boy is nice. He's a nice boy. I like him.'

At six-fifty-five George said: 'He's not coming.'

Two other people had been in the lunch-room. Once George had gone out to the kitchen and made a ham-and-egg sandwich 'to go' that a man wanted to take with him. Inside the kitchen he saw Al, his derby hat tipped back, sitting on a stool beside the wicket with the muzzle of a sawed-off shotgun resting on the ledge. Nick and the cook were back to back in the corner, a towel tied in each of their mouths. George had cooked the sandwich, wrapped it up in oiled paper, put it in a bag, brought it in, and the man had paid for it and gone out.

'Bright boy can do everything,' Max said. 'He can cook and everything. You'd made some girl a nice wife, bright boy.'

'Yes?' George said. 'Your friend, Ole Andreson, isn't going to come.'

'We'll give him ten minutes,' Max said.

Max watched the mirror and the clock. The hands of the clock matched seven o'clock, and then five minutes past seven.

'Come on, Al,' said Max. 'We better go. He's not coming.'

'Better give him five minutes,' Al said from the kitchen.

In the five minutes a man came in, and George explained that the cook was sick.

'Why the hell don't you get another cook?' the man asked. 'Aren't you running a lunch-counter?' He went out.

'Come on, Al,' Max said.

'What about the two bright boys and the nigger?'

'They're all right.'

'You think so?'

'Sure. We're through with it.'

'I don't like it,' said Al. 'It's sloppy. You talk too much.'

'Oh, what the hell,' said Max. 'We got to keep amused, haven't we?'

'You talk too much, all the same,' Al said. He came out from the kitchen. The cut-off barrels of the shotgun made a slight bulge under the waist of his too tight-fitting overcoat. He straightened his coat with his gloved hands.

'So long, bright boy,' he said to George. 'You got a lot of luck.'

'That's the truth,' Max said. 'You ought to play the races, bright boy.'

The two of them went out the door. George watched them, through the window, pass under the arc-light and cross the street. In their right overcoats and derby hats they looked like a vaudeville team. George went back through the swinging-door into the kitchen and untied Nick and the cook.

'I don't want any more of that,' said Sam, the cook. 'I don't want any more of that.'

Nick stood up. He had never had a towel in his mouth before.

'Say,' he said. 'What the hell?' He was trying to swagger it off.

'They were going to kill Ole Andreson,' George said. 'They were going to shoot him when he came in to eat.'

'Ole Andreson?'

'Sure.'

The cook felt the corners of his mouth with his thumbs.

'They all gone?' he asked.

'Yeah,' said George. 'They're gone now.'

'I don't like it,' said the cook. 'I don't like any of it at all.'

'Listen,' George said to Nick. 'You better go see Ole Andreson.'

'All right.'

'You better not have anything to do with it at all,' Sam, the cook, said. 'You better stay way out of it.'

'Don't go if you don't want to,' George said.

'Mixing up in this ain't going to get you anywhere,' the cook said. 'You stay out of it.'

'I'll go see him,' Nick said to George. 'Where does he live?'

The cook turned away.

'Little boys always know what they want to do,' he said.

'He lives up at Hirsch's rooming-house,' George said to Nick.

'I'll go up there.'

Outside the arc-light shone through the bare branches of a tree. Nick walked up the street beside the car-tracks and turned at the next arc-light down a side-street. Three houses up the street was Hirsch's rooming-house. Nick walked up the two steps and pushed the bell. A woman came to the door.

'Is Ole Andreson here?'

'Do you want to see him?'

'Yes, if he's in.'

Nick followed the woman up a flight of stairs and back to the end of the corridor. She knocked on the door.

'Who is it?'

'It's somebody to see you, Mr Andreson,' the woman said.

'It's Nick Adams.'

'Come in.'

Nick opened the door and went into the room. Ole Andreson was lying on the bed with all his clothes on. He had been a heavyweight prize-fighter and he was too long for the bed. He lay with his head on two pillows. He did not look at Nick.

'What was it?' he asked.

'I was up at Henry's,' Nick said, 'and two fellows came in and tied up me and the cook, and they said they were going to kill you.'

It sounded silly when he said it. Ole Andreson said nothing.

'They put us out in the kitchen,' Nick went on. 'They were going to shoot you when you came in to supper.'

Ole Andreson looked at the wall and did not say anything.

'George thought I better come and tell you about it.'

'There isn't anything I can do about it,' Ole Andreson said.

'I'll tell you what they were like.'

'I don't want to know what they were like,' Ole Andreson said. He looked at the wall. 'Thanks for coming to tell me about it.'

'That's all right.'

Nick looked at the big man lying on the bed.

'Don't you want me to go and see the police?'

'No,' Ole Andreson said. 'That wouldn't do any good.'

'Isn't there something I could do?'

'No. There ain't anything to do.'

'Maybe it was just a bluff.'

'No. It ain't just a bluff.'

Ole Andreson rolled over toward the wall.

'The only thing is,' he said, talking toward the wall, 'I just can't make up my mind to go out. I been in here all day.'

'Couldn't you get out of town?'

'No,' Ole Andreson said. 'I'm through with all that running around.'

He looked at the wall.

'There ain't anything to do now.'

'Couldn't you fix it up some way?'

'No. I got in wrong.' He talked in the same flat voice. 'There ain't anything to do. After a while I'll make up my mind to go out.'

'I better go back and see George,' Nick said.

'So long,' said Ole Andreson. He did not look toward Nick. 'Thanks for coming around.'

Nick went out. As he shut the door he saw Ole Andreson with all his clothes on, lying on the bed looking at the wall.

'He's been in his room all day,' the landlady said downstairs. 'I guess he don't feel well. I said to him: "Mr Andreson, you ought to go out and take a walk on a nice fall day like this," but he didn't feel like it.'

'He doesn't want to go out.'

'I'm sorry he don't feel well,' the woman said. 'He's an awfully nice man. He was in the ring, you know.'

'I know it.'

'You'd never know it except for the way his face is,' the woman said. They stood talking just inside the street door. 'He's just as gentle.'

'Well, good-night,' Mrs Hirsch,' Nick said.

'I'm not Mrs Hirsch,' the woman said. 'She owns the place. I just look after it for her. I'm Mrs Bell.'

'Well, good-night, Mrs Bell,' Nick said.

'Good-night,' the woman said.

Nick walked up the dark street to the corner under the arc-light, and then along the car-tracks to Henry's eating-house. George was inside, back of the counter.

'Did you see Ole?'

'Yes,' said Nick. 'He's in his room and he won't go out.' The cook opened the door from the kitchen when he heard Nick's voice.

'I don't even listen to it,' he said and shut the door.

'Did you tell him about it?' George asked.

'Sure. I told him, but he knows what it's all about.'

'What's he going to do?'

'Nothing.'

'They'll kill him.'

'I guess they will.'

'He must have got mixed up in something in Chicago.'

'I guess so,' said Nick.

'It's a hell of a thing.'

'It's an awful thing,' Nick said.

They did not say anything. George reached down for a towel and wiped the counter.

'I wonder what he did?' Nick said.

'Double-crossed somebody. That's what they kill them for.'

'I'm going to get out of this town,' Nick said.

'Yes,' said George. 'That's a good thing to do.'

'I can't stand to think about him waiting in the room and knowing he's going to get it. It's too damned awful.'

'Well,' said George, 'you better not think about it.'

Today is Friday

Three Roman soldiers are in a drinking-place at eleven o'clock at night. There are barrels around the wall. Behind the wooden counter is a Hebrew wine-seller. The three Roman soldiers are a little cockeyed.

1st Roman Soldier – You tried the red?

2nd Soldier – No, I ain't tried it

1st Soldier – You better try it.

2nd Soldier – All right, George, we'll have a round of the red.

Hebrew Wine-seller – Here you are, gentlemen. You'll like that. [*He sets down an earthenware pitcher that he has filled from one of the casks.*] That's a nice little wine.

1st Soldier – Have a drink of it yourself. [*He turns to the third soldier who is leaning on a barrel.*] What's the matter with you?

3rd Soldier – I got a gut-ache.

2nd Soldier – You've been drinking water.

1st Soldier – Try some of the red.

3rd Soldier – I can't drink the damn stuff. It makes my gut sour.

1st Soldier – You been out here too long.

3rd Soldier – Hell, don't I know it?

1st Soldier – Say, George, can't you give this gentleman something to fix up his stomach?

Wine-seller – I got it right here.

[*The third soldier tastes the cup that the wine-seller has mixed for him.*]

3rd Soldier – Hey, what you put in that, camel chips?

Wine-seller – You drink that right down, Lootenant. That'll fix you up right.

3rd Soldier – Well, I couldn't feel any worse.

1st Soldier – Take a chance on it. George fixed me up fine the other day.

417

Wine-seller – You were in bad shape, Lootenant. I know what fixes up a bad stomach.

[*The third soldier drinks the cup down.*]

3rd Soldier –Jesus Christ [*He makes a face.*]

2nd Soldier – That false alarm!

1st Soldier – Oh, I don't know. He was pretty good in there today.

2nd Soldier – Why didn't he come down off the cross?

1st Soldier – He didn't want to come down off the cross. That's not his play.

2nd Soldier – Show me a guy that doesn't want to come down off the cross.

1st Soldier –Aw, hell, you don't know anything about it. Ask George there. Did he want to come down off the cross, George?

Wine-seller –I'll tell you, gentlemen, I wasn't out there. It's a thing I haven't taken any interest in.

2nd Soldier – Listen, I seen a lot of them – here and plenty of other places. Any time you show me one that doesn't want to get down off the cross when the time comes – when the time comes, I mean – I'll climb right up with him.

1st Soldier –I thought he was pretty good in there today.

3rd Soldier – He was all right.

2nd Roman Soldier –You guys don't know what I'm talking about. I'm not saying whether he was good or not. What I mean is, when the time comes. When they first start nailing him, there isn't none of them wouldn't stop it if they could.

1st Soldier – Didn't you follow it, George?

Wine-seller – No, I didn't take any interest in it, Lootenant.

1st Soldier – I was surprised how he acted.

3rd Soldier –The part I don't like is the nailing them on. You know, that must get to you pretty bad.

2nd Soldier – It isn't that that's so bad, as when they first lift 'em up. [*He makes a lifting gesture with his two palms together.*] When the weight starts to pull on 'em. That's when it gets 'em.

3rd Soldier – It takes some of them pretty bad.

1st Soldier – Ain't I seen 'em? I seen plenty of them. I tell you, he was pretty good in there today.

[*The second soldier smiles at the wine-seller.*]

2nd Soldier – You're a regular Christer, big boy.

1st soldier – Sure, go on and kid him. But listen while I tell you something. He was pretty good in there today.

2nd Soldier – What about some more wine?

[*The wine-seller looks up expectantly. The third soldier is sitting with his head down. He does not look well.*]

3rd Soldier – I don't want any more.

2nd Soldier – Just for two, George.

[*The wine-seller puts out a pitcher of wine, a size smaller than the last one. He leans forward on the wooden counter.*]

1st Soldier – You see his girl?

2nd Soldier – Wasn't I standing right by her?

1st Soldier – She's a nice looker.

2nd Soldier – I knew her before he did. [*He winks at the wine-seller.*]

1st Soldier – I used to see her around the town.

2nd Soldier – She used to have a lot of stuff. He never brought *her* no good luck.

1st Soldier – Oh, he ain't lucky. But he looked pretty good to me in there today.

2nd Soldier – What became of his gang?

1st Soldier – Oh, they faded out. Just the women stuck by him.

2nd Soldier – They were a pretty yellow crowd. When they seen him go up there they didn't want any of it.

1st Soldier – The women stuck all right.

2nd Soldier – Sure, they stuck all right.

1st Soldier – You see me slip the old spear into him?

2nd Soldier – You'll get into trouble doing that some day.

1st Soldier – It was the least I could do for him. I'll tell you he looked pretty good to me in there today.

Wine-seller – Gentlemen, you know I got to close.

1st Soldier – We'll have one more round.

2nd Soldier – What's the use? This stuff don't get you anywhere. Come on, let's go.

1st Soldier – Just another round.

3rd Soldier [*getting up from the barrel*] – No, come on. Let's go. I feel like hell tonight.

1st Soldier – Just one more.

2nd Soldier – *No,* come on. We're going to go. Good night,

419

George. Put it on the bill.

Wine-seller – Good night, gentlemen. [*He looks a little worried.*] You couldn't let me have a little something on account, Lootenant?

2nd Soldier – What the hell, George! Wednesday's pay-day.

Wine-seller – It's all right, Lootenant. Good-night, gentlemen.

[*The three soldiers go out the door into the street.*]

[*Outside in the street.*]

2nd Soldier – George is a kike just like all the rest of them.

1st Soldier – Oh, George is a nice fella.

2nd Soldier – Everybody's a nice fella to you tonight.

3rd Soldier – Come on, let's go up to the barracks. I feel like hell tonight.

2nd Soldier – You been out here too long.

3rd Soldier – No, it ain't just that. I feel like hell.

2nd Soldier – You been out here too long. That's all.

CURTAIN

WINNER TAKE NOTHING

A Clean, Well-Lighted Place

It was late and everyone had left the café except an old man who sat in the shadow the leaves of the tree made against the electric light. In the daytime the street was dusty, but at night the dew settled the dust and the old man liked to sit late because he was deaf and now at night it was quiet and he felt the difference. The two waiters inside the café knew that the old man was a little drunk, and while he was a good client they knew that if he became too drunk he would leave without paying, so they kept watch on him.

'Last week he tried to commit suicide,' one waiter said.

'Why?'

'He was in despair.'

'What about?'

'Nothing.'

'How do you know it was nothing?'

'He has plenty of money.'

They sat together at a table that was close against the wall near the door of the café and looked at the terrace where the tables were all empty except where the old man sat in the shadow of the leaves of the tree that moved slightly in the wind. A girl and a soldier went by in the street. The street-light shone on the brass number on his collar. The girl wore no head covering and hurried beside him.

'The guard will pick him up,' one waiter said.

'What does it matter if he gets what he's after?'

'He had better get off the street now. The guard will get him. They went by five minutes ago.'

The old man sitting in the shadow rapped on his saucer with his glass. The younger waiter went over to him. 'What do you want?'

The old man looked at him. 'Another brandy,' he said.

'You'll be drunk,' the waiter said. The old man looked at him. The waiter went away.

'He'll stay all night,' he said to his colleague. 'I'm sleepy now. I never get to bed before three o'clock. He should have killed himself last week.'

The waiter took the brandy bottle and another saucer from the counter inside the café and marched out to the old man's table. He put down the saucer and poured the glass full of brandy.

'You should have killed yourself last week,' he said to the deaf man. The old man motioned with his finger. 'A little more,' he said. The waiter poured on into the glass so that the brandy slopped over and ran down the stem into the top saucer of the pile. 'Thank you,' the old man said. The waiter took the bottle back inside the café. He sat down at the table with his colleague again.

'He's drunk now,' he said.

'He's drunk every night.'

'What did he want to kill himself for?'

'How should I know?'

'How did he do it?'

'He hung himself with a rope.'

'Who cut him down?'

'His niece.'

'Why did they do it?'

'Fear for his soul.'

'How much money has he got?'

'He's got plenty.'

'He must be eighty years old.'

'Anyway I should say he was eighty.'

'I wish he would go home. I never get to bed before three o'clock. What kind of hour is that to go to bed?'

'He stays up because he likes it.'

'He's lonely. I'm not lonely. I have a wife waiting in bed for me.'

'He had a wife once too.'

'A wife would be no good to him now.'

'You can't tell. He might be better with a wife.'

'His niece looks after him.'

'I know. You said she cut him down.'

'I wouldn't want to be that old. An old man is a nasty thing.'

'Not always. This old man is clean. He drinks without spilling. Even now, drunk. Look at him.'

'I don't want to look at him. I wish he would go home. He has no regard for those who must work.'

The old man looked from his glass across the square, then over at the waiters.

'Another brandy,' he said, pointing to his glass. The waiter who was in a hurry came over.

'Finished,' he said, speaking with that omission of syntax stupid people employ when talking to drunken people or foreigners. 'No more tonight. Close now.'

'Another,' said the old man.

'No. Finished.' The waiter wiped the edge of the table with a towel and shook his head.

The old man stood up, slowly counted the saucers, took a leather coin purse from his pocket and paid for the drinks, leaving half a peseta tip.

The waiter watched him go down the street, a very old man walking unsteadily but with dignity.

'Why didn't you let him stay and drink?' the unhurried waiter asked. They were putting up the shutters. 'It is not half past two.'

'I want to go home to bed.'

'What is an hour?'

'More to me than to him.'

'An hour is the same.'

'You talk like an old man yourself. He can buy a bottle and drink at home.'

'It's not the same.'

'No, it is not,' agreed the waiter with a wife. He did not wish to be unjust. He was only in a hurry.

'And you? You have no fear of going home before your usual hour?'

'Are you trying to insult me?'

'No, hombre, only to make a joke.'

'No,' the waiter who was in a hurry said, rising from pulling down the metal shutters. 'I have confidence. I am all confidence.'

'You have youth, confidence, and a job,' the older waiter said. 'You have everything.'

'And what do you lack?'

'Everything but work.'

'You have everything I have.'

'No. I have never had confidence and I am not young.'

'Come on. Stop talking nonsense and lock up.'

'I am of those who like to stay late at the café,' the older waiter said. 'With all those who do not want to go to bed. With all those who need a light for the night.'

'I want to go home and into bed.'

'We are of two different kinds,' the older waiter said. He was dressed now to go home. 'It is not only a question of youth and confidence although those things are very beautiful. Each night I am reluctant to close up because there may be someone who needs the café.'

'Hombre, there are bodegas open all night long.'

'You do not understand. This is a clean and pleasant café. It is well lighted. The light is very good and also, now, there are shadows of the leaves.'

'Good-night,' said the younger waiter.

'Good-night,' the other said. Turning off the electric light he continued the conversation with himself. It is the light of course, but it is necessary that the place be clean and pleasant. You do not want music. Certainly you do not want music. Nor can you stand before a bar with dignity although that is all that is provided for these hours. What did he fear? It was not fear or dread. It was a nothing that he knew too well. It was all a nothing and a man was nothing too. It was only that and light was all it needed and a certain cleanness and order. Some lived in it and never felt it but he knew it all was nada y pues nada y nada y pues nada. Our nada who art in nada, nada be thy name thy kingdom nada thy will be nada in nada as it is in nada. Give us this nada our daily nada and nada us our nada as we nada our nadas and nada us not into nada but deliver us from nada; pues nada. Hail nothing full of nothing, nothing is with thee. He smiled and stood before a bar with a shining steam pressure coffee machine.

'What's yours?' asked the barman.

'Nada.'

'Otro loco mas,' said the barman and turned away.

'A little cup,' said the waiter.

The barman poured it for him.

'The light is very bright and pleasant but the bar is unpolished,' the waiter said.

The barman looked at him but did not answer. It was too late at night for conversation.

'You want another copita?' the barman asked.

'No, thank you,' said the waiter and went out. He disliked bars and bodegas. A clean, well-lighted café was a very different thing. Now, without thinking further, he would go home to his room. He would lie in the bed and finally, with daylight, he would go to sleep. After all, he said to himself, it is probably only insomnia. Many must have it.

The Light of the World

When he saw us come in the door the bartender looked up and then reached over and put the glass covers on the two free-lunch bowls.

'Give me a beer,' I said. He drew it, cut the top off with the spatula and then held the glass in his hand. I put the nickel on the wood and he slid the beer toward me.

'What's yours?' he said to Tom.

'Beer.'

He drew that beer and cut it off and when he saw the money he pushed the beer across to Tom.

'What's the matter?' Tom asked.

The bartender didn't answer him. He just looked over our heads and said, 'What's yours?' to a man who'd come in.

'Rye,' the man said. The bartender put out the bottle and glass and a glass of water.

Tom reached over and took the glass off the free-lunch

bowl. It was a bowl of pickled pigs' feet and there was a wooden thing that worked like a scissors, with two wooden forks at the end to pick them up with.

'No,' said the bartender and put the glass cover back on the bowl. Tom held the wooden scissors fork in his hand. 'Put it back,' said the bartender.

'You know where,' said Tom.

The bartender reached a hand forward under the bar, watching us both. I put fifty cents on the wood and he straightened up.

'What was yours?' he said.

'Beer,' I said, and before he drew the beer he uncovered both the bowls.

'Your goddam pig's feet stink,' Tom said, and spit what he had in his mouth on the floor. The bartender didn't say anything. The man who had drunk the rye paid and went out without looking back.

'You stink yourself,' the bartender said. 'All you punks stink.'

'He says we're punks,' Tommy said to me.

'Listen,' I said. 'Let's get out.'

'You punks clear the hell out of here,' the bartender said.

'I said we were going out,' I said. 'It wasn't your idea.'

'We'll be back,' Tommy said.

'No you won't,' the bartender told him.

'Tell him how wrong he is,' Tom turned to me.

'Come on,' I said.

Outside it was good and dark.

'What the hell kind of place is this?' Tommy said.

'I don't know,' I said. 'Let's go down to the station.'

We'd come in that town at one end and we were going out the other. It smelled of hides and tan bark and the big piles of sawdust. It was getting dark as we came in, and now that it was dark it was cold and the puddles of water in the road were freezing at the edges.

Down at the station there were five whores waiting for the train to come in, and six white men and four Indians. It was crowded and hot from the stove and full of stale smoke. As we came in nobody was talking and the ticket window was down.

426

'Shut the door, can't you!' somebody said.

I looked to see who said it. It was one of the white men. He wore stagged trousers and lumbermen's rubbers and a mackinaw shirt like the others, but he had no cap and his face was white and his hands were white and thin.

'Aren't you going to shut it?'

'Sure,' I said, and shut it.

'Thank you,' he said. One of the other men snickered.

'Ever interfere with a cook?' he said to me.

'No.'

'You can interfere with this one,' he looked at the cook. 'He likes it.'

The cook looked away from him holding his lips tight together.

'He puts lemon juice on his hands,' the man said. 'He wouldn't get them in dishwater for anything. Look how white they are.'

One of the whores laughed out loud. She was the biggest whore I ever saw in my life and the biggest woman. And she had on one of those silk dresses that change colours. There were two other whores that were nearly as big but the big one must have weighed three hundred and fifty pounds. You couldn't believe she was real when you looked at her. All three had those changeable silk dresses. They sat side by side on the bench. They were huge. The other two were just ordinary looking whores, peroxide blondes.

'Look at his hands,' the man said and nodded his head at the cook. The whore laughed again and shook all over.

The cook turned and said to her quickly. 'You big disgusting mountain of flesh.'

She just kept on laughing and shaking.

'Oh, my Christ,' she said. She had a nice voice. 'Oh, my sweet Christ.'

The other two whores, the big ones, acted very quiet and placid as though they didn't have much sense, but they were big, nearly as big as the biggest one. They'd have both gone well over two hundred and fifty pounds. The other two were dignified.

Of the men, besides the cook and the one who talked, there

were two other lumberjacks, one that listened, interested but bashful, and the other that seemed getting ready to say something, and two Swedes. Two Indians were sitting down at the end of the bench and one standing up against the wall.

The man who was getting ready to say something spoke to me very low, 'Must be like getting on top of a hay mow.'

I laughed and said it to Tommy.

'I swear to Christ I've never been anywhere like this,' he said. 'Look at the three of them.' Then the cook spoke up.

'How old are you boys?'

'I'm ninety-six and he's sixty-nine,' Tommy said.

'Ho! Ho! Ho!' the big whore shook with laughing. She had a really pretty voice. The other whores didn't smile.

'Oh, can't you be decent?' the cook said. 'I asked just to be friendly.'

'We're seventeen and nineteen,' I said.

'What's the matter with you?' Tommy turned to me.

'That's all right.'

'You can call me Alice,' the big whore said and then she began to shake again.

'Is that your name?' Tommy asked.

'Sure,' she said. 'Alice. Isn't it?' she turned to the man who sat by the cook.

'Alice. That's right.'

'That's the sort of name you'd have,' the cook said.

'It's my real name,' Alice said.

'What's the other girls' names?' Tom asked.

'Hazel and Ethel,' Alice said. Hazel and Ethel smiled. They weren't very bright.

'What's your name?' I said to one of the blondes.

'Frances,' she said.

'Frances what?'

'Frances Wilson. What's it to you?'

'What's yours?' I asked the other one.

'Oh, don't be fresh,' she said.

'He just wants us all to be friends,' the man who talked said. 'Don't you want to be friends?'

'No,' the peroxide one said. 'Not with you.'

'She's just a spitfire,' the man said. 'A regular little spitfire.'

428

The one blonde looked at the other and shook her head.

'Goddamned mossbacks,' she said.

Alice commenced to laugh again and to shake all over.

'There's nothing funny,' the cook said. 'You all laugh but there's nothing funny. You two young lads; where are you bound for?'

'Where are you going yourself?' Tom asked him.

'I want to go to Cadillac,' the cook said. 'Have you ever been there? My sister lives there.'

'He's a sister himself,' the man in the stagged trousers said.

'Can't you stop that sort of thing?' the cook asked. 'Can't we speak decently?'

'Cadillac is where Steve Ketchel came from and where Ad Wolgast is from,' the shy man said.

'Steve Ketchel,' one of the blondes said in a high voice as though the name had pulled a trigger in her. 'His own father shot and killed him. Yes, by Christ, his own father. There aren't any more men like Steve Ketchel.'

'Wasn't his name Stanley Ketchel?' asked the cook.

'Oh, shut up,' said the blonde. 'What do you know about Steve? Stanley. He was no Stanley. Steve Ketchel was the finest and most beautiful man that ever lived. I never saw a man as clean and as white and as beautiful as Steve Ketchel. There never was a man like that. He moved just like a tiger and he was the finest, free-est spender that ever lived.'

'Did you know him?' one of the men asked.

'Did I know him? Did I know him? Did I love him? You ask me that? I knew him like you know nobody in the world and I loved him like you love God. He was the greatest, finest, whitest, most beautiful man that ever lived, Steve Ketchel, and his own father shot him down like a dog.'

'Were you out on the coast with him?'

'No. I knew him before that. He was the only man I ever loved.'

Everyone was very respectful to the peroxide blonde, who said all this in a high stagey way, but Alice was beginning to shake again. I felt it sitting by her.

'You should have married him,' the cook said.

'I wouldn't hurt his career,' the peroxide blonde said. 'I

wouldn't be a drawback to him. A wife wasn't what he needed. Oh, my God, what a man he was.'

'That was a fine way to look at it,' the cook said. 'Didn't Jack Johnson knock him out though?'

'It was a trick,' Peroxide said. 'That big dinge took him by surprise. He'd just knocked Jack Johnson down, the big black bastard. That nigger beat him by a fluke.'

The ticket window went up and the three Indians went over to it.

'Steve knocked him down,' Peroxide said. 'He turned to smile at me.'

'I thought you said you weren't on the coast,' someone said.

'I went out just for that fight. Steve turned to smile at me and that black son of a bitch from hell jumped up and hit him by surprise. Steve could lick a hundred like that black bastard.'

'He was a great fighter,' the lumberjack said.

'I hope to God he was,' Peroxide said. 'I hope to God they don't have fighters like that now. He was like a god, he was. So white and clean and beautiful and smooth and fast and like a tiger or like lightning.'

'I saw him in the moving pictures of the fight,' Tom said. We were all very moved. Alice was shaking all over and I looked and saw she was crying. The Indians had gone outside on the platform.

'He was more than any husband could ever be,' Peroxide said. 'We were married in the eyes of God and I belong to him right now and always will and all of me is his. I don't care about my body. They can take my body. My soul belongs to Steve Ketchel. By God, he was a man.'

Everybody felt terribly. It was sad and embarrassing. Then Alice, who was still shaking, spoke. 'You're a dirty liar,' she said in that low voice. 'You never laid Steve Ketchel in your life and you know it.'

'How can you say that?' Peroxide said proudly.

'I say it because it's true,' Alice said. 'I'm the only one here that ever knew Steve Ketchel and I come from Mancelona and I knew him there and it's true and you know it's true and God can strike me dead if it isn't true.'

'He can strike me too,' Peroxide said.

'This is true, true, true, and you know it. Not just made up and I know exactly what he said to me.'

'What did he say?' Peroxide asked, complacently.

Alice was crying so she could hardly speak from shaking so. 'He said, "You're a lovely piece, Alice." That's exactly what he said.'

'It's a lie,' Peroxide said.

'It's true,' Alice said. 'That's truly what he said.'

'It's a lie,' Peroxide said proudly.

'No, it's true, true, true, to Jesus and Mary true.'

'Steve couldn't have said that. It wasn't the way he talked,' Peroxide said happily.

'It's true,' said Alice in her nice voice. 'And it doesn't make any difference to me whether you believe it or not.' She wasn't crying any more and she was calm.

'It would be impossible for Steve to have said that,' Peroxide declared.

'He said it,' Alice said and smiled. 'And I remember when he said it and I *was* a lovely piece then exactly as he said, and right now I'm a better piece than you, you dried-up old hot water-bottle.'

'You can't insult me,' said Peroxide. 'You big mountain of pus. I have my memories.'

'No,' Alice said in that sweet lovely voice, 'you haven't got any real memories except having your tubes out and when you started C. and M. Everything else you just read in the papers. I'm clean and you know it, and men like me, even though I'm big, and you know it, and I never lie and you know it.'

'Leave me with my memories,' Peroxide said. 'With my true, wonderful memories.'

Alice looked at her and then at us and her face lost that hurt look and she smiled and she had the prettiest face I ever saw. She had a pretty face and a nice smooth skin and a lovely voice and she was nice all right and really friendly. But my God she was big. She was big as three women. Tom saw me looking at her and said, 'Come on. Let's go.'

'Good-bye,' said Alice. She certainly had a nice voice.

'Good-bye,' I said.

'Which way are you boys going?' asked the cook.

'The other way from you,' Tom told him.

A Way You'll Never Be

The attack had gone across the field, been held up by machine-gun fire from the sunken road and from the group of farmhouses, encountered no resistance in the town, and reached the bank of the river. Coming along the road on a bicycle, getting off to push the machine when the surface of the road became too broken, Nicholas Adams saw what had happened by the position of the dead.

They lay alone or in clumps in the high grass of the field and along the road, their pockets out, and over them were flies and around each body or group of bodies were the scattered papers.

In the grass and the grain, beside the road, and in some places scattered over the road, there was much material: a field kitchen, it must have come over when things were going well; many of the calf-skin-covered haversacks, stick bombs, helmets, rifles, sometimes one butt-up, the bayonet struck in the dirt, they had dug quite a little at the last; stick bombs, helmets, rifles, entrenching tools, ammunition boxes, star-shell pistols, their shells scattered about, medical kits, gas masks, empty gas-mask cans, a squat, tripoded machine-gun in a nest of empty shells, full belts protruding from the boxes, the water-cooling can empty and on its side, the breech block gone, the crew in odd positions, and around them, in the grass, more of the typical papers.

There were mass prayer books, group postcards showing the machine-gun unit standing in ranked and ruddy cheerfulness as in a football picture for a college annual; now they were humped and swollen in the grass; propaganda post-cards showing a soldier in Austrian uniform bending a woman backward over a bed; the figures were impressionistically drawn; very attractively depicted and had nothing in common with actual rape in which the woman's skirts are pulled over her

432

head to smother her, one comrade sometimes sitting upon the head. There were many of these inciting cards which had evidently been issued just before the offensive. Now they were scattered with the smutty post-cards, photographic; the small photographs of village girls by village photographers, the occasional pictures of children, and the letters, letters, letters. There was always much paper about the dead and the debris of this attack was no exception.

These were new dead and no one had bothered with anything but their pockets. Our own dead, or what he thought of, still, as our own dead, were surprisingly few, Nick noticed. Their coats had been opened too and their pockets were out, and they showed, by their positions, the manner and the skill of the attack. The hot weather had swollen them all alike regardless of nationality.

The town had evidently been defended, at the last, from the line of the sunken road and there had been few or no Austrians to fall back into it. There were only three bodies in the street and they looked to have been killed running. The houses of the town were broken by the shelling and the street had much rubble of plaster and mortar and there were broken beams, broken tiles, and many holes, some of them yellow-edged from the mustard gas. There were many pieces of shell, and shrapnel balls were scattered in the rubble. There was no one in the town at all.

Nick Adams had seen no one since he had left Fornaci, although, riding along the road through the over-foliaged country, he had seen guns hidden under screens of mulberry leaves to the left of the road, noticing them by the heat-waves in the air above the eaves where the sun hit the metal. Now he went on through the town, surprised to find it deserted, and came out on the low road beneath the bank of the river. Leaving the town there was a bare open space where the road slanted down and he could see the placid reach of the river and the low curve of the opposite bank and the whitened, sun-baked mud where the Austrians had dug. It was all very lush and over-green since he had seen it last and becoming historical had made no change in this, the lower river.

The battalion was along the bank to the left. There was a

series of holes in the top of the bank with a few men in them. Nick noticed where the machine-guns were posted and the signal rockets in their racks. The men in the holes in the side of the bank were sleeping. No one challenged. He went on and as he came around a turn in the mud bank a young second lieutenant with a stubble of beard and red-rimmed, very bloodshot eyes pointed a pistol at him.

'Who are you?'

Nick told him.

'How do I know this?'

Nick showed him the tessera with photograph and identification and the seal of the third army. He took hold of it.

'I will keep this.'

'You will not,' Nick said. 'Give me back the card and put your gun away. There. In the holster.'

'How am I to know who you are?'

'The tessera tells you.'

'And if the tessera is false? Give me that card.'

'Don't be a fool,' Nick said cheerfully. 'Take me to your company commander.'

'I should send you to battalion headquarters.'

'All right,' said Nick. 'Listen, do you know the Captain Paravicini? The tall one with the small moustache who was an architect and speaks English?'

'You know him?'

'A little.'

'What company does he command?'

'The second.'

'He is commanding the battalion.'

'Good,' said Nick. He was relieved to know that Para was all right. 'Let us go to the battalion.'

As Nick had left the edge of the town three shrapnel had burst high and to the right over one of the wrecked houses and since then there had been no shelling. But the face of this officer looked like the face of a man during a bombardment. There was the same tightness and the voice did not sound natural. His pistol made Nick nervous.

'Put it away,' he said. 'There's the whole river between them and you.'

'If I thought you were a spy I would shoot you now,' the second lieutenant said.

'Come on,' said Nick. 'Let us go to the battalion.' This officer made him very nervous.

The Captain Paravicini, acting major, thinner and more English looking than ever, rose when Nick saluted from behind the table in the dug-out that was battalion headquarters.

'Hello,' he said. 'I didn't know you. What are you doing in that uniform?'

'They've put me in it.'

'I am very glad to see you, Nicolo.'

'Right. You look well. How was the show?'

'We made a very fine attack. Truly. A very fine attack. I will show you. Look.'

He showed on the map how the attack had gone.

'I came from Fornaci,' Nick said. 'I could see how it had been. It was very good.'

'It was extraordinary. Altogether extraordinary. Are you attached to the regiment?'

'No. I am supposed to move around and let them see the uniform.'

'How odd.'

'If they see one American uniform that is supposed to make them believe others are coming.'

'But how will they know it is an American uniform?'

'You will tell them.'

'Oh. Yes, I see. I will send a corporal with you to show you about and you will make a tour of the lines.'

'Like a bloody politician,' Nick said.

'You would be much more distinguished in civilian clothes. They are what is really distinguished.'

'With a homburg hat,' said Nick.

'Or with a very furry fedora.'

'I'm supposed to have my pockets full of cigarettes and postal cards and such things,' Nick said. 'I should have a musette full of chocolate. These I should distribute with a kind word and a pat on the back. But there weren't any cigarettes and post cards and no chocolate. So they said to circulate around anyway.'

'I'm sure your appearance will be very heartening to the troops.'

'I wish you wouldn't,' Nick said. 'I feel badly enough about it as it is. In principle, I would have brought you a bottle of brandy.'

'In principle,' Para said and smiled, for the first time, showing yellowed teeth. 'Such a beautiful expression. Would you like some Grappa?'

'No, thank you,' Nick said.

'It hasn't any ether in it.'

'I can taste that still,' Nick remembered suddenly and completely.

'You know I never knew you were drunk until you started talking coming back in the camions.'

'I was stinking in every attack,' Nick said.

'I can't do it,' Para said. 'I took it in the first show, the very first show, and it only made me very upset and then frightfully thirsty.'

'You don't need it.'

'You're much braver in an attack than I am.'

'No,' Nick said. 'I know how I am and I prefer to get stinking. I'm not ashamed of it.'

'I've never seen you drunk.'

'No?' said Nick. 'Never? Not when we rode from Mestre to Portogrande that night and I wanted to go to sleep and used the bicycle for a blanket and pulled it up under my chin?'

'That wasn't in the lines.'

'Let's not talk about how I am,' Nick said. 'It's a subject I know too much about to want to think about it any more.'

'You might as well stay here a while,' Paravicini said. 'You can take a nap if you like. They didn't do much to this in the bombardment. It's too hot to go out yet.'

'I suppose there is no hurry.'

'How are you really?'

'I'm fine. I'm perfectly all right.'

'No. I mean really.'

'I'm all right. I can't sleep without a light of some sort. That's all I have now.'

'I said it should have been trepanned. I'm no doctor but I know that.'

'Well, they thought it was better to have it absorb, and that's what I got. What's the matter? I don't seem crazy to you, do I?'

'You seem in top-hole shape.'

'It's a hell of a nuisance once they've had you certified as nutty,' Nick said. 'No one ever has any confidence in you again.'

'I would take a nap, Nicolo,' Paravicini said. 'This isn't battalion headquarters as we used to know it. We're just waiting to be pulled out. You oughtn't to go out in the heat now – it's silly. Use that bunk.'

'I might just lie down,' Nick said.

Nick lay on the bunk. He was very disappointed that he felt this way and more disappointed, even, that it was so obvious to Captain Paravicini. This was not as large a dug-out as the one where that platoon of the class of 1899, just out at the front, got hysterics during the bombardment before the attack, and Para had had him walk them two at a time outside to show them nothing would happen, he wearing his own chin strap tight across his mouth to keep his lips quiet. Knowing they could not hold it when they took it. Knowing it was all a bloody balls – If he can't stop crying, break his nose to give him something else to think about. I'd shoot one but it's too late now. They'd all be worse. Break his nose. They've put it back to five-twenty. We've only got four minutes more. Break that other silly bugger's nose and kick his silly arse out of here. Do you think they'll go over? If they don't, shoot two and try to scoop the others out some way. Keep behind them, sergeant. It's no use to walk ahead and find there's nothing coming behind you. Bail them out as you go. What a bloody balls. All right. That's right. Then, looking at the watch, in that quiet tone, that valuable quiet tone, 'Savoia'. Making it cold, no time to get it, he couldn't find his own after the cave-in, one whole end had caved in; it was that started them; making it cold up that slope the only time he hadn't done it stinking. And after they came back the teleferica house burned, it seemed, and some of the wounded got down four days later and some did not get down, but we went up and we went back and we came down – we always came down. And there was Gaby Deslys, oddly enough, with feathers on; you called me baby doll a year ago tadada you said that I was rather nice to know tadada with feathers on, with feathers off, the great Gaby, and my name's Harry Pilcer, too, we used to step out of the far side of the taxis when it got steep going up the hill and he could see that hill every night when he dreamed with Sacré Cœur, blown white, like a soap bubble. Sometimes his girl was there and sometimes she was with someone else and he could not understand that, but those were the nights the river ran so much wider and stiller than it should and outside of Fossalta there was a low house painted yellow with willows all around it and a low stable and there was a canal, and he had been there a thousand times and never seen it, but there it was every night as plain as the hill, only it frightened him. That house meant more than anything and every night he had it. That was what he needed but it frightened him especially when the boat lay there quietly in the willows on the canal, but the banks weren't like this river. It was all lower, as it was at Portogrande, where they had seen them come wallowing across the flooded ground holding the rifles high until they fell with them in the water. Who ordered that one? If it didn't get so damned mixed up he could follow it all right. That was why he noticed everything in such detail to keep it all straight so he would know just where he was, but suddenly it confused without reason as now, he lying in a bunk at battalion headquarters, with Para commanding a battalion and he in a bloody American uniform. He sat up and looked around; they all watching him. Para was gone out. He lay down again.

The Paris part came earlier and he was not frightened of it except when she had gone off with someone else and the fear that they might take the same driver twice. That was what frightened about that. Never about the front. He never dreamed about the front now any more but what frightened him so that he could not get rid of it was that long yellow house and the different width of the river. Now he was back here at the river, he had gone through that same town, and there was no house. Nor was the river that way. Then where did he go each night and what was the peril, and why would he wake, soaking wet, more frightened than he had ever been in a bombardment, because of a house and a long stable and a canal?

He sat up, swung his legs carefully down; they stiffened any time they were out straight for long; returned the stares of the adjutant, the signallers and the two runners by the door and put on his cloth-covered trench helmet.

'I regret the absence of the chocolate, the postal cards and cigarettes,' he said. 'I am, however, wearing the uniform.'

'The major is coming back at once,' the adjutant said. In that army the adjutant is not a commissioned officer.

'The uniform is not very correct,' Nick told them. 'But it gives you the idea. There will be several millions of Americans here shortly.'

'Do you think they will send Americans down here?' asked the adjutant.

'Oh, absolutely. Americans twice as large as myself, healthy, with clean hearts, sleep at night never been wounded, never been blown up, never had their heads caved in, never been scared, don't drink, faithful to the girls they left behind them, many of them never had crabs, wonderful chaps. You'll see.'

'Are you an Italian?' asked the adjutant.

'No, American. Look at the uniform. Spagnolini made it but it's not quite correct.'

'A North or South American?'

'North,' said Nick. He felt it coming on now. He would quiet down.

'But you speak Italian.'

'Why not? Do you mind if I speak Italian? Haven't I a right to speak Italian?'

'You have Italian medals.'

'Just the ribbons and the papers. The medals come later. Or you give them to people to keep and the people go away; or they are lost with your baggage. You can purchase others in Milan. It is the papers that are of importance. You must not feel badly about them. You will have some yourself if you stay at the front long enough.'

'I am a veteran of the Iritrea campaign,' said the adjutant stiffly. 'I fought in Tripoli.'

'It's quite something to have met you,' Nick put out his hand. 'Those must have been trying days. I noticed the ribbons. Were you, by any chance, on the Carso?'

'I have just been called up for this war. My class was too old.'

'At one time I was under the age limit,' Nick said. 'But now I am reformed out of the war.'

'But why are you here now?'

'I am demonstrating the American uniform,' Nick said. 'Don't you think it is very significant? It is a little tight in the collar but soon you will see untold millions wearing this uniform swarming like locusts. The grasshopper, you know, what we call the grasshopper in American, is really a locust. The true grasshopper is small and green and comparatively feeble. You must not, however, make a confusion with the seven-year locust or cicada which emits a peculiar sustained sound which at the moment I cannot recall. I try to recall it but I cannot. I can almost hear it and then it is quite gone. You will pardon me if I break off our conversation?'

'See if you can find the major,' the adjutant said to one of the two runners. 'I can see you have been wounded,' he said to Nick.

'In various places,' Nick said. 'If you are interested in scars I can show you some very interesting ones but I would rather talk about grasshoppers. What we call grasshoppers that is; and what are, really, locusts. These insects at one time played a very important part in my life. It might interest you and you can look at the uniform while I am talking.'

The adjutant made a motion with his hand to the second runner who went out.

'Fix your eyes on the uniform: Spagnolini made it, you know. You might as well look, too,' Nick said to the signallers. 'I really have no rank. We're under the American consul. It's perfectly all right for you to look. You can stare, if you like. I will tell you about the American locust. We always preferred one that we called the medium-brown. They last the best in the water and fish prefer them. The larger ones that fly making a noise somewhat similar to that produced by a rattlesnake rattling his rattlers, a very dry sound, have vivid coloured wings, some are bright red, others yellow barred with black, but their wings go to pieces in the water and they make a very blowsy bait, while the medium-brown is a plump, compact, succulent hopper than I can recommend as far as one may well recommend something you gentlemen will probably never encounter. But I must insist that you will never gather a sufficient supply of these insects for a day's fishing by pursuing them with your hands or trying to hit them with a bat. That is sheer nonsense and a useless waste of time. I repeat, gentlemen, that you will get nowhere at it. The correct procedure, and one which should be taught all young officers at every small-arms course if I had anything to say about it, and who knows but what I will have, is the employment of a seine or net made of common mosquito netting. Two officers holding this length of netting at alternate ends, or let us say one at each end, stoop, hold the bottom extremity of the net in one hand and the top extremity in the other and run into the wind. The hoppers, flying with the wind, fly against the length of netting and are imprisoned in its folds. It is no trick at all to catch a very great quantity indeed, and no officer, in my opinion, should be without a length of mosquito netting suitable for the improvisation of one of these grasshopper seines. I hope I have made myself clear, gentlemen. Are there any questions? If there is anything in the course you do not understand please ask questions. Speak up. None? Then I would like to close on this note. In the words of that great soldier and gentleman, Sir Henry Wilson: Gentlemen, either you must govern or you must be governed. Let me repeat it. Gentlemen, there is one thing I would like to have you remember. One thing I would like you to take with you as you leave this room. Gentlemen, either you must govern – or you must be governed. That is all, gentlemen. Good-day.'

He removed his cloth-covered helmet, put it on again and, stooping, went out the low entrance of the dug-out. Para, accompanied by the two runners, was coming down the line of the sunken road. It was very hot in the sun and Nick removed the helmet.

'There ought to be a system for wetting these things,' he said. 'I shall wet this one in the river,' He started up the bank.

'Nicolo,' Paravicini called. 'Nicolo. Where are you going?'

'I don't really have to go.' Nick came down the slope, holding the helmet in his hands. 'They're a damned nuisance wet or dry. Do you wear yours all the time?'

'All the time,' said Para. 'It's making me bald. Come inside.' Inside Para told him to sit down.

'You know they're absolutely no damned good,' Nick said. 'I remember when they were a comfort when we first had them, but I've seen them full of brains too many times.'

'Nicolo,' Para said. 'I think you should go back. I think it would be better if you didn't come up to the line until you have had those supplies. There's nothing here for you to do. If you move around, even with something worth giving away, the men will group and that invites shelling. I won't have it.'

'I know it's silly,' Nick said. 'It wasn't my idea. I heard the brigade was here so I thought I would see you or someone else I knew. I could have gone to Zenzon or to San Dona. I'd like to go to San Dona to see the bridge again.'

'I won't have you circulating around to no purpose,' Captain Paravicini said.

'All right,' said Nick. He felt it coming on again.

'You understand?'

'Of course,' said Nick. He was trying to hold it in.

'Anything of that sort should be done at night.'

'Naturally,' said Nick. He knew he could not stop it now.

'You see, I am commanding the battalion,' Para said.

'And why shouldn't you be?' Nick said. Here it came. 'You can read and write, can't you?'

'Yes,' said Para gently.

'The trouble is you have a damned small battalion to command. As soon as it gets to strength again they'll give you back your company. Why don't they bury the dead? I've seen them now. I don't care about seeing them again. They can bury them any time as far as I'm concerned and it would be much better for you. You'll all get bloody sick.'

'Where did you leave your bicycle?'

'Inside the last house.'

'Do you think it will be all right?'

'Don't worry,' Nick said. 'I'll go in a little while.'

'Lie down a little while, Nicolo.'

442

'All right.'

He shut his eyes, and in place of the man with the beard who looked at him over the sights of the rifle, quite calmly before squeezing off, the white flash and club-like impact, on his knees, hot-sweet choking, coughing it on to the rock while they went past him, he saw a long yellow house with a low stable and the river much wider than it was and stiller. 'Christ,' he said, 'I might as well go.'

He stood up.

'I'm going, Para,' he said. 'I'll ride back now in the afternoon. If any supplies have come I'll bring them down tonight. If not I'll come at night when I have something to bring.'

'It is still hot to ride,' Captain Paravicini said.

'You don't need to worry,' Nick said. 'I'm all right now for quite a while. I had one then but it was easy. They're getting much better. I can tell when I'm going to have one because I talk so much.'

'I'll send a runner with you.'

'I'd rather you didn't. I know the way.'

'You'll be back soon?'

'Absolutely.'

'Let me send –

'No,' said Nick. 'As a mark of confidence.'

'Well, Ciaou then.'

'Ciaou,' said Nick. He started back along the sunken road toward where he had left his bicycle. In the afternoon the road would be shady once he had passed the canal. Beyond that there were trees on both sides that had not been shelled at all. It was on that stretch that, marching, they had once passed the Terza Savoia cavalry regiment riding in the snow with their lances. The horses' breath made plumes in the cold air. No, that was somewhere else. Where was that?

'I'd better get to that damned bicycle,' Nick said to himself. 'I don't want to lose the way to Fornaci.'

THE SHORT HAPPY LIFE OF FRANCIS MACOMBER

It was now lunch time and they were all sitting under the double green fly of the dining-tent pretending that nothing had happened.

'Will you have lime juice or lemon squash?' Macomber asked.

'I'll have a gimlet,' Robert Wilson told him.

'I'll have a gimlet too. I need something,' Macomber's wife said.

'I suppose it's the thing to do,' Macomber agreed. 'Tell him to make three gimlets.'

The mess boy had started them already, lifting the bottles out of the canvas cooling bags that sweated wet in the wind that blew through the trees that shaded the tents.

'What had I ought to give them?' Macomber asked.

'A quid would be plenty,' Wilson told him. 'You don't want to spoil them.'

'Will the headman distribute it?'

'Absolutely.'

Francis Macomber had, half an hour before, been carried to his tent from the edge of the camp in triumph on the arms and shoulders of the cook, the personal boys, the skinner and the porters. The gun-bearers had taken no part in the demonstration. When the native boys put him down at the door of his tent, he had shaken all their hands, received their congratulations, and then gone into the tent and sat on the bed until his wife came in. She did not speak to him when she came in and he left the tent at once to wash his face and hands in the portable wash basin outside and go over to the dining-tent to sit in a comfortable canvas chair in the breeze and the shade.

'You've got your lion,' Robert Wilson said to him, 'and a

damned fine one too.'

Mrs Macomber looked at Wilson quickly. She was an extremely handsome and well-kept woman of the beauty and social position which had, five years before, commanded five thousand dollars as the price of endorsing, with photographs, a beauty product which she had never used. She had been married to Francis Macomber for eleven years.

'He is a good lion, isn't he?' Macomber said. His wife looked at him now. She looked at both these men as though she had never seen them before.

One, Wilson, the white hunter, she knew she had never truly seen before. He was about middle height with sandy hair, a stubby moustache, a very red face and extremely cold blue eyes with faint white wrinkles at the corners that grooved merrily when he smiled. He smiled at her now and she looked away from his face at the way his shoulders sloped in the loose tunic he wore with the four big cartridges held in loops where the left breast pocket should have been, at his big brown hands, his old slacks, his very dirty boots, and back to his red face again. She noticed where the baked red of his face stopped in a white line that marked the circle left by his Stetson hat that hung now from one of the pegs of the tent pole.

'Well, here's to the lion,' Robert Wilson said. He smiled at her again and, not smiling, she looked curiously at her husband.

Francis Macomber was very tall, very well built if you did not mind that length of bone, dark, his hair cropped like an oarsman, rather thin-lipped, and was considered handsome. He was dressed in the same sort of safari clothes that Wilson wore except that his were new, he was thirty-five years old, kept himself very fit, was good at court games, had a number of big-game fishing records, and had just shown himself, very publicly, to be a coward.

'Here's to the lion,' he said. 'I can't ever thank you for what you did.'

Margaret, his wife, looked away from him and back to Wilson.

'Let's not talk about the lion,' she said.

Wilson looked over at her without smiling and now she smiled at him.

'It's been a very strange day,' she said. 'Hadn't you ought to

445

put your hat on even under the canvas at noon? You told me that, you know.'

'Might put it on,' said Wilson.

'You know you have a very red face, Mr Wilson,' she told him and smiled again.

'Drink,' said Wilson.

'I don't think so,' she said. 'Francis drinks a great deal, but his face is never red.'

'It's red today,' Macomber tried a joke.

'No,' said Margaret. 'It's mine that's red today. But Mr Wilson's is always red.'

'Must be racial,' said Wilson. 'I say, you wouldn't like to drop my beauty as a topic, would you?'

'I've just started on it.'

'Let's chuck it,' said Wilson.

'Conversation is going to be so difficult,' Margaret said.

'Don't be silly, Margot,' her husband said.

'No difficulty,' Wilson said. 'Got a damn fine lion.'

Margot looked at them both and they both saw that she was going to cry. Wilson had seen it coming for a long time and he dreaded it. Macomber was past dreading it.

'I wish it hadn't happened. Oh, I wish it hadn't happened,' she said and started for her tent. She made no noise of crying but they could see that her shoulders were shaking under the rose-coloured, sun-proofed shirt she wore.

'Women upset,' said Wilson to the tall man. 'Amounts to nothing. Strain on the nerves and one thing'n another.'

'No,' said Macomber. 'I suppose that I rate that for the rest of my life now.'

'Nonsense. Let's have a spot of the giant killer,' said Wilson. 'Forget the whole thing. Nothing to it anyway.'

'We might try,' said Macomber. 'I won't forget what you did for me though.'

'Nothing,' said Wilson. 'All nonsense.'

So they sat there in the shade where the camp was pitched under some wide-topped acacia trees with a boulder-strewn cliff behind them, and a stretch of grass that ran to the bank of a boulder-filled stream in front with forest beyond it, and drank their just-cool lime drinks and avoided one another's eyes while the boys set the table for lunch. Wilson could tell that the boys all knew about it now and when he saw Macomber's personal boy looking curiously at his master while he was putting dishes on the table he snapped at him in Swahili. The boy turned away with his face blank.

'What were you telling him?' Macomber asked.

'Nothing. Told him to look alive or I'd see he got about fifteen of the best.'

'What's that? Lashes?'

'It's quite illegal,' Wilson said. 'You're supposed to fine them.'

'Do you still have them whipped?'

'Oh, yes. They could raise a row if they chose to complain. But they don't. They prefer it to the fines.'

'How strange!' said Macomber.

'Not strange, really,' Wilson said. 'Which would you rather do? Take a good birching or lose your pay?'

Then he felt embarrassed at asking it and before Macomber could answer he went on, 'We all take a beating every day, you know, one way or another.'

This was no better. 'Good God,' he thought. 'I am a diplomat, aren't I?'

'Yes, we take a beating,' said Macomber, still not looking at him. 'I'm awfully sorry about that lion business. It doesn't have to go any further, does it? I mean no one will hear about it, will they?'

'You mean will I tell it at the Mathaiga Club?' Wilson looked at him now coldly. He had not expected this. So he's a bloody four-letter man as well as a bloody coward, he thought. I rather liked him too until today. But how is one to know about an American?

'No,' said Wilson. 'I'm a professional hunter. We never talk about our clients. You can be quite easy on that. It's supposed to be bad form to ask us not to talk though.'

He had decided now that to break would be much easier. He would eat, then, by himself and could read a book with his meals. They would eat by themselves. He would see them through the safari on a very formal basis – what was it the French called it? Distinguished consideration – and it would be a damn sight easier than having to go through this emotional

447

trash. He'd insult him and make a good clean break. Then he could read a book with his meals and he'd still be drinking their whisky. That was the phrase for it when a safari went bad. You ran into another white hunter and you asked, 'How is everything going?' and he answered, 'Oh, I'm still drinking their whisky,' and you knew everything had gone to pot.

'I'm sorry,' Macomber said and looked at him with his American face that would stay adolescent until it became middle-aged, and Wilson noted his crew-cropped hair, fine eyes only faintly shifty, good nose, thin lips and handsome jaw. 'I'm sorry I didn't realize that. There are lots of things I don't know.'

So what could he do, Wilson thought. He was all ready to break it off quickly and neatly and here the beggar was apologizing after he had just insulted him. He made one more attempt. 'Don't worry about me talking,' he said. 'I have a living to make. You know in Africa no woman ever misses her lion and no white man ever bolts.'

'I bolted like a rabbit,' Macomber said.

Now what in hell were you going to do about a man who talked like that? Wilson wondered.

Wilson looked at Macomber with his flat, blue, machine-gunner's eyes and the other smiled back at him. He had a pleasant smile if you did not notice how his eyes showed when he was hurt.

'Maybe I can fix it up on buffalo,' he said. 'We're after them next, aren't we?'

'In the morning if you like,' Wilson told him. Perhaps he had been wrong. This was certainly the way to take it. You most certainly could not tell a damned thing about an American. He was all for Macomber again. If you could forget the morning. But, of course, you couldn't. The morning had been about as bad as they come.

'Here comes the Memsahib,' he said. She was walking over from her tent looking refreshed and cheerful and quite lovely. She had a very perfect oval face, so perfect that you expected her to be stupid. But she wasn't stupid, Wilson thought, no, not stupid.

'How is the beautiful red-faced Mr Wilson? Are you feeling better, Francis, my pearl?'

'Oh, much,' said Macomber.

'I've dropped the whole thing,' she said, sitting down at the table. 'What importance is there to whether Francis is any good at killing lions? That's not his trade. That's Mr Wilson's trade. Mr Wilson is really very impressive killing anything. You do kill anything, don't you?'

'Oh, anything,' said Wilson. 'Simply anything.' They are, he thought, the hardest in the world; the hardest, the cruellest, the most predatory and the most attractive and their men have softened or gone to pieces nervously as they have hardened. Or is it that they pick men they can handle? They can't know that much at the age they marry, he thought. He was grateful that he had gone through his education on American women before now because this was a very attractive one.

'We're going after buff in the morning,' he told her.

'I'm coming,' she said.

'No you're not.'

'Oh, yes, I am. Mayn't I, Francis?'

'Why not stay in camp?'

'Not for anything,' she said. 'I wouldn't miss something like today for anything.'

When she left, Wilson was thinking, when she went off to cry she seemed a hell of a fine woman. She seemed to understand, to realize, to be hurt for him and for herself and to know how things really stood. She is away for twenty minutes and now she is back, simply enamelled in that American female cruelty. They are the damnedest women. Really the damnedest.

'We'll put on another show for you tomorrow,' Francis Macomber said.

'You're not coming,' Wilson said.

'You're very mistaken,' she told him. 'And I want *so* to see you perform again. You were lovely this morning. That is if blowing things' heads off is lovely.'

'Here's the lunch,' said Wilson. 'You're very merry, aren't you?'

'Why not? I didn't come out here to be dull.'

'Well, it hasn't been dull,' Wilson said. He could see the boulders in the river and the high bank beyond with the trees and he remembered the morning.

449

'Oh, no,' she said. 'It's been charming. And tomorrow. You don't know how I look forward to tomorrow.'

'That's eland he's offering you,' Wilson said.

'They're the big cowy things that jump like hares, aren't they?'

'I suppose that describes them,' Wilson said.

'It's very good meat,' Macomber said.

'Did you shoot it, Francis?' she asked.

'Yes.'

'They're not dangerous, are they?'

'Only if they fall on you,' Wilson told her.

'I'm so glad.'

'Why not let up on the bitchery just a little, Margot,' Macomber said, cutting the eland steak and putting some mashed potato, gravy and carrot on the down-turned fork that tined through the piece of meat.

'I suppose I could,' she said, 'since you put it so prettily.'

'Tonight we'll have champagne for the lion,' Wilson said. 'It's a bit too hot at noon.'

'Oh, the lion,' Margot said. 'I'd forgotten the lion!'

So, Robert Wilson thought to himself, she *is* giving him a ride, isn't she? Or do you suppose that's her idea of putting up a good show? How should a woman act when she discovers her husband is a bloody coward? She's damned cruel but they're all cruel. They govern, of course, and to govern one has to be cruel sometimes. Still, I've seen enough of their damn terrorism.

'Have some more eland,' he said to her politely.

That afternoon, late, Wilson and Macomber went out in the motor car with the native driver and the two gun-bearers. Mrs Macomber stayed in the camp. It was too hot to go out, she said, and she was going with them in the early morning. As they drove off Wilson saw her standing under the big tree looking pretty rather than beautiful in her faintly rosy khaki, her dark brown hair drawn back off her forehead and gathered in a knot low on her neck, her face as fresh, he thought, as though she were in England. She waved to them as the car went off through the swale of high grass and curved through the trees into the small hills of orchard bush.

In the orchard bush they found a herd of impala, and leaving

450

the car they stalked one old ram with long, widespread horns and Macomber killed it with a very creditable shot that knocked the buck down at a good two hundred yards and sent the herd off bounding wildly and leaping over one another's backs in long, leg-drawn-up leaps as unbelievable and as floating as those one makes sometimes in dreams.

'That was a good shot,' Wilson said. 'They're a small target.'

'Is it a worth-while head?' Macomber asked.

'It's excellent,' Wilson told him. 'You shoot like that and you'll have no trouble.'

'Do you think we'll find buffalo tomorrow?'

'There's a good chance of it. They feed out early in the morning and with luck we may catch them in the open.'

'I'd like to clear away that lion business,' Macomber said. 'It's not very pleasant to have your wife see you do something like that.'

I should think it would be even more unpleasant to do it, Wilson thought, wife or no wife, or to talk about it having done it. But he said, 'I wouldn't think about that any more. Anyone could be upset by his first lion. That's all over.'

But that night after dinner and a whisky and soda by the fire before going to bed, as Francis Macomber lay on his cot with the mosquito bar over him and listened to the night noises it was not all over. It was neither all over nor was it beginning. It was there exactly as it happened with some parts of it indelibly emphasized and he was miserably ashamed of it. But more than shame he felt cold, hollow fear in him. The fear was still there like a cold slimy hollow in all the emptiness where once his confidence had been and it made him feel sick. It was still there with him now.

It had started the night before when he had awakened and heard the lion roaring somewhere up along the river. It was a deep sound and at the end there were sort of coughing grunts that made him seem just outside the tent, and when Francis Macomber woke in the night to hear it he was afraid. He could hear his wife breathing quietly, asleep. There was no one to tell he was afraid, nor to be afraid with him, and, lying alone, he did not knew the Somali proverb that says a brave man is always frightened three times by a lion; when he first sees his track, when he first hears him roar and when he first confronts

451

him. Then while they were eating breakfast by lantern light out in the dining-tent, before the sun was up, the lion roared again and Francis thought he was just at the edge of camp.

'Sounds like an old-timer,' Robert Wilson said, looking up from his kippers and coffee. 'Listen to him cough.'

'Is he very close?'

'A mile or so up the stream.'

'Will we see him?'

'We'll have a look.'

'Does his roaring carry that far? It sounds as though he were right in camp.'

'Carries a hell of a long way,' said Robert Wilson. 'It's strange the way it carries. Hope he's a shootable cat. The boys said there was a very big one about here.'

'If I get a shot, where should I hit him,' Macomber asked, 'to stop him?'

'In the shoulders,' Wilson said. 'In the neck if you can make it. Shoot for bone. Break him down.'

'I hope I can place it properly,' Macomber said.

'You shoot very well,' Wilson told him. 'Take your time. Make sure of him. The first one in is the one that counts.'

'What range will it be?'

'Can't tell. Lion has something to say about that. Don't shoot unless it's close enough so you can make sure.'

'At under a hundred yards?' Macomber asked.

Wilson looked at him quickly.

'Hundred's about right. Might have to take him a bit under. Shouldn't chance a shot at much over that. A hundred's a decent range. You can hit him wherever you want at that. Here comes the Memsahib.'

'Good morning,' she said. 'Are we going after that lion?'

'As soon as you deal with your breakfast,' Wilson said. 'How are you feeling?'

'Marvellous,' she said. 'I'm very excited.'

'I'll just go and see that everything is ready.' Wilson went off. As he left the lion roared again.

'Noisy beggar,' Wilson said. 'We'll put a stop to that.'

'What's the matter, Francis?' his wife asked him.

'Nothing,' Macomber said.

'Yes, there is,' she said. 'What are you upset about?'

'Nothing,' he said.

'Tell me,' she looked at him. 'Don't you feel well?'

'It's that damned roaring,' he said. 'It's been going on all night, you know.'

'Why didn't you wake me?' she said. 'I'd love to have heard it.'

'I've got to kill the damned thing,' Macomber said, miserably.

'Well, that's what you're out here for, isn't it?'

'Yes. But I'm nervous. Hearing the thing roar gets on my nerves.'

'Well then, as Wilson said, kill him and stop his roaring.'

'Yes, darling,' said Francis Macomber. 'It sounds easy, doesn't it?'

'You're not afraid, are you?'

'Of course not. But I'm nervous from hearing him roar all night.'

'You'll kill him marvellously,' she said. 'I know you will. I'm awfully anxious to see it.'

'Finish your breakfast and we'll be starting.'

'It's not light yet,' she said. 'This is a ridiculous hour.'

Just then the lion roared in a deep-chested moaning, suddenly guttural, ascending vibration that seemed to shake the air and ended in a sigh and a heavy, deep-chested grunt.

'He sounds almost here,' Macomber's wife said.

'My God,' said Macomber. 'I hate that damned noise.'

'It's very impressive.'

'Impressive. It's frightful.'

Robert Wilson came up then carrying his short, ugly, shockingly big-bored ·505 Gibbs and grinning.

'Come on,' he said. 'Your gun-bearer has your Springfield and the big gun. Everything's in the car. Have you solids?'

'Yes.'

'I'm ready,' Mrs Macomber said.

'Must make him stop that racket,' Wilson said. 'You get in front. The Memsahib can sit back here with me.'

They climbed into the motor car and, in the grey first daylight, moved off up the river through the trees. Macomber opened the breech of his rifle and saw he had metal-cased bullets, shut the bolt and put the rifle on safety. He saw his hand was trembling. He felt in his pocket for more cartridges and moved his fingers over the cartridges in the loops of his tunic front. He turned back to where Wilson sat in the rear seat of the doorless, box-bodied motor car beside his wife, them both grinning with excitement, and Wilson leaned forward and whispered.

'See the birds dropping. Means the old boy has left his kill.'

On the far bank of the stream Macomber could see, above the trees, vultures circling and plummeting down.

'Chances are he'll come to drink along here,' Wilson whispered. 'Before he goes to lay up. Keep an eye out.'

They were driving slowly along the high bank of the stream which here cut deeply to its boulder-filled bed, and they wound in and out through big trees as they drove. Macomber was watching the opposite bank when he felt Wilson take hold of his arm. The car stopped.

'There he is,' he heard the whisper. 'Ahead and to the right. Get out and take him. He's a marvellous lion.'

Macomber saw the lion now. He was standing almost broadside, his great head up and turned toward them. The early morning breeze that blew toward them was just stirring his dark mane, and the lion looked huge, silhouetted on the rise of bank in the grey morning light, his shoulders heavy, his barrel of a body bulking smoothly.

'How far is he?' asked Macomber, raising his rifle.

'About seventy-five. Get out and take him.'

'Why not shoot from where I am?'

'You don't shoot them from cars,' he heard Wilson saying in his ear. 'Get out. He's not going to stay there all day.'

Macomber stepped out of the curved opening at the side of the front seat, on to the step and down on to the ground. The lion still stood looking majestically and coolly toward this object that his eyes only showed in silhouette, bulking like some super-rhino. There was no man smell carried toward him and he watched the object, moving his great head a little from side to side. Then watching the object, not afraid, but hesitating before going down the bank to drink with such a thing opposite him, he saw a man figure detach itself from it and he turned his heavy head and swung away toward the cover of the trees as he heard a cracking crash and felt the slam of a 30–06 220-grain solid bullet that bit his flank and ripped in sudden hot scalding nausea through his stomach. He trotted, heavy, big-footed, swinging wounded full-bellied, through the trees toward the tall grass and cover, and the crash came again to go past him ripping the air apart. Then it crashed again and he felt the blow as it hit his lower ribs and ripped on through, blood sudden hot and frothy in his mouth, and he galloped toward the high grass where he could crouch and not be seen and make them bring the crashing thing close enough so he could make a rush and get the man that held it.

Macomber had not thought how the lion felt as he got out of the car. He only knew his hands were shaking and as he walked away from the car it was almost impossible for him to make his legs move. They were stiff in the thighs, but he could feel the muscles fluttering. He raised the rifle, sighted on the junction of the lion's head and shoulders and pulled the trigger. Nothing happened though he pulled until he thought his finger would break. Then he knew he had the safety on and as he lowered the rifle to move the safety over he moved another frozen pace forward and the lion seeing his silhouette now clear of the silhouette of the car, turned and started off at a trot, and, as Macomber fired, he heard a whunk that meant the bullet was home; but the lion kept on going. Macomber shot again and everyone saw the bullet throw a spout of dirt beyond the trotting lion. He shot again, remembering to lower his aim, and they all heard the bullet hit, and the lion went into a gallop and was in the tall grass before he had the bolt pushed forward.

Macomber stood there feeling sick at his stomach, his hands that held the Springfield still cocked, shaking, and his wife and Robert Wilson were standing by him. Beside him too were the gun-bearers chattering in Wakamba.

'I hit him,' Macomber said. 'I hit him twice.'

'You gut-shot him and you hit him somewhere forward,' Wilson said without enthusiasm. The gun-bearers looked very grave. They were silent now.

'You may have killed him,' Wilson went on. 'We'll have to wait a while before we go in to find out.'

'What do you mean?'

'Let him get sick before we follow him up.'

'Oh,' said Macomber.

'He's a hell of a fine lion,' Wilson said cheerfully. 'He's gotten into a bad place though.'

'Why is it bad?'

'Can't see him until you're on him.'

'Oh,' said Macomber.

'Come on,' said Wilson. 'The Memsahib can stay here in the car. We'll go to have a look at the blood spoor.'

'Stay here, Margot,' Macomber said to his wife. His mouth was very dry and it was hard for him to talk.

'Why?' she asked.

'Wilson says to.'

'We're going to have a look,' Wilson said. 'You stay here. You can see even better from here.'

'All right.'

Wilson spoke in Swahili to the driver. He nodded and said, 'Yes, Bwana.'

Then they went down the steep bank and across the stream, climbing over and around the boulders and up the other bank, pulling up by some projecting roots, and along it until they found where the lion had been trotting when Macomber first shot. There was dark blood on the short grass that the gun-bearers pointed out with grass stems, and that ran away behind the river bank trees.

'What do we do?' asked Macomber.

'Not much choice,' said Wilson. 'We can't bring the car over. Bank's too steep. We'll let him stiffen up a bit and then you and I'll go in and have a look for him.'

'Can't we set the grass on fire?' Macomber asked.

'Too green.'

'Can't we send beaters?'

Wilson looked at him appraisingly. 'Of course we can,' he said. 'But it's just a touch murderous. You see we know the lion's wounded. You can drive an unwounded lion – he'll move on ahead of a noise – but a wounded lion's going to charge. You can't see him until you're right on him. He'll make himself perfectly flat in cover you wouldn't think would hide a hare. You can't very well send boys in there to that sort of a show. Somebody bound to get mauled.'

'What about the gun-bearers?'

'Oh, they'll go with us. It's their *shauri*. You see, they signed on for it. They don't look too happy though, do they?'

'I don't want to go in there,' said Macomber. It was out before he knew he'd said it.

'Neither do I,' said Wilson very cheerily. 'Really no choice though.' Then, as an afterthought, he glanced at Macomber and saw suddenly how he was trembling and the pitiful look on his face.

'You don't have to go in, of course,' he said. 'That's what I'm hired for, you know. That's why I'm so expensive.'

'You mean you'd go in by yourself? Why not leave him there?'

Robert Wilson, whose entire occupation had been with the lion and the problem he presented, and who had not been thinking about Macomber except to note that he was rather windy, suddenly felt as though he had opened the wrong door in an hotel and seen something shameful.

'What do you mean?'

'Why not just leave him?'

'You mean pretend to ourselves he hasn't been hit?'

'No. Just drop it.'

'It isn't done.'

'Why not?'

'For one thing, he's certain to be suffering. For another, someone else might run on to him.'

'I see.'

'But you don't have to have anything to do with it.'

'I'd like to,' Macomber said. 'I'm just scared, you know.'

'I'll go ahead when we go in,' Wilson said, 'with Kongoni tracking. You keep behind me and a little to one side. Chances are we'll hear him growl. If we see him we'll both shoot. Don't worry about anything. I'll keep you backed up. As a matter of fact, you know, perhaps you'd better not go. It might be much better. Why don't you go over and join the Memsahib while I just get it over with?'

'No, I want to go.'

'All right,' said Wilson.' But don't go in if you don't want to. This is my *shauri* now, you know.'

'I want to go,' said Macomber.

They sat under a tree and smoked.

'Want to go back and speak to the Memsahib while we're waiting?' Wilson asked.

'No.'

'I'll just step back and tell her to be patient.'

'Good,' said Macomber. He sat there, sweating under his arms, his mouth dry, his stomach hollow feeling, wanting to find courage to tell Wilson to go on and finish off the lion without him. He could not know that Wilson was furious because he had not noticed the state he was in earlier and sent him back to his wife. While he sat there Wilson came up. 'I have your big gun,' he said. 'Take it. We've given him time, I think. Come on.'

Macomber took the big gun and Wilson said:

'Keep behind me and about five yards to the right and do exactly as I tell you.' Then he spoke in Swahili to the two gun-bearers who looked the picture of gloom.

'Let's go,' he said.

'Could I have a drink of water?' Macomber asked. Wilson spoke to the older gun-bearer, who wore a canteen on his belt, and the man unbuckled it, unscrewed the top and handed it to Macomber, who took it noticing how heavy it seemed and how hairy and shoddy the felt covering was in his hand. He raised it to drink and looked ahead at the high grass with the flat-topped trees behind it. A breeze was blowing toward them and the grass rippled gently in the wind. He looked at the gun-bearer and he could see the gun-bearer was suffering too with fear.

Thirty-five yards into the grass the big lion lay flattened out along the ground. His ears were back and his only movement was a slight twitching up and down of his long, black-tufted tail. He had turned at bay as soon as he had reached this cover and he was sick with the wound through his full belly, and weakening with the wound through his lungs that brought a thin foamy red to his mouth each time he breathed. His flanks were wet and hot and flies were on the little opening the solid bullets had made in his tawny hide, and his big yellow eyes, narrowed with hate, looking straight ahead, only blinking when the pain came as he breathed, and his claws dug in the soft baked earth. All of him, pain, sickness, hatred and all of his remaining strength, was tightening into an absolute concentration for a rush. He could hear the men talking and he waited, gathering all of himself into this preparation for a charge as soon as the men would come into the grass. As he heard their voices his tail stiffened to twitch up and down, and, as they came into the edge of the grass, he made a coughing grunt and charged.

Kongoni, the old gun-bearer, in the lead watching the blood spoor, Wilson watching the grass for any movement, his big gun ready, the second gun-bearer looking ahead and listening, Macomber close to Wilson, his rifle cocked, they had just moved into the grass when Macomber heard the blood-choked coughing grunt, and saw the swishing rush in the grass. The next thing he knew he was running; running wildly, in panic in the open, running toward the stream.

He heard the *carawong!* of Wilson's big rifle, and again in a second crashing *carawong!* and turning saw the lion, horrible-looking now, with half his head seeming to be gone, crawling toward Wilson in the edge of the tall grass while the red-faced man worked the bolt on the short ugly rifle and aimed carefully as another blasting *carawong!* came from the muzzle, and the crawling, heavy, yellow bulk of the lion stiffened and the huge, mutilated head slid forward and Macomber, standing by himself in the clearing where he had run, holding a loaded rifle, while two black men and a white man looked back at him in contempt, knew the lion was dead. He came toward Wilson, his tallness all seeming a naked reproach, and Wilson looked at him and said:

'Want to take pictures?'

'No,' he said.

That was all anyone had said until they reached the motor car. Then Wilson had said:

'Hell of a fine lion. Boys will skin him out. We might as well stay here in the shade.'

Macomber's wife had not looked at him nor he at her and he had sat by her in the back seat with Wilson sitting in the front seat. Once he had reached over and taken his wife's hand without looking at her and she had removed her hand from his. Looking across the stream to where the gun-bearers were skinning out the lion he could see that she had been able to see the whole thing.

While they sat there his wife had reached forward and put her hand on Wilson's shoulder. He turned and she had leaned forward over the low seat and kissed him on the mouth.

'Oh, I say,' said Wilson, going redder than his natural baked colour.

'Mr Robert Wilson,' she said. 'The beautifully red-faced Mr Robert Wilson.'

Then she sat down beside Macomber again and looked away across the stream to where the lion lay, with uplifted, white-muscled, tendon-marked naked forearms, and white bloating belly, as the black men fleshed away the skin. Finally the gun-bearers brought the skin over, wet and heavy, and climbed in behind with it, rolling it up before they got in, and the motor car started. No one had said anything more until they were back in camp.

That was the story of the lion. Macomber did not know how the lion had felt before he started his rush, nor during it when the unbelievable smash of the ·505 with a muzzle velocity of two tons had hit him in the mouth, nor what kept him coming after that, when the second ripping crash had smashed his hind quarters and he had come crawling on toward the crashing, blasting thing that had destroyed him. Wilson knew something about it and only expressed it by saying, 'Damned fine lion', but Macomber did not know how Wilson felt about things either. He did not know how his wife felt except that she was through with him.

His wife had been through with him before but it never lasted. He was very wealthy, and would be much wealthier, and he knew she would not leave him ever now. That was one of the few things he really knew. He knew about that, about motor cycles – that was earliest – about motor cars, about duck-shooting, about fishing, trout, salmon and big-sea, about sex in books, many books, too many books, about all court games, about dogs, not much about horses, about hanging on to his money, about most of the other things his world dealt in, and about his wife not leaving him. His wife had been a great beauty and she was still a great beauty in Africa, but she was not a great enough beauty any more at home to be able to leave him and better herself and she knew it and he knew it. She had missed the chance to leave him and he knew it. If he had been better with women she would probably have started to worry about him getting another new, beautiful wife; but she knew too much about him to worry about him either. Also, he had always had a great tolerance which seemed the nicest thing about him if it were not the most sinister.

All in all they were known as a comparatively happily married couple, one of those whose disruption is often rumoured but never occurs, and as the society columnist put it, they were adding more than a spice of *adventure* to their much envied and ever-enduring *Romance* by *a Safari* in what was known as *Darkest Africa* until the Martin Johnsons lighted it on so many silver screens where they were pursuing *Old Simba* the lion, the buffalo, *Tembo* the elephant and as well collecting specimens for the Museum of Natural History. This same columnist had reported them *on the verge* at least three times in the past and they had been. But they always made it up. They had a sound basis of union. Margot was too beautiful for Macomber to divorce her and Macomber had too much money for Margot ever to leave him.

It was now about three o'clock in the morning and Francis Macomber, who had been asleep a little while after he had stopped thinking about the lion, wakened and then slept again, woke suddenly, frightened in a dream of the bloody-headed lion standing over him, and listening while his heart pounded, he realized that his wife was not in the other cot in the tent. He lay awake with that knowledge for two hours.

At the end of that time his wife came into the tent, lifted her mosquito bar and crawled cosily into bed.

'Where have you been?' Macomber asked in the darkness.

'Hello,' she said. 'Are you awake?'

'Where have you been?'

'I just went out to get a breath of air.'

'You did, like hell.'

'What do you want me to say, darling?'

'Where have you been?'

'Out to get a breath of air.'

'That's a new name for it. You *are* a bitch.'

'Well, you're a coward.'

'All right,' he said. 'What of it?'

'Nothing as far as I'm concerned. But please let's not talk, darling, because I'm very sleepy.'

'You think that I'll take anything.'

'I know you will, sweet.'

'Well, I won't.'

'Please, darling, let's not talk. I'm so very sleepy.'

'There wasn't going to be any of that. You promised there wouldn't be.'

'Well, there is now,' she said sweetly.

'You said if we made this trip there would be none of that. You promised.'

'Yes, darling. That's the way I meant it to be. But the trip was spoiled yesterday. We don't have to talk about it, do we?'

'You don't wait long when you have an advantage, do you?'

'Please, let's not talk. I'm so sleepy, darling.'

'I'm going to talk.'

'Don't mind me then, because I'm going to sleep.' And she did.

At breakfast they were all three at the table before daylight and Francis Macomber found that, of all the many men that he had hated, he hated Robert Wilson the most.

'Sleep well?' Wilson asked in his throaty voice, filling a pipe.

'Did you?'

'Topping,' the white hunter told him.

You bastard, thought Macomber, you insolent bastard.

So she woke him when she came in, Wilson thought, looking at them both with his flat, cold eyes. Well, why doesn't he keep his wife where she belongs? What does he think I am, a bloody plaster saint? Let him keep her where she belongs. It's his own fault.

'Do you think we'll find buffalo?' Margot asked, pushing away a dish of apricots.

'Chance of it,' Wilson said and smiled at her. 'Why don't you stay in camp?'

'Not for anything,' she told him.

'Why not order her to stay in camp?' Wilson said to Macomber.

'You order her,' said Macomber coldly.

'Let's not have any ordering, nor,' turning to Macomber,

462

'any silliness, Francis,' Margot said quite pleasantly.

'Are you ready to start?' Macomber asked.

'Any time,' Wilson told him. 'Do you want the Memsahib to go?'

'Does it make any difference whether I do or not?'

The hell with it, thought Robert Wilson. The utter complete hell with it. So this is what it's going to be like. Well, this is what it's going to be like then.

'Makes no difference,' he said.

'You're sure you wouldn't like to stay in camp with her yourself and let me go out and hunt the buffalo?' Macomber asked.

'Can't do that,' said Wilson. 'Wouldn't talk rot if I were you.'

'I'm not talking rot. I'm disgusted.'

'Bad word, disgusted.'

'Francis, will you please try to speak sensibly?' his wife said.

'I speak too damned sensibly,' Macomber said. 'Did you ever eat such filthy food?'

'Something wrong with the food?' asked Wilson quietly.

'No more than with everything else.'

'I'd pull yourself together, laddybuck,' Wilson said very quietly. 'There's a boy waits at table that understands a little English.'

'The hell with him.'

Wilson stood up and puffing on his pipe strolled away, speaking a few words in Swahili to one of the gun-bearers who was standing waiting for him. Macomber and his wife sat on at the table. He was staring at his coffee cup.

'If you make a scene I'll leave you, darling,' Margot said quietly.

'No, you won't.'

'You can try it and see.'

'You won't leave me.'

'No,' she said. 'I won't leave you and you'll behave yourself.'

'Behave myself? That's a way to talk. Behave myself.'

'Yes. Behave yourself.'

'Why don't *you* try behaving?'

'I've tried it so long. So very long.'

'I hate that red-faced swine,' Macomber said. 'I loathe the sight of him.'

'He's really *very* nice.'

'Oh, *shut up*,' Macomber almost shouted. Just then the car came up and stopped in front of the dining tent and the driver and the two gun-bearers got out. Wilson walked over and looked at the husband and wife sitting there at the table.

'Going shooting?' he asked.

'Yes,' said Macomber, standing up. 'Yes.'

'Better bring a woolly. It will be cool in the car,' Wilson said.

'I'll get my leather jacket,' Margot said.

'The boy has it,' Wilson told her. He climbed into the front with the driver and Francis Macomber and his wife sat, not speaking, in the back seat.

Hope the silly beggar doesn't take a notion to blow the back of my head off, Wilson thought to himself. Women *are* a nuisance on safari.

The car was grinding down to cross the river at a pebbly ford in the grey daylight and then climbed, angling up the steep bank, where Wilson had ordered a way shovelled out the day before so they could reach the parklike wooded rolling country on the far side.

It was a good morning, Wilson thought. There was a heavy dew and as the wheels went through the grass and low bushes he could smell the odour of the crushed fronds. It was an odour like verbena and he liked this early morning smell of the dew, the crushed bracken and the look of the tree trunks showing black through the early morning mist, as the car made its way through the untracked, parklike country. He had put the two in the back seat out of his mind now and was thinking about buffalo. The buffalo that he was after stayed in the daytime in a thick swamp where it was impossible to get a shot, but in the night they fed out into an open stretch of country and if he could come between them and their swamp with the car, Macomber would have a good chance at them in the open. He did not want to hunt buff with Macomber in thick cover. He did not want to hunt buff or anything else with Macomber at all, but he was a professional hunter and he had hunted with some rare ones in

464

his time. If they got buff today there would only be rhino to come and the poor man would have gone through his dangerous game and things might pick up. He'd have nothing more to do with the woman and Macomber would get over that too. He must have gone through plenty of that before by the look of things. Poor beggar. He must have a way of getting over it. Well, it was the poor sod's own bloody fault.

He, Robert Wilson, carried a double size cot on safari to accommodate any windfalls he might receive. He had hunted for a certain clientele, the international, fast, sporting set, where the women did not feel they were getting their money's worth unless they had shared that cot with the white hunter. He despised them when he was away from them although he liked some of them well enough at the time, but he made his living by them; and their standards were his standards as long as they were hiring him.

They were his standards in all except the shooting. He had his own standards about the killing and they could live up to them or get someone else to hunt them. He knew, too, that they all respected him for this. This Macomber was an odd one though. Damned if he wasn't. Now the wife. Hell, the wife. Yes, the wife. Mm, the wife. Well, he'd dropped all that. He looked around at them. Macomber sat grim and furious. Margot smiled at him. She looked younger today, more innocent and fresher and not so professionally beautiful. What's in her heart God knows, Wilson thought. She hadn't talked much last night. At that it was a pleasure to see her.

The motor car climbed up a slight rise and went on through the trees and then out into a grassy prairie-like opening and kept in the shelter of the trees along the edge, the driver going slowly and Wilson looking carefully out across the prairie and all along its far side. He stopped the car and studied the opening with his field glasses. Then he motioned the driver to go on and the car moved slowly along, the driver avoiding warthog holes and driving around the mud castles ants had built. Then, looking across the opening, Wilson suddenly turned and said:

'By God, there they are!'

And looking where he pointed, while the car jumped forward and Wilson spoke in rapid Swahili to the driver, Macomber saw three huge black animals looking almost cylindrical in their long heaviness, like big black tank cars, moving at a gallop across the far edge of the open prairie. They moved at a stiff-necked, stiff-bodied gallop and he could see the upswept wide black horns on their heads as they galloped heads out; the heads not moving.

'They're three old bulls,' Wilson said. 'We'll cut them off before they get to the swamp.'

The car was going a wild forty-five miles an hour across the open and as Macomber watched, the buffalo got bigger and bigger until he could see the grey, hairless, scabby look of one huge bull and how his neck was a part of his shoulders and the shiny black of his horns as he galloped a little behind the others that were strung out in that steady plunging gait; and then, the car swaying as though it had just jumped a road, they drew up close and he could see the plunging hugeness of the bull, and the dust in his sparsely haired hide, the wide boss of horn and his outstretched, wide-nostrilled muzzle, and he was raising his rifle when Wilson shouted, 'Not from the car, you fool!' and he had no fear, only hatred of Wilson, while the brakes clamped on and the car skidded, ploughing sideways to an almost stop and Wilson was out on one side and he on the other, stumbling as his feet hit the still speeding-by of the earth, and then he was shooting at the bull as he moved away, hearing the bullets whunk into him, emptying his rifle at him as he moved steadily away, finally remembering to get his shots forward into the shoulder, and as he fumbled to re-load, he saw the bull was down. Down on his knees, his big head tossing, and seeing the other two still galloping he shot at the leader and hit him. He shot again and missed and he heard the *carawonging* roar as Wilson shot and saw the leading bull slide forward on to his nose.

'Get that other,' Wilson said. 'Now you're shooting!'

But the other bull was moving steadily at the same gallop and he missed, throwing a spout of dirt, and Wilson missed and the dust rose in a cloud and Wilson shouted, 'Come on. He's too far!' and grabbed his arm and they were in the car again, Macomber and Wilson hanging on the sides and rocketing swayingly over the uneven ground, drawing up on the steady, plunging, heavy-necked, straight-moving gallop of the bull.

They were behind him and Macomber was filling his rifle, dropping shells on to the ground, jamming it, clearing the jam, then they were almost up with the bull when Wilson yelled 'Stop,' and the car skidded so that it almost swung over and Macomber fell forward on to his feet, slammed his bolt forward and fired as far forward as he could aim into the galloping, rounded black back, aimed and shot again, then again, then again, and the bullets, all of them hitting, had no effect on the buffalo that he could see. Then Wilson shot, the roar deafening him, and he could see the bull stagger. Macomber shot again, aiming carefully, and down he came, on to his knees.

'All right,' Wilson said. 'Nice work. That's the three.'

Macomber felt a drunken elation.

'How many times did you shoot?' he asked.

'Just three,' Wilson said. 'You killed the first bull. The biggest one. I helped you finish the other two. Afraid they might have got into cover. You had them killed. I was just mopping up a little. You shot damn well.'

'Let's go to the car,' said Macomber. 'I want a drink.'

'Got to finish off that buff first,' Wilson told him. The buffalo was on his knees and he jerked his head furiously and bellowed in pig-eyed, roaring rage as they came toward him.

'Watch he doesn't get up,' Wilson said. Then, 'Get a little broadside and take him in the neck just behind the ear.'

Macomber aimed carefully at the centre of the huge, jerking, rage-driven neck and shot. At the shot the head dropped forward.

'That does it,' said Wilson. 'Got the spine. They're a hell of a looking thing, aren't they?'

'Let's get the drink,' said Macomber. In his life he had never felt so good.

In the car Macomber's wife sat very white faced. 'You were marvellous, darling,' she said to Macomber. 'What a ride.'

'Was it rough?' Wilson asked.

'It was frightful. I've never been more frightened in my life.'

'Let's all have a drink,' Macomber said.

'By all means,' said Wilson. 'Give it to the Memsahib.' She drank the neat whisky from the flask and shuddered a little when she swallowed. She handed the flask to Macomber who handed it to Wilson.

'It was frightfully exciting,' she said. 'It's given me a dreadful headache. I didn't know you were allowed to shoot them from cars though.'

'No one shot from cars,' said Wilson coldly.

'I mean chase them from cars.'

'Wouldn't ordinarily,' Wilson said. 'Seemed sporting enough to me though while we were doing it. Taking more chance driving that way across a plain full of holes and one thing and another than hunting on foot. Buffalo could have charged us each time we shot if he liked. Gave him every chance. Wouldn't mention it to anyone though. It's illegal if that's what you mean.'

'It seemed very unfair to me,' Margo said, 'chasing those big helpless things in a motor car.'

'Did it?' said Wilson.

'What would happen if they heard about that in Nairobi?'

'I'd lose my licence for one thing. Other unpleasantnesses,' Wilson said, taking a drink from the flask. 'I'd be out of business.'

'Really?'

'Well,' said Macomber, and he smiled for the first time all day. 'Now she has something on you.'

'You have such a pretty way of putting things, Francis,' Margot Macomber said. Wilson looked at them both. If a four-letter man marries a five-letter woman, he was thinking, what number of letters would their children be? What he said was 'We lost a gun-bearer. Did you notice it?'

'My God, no,' Macomber said.

'Here he comes,' Wilson said. 'He's all right. He must have fallen off when we left the first bull.'

Approaching them was the middle-aged gun-bearer, limping along in his knitted cap, khaki tunic, shorts and rubber sandals, gloomy-faced and disgusted looking. As he came up he called out to Wilson in Swahili and they all saw the change in the white hunter's face.

'What does he say?' asked Margot.

'He says the first bull got up and went into the bush,' Wilson said with no expression in his voice.

'Oh,' said Macomber blankly.

'Then it's going to be just like the lion,' said Margot, full of anticipation.

'It's not going to be a damned bit like the lion,' Wilson told her. 'Did you want another drink, Macomber?'

'Thanks, yes,' Macomber said. He expected the feeling he had had about the lion to come back but it did not. For the first time in his life he really felt wholly without fear. Instead of fear he had a feeling of definite elation.

'We'll go and have a look at the second bull,' Wilson said. 'I'll tell the driver to put the car in the shade.'

'What are you going to do?' asked Margot Macomber.

'Take a look at the buff,' Wilson said.

'I'll come.'

'Come along.'

The three of them walked over to where the second buffalo bulked blackly in the open, head forward on the grass, the massive horns swung wide,

'He's a very good head,' Wilson said. ''That's close to a fifty-inch spread.'

Macomber was looking at him with delight.

'He's hateful looking,' said Margot. 'Can't we go into the shade?'

'Of course,' Wilson said. 'Look,' he said to Macomber, and pointed. 'See that patch of bush?'

'Yes.'

'That's where the first bull went in. The gun-bearer said when he fell off the bull was down. He was watching us helling along and the other two buff galloping. When he looked up there was the bull up and looking at him. Gun-bearer ran like hell and the bull went off slowly into that bush.'

'Can we go in after him now?' asked Macomber eagerly.

Wilson looked at him appraisingly. Damned if this isn't a strange one, he thought. Yesterday he's scared sick and today he's a ruddy fire-eater.

'No, we'll give him a while.'

'Let's please go into the shade,' Margot said. Her face was white and she looked ill.

They made their way to the car where it stood under a single wide-spreading tree and all climbed in.

'Chances are he's dead in there,' Wilson remarked. 'After a little we'll have a look.'

Macomber felt a wild unreasonable happiness that he had never known before.

'By God, that was a chase,' he said. 'I've never felt any such feeling. Wasn't it marvellous, Margot?'

'I hated it.'

'Why?,'

'I hated it,' she said bitterly. 'I loathed it.'

'You know, I don't think I'd be afraid of anything again,' Macomber said to Wilson. 'Something happened in me after we first saw the buff and started after him. Like a dam bursting. It was pure excitement.'

'Cleans out your liver,' said Wilson. 'Damn funny things happen to people.'

Macomber's face was shining. 'You know, something did happen to me,' he said, 'I feel absolutely different.'

His wife said nothing and eyed him strangely. She was sitting far back in the seat and Macomber was sitting forward talking to Wilson who turned sideways talking over the back of the front seat.

'You know, I'd like to try another lion,' Macomber said. 'I'm not really afraid of them now. After all, what can they do to you?'

'That's it,' said Wilson. 'Worst one can do is kill you. How does it go? Shakespeare. Damned good. See if I can remember. Oh, damned good. Used to quote it to myself at one time. Let's see. "By my troth, I care not; a man can die but once; we owe God a death and let it go which way it will he that dies this year is quit for the next." Damned fine, eh?'

He was very embarrassed, having brought out this thing he had lived by, but he had seen men come of age before and it always moved him. It was not a matter of their twenty-first birthday.

It had taken a strange chance of hunting, a sudden precipitation into action without opportunity for worrying beforehand, to bring this about with Macomber, but regardless of how it had happened it had most certainly happened. Look at the beggar now, Wilson thought. It's that some of them stay little boys so long, Wilson thought. Sometimes all their lives. Their figures stay boyish when they're fifty. The great American boy-men. Damned strange people. But he liked this Macomber now. Damned strange fellow. Probably meant the end of cuckoldry too. Well, that would be a damned good thing. Damned good thing. Beggar had probably been afraid all his life. Don't know what started it. But over now. Hadn't had time to be afraid with the buff. That and being angry too. Motor car too. Motor cars made it familiar. Be a damn fire-eater now. He'd seen it in the war work the same way. More of a change than any loss of virginity. Fear gone like an operation. Something else grew in its place. Main thing a man had. Made him into a man. Women knew it too. No bloody fear.

From the far corner of the seat Margaret Macomber looked at the two of them. There was no change in Wilson. She saw Wilson as she had seen him the day before when she had first realized what his great talent was. But she saw the change in Francis Macomber now.

'Do you have that feeling of happiness about what's going to happen?' Macomber asked, still exploring his new wealth.

'You're not supposed to mention it,' Wilson said, looking in the other's face. 'Much more fashionable to say you're scared. Mind you, you'll be scared too, plenty of times.'

'But you *have a* feeling of happiness about action to come?'

'Yes,' said Wilson. 'There's that. Doesn't do to talk too much about all this. Talk the whole thing away. No pleasure in anything if you mouth it up too much.'

'You're both talking rot,' said Margot. 'Just because you've chased some helpless animals in a motor car you talk like heroes.'

'Sorry,' said Wilson. 'I have been gassing too much.' She's worried about it already, he thought.

'If you don't know what we're talking about, why not keep out of it?' Macomber asked his wife.

'You've gotten awfully brave, awfully suddenly,' his wife said contemptuously, but her contempt was not secure. She was very afraid of something.

Macomber laughed, a very natural hearty laugh. 'You know *I have,*' he said. 'I really have.'

'Isn't it sort of late?' Margot said bitterly. Because she had done the best she could for many years back and the way they were together now was no one person's fault.

'Not for me,' said Macomber.

Margot said nothing but sat back in the corner of the seat.

'Do you think we've given him time enough?' Macomber asked Wilson cheerfully.

'We might have a look,' Wilson said. 'Have you any solids left?'

'The gun-bearer has some.'

Wilson called in Swahili and the older gun-bearer, who was skinning out one of the heads, straightened up, pulled a box of solids out of his pocket, and brought them over to Macomber, who filled his magazine and put the remaining shells in his pocket.

'You might as well shoot the Springfield,' Wilson said. 'You're used to it. We'll leave the Mannlicher in the car with the Memsahib. Your gun-bearer can carry your heavy gun. I've this damned cannon. Now let me tell you about them.' He had saved this until the last because he did not want to worry Macomber. 'When a buff comes he comes with his head high and thrust straight out. The boss of the horns covers any sort of a brain shot. The only shot is straight into the nose. The only other shot is into his chest or, if you're to one side, into the neck or the shoulders. After they've been hit once they take a hell of a lot of killing. Don't try anything fancy. Take the easiest shot there is. They've finished skinning out that head now. Should we get started?'

He called to the gun-bearers, who came up wiping their hands, and the older one got into the back.

'I'll only take Kongoni,' Wilson said. 'The other can watch to keep the birds away.'

As the car moved slowly across the open space toward the island of brushy trees that ran in a tongue of foliage along a dry water course that cut the open swale, Macomber felt his heart pounding and his mouth was dry again, but it was excitement, not fear.

'Here's where he went in,' Wilson said. Then to the gun-bearer in Swahili, 'Take the blood spoor.'

The car was parallel to the patch of bush. Macomber, Wilson and the gun-bearer got down. Macomber, looking back, saw his wife, with the rifle by her side, looking at him. He waved to her and she did not wave back.

The brush was very thick ahead and the ground was dry. The middle-aged gun-bearer was sweating heavily and Wilson had his hat down over his eyes and his red neck showed just ahead of Macomber. Suddenly the gun-bearer said something in Swahili to Wilson and ran forward.

'He's dead in there,' Wilson said. 'Good work,' and he turned to grip Macomber's hand and as they shook hands, grinning at each other, the gun-bearer shouted wildly and they saw him coming out of the bush sideways, fast as a crab, and the bull coming, nose out, mouth tight closed, blood dripping, massive head straight out, coming in a charge, his little pig eyes bloodshot as he looked at them. Wilson, who was ahead, was kneeling shooting, and Macomber, as he fired, unhearing his shot in the roaring of Wilson's gun, saw fragments like slate burst from the huge boss of the horns, and the head jerked, he shot again at the wide nostrils and saw the horns jolt again and fragments fly, and he did not see Wilson now and, aiming carefully, shot again with the buffalo's huge bulk almost on him and his rifle almost level with the oncoming head, nose out, and he could see the little wicked eyes and the head started to lower and he felt a sudden white-hot, blinding flash explode inside his head and that was all he ever felt.

Wilson had ducked to one side to get in a shoulder shot. Macomber had stood solid and shot for the nose, shooting a touch high each time and hitting the heavy horns, splintering and chipping them like hitting a slate roof, and Mrs Macomber in the car, had shot at the buffalo with the 6·5 Mannlicher as it seemed about to gore Macomber and had hit her husband about two inches up and a little to one side of the base of his skull.

Francis Macomber lay now, face down, not two yards from where the buffalo lay on his side and his wife knelt over him with Wilson beside her.

'I wouldn't turn him over,' Wilson said.

The woman was crying hysterically.

'I'd get back in the car,' Wilson said. 'Where's the rifle?'

She shook her head, her face contorted. The gun-bearer picked up the rifle.

'Leave it as it is,' said Wilson. Then, 'Go get Abdulla so that he may witness the manner of the accident.'

He knelt down, took a handkerchief from his pocket, and spread it over Francis Macomber's crew-cropped head where it lay. The blood sank into the dry, loose earth.

Wilson stood up and saw the buffalo on his side, his legs out, his thinly-haired belly crawling with ticks. 'Hell of a good bull,' his brain registered automatically. 'A good fifty inches, or better. Better.' he called to the driver and told him to spread a blanket over the body and stay by it. Then he walked over to the motor car where the woman sat crying in the corner.

'That was a pretty thing to do,' he said in a toneless voice. 'He *would* have left you too.'

'Stop it,' she said.

'Of course it's an accident,' he said. 'I know that.'

'Stop it,' she said.

'Don't worry,' he said. 'There will be a certain amount of unpleasantness but I will have some photographs taken that will be very useful at the inquest. There's the testimony of the gun-bearers and the driver too. You're perfectly all right.'

'Stop it,' she said.

'There's a hell of a lot to be done,' he said. 'And I'll have to send a truck off to the lake to wireless for a plane to take the three of us into Nairobi. Why didn't you poison him? That's what they do in England.'

'Stop it. Stop it. Stop it,' the woman cried.

Wilson looked at her with his flat blue eyes.

'I'm through now,' he said. 'I was a little angry. I'd begun to like your husband.'

'Oh, please stop it,' she said. 'Please, please stop it.'

'That's better,' Wilson said. 'Please is much better. Now I'll stop.'

THE SNOWS OF KILIMANJARO

Kilimanjaro is a snow covered mountain 19,710 feet high, and is said to be the highest mountain in Africa. Its western summit is called 'Ngàje Ngài', the House of God. Close to the western summit there is the dried and frozen carcass of a leopard. No one has explained what the leopard was seeking at that altitude.

'The marvellous thing is that it's painless,' he said. 'That's how you know when it starts.'

'Is it really?'

'Absolutely. I'm awfully sorry about the odour, though. That must bother you.'

'Don't! Please don't.'

'Look at them,' he said. 'Now is it sight or is it scent that brings them like that?'

The cot the man lay on was in the wide shade of a mimosa tree and as he looked out past the shade on to the glare of the plain there were three of the big birds squatted obscenely, while in the sky a dozen more sailed, making quick-moving shadows as they passed.

'They've been there since the day the truck broke down,' he said. 'Today's the first time any have lit on the ground. I watched the way they sailed very carefully at first in case I ever wanted to use them in a story. That's funny now.'

'I wish you wouldn't,' she said.

'I'm only talking,' he said. 'It's much easier if I talk. But I don't want to bother you.'

'You know it doesn't bother me,' she said. 'It's that I've gotten so very nervous not being able to do anything. I think we might make it as easy as we can until the plane comes.'

'Or until the plane doesn't come.'

'Please tell me what I can do. There must be something I can do.'

'You can take the leg off and that might stop it, though I doubt it. Or you can shoot me. You're a good shot now. I taught you to shoot didn't I?'

'Please don't talk that way. Couldn't I read to you?'

'Read what?'

'Anything in the book bag that we haven't read.'

'I can't listen to it,' he said. 'Talking is the easiest. We quarrel and that makes the time pass.'

'I don't quarrel. I never want to quarrel. Let's not quarrel any more. No matter how nervous we get. Maybe they will be back with another truck today. Maybe the plane will come.'

'I don't want to move,' the man said. 'There is no sense in moving now except to make it easier for you.'

'That's cowardly.'

'Can't you let a man die as comfortably as he can without calling him names? What's the use of slanging me?'

'You're not going to die.'

'Don't be silly. I'm dying now. Ask those bastards.' He looked over to where the huge, filthy birds sat, their naked head sunk in the hunched feathers. A fourth planed down, to run quick-legged and then waddle slowly towards the others.

'They are around every camp. You never notice them. You can't die if you don't give up.'

'Where did you read that? You're such a bloody fool.'

'You might think about someone else.'

'For Christ's sake,' he said, 'that's been my trade.'

He lay then and was quiet for a while and looked across the heat shimmer of the plain to the edge of the bush. There were a few Tommies that showed minute and white against the yellow and, far off, he saw a herd of zebra, white against the green of the bush. This was a pleasant camp under big trees against a hill, with good water, and close by, a nearly dry water hole where sand grouse flighted in the mornings.

'Wouldn't you like me to read?' she asked. She was sitting on a canvas chair beside the cot. 'There's a breeze coming up.'

'No thanks.'

'Maybe the truck will come.'

'I don't give a damn about the truck.'

'I do.'

'You give a damn about so many things that I don't.'

'Not so many, Harry.'

'What about a drink?'

'It's supposed to be bad for you. It said in Black's to avoid all alcohol. You shouldn't drink.'

'Molo!' he shouted.

'Yes, Bwana.'

'Bring whisky-soda.'

'Yes, Bwana.'

'You shouldn't,' she said. 'That's what I mean by giving up. It says it's bad for you. I know it's bad for you.'

'No,' he said. 'It's good for me.'

So now it was all over, he thought. So now he would never have a chance to finish it. So this was the way it ended in a bickering over a drink. Since the gangrene started in his right leg he had no pain and with the pain the horror had gone and all he felt now was a great tiredness and anger that this was the end of it. For this, that now was coming, he had very little curiosity. For years it had obsessed him; but now it meant nothing in itself. It was strange how easy being tired enough made it.

Now he would never write the things that he had saved to write until he knew enough to write them well. Well, he would not have to fail at trying to write them either. Maybe you could never write them, and that was why you put them off and delayed the starting. Well, he would never know, now.

'I wish we'd never come,' the woman said. She was looking at him holding the glass and biting her lip. 'You never would have gotten anything like this in Paris. You always said you loved Paris. We could have stayed in Paris or gone anywhere. I'd have gone anywhere. I said I'd go anywhere you wanted. If you wanted to shoot we could have gone shooting in Hungary and been comfortable.'

'Your bloody money,' he said.

'That's not fair,' she said. 'It was always yours as much as mine. I left everything and I went wherever you wanted to go and I've done what you wanted to do. But I wish we'd never come here.'

'You said you loved it.'

'I did when you were all right. But now I hate it. I don't see why that had to happen to your leg. What have we done to have that happen to us?'

'I suppose what I did was to forget to put iodine on it when I first scratched it. Then I didn't pay any attention to it because I never infect. Then, later, when it got bad, it was probably using that weak carbolic solution when the other antiseptics ran out that paralysed the minute blood vessels and started the gangrene.' He looked at her, 'What else?'

'I don't mean that.'

'If we would have hired a good mechanic instead of a half-baked kikuyu driver, he would have checked the oil and never burned out that bearing in the truck.'

'I don't mean that.'

'If you hadn't left your own people, your goddamned Old Westbury, Saratoga, Palm Beach people to take me on –'

'Why, I loved you. That's not fair. I love you now. I'll always love you. Don't you love me?'

'No,' said the man. 'I don't think so. I never have.'

'Harry, what are you saying? You're out of your head.'

'No. I haven't any head to go out of.'

'Don't drink that,' she said. 'Darling, please don't drink that. We have to do everything we can.'

'You do it,' he said. 'I'm tired.'

Now in his mind he saw a railway station at Karagatch and he was standing with his pack and that was the headlight of the Simplon – Orient cutting the dark now and he was leaving Thrace then after the retreat. That was one of the things he had saved to write, with, in the morning at breakfast, looking out the window and seeing snow on the mountains in Bulgaria and Nansen's Secretary asking the old man if it were snow and the old man looking at it and saying, No, that's not snow. It's too early for snow. And the Secretary repeating to the other girls, No, you see. It's not snow and them all saying, it's not snow, we were mistaken. But it was the snow all right and he sent them on into

478

it when he evolved exchange of populations. And it was snow they tramped along in until they died that winter.

It was snow too that fell all Christmas week that year up in the Gauertal, that year they lived in the woodcutter's house with the big square porcelain stove that filled half the room, and they slept on mattresses filled with beech leaves, the time the deserter came with his feet bloody in the snow. He said the police were right behind him and they gave him woollen socks and held the gendarmes talking until the tracks had drifted over.

In Schrunz, on Christmas day, the snow was so bright it hurt your eyes when you looked out from the weinstube and saw everyone coming home from church. That was where they walked up the sleigh-smoothed urine-yellowed road along the river with the steep pine hills, skis heavy on the shoulder, and where they ran that great run down the glacier above the Madlener-Haus, the snow as smooth to see as cake frosting and as light as powder and he remembered the noiseless rush the speed made as you dropped down like a bird.

They were snow-bound a week in the Madlener-Haus that time in the blizzard playing cards in the smoke by the lantern light and the stakes were higher all the time as Herr Lent lost more. Finally he lost it all. Everything, the skischule money and all the season's profit and then his capital. He could see him with his long nose, picking up the cards and then opening, 'Sans Voir'. There was always gambling then. When there was no snow you gambled and when there was too much you gambled. He thought of all the time in his life he had spent gambling.

But he had never written a line of that, nor of that cold, bright Christmas day with the mountains showing across the plain that Johnson had flown across the lines to bomb the Austrian officers' leave train, machine-gunning them as they scattered and ran. He remembered Johnson afterward coming into the mess and starting to tell about it. And how quiet it got and then somebody saying: 'You bloody murderous bastard!'

They were the same Austrians they killed then that he skied with later. No, not the same. Hans, that he skied with all that year, had been in the Kaiser Jägers and when they went hunting hares together up the little valley above the saw-mill they had talked of the fighting on Pasubio and of the attack on Pertica and Asalone and he had never written a word of that. Nor of Monte Corno, nor the Siete Commum, nor of Arsiedo.

How many winters had he lived in the Voralberg and the Arlberg? It was four and then he remembered the man who had the fox to sell when they had walked into Bludenz, that time to buy presents, and the cherry-pip taste of the good kirsch, the fast-slipping rush of running powder-snow on crust, singing 'Hi! Ho! said Rolly!' as you ran down the last stretch to the steep drop, taking it straight, then running the orchard in three turns and out across the ditch and on to the icy road behind the inn. Knocking your bindings loose, kicking the skis free and leaning them up against the wooden wall of the inn, the lamplight coming from the window, where inside, in the smokey, new-wine smelling warmth, they were playing the accordion.

'Where did we stay in Paris?' he asked the woman who was sitting by him in a canvas chair, now, in Africa.

'At the Crillon. You know that.'

'Why do I know that?'

'That's where we always stayed.'

'No. Not always.'

'There and at the Pavillion Henri-Quatre in St Germain. You said you loved it there.'

'Love is a dunghill,' said Harry. 'And I'm the cock that gets on it to crow.'

'If you have to go away,' she said, 'is it absolutely necessary to kill off everything you leave behind? I mean do you have to take away everything? Do you have to kill your horse, and your wife and burn your saddle and your armour?'

'Yes,' he said. 'Your damned money was my armour. My Swift and my Armour.'

'Don't.'

'All right. I'll stop that. I don't want to hurt you.'

'It's a little bit late now.'

'All right then. I'll go on hurting you. It's more amusing. The only thing I ever really liked to do with you I can't do now.'

'No, that's not true. You liked to do many things and everything you wanted to do I did.'

480

'Oh, for Christ sake stop bragging, will you?'

He looked at her and saw her crying.

'Listen,' he said. 'Do you think that it is fun to do this? I don't know why I'm doing it. It's trying to kill to keep yourself alive, I imagine. I was all right when we started talking. I didn't mean to start this, and now I'm crazy as a coot and being as cruel to you as I can be. Don't pay any attention, darling, to what I say. I love you, really. You know I love you. I've never loved anyone else the way I love you.'

He slipped into the familiar lie he made his bread and butter by.

'You're sweet to me.'

'You bitch,' he said. 'You rich bitch. That's poetry. I'm full of poetry now. Rot and poetry. Rotten poetry.'

'Stop it. Harry, why do you have to turn into a devil now?'

'I don't like to leave anything,' the man said. 'I don't like to leave things behind.'

It was evening now and he had been asleep. The sun was gone behind the hill and there was a shadow all across the plain and the small animals were feeding close to camp; quick dropping heads and switching tails, he watched them keeping well out away from the bush now. The birds no longer waited on the ground. They were all perched heavily in a tree. There were many more of them. His personal boy was sitting by the bed.

'Memsahib's gone to shoot,' the boy said. 'Does Bwana want?'

'Nothing.'

She had gone to kill a piece of meat and, knowing how he liked to watch the game, she had gone well away so she would not disturb this little pocket of the plain that he could see. She was always thoughtful, he thought. On anything she knew about, or had read, or what she had ever heard.

It was not her fault that when he went to her he was already over. How could a woman know that you meant nothing that you said; that you spoke only from habit and to be comfortable? After he no longer meant what he said, his lies were more successful with women than when he had told them the truth.

It was not so much that he lied as that there was no truth to tell. He had had his life and it was over and then he went on living it again with different people and more money, with the best of the same places, and some new ones.

You kept from thinking and it was all marvellous. You were equipped with good insides so that you did not go to pieces that way, the way most of them had, and you made an attitude that you cared nothing for the work you used to do, now that you could no longer do it. But, in yourself, you said that you would write about people; about the very rich; that you were really not of them but a spy in their country; that you would leave it and write of it and for once it would be written by someone who knew what he was writing of. But he would never do it, because each day of not writing, of comfort, of being that which he despised, dulled his ability and softened his will to work so that, finally, he did no work at all. The people he knew now were all much more comfortable when he did not work. Africa was where he had been happiest in the good time of his life, so he had come out here to start again. They had made this safari with the minimum of comfort. There was no hardship; but there was no luxury and he had thought that he could get back into training that way. That in some way he could work the fat off his soul the way a fighter went into the mountains to work and train in order to burn it out of his body.

She had liked it. She said she loved it. She loved anything that was exciting, that involved a change of scene, where there were new people and where things were pleasant. And he had felt the illusion of returning strength of will to work. Now if this was how it ended, and he knew it was, he must not turn like some snake biting itself because its back was broken. It wasn't this woman's fault. If it had not been she it would have been another. If he lived by a lie he should try to die by it. He heard a shot beyond the hill.

She shot very well, this good, this rich bitch, this kindly caretaker and destroyer of his talent. Nonsense. He had destroyed his talent himself. Why should he blame this woman because she kept him well? He had destroyed his talent by not using it, by betrayals of himself and what he believed in, by drinking so much that he blunted the edge of his perceptions,

482

by laziness, by sloth, and by snobbery, by pride and by prejudice, by hook and by crook. What was this? A catalogue of old books? What was his talent anyway? It was a talent all right but instead of using it, he had traded on it. It was never what he had done, but always what he could do. And he had chosen to make his living with something else instead of a pen or a pencil. It was strange, too, wasn't it, that when he fell in love with another woman, that woman should always have more money than the last one? But when he no longer was in love, when he was only lying, as to this woman, now, who had the most money of all, who had all the money there was, who had had a husband and children, who had taken lovers and been dissatisfied with them, and who loved him dearly as a writer, as a man, as a companion and as a proud possession; it was strange that when he did not love her at all and was lying, that he should be able to give her more for her money than when he had really loved.

We must all be cut out for what we do, he thought. However you make your living is where your talent lies. He had sold vitality, in one form or another, all his life and when your affections are not too involved you give much better value for the money. He had found that out but he would never write that, now, either. No, he would not write that, although it was well worth writing.

Now she came in sight, walking across the open toward the camp. She was wearing jodhpurs and carrying her rifle. The two boys had a Tommie slung and they coming along behind her. She was still a good-looking woman, he thought, and she had a pleasant body. She had a great talent and appreciation for the bed, she was not pretty, but he liked her face, she read enormously, liked to ride and shoot and, certainly, she drank too much. Her husband had died when she was still a comparatively young woman and for a while she had devoted herself to her two just-grown children, who did not need her and were embarrassed at having her about, to her stable of horses, to books, and to bottles. She liked to read in the evening before dinner and she drank Scotch and soda while she read. By dinner she was fairly drunk and after a bottle of wine at dinner she was usually drunk enough to sleep.

That was before the lovers. After she had the lovers she did not drink so much because she did not have to be drunk to sleep. But the lovers bored her. She had been married to a man who never bored her and these people bored her very much.

Then one of her two children was killed in a plane crash and after that was over she did not want the lovers, and drink being no anaesthetic she had to make another life. Suddenly she had been acutely frightened of being alone. But she wanted someone that she respected with her.

It had begun very simply. She liked what he wrote and she had always envied the life he led. She thought he did exactly what he wanted to. The steps by which she had acquired him and the way in which she had finally fallen in love with him were all part of a regular progression in which she had built herself a new life and he had traded away what remained of his old life.

He had traded it for security, for comfort too, there was no denying that, and for what else? He did not know. She would have bought him anything he wanted. He knew that. She was a damned nice woman too. He would as soon be in bed with her as anyone; rather with her, because she was richer, because she was very pleasant and appreciative and because she never made scenes. And now this life that she had built again was coming to a term because he had not used iodine two weeks ago when a thorn had scratched his knee as they moved forward trying to photograph a herd of waterbuck standing, their heads up, peering while their nostrils searched the air, their ears spread wide to hear the first noise that would send them rushing into the bush. They had bolted, too, before he got the picture.

Here she came now.

He turned his head on the cot to look toward her. 'Hello,' he said.

'I shot a Tommy ram,' she told him. 'He'll make you good broth and I'll have them mash some potatoes with the Klim. How do you feel?'

'Much better.'

'Isn't that lovely? You know I thought perhaps you would. You were sleeping when I left.'

'I had a good sleep. Did you walk far?'

484

'No. Just around the hill. I made quite a good shot on the Tommy.'

'You shoot marvellously, you know.'

'I love it. I've loved Africa. Really. If *you're* all right it's the most fun that I've ever had. You don't know the fun it's been to shoot with you. I've loved the country.'

'I love it too.'

'Darling, you don't know how marvellous it is to see you feeling better. I couldn't stand it when you felt that way. You won't talk to me like that again, will you? Promise me?'

'No,' he said. 'I don't remember what I said.'

'You don't have to destroy me. Do you? I'm only a middle-aged woman who loves you and wants to do what you want to do. I've been destroyed two or three times already. You wouldn't want to destroy me again, would you?'

'I'd like to destroy you a few times in bed,' he said.

'Yes. That's the good destruction. That's the way we're made to be destroyed. The plane will be here tomorrow.'

'How do you know?'

'I'm sure. It's bound to come. The boys have the wood all ready and the grass to make the smudge. I went down and looked at it again today. There's plenty of room to land and we have the smudges ready at both ends.'

'What makes you think it will come tomorrow?'

'I'm sure it will. It's overdue now. Then, in town, they will fix up your leg and then we will have some good destruction. Not that dreadful talking kind.'

'Should we have a drink? The sun is down.'

'Do you think you should?'

'I'm having one.'

'We'll have one together. *Molo, letti dui whisky-soda!*' she called.

'You'd better put on your mosquito boots,' he told her.

'I'll wait till I bathe . . . .'

While it grew dark they drank and just before it was dark and there was no longer enough light to shoot, a hyena crossed the open on his way around the hill.

'That bastard crosses there every night,' the man said. 'Every night for two weeks.'

'He's the one makes the noise at night. I don't mind it. They're a filthy animal though.'

Drinking together, with no pain now except the discomfort of lying in the one position, the boys lighting a fire, its shadow jumping on the tents, he could feel the return of acquiescence in this life of pleasant surrender. She *was* very good to him. He had been cruel and unjust in the afternoon. She was a fine woman, marvellous really. And just then it occurred to him that he was going to die.

It came with a rush; not as a rush of water nor of wind; but of a sudden evil-smelling emptiness and the odd thing was that the hyena slipped lightly along the edge of it.

'What is it, Harry?' she asked him.

'Nothing,' he said. 'You had better move over to the other side. To windward.'

'Did Molo change the dressing?'

'Yes. I'm just using the boric now.'

'How do you feel?'

'A little wobbly.'

'I'm going in to bathe,' she said. 'I'll be right out. I'll eat with you and then we'll put the cot in.'

So, he said to himself, we did well to stop the quarrelling. He had never quarrelled much with this woman, while with the women that he loved he had quarrelled so much they had finally, always, with the corrosion of the quarrelling, killed what they had together. He had loved too much, demanded too much, and he wore it all out.

He thought about alone in Constantinople that time, having quarrelled in Paris before he had gone out. He had whored the whole time and then, when that was over, and he had failed to kill his loneliness, but only made it worse, he had written her, the first one, the one who left him, a letter telling her how he had never been able to kill it ... How when he thought he saw her outside the Regence one time it made him go all faint and sick inside, and that he would follow a woman who looked like her in some way, along the Boulevard, afraid to see it was not she, afraid to lose the feeling it gave him. How everyone he had slept with had only made him miss her more. How what she had done could never

*matter since he knew he could not cure himself of loving her. He
wrote this letter at the Club, cold sober, and mailed it to New
York asking her to write him at the office in Paris. That seemed
safe. And that night missing her so much made him feel hollow
sick inside, he wandered up past Taxim's, picked a girl up and
took her out to supper. He had gone to a place to dance with her
afterward, she danced badly, and left her for a hot Armenian
slut, that swung her belly against him so it almost scalded. He
took her away from a British gunner subaltern after a row. The
gunner asked him outside and they fought in the street on the
cobbles in the dark. He'd hit him twice, hard, on the side of the
jaw and when he didn't go down he knew he was in for a fight.
The gunner hit him in the body, then beside his eye. He swung
with his left again and landed and the gunner fell on him and
grabbed his coat and tore the sleeve off and he clubbed him twice
behind the ear and then smashed him with his right as he pushed
him away. When the gunner went down his head hit first and he
ran with the girl because they heard the M.P.s coming. They got
into a taxi and drove out to Rimmily Hissa along the Bosphorus,
and around, and back in the cool night and went to bed and she
felt as over-ripe as she looked but smooth, rose-petal, syrupy,
smooth-bellied, big-breasted and needed no pillow under her
buttocks, and he left her before she was awake and looking blowzy
enough in the first daylight and turned up at the Pera Palace
with a black eye, carrying his coat because one sleeve was missing.*

*That same night he left for Anatolia and he remembered, later
on that trip, riding all day through fields of poppies that they
raised for opium and how strange it made you feel, finally, and
all the distances seemed wrong, to where they had made the attack
with the newly arrived Constantine officers, that did not know a
god-damned thing, and the artillery had fired into the troops and
the British observer had cried like a child.*

*That was the day he'd first seen dead men wearing white ballet
skirts and upturned shoes with pompoms on them. The Turks had
come steadily and lumpily and he had seen the skirted men
running and the officers shooting into them and running then
themselves and he and the British observer had run too until his
lungs ached and his mouth was full of the taste of pennies and
they stopped behind some rocks and there were the Turks coming*

as lumpily as ever. Later he had seen the things that he could never think of and later still he had seen much worse. So when he got back to Paris that time he could not talk about it or stand to have it mentioned. And there in the café as he passed was that American poet with a pile of saucers in front of him and a stupid look on his potato face talking about the Dada movement with a Roumanian who said his name was Tristan Tzara, who always wore a monocle and had a headache, and, back at the apartment with his wife that now he loved again, the quarrel all over, the madness all over, glad to be home, the office sent his mail up to the flat. So then the letter in answer to the one he'd written came in on a platter one morning and when he saw the hand-writing he went cold all over and tried to slip the letter underneath another. But his wife said, 'Who is that letter from, dear?' and that was the end of the beginning of that.

He remembered the good times with them all, and the quarrels. They always picked the finest places to have quarrels. And why had they always quarrelled when was he feeling best? He had never written any of that because, at first, he never wanted to hurt anyone and then it seemed as though there was enough to write without it. But he had always thought that he would write it finally. There was so much to write. He had seen the world change; not just the events; although he had seen many of them and had watched the people, but he had seen the subtler change and he could remember how the people were at different times. He had been in it and he had watched it and it was his duty to write of it; but now he never would.

'How do you feel?' she said. She had come out from the tent now after her bath.

'All right.'

'Could you eat now?' He saw Molo behind her with the folding table and the other boy with the dishes.

'I want to write,' he said.

'You ought to take some broth to keep your strength up.'

'I'm going to die tonight,' he said. 'I don't need my strength up.'

'Don't be melodramatic, Harry, please,' she said.

'Why don't you use your nose? I'm rotted half way up my

thigh now. What the hell should I fool with broth for? Molo, bring whisky-soda.'

'Please take the broth,' she said gently.

'All right.'

The broth was too hot. He had to hold it in the cup until it cooled enough to take it and then he just got it down without gagging.

'You're a fine woman,' he said. 'Don't pay any attention to me.'

She looked at him with her well-known, well-loved face from *Spur* and *Town and Country*, only a little the worse for drink, only a little the worse for bed, but *Town and Country* never showed those good breasts and those useful thighs and those lightly small-of-back-caressing hands, and as he looked and saw her well-known pleasant smile, he felt death come again. This time there was no rush. It was a puff, as of a wind that makes a candle flicker and the flame go tall.

'They can bring my net out later and hang it from the tree and build the fire up. I'm not going in the tent tonight. It's not worth moving. It's a clear night. There won't be any rain.'

So this was how you died, in whispers that you did not hear. Well, there would be no more quarrelling. He could promise that. The one experience that he had never had he was not going to spoil now. He probably would. You spoiled everything. But perhaps he wouldn't.

'You can't take dictation, can you?'

'I never learned,' she told him.

'That's all right.'

There wasn't time, of course, although it seemed as though it telescoped so that you might put it all into one paragraph if you could get it right.

There was a log house, chinked white with mortar, on a hill above the lake. There was a bell on a pole by the door to call the people in to meals. Behind the house were fields and behind the fields was the timber. A line of lombardy poplars ran from the house to the dock. Other poplars ran along the point. A road went up to the hills along the edge of the timber and along that road he picked blackberries. Then that log house was burned down and all the

guns that had been on deer foot racks above the open fire place
were burned and afterward their barrels, with the lead melted in
the magazines, and the stocks burned away, lay out on the heap of
ashes that were used to make lye for the big iron soap kettles, and
you asked Grandfather if you could have them to play with, and
he said, no. You see they were his guns and he never bought any
others. Nor did he hunt any more. The house was rebuilt in the
same place out of lumber now and painted white and from its
porch you saw the poplars and the lake beyond; but there were
never any more guns. The barrels of the guns that had hung on
the deer feet on the wall of the log house lay out there on the heap
of ashes and no one ever touched them.

In the Black Forest, after the war, we rented a trout stream
and there were two ways to walk it. One was down the valley from
Triberg and around the valley road in the shade of the trees that
bordered the white road, and then up a side road that went up
through the hills, past many small farms, with the big
Schwarzwald houses, until that road crossed the stream. That was
where our fishing began.

The other way was to climb steeply up to the edge of the woods
and then go across the top of the hills through the pine woods, and
then out to the edge of a meadow and down across this meadow to
the bridge. There were birches along the stream and it was not big,
but narrow, clear and fast, with pools where it had cut under the
roots of the birches. At the Hotel in Triberg the proprietor had a
fine season. It was very pleasant and we were all great friends.
The next year came the inflation and the money he had made the
year before was not enough to buy supplies to open the hotel and he
hanged himself.

You could dictate that, but you could not dictate the Place
Contrescarpe where the flower sellers dyed their flowers in the
street and the dye ran over the paving where the autobus started
and the old men and the women, always drunk on wine and bad
marc; and the children with their noses running in the cold; the
smell of dirty sweat and poverty and drunkenness at the Café des
Amateurs and the whores at the Bal Musette they lived above. The
Concierge who entertained the trooper of the Garde Republicaine
in her loge, his horse-hair-plumed helmet on a chair. The
locataire across the hall whose husband was a bicycle racer and

her joy that morning at the Crémerie when she had opened L'Auto and seen where he placed third in Paris–Tours, his first big race. She had blushed and laughed and then gone upstairs crying with the yellow sporting paper in her hand. The husband of the woman who ran the Bal Musette drove a taxi and when he, Harry, had to take an early plane the husband knocked upon the door to wake him and they each drank a glass of white wine at the zinc of the bar before they started. He knew his neighbours in that quarter then because they all were poor.

Around the Place there were two kinds: the drunkards and the sportifs. The drunkards killed their poverty that way; the sportifs took it out in exercise. They were the descendants of the Communards and it was no struggle for them to know their politics. They knew who had shot their fathers, their relatives, their brothers, and their friends when the Versailles troops came in and took the town after the Commune and executed anyone they could catch with calloused hands, or who wore a cap, or carried any other sign he was a working man. And in that poverty, and in that quarter across the street from a Boucherie Chevaline and a wine co-operative he had written the start of all he was to do. There never was another part of Paris that he loved like that, the sprawling trees, the old white plastered houses painted brown below, the long green of the autobus in that round square, the purple flower dye upon the paving, the sudden drop down the hill of the rue Cardinal Lemoine to the River, and the other way the narrow crowded world of the rue Mouffetard. The street that ran up toward the Pantheon and the other that he always took with the bicycle, the only asphalted street in all that quarter, smooth under the tyres, with the high narrow houses and the cheap tall hotel where Paul Verlaine had died. There were only two rooms in the apartments where they lived and he had a room on the top floor of that hotel that cost him sixty francs a month where he did his writing, and from it he could see the roofs and chimney pots and all the hills of Paris.

From the apartment you could only see the wood and coal man's place. He sold wine, too, bad wine. The golden horse's head outside the Boucherie Chevaline where the carcasses hung yellow gold and red in the open window, and the green painted co-operative where they bought their wine; good wine and cheap. The *rest was plaster walls and the windows of the neighbours. The neighbours who, at night, when someone lay drunk in the street, moaning and groaning in typical French ivresse that you were propaganded to believe did not exist, would open their windows and then the murmur of talk.*

'Where is the policeman? When you don't want him the bugger is always there. He's sleeping with some concierge. Get the Agent.' Till someone threw a bucket of water from a window and the moaning stopped. 'What's that? Water. Ah, that's intelligent.' And the windows shutting. Marie, his femme de ménage, protesting against the eight-hour day saying, 'If a husband works until six he only gets a little drunk on the way home and does not waste too much. If he works only until five he is drunk every night and one has no money. It is the wife of the working man who suffers from this shortening of hours.'

'Wouldn't you like some more broth?' the woman asked him now.

'No, thank you very much. It is awfully good.'

'Cry just a little.'

'I would like a whisky-soda.'

'It's not good for you.'

'No. It's bad for me. Cole Porter wrote the words and the music. This knowledge that you're going mad for me.'

'You know I like you to drink.'

'Oh yes. Only it's bad for me.'

When she goes, he thought, I'll have all I want. Not all I want but all there is. Ayee he was tired. Too tired. He was going to sleep a little while. He lay still and death was not there. It must have gone around another street. It went in pairs, on bicycles, and moved absolutely silently on the pavements.

No, he had never written about Paris. Not the Paris that he cared about. But what about the rest that he had never written?

What about the ranch and the silvered grey of the sage brush, the quick, clear water in the irrigation ditches, and the heavy green of the alfalfa. The trail went up into the hills and the cattle in the summer were shy as deer. The bawling and the steady noise and slow moving mass raising dust as you brought them down in the fall. And behind the mountains, the clear sharpness of the peak in the evening light and, riding down along the trail in the moonlight, bright across the valley. Now he remembered coming down through the timber in the dark holding the horse's tail when you could not see and all the stories that he meant to write.

About the half-wit chore boy who was left at the ranch that time and told not to let anyone get any hay, and that old bastard from the Forks who had beaten the boy when he had worked for him stopping to get some feed. The boy refusing and the old man saying he would beat him again. The boy got the rifle from the kitchen and shot him when he tried to come into the barn and when they came back to the ranch he'd been dead a week, frozen in the corral, and the dogs had eaten part of him. But what was left you packed on a sled wrapped in a blanket and roped on and you got the boy to help you haul it, and the two of you took it out over the road on skis, and sixty miles down to town to turn the boy over. He having no idea that he would be arrested. Thinking he had done his duty and that you were his friend and he would be rewarded. He'd helped to haul the old man in so everybody could know how bad the old man had been and how he'd tried to steal some feed that didn't belong to him, and when the sheriff put the handcuffs on the boy he couldn't believe it. Then he started to cry. That was one story he had saved to write. He knew at least twenty good stories from out there and he had never written one. Why?

'You tell them why,' he said.

'Why what, dear?'

'Why nothing.'

She didn't drink so much, now, since she had him. But if he lived he would never write about her, he knew that now. Nor about any of them. The rich were dull and they drank too much, or they played too much backgammon. They were dull and they were repetitious. He remembered poor Julian and his romantic awe of them and how he had started a story once that began, 'The very rich are different from you and me.' And how someone had said to Julian, Yes, they have more money. But that was not humorous to Julian. He thought they were a special glamorous race and when he found they weren't it

493

wrecked him just as much as any other thing that wrecked him.

He had been contemptuous of those who wrecked. You did not have to like it because you understood it. He could beat anything, he thought, because nothing could hurt him if he did not care.

All right. Now he would not care for death. One thing he had always dreaded was the pain. He could stand pain as well as any man, until it went on too long, and wore him out, but here he had something that had hurt frightfully and just when he had felt it breaking him, the pain had stopped.

He remembered long ago when Williamson, the bombing officer, had been hit by a stick bomb someone in a German patrol had thrown as he was coming in through the wire that night and, screaming, had begged everyone to kill him. He was a fat man, very brave, and a good officer, although addicted to fantastic shows. But that night he was caught in the wire, with a flare lighting him up and his bowels spilled out into the wire, so when they brought him in, alive, they had to cut him loose. Shoot me, Harry. For Christ sake shoot me. They had had an argument one time about our Lord never sending you anything you could not bear and someone's theory had been that meant that at a certain time the pain passed you out automatically. But he had always remembered Williamson, that night. Nothing passed out Williamson until he gave him all his morphine tablets that he had always saved to use himself and then they did not work right away.

Still this now, that he had, was very easy; and if it was no worse as it went on there was nothing to worry about. Except that he would rather be in better company.

He thought a little about the company that he would like to have.

No, he thought, when everything you do, you do too long, and do too late, you can't expect to find the people still there. The people all are gone. The party's over and you are with your hostess now.

I'm getting bored with dying as with everything else, he thought.

'It's a bore,' he said out loud.

'What is, my dear?'

'Anything you do too bloody long.'

He looked at her face between him and the fire. She was leaning back in the chair and the firelight shone on her pleasantly lined face and he could see that she was sleepy. He heard the hyena make a noise just outside the range of the fire.

'I've been writing,' he said. 'But I got tired.'

'Do you think you will be able to sleep?'

'Pretty sure. Why don't you turn in?'

'I like to sit here with you.'

'Do you feel anything strange?' he asked her.

'No. Just a little sleepy.'

'I do,' he said.

He had just felt death come by again.

'You know the only thing I've never lost is curiosity,' he said to her.

'You've never lost anything. You're the most complete man I've ever known.'

'Christ,' he said. 'How little a woman knows. What is that? Your intuition?'

Because, just then, death had come and rested its head on the foot of the cot and he could smell its breath.

'Never believe any of that about a scythe and a skull,' he told her. 'It can be two bicycle policemen as easily, or be a bird. Or it can have a wide snout like a hyena.'

It had moved up on him now, but it had no shape any more. It simply occupied space.

'Tell it to go away.'

It did not go away but moved a little closer.

'You've got a hell of a breath,' he told it. 'You stinking bastard.'

It moved up closer to him still and now he could not speak to it, and when it saw he could not speak it came a little closer, and now he tried to send it away without speaking, but it moved in on him so its weight was all upon his chest, and while it crouched there and he could not move, or speak, he heard the woman say, 'Bwana is asleep now. Take the cot up very gently and carry it into the tent.'

He could not speak to tell her to make it go away and it crouched now heavier, so he could not breathe. And then, while they lifted the cot, suddenly it was all right and the weight went from his chest.

It was morning and had been morning for some time and he heard the plane. It showed very tiny and then made a wide circle and the boys ran out and lit the fires, using kerosene, and piled on grass so there were two big smudges at each end of the level place and the morning breeze blew them toward the camp and the plane circled twice more, low this time, and then glided down and levelled off and landed smoothly and, coming walking toward him, was old Compton in slacks, a tweed jacket and a brown felt hat.

'What's the matter, old cock?' Compton said.

'Bad leg,' he told him. 'Will you have some breakfast?'

'Thanks. I'll just have some tea. It's the Puss Moth you know. I won't be able to take the Memsahib. There's only room for one. Your lorry is on the way.'

Helen had taken Compton aside and was speaking to him. Compton came back more cheery than ever.

'We'll get you right in,' he said. 'I'll be back for the Mem. Now I'm afraid I'll have to stop at Arusha to refuel. We'd better get going.'

'What about the tea?'

'I don't really care about it you know.'

The boys had picked up the cot and carried it around the green tents and down along the rock and out on to the plain and along past the smudges that were burning brightly now, the grass all consumed, and the wind fanning the fire, to the little plane. It was difficult getting him in, but once he lay back in the leather seat, and the leg was stuck straight out to one side of the seat where Compton sat. Compton started the motor and got in. He waved to Helen and to the boys and, as the clatter moved into the old familiar roar, they swung around with Compie watching for warthog holes and roared, bumping, along the stretch between the fires and with the last bump rose and he saw them all standing below, waving, and the camp beside the hill, flattening now, and the plain spreading, clumps of trees, and the bush flattening, while the game trails ran now smoothly to the dry waterholes, and there was a new water that he had never known of. The zebra, small rounded back snow, and the wildebeeste, big-headed dots seeming to climb as they moved in long fingers across the plain, now scattering as the shadow came toward them, they were tiny now, and the movement had no gallop, and the plain as far as you could see, gray-yellow now and ahead old Compie's tweed back and the brown felt hat. Then they were over the first hills and the wildebeeste were trailing up them, and then they were over mountains with sudden depths of green-rising forest and the solid bamboo slopes, and then the heavy forest again, sculptured into peaks and hollows until they crossed, and hills sloped down and then another plain, hot now, and purple brown, bumpy with heat and Compie looking back to see how he was riding. Then there were other mountains dark ahead.

And then instead of going on to Arusha they turned left, he evidently figured that they had the gas, and looking down he saw a pink sifting cloud, moving over the ground, and in the air, like the first snow in a blizzard, that comes from nowhere, and he knew the locusts were coming up from the south. Then they began to climb and they were going to the east it seemed, and then it darkened and they were in a storm, the rain so thick it seemed like flying through a waterfall, and then they were out and Compie turned his head and grinned and pointed and there, ahead, all he could see, as wide as all the world, great, high, and unbelievably white in the sun, was the square top of Kilimanjaro. And then he knew that there was where he was going.

Just then the hyena stopped whimpering in the night and started to make a strange, human, almost crying sound. The woman heard it and stirred uneasily. She did not wake. In her dream she was at the house on Long Island and it was the night before her daughter's debut. Somehow her father was there and he had been very rude. Then the noise the hyena made was so loud she woke and for a moment she did not know where she was and she was very afraid. Then she took a flashlight and shone it on the other cot that they had carried in after Harry had gone to sleep. She could see his bulk under the mosquito bar but somehow he had gotten his leg out and it hung down alongside the cot. The dressings had all come down and she could not look at it.

'Molo,' she called, 'Molo! Molo!'

Then she said, 'Harry, Harry!' Then her voice rising, 'Harry! Please, Oh Harry!'

There was no answer and she could not hear him breathing.

Outside the tent the hyena made the same strange noise that had awakened her. But she did not hear him for the beating of her heart.

DEATH IN THE AFTERNOON

Epilogue

If I could have made this enough of a book it would have had everything in it. The Prado, looking like some big American college building, with sprinklers watering the grass early in the bright Madrid summer morning; the bare white mud hills looking across toward Carabanchel; days on the train in August with the blinds pulled down on the side against the sun and the wind blowing them; chaff blown against the car in the wind from the hard earthen threshing floors; the odour of grain and the stone windmills. It would have had the change when you leave the green country behind at Alsasua; it would have had Burgos far across the plain and eating the cheese later up in the room; it would have had the boy taking the wicker-bound jugs of wine on the train as samples; his first trip to Madrid and opening them in enthusiasm and they all got drunk including the pair of Guardia Civil and I lost the tickets and we were taken through the wicket by the two Guardia Civil (who took us out as though prisoners because there were no tickets and then saluted as they put us in the cab); Hadley, with the bull's ear wrapped in a handkerchief, the ear was very stiff and dry and the hair all wore off it and the man who cut the ear is bald now too and slicks long strips of hair over the top of his head and he was beau then. He was, all right.

It should make clear the change in the country as you come down out of the mountains and into Valencia in the dusk on the train holding a rooster for a woman who was bringing it to her sister; and it should show the wooden ring at Alciras where they dragged the dead horses out in the field and you had to pick your way over them; and the noise in the streets in Madrid after midnight and the fair that goes on all night long, in June, and walking home on Sundays from the ring; or with Rafael in the cab. Que tal? Malo, hombre, malo; with that lift of the shoulders, or with Roberto, Don Roberto, Don Ernesto, so polite always, so gentle and such a good friend. Also the house where Rafael lived before being a republican, became respectable with the mounted head of the bull Gitanillo had killed and the great oil jar and always presents and the excellent cooking.

It should have the smell of burnt powder and the smoke and the flash and the noise of the traca going off through the green leaves of the trees and it should have the taste of horchata, ice-cold horchata, and the new-washed streets in the sun, and the melons and beads of cool on the outside of the pitchers of beer; the storks on the houses in Barco de Avila and wheeling in the sky and the red-mud colour of the ring; and at night dancing to the pipes and the drum with the lights through the green leaves and the portrait of Garibaldi framed in leaves. It should, if it were enough of a book, have the forced smile of Lagartito; it was once a real smile, and the unsuccessful matadors swimming with the cheap whores out on the Manzanares along the Pardo road; beggars can't be choosers, Luis said; playing ball on the grass by the stream where the fairy marquis came out in his car with the boxer; where we made the paellas and walked home in the dark with the cars coming fast along the road; and with electric lights through the green leaves and the dew settling the dust, in the cool at night; cider in Bombilla and the road to Pontevedra from Santiago de Compostella with the high turn in the pines and blackberries beside the road; Algabeno the worst faker of them all; and Maera up in the room at Quintana's changing outfits with the priest the one year everyone drank so much and no one was nasty. There really was such a year, but this is not enough of a book.

Make all that come true again; throw grasshoppers to the trout in the Tambre on the bridge in the evening; have the serious brown face of Felix Merino at the old Aguilar; have the brave, awkward, wall-eyed Pedro Montes dressing away from home because he had promised his mother he had stopped fighting after Mariano, his brother, was killed at Tetuan; and Litri, like a little rabbit, his eyes winking nervously as the bull came; he was very bow-legged and brave and those three are all killed and never any mention made about the beer place on the cool side of the street underneath the Palace where he sat with his father and how it is a Citroen showroom now; nor about them carrying Pedro Carreño, dead, through the streets with torches and finally into the church and put him naked on the altar.

There is nothing in this book about Francisco Gomez, Aldeano, who worked in Ohio in a steel plant and came home to be a matador and now is scarred and marked worse than anyone except Freg, his eye twisted so a tear runs down his nose. Nor Gavira dead at the very instant as the bull with the same cornada that killed El Espartero. Nor does it tell about Zaragossa, at night on the bridge watching the Ebro, and the parachute jumper the next day and Rafael's cigars; nor the jota contests in the old red plush theatre and the wonderful boy and girl pairs; nor when they killed the Noy de Sucre in Barcelona, nor about any of that; nor anything about Navarra; nor about the lousy town Leon is; nor about lying with a muscle torn in a hotel on the sunny side of the street in Valencia where it was hot and you do not know what hot is when you have not been there; nor on the road where dust is deeper than the hubs between Requena and Madrid; nor when it was one hundred and twenty in the shade in Aragon and the car, with no carbon nor anything wrong, would boil the water out of the radiator in fifteen miles on a level road.

If it were more of a book it would make the last night of feria when Maera fought Alfredo David in the Café Kutz; and it should show the bootblacks. My God, you could not get in all the bootblacks; nor all the fine girls passing; nor the whores; nor all of us ourselves as we were then. Pamplona now is changed; they have built new apartment buildings out over all the sweep of plain that ran to the edge of the plateau; so now you cannot see the mountains. They tore down the old Gayarre and spoiled the square to cut a wide thoroughfare to the ring and in the old days there was Chicuelo's uncle sitting drunk in the upstairs dining room watching the dancing in the square; Chicuelo was in his room alone, and the cuadrilla in the café and around the town. I wrote a story about it called *A*

501

Lack of Passion, but it was not good enough although when they threw the dead cats at the train and afterward the wheels clicking and Chicuelo in the berth, alone; able to do it alone; it was fair enough.

It should, if it had Spain in it, have the tall thin boy, eight feet six inches, he advertised the Empastre show before they came to town, and that night, at the feria de ganado, the whores wouldn't have anything to do with the dwarf, he was full size except that his legs were only six inches long, and he said, 'I'm a man like any man,' and the whore said, 'No you're not and that's the trouble.' There are many dwarfs in Spain and cripples that you wouldn't believe that follow all the fairs.

In the morning there we would have breakfast and then go out to swim in the Irati at Aoiz, the water clear as light, and varying in temperature as you sunk down, cool, cold, and the shade from the trees on the bank when the sun was hot, the ripe wheat in the wind up on the other side and sloping to the mountain. There was an old castle at the head of the valley where the river came out between two rocks; and we lay naked on the short grass in the sun and later in the shade. The wine at Aoiz was no good so then we brought our own, and neither was the ham, so the next time we brought a lunch from Quintana's. Quintana, the best aficionado and most loyal friend in Spain, and with a fine hotel with all the rooms full. Que tal Juanito? Que tal, hombre, que tal?

And why should it not have the cavalry crossing another stream at a ford, the shadow of the leaves on the horses, if it is Spain, and why not have them marching out from the machine-gun school across the clay-white ground, very small so far away, and looking beyond from Quintanilla's window were the mountains. Or waking in the morning, the streets empty on Sunday, and the shouting far away and then the firing. That happens many times if you live long enough and move around.

And if you ride and if your memory is good you may ride still through the forest of the Irati with trees like drawings in a child's fairy book. They cut those down. They ran logs down the river and they killed the fish, or in Galicia they bombed and poisoned them; results the same; so in the end it's just like home except for yellow gorse on the high meadows and the thin rain. Clouds come across the mountains from the sea but when the wind is from the south Navarra is all the colour of wheat except it does not grow on level plains but up and down the sides of hills and cut by roads with trees and many villages with bells, pelota courts, the smell of sheep manure and squares with standing horses.

If you could make the yellow flames of candles in the sun; that shines on steel of bayonets freshly oiled and yellow patent-leather belts of those who guard the Host; or hunt in pairs through scrub oak in the mountains for the ones who fell into the trap at Deva (it was a bad long way to come from the Café Rotonde to be garrotted in a draughty room with consolation of the church at order of the state, acquitted once and held until the captain general of Burgos reversed the finding of the court) and in the same town where Loyola got his wound that made him think, the bravest of those who were betrayed that year dived from the balcony on to the paving of the court, head first, because he had sworn they would not kill him (his mother tried to make him promise not to take his life because she worried most about his soul but he dived well and cleanly with his hands tied while they walked with him praying); if I could make him; make a bishop; make Candido Tiebas and Toron; make clouds come fast in shadows moving over wheat and the small, careful stepping horses; the smell of olive oil; the feel of leather; rope-soled shoes; the loops of twisted garlics; earthen pots; saddle bags carried across the shoulder; wine skins; the pitchforks made of natural wood (the tines were branches); the early morning smells; the cold mountain nights and long hot days of summer, with always trees and shade under the trees, then you would have a little of Navarra. But it's not in this book.

There ought to be Astorga, Lugo, Orense, Soria, Tarragona and Calatayud, the chestnut woods on the high hills, the green country and the rivers, the red dust, the small shade beside the dry rivers and the white, baked clay hills; cool walking under palms in the old city on the cliff above the sea, cool in the evening with the breeze; mosquitoes at night but in the morning the water clear and the sand white; then sitting in the heavy twilight at Miro's; vines as far as you can see, cut by the hedges and the road; the railroad and the sea with pebbly beach and tall papyrus grass. There were earthen jars for the different years of wine, twelve feet high, set side by side in a dark room; a tower on the house to climb to in the evening to see the vines, the villages and the mountains and to listen and hear how quiet it was. In front of the barn a woman held a duck whose throat she had cut and stroked him gently while a little girl held up a cup to catch the blood for making gravy. The duck seemed very contented and when they put him down (the blood all in the cup) he waddled twice and found that he was dead. We ate him later, stuffed and roasted; and many other dishes, with the wine of that year and the year before and the great year four years before that and other years that I lost track of while the long arms of a mechanical fly chaser that wound by clockwork went round and round and we talked French. We all knew Spanish better.

That is Montroig, pronounced Montroych, one of many places in Spain, where there are also the streets of Santiago in the rain; seeing the town down in the cups of hills as you come home across the high country; and all the carts that roll, piled high, on smooth stone tracks along the road to Grau should be there with the temporary wooden ring in Noya, smelling of fresh cut boards; Chiquito with his girl's face, a great artist, fine muy fino, pero frio. Valencia II with his eye they sewed up wrong so that the inside of the lid showed and he could not be arrogant any more. Also the boy who missed the bull entirely when he went in to kill and missed him again the second time. If you could stay awake for the nocturnals you saw them funny.

In Madrid the comic bullfighter, beaten up twice by Rodalito stabbing him in the belly because he thought there was another beating coming. Aguero eating with his whole family in the dining room; they all looking alike in different ages. He looked like a shortstop or a quarterback, not like a matador. Cagancho eating in his room with his fingers because he could not use a fork. He could not learn it, so when he had enough money he never ate in public. Ortega engaged to Miss España, the ugliest and the prettiest, and who was the wittiest? Derperdicios in la Gaceta del Norte was the wittiest; the wittiest I ever read.

And up in Sidney's rooms, the ones coming to ask for work when he was fighting, the ones to borrow money, the ones for an old shirt, a suit of clothes; all bullfighters, all well known somewhere at the hour of eating, all formally polite, all out of luck; the muletas folded and piled; the capes all folded flat; swords in the embossed leather case; all in the armoire; muleta sticks are in the bottom drawer, suits hung in the trunk, cloth covered to protect the gold; my whisky in an earthen crock; Mercédes, bring the glasses; she says he had a fever all night long and only went out an hour ago. So then he comes in. How do you feel? Great. She says you had fever. But I feel great now. What do you say, Doctor, why not eat here? She can get something and make a salad. Mércedes oh Mercédes.

Then you could walk across the town and to the café where they say you get your education learning who owed who money and who chiselled this from who and why he told him he could kiss his what and who had children by who and who married who before and after what and how long it took for this and that and what the doctor said. Who was so pleased because the bulls were delayed, being unloaded only the day of the fight, naturally weak in the legs, just two passes, poom, and it is all over, he said, and then it rained and the fight postponed a week and that was when he got it. Who wouldn't fight with who and when and why and does she, of course she does, you fool you didn't know she does? Absolutely and that's all and in no other fashion, she gobbles them alive, and all such valuable news you learn in cafés. In cafés where the boys are never wrong; in cafés where they are all brave; in cafés where the saucers pile and drinks are figured in pencil on the marble table tops among the shucked shrimps of seasons lost and feeling good because there are no other triumphs so secure and every man a success by eight o'clock if somebody can pay the score in cafés.

What else should it contain about a country you love very much? Rafael says things are very changed and he won't go to Pamplona any more. *La Libertad* I find is getting like *Le Temps*. It is no longer the paper where you could put a notice and know the pickpocket would see it now that Republicans are all respectable and Pamplona is changed, of course, but not as much as we are older. I found that if you took a drink that it got very much the same as it was always. I know things change now and I do not care. It's all been changed for me. Let it all change. We'll all be gone before it's changed too much and if no deluge comes when we are gone it still will rain in summer in the north and hawks will nest in the Cathedral at Santiago and in La Granja, where we practised with the cape on the long gravelled paths between the shadows, it makes no difference if the fountains play or not. We never will ride back from Toledo in the dark, washing the dust out with Fundador, nor will there be that week of what happened in the night in that July in Madrid. We've all seen it go and we'll watch it go again. The great thing is to last and get your work done and see and hear and learn and understand; and write when there is something that you know; and not before; and not too damned much after. Let those who want to save the world if you can get to see it clear and as a whole. Then any part you make will represent the whole if it's made truly. The thing to do is work and learn to make it. No. It is not enough of a book, but still there were a few things to be said. There were a few practical things to be said.